THE POSEIDON PROJECT

A Novel by

Tracy Vetter

ISBN 978-1-966012-03-0 (paperback)
ISBN 978-1-966012-04-7 (hardcover)
ISBN 978-1-966012-05-4 (digital)

Printed in the United States of America

CHAPTER 1

Don Merrick stood alone in the huge freight elevator as it traveled downward. In one arm he clutched a laptop computer, larger than most and the leather traveling case slightly worn at the edges, but still reliable and packed to the maximum with information. In his other hand, pulling heavily on his shoulder was a briefcase, piled full with papers and small, precision hand tools which added to the weight. He wore simple gray pants and a button up, blue plaid shirt. A series of large identification tags dangled from his neck, absolutely the top clearance given to a civilian. He could travel through doors where the President of the United States could not. At least not where the President would not have a couple of M-sixteen's pointed at him.

He had adopted the huge freight elevator the moment he had found out there was no smoking allowed in the personnel elevator. No smoking allowed in the upper reaches and any smoking down below it was the last chance of the day for him. But that was all he needed. At five foot nine inches tall and forty-three-year-old, he carried a well-muscled frame of one hundred-seventy-five pounds. He kept his dirty blonde hair short and parted, and hated shaving, but did so every morning. He maintained his boyish good looks with bright blue eyes.

The elevator he rode was massive, being a thirty-by-thirty square and capable of holding 10 tons of materials. It smelled of hydraulic fluid, oil, a cleaning fluid that had leaked onto the floor, rotting wood and old sweat. He stood alone in the center of the huge lift, utterly content with himself at wasting that much power. He did things his way with frustrating accuracy.

As the immense doors slid up and out of the way, Merrick crossed an open warehouse area, but his mind was on the interior. A very complicated machine that he had engineered and the bane of his existence for the past five years. The last two in complete immersion.

The building itself was an engineering feat. Off the coast of California, at the home of the second largest naval base in the United States, Naval Base San Diego. This facility had been designed for one purpose. To assemble a submarine, undetected.

The massive installation was the home of the Pacific Fleet. Nine hundred seventy-seven acres of docks, large buildings and around one hundred-fifty ships at any given time dotted the coastal facility. At the northern tip was an unobtrusive warehouse type building. But underneath was the final assembly and testing area of submarines. Going through normal channels one would pass through the main office complex, then into the last of three assembly facilities. From there a person passed into a restricted area, still above ground, then into a Secret area with restricted access. This was the above ground assembly facility for the Poseidon Project as this current project had been nicknamed. Then into the building sight for the sub, and another check of a person's credentials, finally took them to the elevators. From the sky or a satellite's eye view, it looked like any other warehouse of the Naval Facility. Like an iceberg, the bulk of the installation was underground.

The Poseidon's Projects underground final assembly point was longer than two football fields. Massive cranes on either side of the open water, several large hoists spanning the ceiling, more than fifty feet in the air and moveable cat walks suspended over the water. Everything was adjustable, moveable, and utterly top secret. Ninety percent of the people that worked directly overhead would never see what they worked on.

As normal, a cement dock circled the submarine, but on the south side, hydraulics could push the dock too within inches of any boat the facility was working on. The one hundred twenty-eight lights hanging from the ceiling were all one-thousand-watt LED lighting. By remote control they could be moved, lowered or all focused on one item, without leaving the hint of a shadow. Sectionally they could bring to full brightness or dimmed to a mere ten percent. Very seldom were they all on at any one time. A large underwater tunnel through which only a submarine could navigate extended out to the sea. Large locking doors kept anything from coming in.

The north side of the facility was a multitude of rooms. A drafting room, several assembly rooms, meeting and strategy venues. Extending underground, it was the interior office complex that kept the boat afloat. They included simple rooms for day-to-day life, such as a lunch room and a guard room. A large tool locker and an electronics storehouse were next to the assembly room, which was conveniently located next to the freight elevator. Small offices helped keep builders and commanders note and papers separate and a communications room kept them in touch with the outside world. On a coded frequency.

The most unusual design of the North side was its immense open window design. Every office that graced the South wall of the North side had double pane insulated glass walls, separating itself from the sub. Within any room was a large-scale view of the vessel that sat stoically in the water. It reminded everyone on a day-to-day basis what they were building.

The West side was the largest open area where the Submarine was built in sections. It was where the freight elevator dropped to, conveniently opening on all four sides to deposit new products.

Donald Merrick pulled a cigar out of his breast pocket, flipped open his old Zippo lighter and puffed carefully. There were at least thirty signs in the facility stating "NO SMOKING." He did not care today. It was his submarine and he was going to do what he wanted to do. Besides, that early in the morning there was only the guard to consider. Don had a reputation for being a fair individual, and yet, he was the end all to the questions that came up on a daily basis.

Merrick was a man unto himself. Married only to his job, his one and only hobby was collecting Star Trek memorabilia concerning specifically, the crafts or starships. And yet, he was not a Trekkie. He did not care one bit about the cast members or going to conventions. At a young age he wanted to know how things worked in the Star Trek Universe. He would have designed them differently. At the age of six he figured out that the Enterprise of the Star Trek universe was graceful, and yet, simply a model, having nothing to do with the complexities of anti-matter engines. He sincerely doubted that the Federation Starship Enterprise would ever fly. He also figured that the boxy shuttle crafts were made by underpaid carpenters and lacked any kind of designing at all, and should have burned up going in and out of Earth's atmosphere, for it was not large enough for a shield generator. Stuff like that irritated the hell out of him.

A team of scientists and top-notch engineers had been assembled for the Poseidon Project has it had been named. Own by the PDM Boat Builders LLC. The new submarine was rethought from square one. Leave no conventions to chance. Question any standard procedure in building. That was why it took Donald five years.

This was not the standard steel-plated behemoth that was churned out at the Electric Boat yards. It was cutting edge by the new boat company that specialized in submarines.

Very much like the jagged Stealth Bomber next to the old B- 52's, this barely resembled a submarine. It lay low in the water, shaped like a shark with a large open maw at the front. Unlike the round subs built for resistance to the crushing pressure of extreme water depths, this submarine suffered no such problems. So, Donald designed it to be sleek and fast.

Flat on the bottom, its nose angling up to recede into a small conning tower. The tower or sail itself, rose up at a forty-five-degree angle, enabling it to slice through the water. Only twelve feet above the rounded deck, it tapered slightly behind it, not reaching the original deck surface until the very rear of the submarine. Its aerodynamic and sleek design was also devoid of the traditional masts associated with a normal submarine. Gone were the Electronic Counter measure mast, periscope, radio aerial, and associated ports. The only evident thing was a hundred, six-foot fins, being the satellite aerial built into the slopping front end of the conning tower, becoming part of the sub itself. The diving planes were also tapered back, which made them look like delta wings on the fighter plane. It was built for speed and maneuverability.

The opening under the water, was much like the turbo air intakes of an Indianapolis styled race cars. For much the same purpose. It pulled the water through and forced it out like the shot of a squirt gun, with the water expelling under the boat. Making no sound or wake, it was as silent as a whale slicing through the water.

As singular and innovative as the engine and design was, it was the body composition that was the most scientific and creative. Amorphous Metal, surrounding the ship and making the core, made the ship not only stronger than any known steel but uniformly smooth, capable of displacing water over its smooth surface quickly. Injected molded like plastic, the process offering more strength than cut steel. Liquidmetal, in various stages of transformations, had been in experimentation for years. Don's company had perfected its own where the ship itself would never need scaling, or painting. What would define the color of the sub was actually worked into the liquid metal. Radar bouncing crystals gave the entire ship a translucent reflection.

The surface of the craft, due to the cooling effects of the Liquidmetal allowed the ship to reflect back whatever water and sky configurations that it traveled in. It was almost like a mirror, and, like the stealth fighter, signals were not absorbed, but refracted. In the ship yard, only the bright lights that were bouncing off the skin, gave it any depth. The lower part of the ship where it blended in with the water took on an oily hue, the microscopic crystal construction reflecting back the surface. Out in open water it would be visible, but not as a submarine. It would appear as something shadowy slicing cleanly through the water. In the dark it would be damned near impossible to see until it crossed the moonlight, its shadow still not carving much of a sub's shape. To keep from people being blinded by an errant shaft of bright light, they covered the exposed skin that was not being worked on at the moment.

The ship itself had been built in a smaller facility in Seattle that the Submariner Group owned, then silently towed down to San Diego for its final fitting and assembly. Don preferred his smaller place and argued vehemently against towing his little sub around the damned ocean, but was out-voted. The US Navy was paying the bills.

Merrick puffed joyously on his cigar. He finally reached the dock floor and looked around. At five-thirty in the morning there was little activity, except for the security that surrounded the submarine. Already, a guard was crossing the dock to greet him. Even though he had passed through a rigorous security check up above, they would check him one more time before letting him continue. Through the music system came the sweet refrains of Dean Martin. It had been Don's choice of music set ups, which some of the guards objected to. He was not there to make friends.

"Mr. Merrick! Good morning, sir," said the beefy guard as Merrick stood silently as the guard again checked his badge, with a small hand-held scanner, connected to a back pack computer. "Mr. Merrick?" The guard waved at the cigar. This too was a ritual, as Don gave the guard a nasty look and dropped the cigar to the concrete. Donald would never argue as it was the only smoke of the day for him.

"So, when is the big day?" mentioned the guard, whose name Merrick never remembered.

Merrick looked at the man disgustedly. "Today was the big day a month ago. Now it is two weeks away. The Navy has an unerring way of botching things, as usual."

The Naval MP guard smiled. "Well, I will have to be sure to be around when she does set sail."

"Want to see it sink?" Merrick said in return, his caustic temper flaring up.

"Not at all sir. I'll just feel a sense of accomplishment when she sets sail. That's all. Oh, by the way, the chief is already on board."

Merrick smiled and nodded his head. "Of course he is. The man lives in that thing."

They were referring to the Chief of Engineering, Senior Chief Petty Officer Gunther Schmidt. Or Schmitty as most called him. The only crew member to be picked from the very start, he helped engineer the small but a powerful nuclear reactor for the submarine. Too many times Merrick had left for the night with Schmitty working, only to return the next morning to find the man still there. Small and wiry, he could fit into the cramped spaces that most could not. With a technical mind and a never say die attitude, the man used his nimble fingers to solve many a problem.

With his badges thoroughly checked for the last time, Merrick returned his gaze back to the Submarine. Unlike the first Submarine that The PDM Group designed and built, this was not a multipurpose attack Sub. It was a first of its kind Stealth Submarine. The entire thing would fit into the missile bay of a standard Ballistic Submarine. It was only one hundred ninety-eight feet long and carried only nineteen crew members. Its top speed was formulated at more than ninety knots. And that was underwater. There was not a war ship afloat that would keep up with the little boat.

Rear-Admiral Cartwright had halted the commissioning the previous week. The name had been changed one more time. Staff was being reconfigured once again. It was packed and stocked and ready to go and the US Navy played waiting games. As usual.

Merrick disliked working with the Navy. All he wanted to do was take the thing out for a spin. That had been the deal with the Admiral. He was going on the first voyage. His ship. And he wanted to drive.

Spending the next two hours in the drafting room off to one side, a large window open to view the submarine floating easily in the water, Merrick was submerged in checking and double checking every possible system and their failures. He hated surprises. And submarines, like helicopters, were the worst place in the world to find out something did not work. The ghostly visage of the USS Thresher was always in the back of his mind. State of the art, on its maiden voyage, and it sunk. The crew of one hundred twenty-nine people, including civilians testing their new Submarine all died. Supposedly from a watery short circuit. Don had no intention of dying that way.

When the door opened, he did not look around to see who it was. There were only a dozen other people allowed in the room and most of the other engineers had been redeployed.

"Ralphie," mentioned Merrick casually glancing up.

Captain Ralph Wolfson had all the credentials for this project. Having sailed under two other nuclear banners and a sub of his own, he relished this assignment. And his temperament was one of quiet confidence. He constantly soothed Merrick's ruffled feathers. A couple of inches above six-foot inches, he was tall for any man let alone a stealthy submarine meant for sneaking around. A handsome face, and broad shoulders, a bushy mustache neatly trimmed, he was the epitome of a Naval Hero.

"Donny! We have a new date to set sail and the Admiral promises us this is the one," said Captain Wolfson enthusiastically, bursting through the door.

Don cringed. He hated the name, Donny. "So you got the word too. Admiral Cartwright is going to screw around until this thing sinks, or becomes obsolete," responded Merrick dejectedly. And yet, he was actually happy for the extended time. There was always something to consider changing on the sub.

Captain Wolfson clapped Merrick on the back and said, "The Tiger Shark will set sail with us aboard. Next week. I promise."

"The Tiger Shark huh? Is that the new name? Last week it was the Speed Star and the week before it was the Manta Ray. Next week it will be the Flounder," Don noted with a comic air.

"Sorry. I know you had your heart set on the Poseidon, but the name is already taken. They could have stuck us with the George Bush after the ex-president that died a few years back," replied Wolfson. He was very used to the give and take with Merrick. Working with the man had given Wolfson an intuition as to when Don was kidding, and when he was not.

Merrick looked over at the handsome man dressed in starched khakis. "Cartwrights' assistant wanted to call the damned thing the Chameleon." Then Merrick smiled and shook the man's hand. It was one of the few men on this project that Merrick liked even though Wolfson's enthusiasm reminded him of a school boy.

"Cartwrights' assistant, does not know the difference between a state of the art Submarine and a bath tub toy." The Captain said eloquently.

Merrick chuckled appreciatively. Ralph knew to get in Merrick's good graces for the day, was to insult somebody and make it funny.

"You run into Cartwrights lists of crew members yet?" asked the Captain.

Merrick turned around and sat down on the drafting stool. "Don't care about a list. I want bodies so that they can have an idea of what the hell they're doing," he said.

Captain Wolfson nodded his head. It had been an argument between Merrick and the Admiral starting several months ago. Merrick wanted the crew in place and being trained on the new sub as it was being built. The Admiral however, did not want any more people to know about it than was necessary. The Admiral maintained that the crew would be assembled from the brightest and the best and a submarine was a submarine, no matter how fancy. On this one Wolfson agreed with Merrick. The Admiral did not always appreciate how much this was redesigned for a typical sub. It would be nice to have a knowledgeable crew.

Wolfson nodded his head in agreement. "The skills will be there but yeah; we'll need to bring everyone up to speed in a hurry. At least we have another week."

"You run into the Wizard?" asked Merrick suddenly.

"Passed him in the hallway. Why?"

"I want to run another test of the GP Satellite one more time."

Wolfson looked sideways at the man. "Why? We've run that thing to death. One hundred feet below the surface and it can detect a heartbeat. Why another test?"

"I want to take it off line and reboot the system using only the battery back-up. Then I'm going to install fresh batteries and do it again."

Wolfson smiled. He had not thought of that. All the battery systems in the sub were already over a year old. "Don't tell Schmitty you think his nuclear reactor will malfunction. You'll never hear the end of it."

"I have all the confidence in the world in PDM's design and Schmitty's abilities. But things happen and I want capable back up."

"I'll go find Willy." Captain Wolfson turned and walked out of the room. The Wizard, better known as Lt. Willy Williams was the electronics specialist on board the sub. Barely twenty-five years old he had run into Merrick a year previously at an electronics seminar. Brought in two months ago at Merrick's insistence that at least someone in the damned Naval mess was familiar with the electronics aboard the floating Radio Shack. Like a child in a toy store, there was nothing that Willy did not want to tinker with. And upgrade and fix. Wearing wire rim glasses with a pair of magnified glasses pivoting off the top of the glasses, Merrick had quickly nicknamed him the Wizard. Which Willy did not object too. And yet, people that knew him knew better than to think he was a geek. He was as solid as that proverbial brick wall people dd not want to run into.

When Wolfson found Willy in the part's room and told him of Merrick's plans, Willy quickly thought it was a good idea.

"But is Don looking at replacing the battery system for the whole sub or just the ones that run the satellite system? Because I just read an article about a new Ion battery that GE has developed that should replace the ones we have for the satellite," asked Willy. Merrick had encouraged the young man to always think outside the box. So he kept up on his trade journals. He secretly hoped to work with Merrick someday.

"Sorry, I didn't ask. I'm assuming it's just the Satellites system though that he wants to replace," Wolfson replied looking down through the magnified glasses of the young man. It had happened before on the Poseidon Project. A new technology becomes available, and Don scraps what he has going and replaces midstream. Wolfson was eager to get the boat on the high seas before Don tinkered it to death.

"I'm going to check procurement. See if we can get those suckers. In a week if possible."

"Captain Wolfson, you are wanted in the staffing room," came over the intercom.

"The Admirals here," acknowledged the Captain.

Willy smiled and responded, "All the technology in the world and you guys are going to go sit with a bunch of loose leaf binders and try and figure out people. Good Luck."

Rear Admiral Cartwright was a stately man with bristly, grey hair and a chiseled face, and pencil thin mustache. One would say he was African American but he would tell you otherwise. He was a Black American, proudly from the state of Ohio. Wolfson got along with the Admiral well enough and had enjoyed his company on a social occasion a time or two. The meeting was directed at picking the roster of crew members.

The meeting room itself was understated. A large mahogany table filled the center with twelve gray padded chairs circled around. A small sink and coffee bar on one wall, several computer monitors on the other and a large screen television with satellite hookup and playback. But on the outside wall was double thick glass and a view of the stern of the new submarine.

For two hours they hammered through the files of each individual. The pros, the cons, the availability. There were more than two hundred files for just sixteen positions. The real challenge of the arrangement was that a lot of positions had to be dual or even three manned. Unlike a Ballistic sub which had room for several cooks, this sub needed someone to both run the radar and cook. And not burn the meatloaf.

At one point the Admiral refreshed his cup of coffee then asked, "I noticed that every time I bring up a very competent woman, you shoot her down for one reason or another. I'm beginning to detect a pattern. Any reasons or are you just superstitious?"

Wolfson leaned back in his chair and stretched out his long frame. After a moment he replied, "No chauvinistic tendencies, Admiral. You know me better than that. In fact, I think a Submarine is a very apt warship for a woman of the highest caliber. It's expertise we're interested in, not brute strength. I also realize there are now three women on board the Alabama and two on the Nautilus Two."

Cartwright nodded, flinching slightly at the thought of the Nautilus Two. "So, the problem is?"

"Actually, two problems. One being simple logistics. We'll be hot bunking eight crew members to run a gold and blue shift. And the officers in turn have to share quarters. Hell, the captain doesn't even have his own stateroom. So, if we get a woman, she will have to share. No way to get around it."

The Admiral nodded his head then said, "Yeah, I'm aware of that. I've seen the stats on aircraft carriers like the Eisenhauer. I don't remember the exact numbers but typically ten to fifteen women a tour get pregnant. But as of yet, we have had no problems with women on board a sub. Military being what it is, one touch and your screwed for life. No pun intended. And the second reason?"

Wolfson smiled then said, "Merrick."

The Admiral chuckled. "Oh, yes. Mr. Merrick."

"He would go ballistic. Create too much confusion and distraction, on the maiden voyage of his super-secret submarine."

"What if we scrubbed him from this mission?" Cartwright mentioned hopefully, actually toying with the idea.

The question caught Captain Wolfson off guard. Merrick, not go? "Sir, if Don were told he was not going on the maiden voyage of this ship, we would walk in one morning and it would not be there. He and that notebook computer of his could automate that thing and set sail by himself. Remember, the AI program on that little sub is his design."

Admiral Cartwright sighed visibly. "That's what I thought. And yet the Pentagon is having second thoughts on letting a civilian on board."

"Surely, that has nothing to do with Don, does it?" asked Wolfson with concern edging his voice. He was, no doubt qualified to command this submarine. But nothing was the same as any other sub he had ever been on.

Admiral Cartwright waved his hand in dismissal. "No, no. No political overtones or extremism. Hell, I don't think Don even votes. It's just that there's been a situation and right now isn't a good time."

"You mean Chechnya, Ukraine and North Korea."

"You read your memo's."

"This is a training voyage Admiral. A one month shake down. And nothing in the memo said anything about an escalation of forces or US commitment."

"I'm well aware of that."

"Then you're well aware that if anything goes wrong on board that ship, Don is the one man I want right there to fix it. I base that on the fact that he's the best AND you've given me exactly three crewmen to have any confidence in." Wolfson glared over at the Admiral, aware that there was an admonishment in his voice.

The Admiral, in turn smiled at the Captain. Finally, he said, "All things being equal, what the Pentagon doesn't know when this ship shoves off, won't hurt them."

"Then, we're in agreement."

"We're in agreement about Don. But let me tell you this. The Pentagon thinks differently about things. Do not be surprised if all our choices are taken. Remember, even though Don lives with that thing, it is not his boat, your boat, or even my boat. It is, in the end, their boat. And they will do what they want to do."

Capt. Wolfson took the stinging statement to heart then quickly brushed it aside and waited for the next selection from the Admiral.

The Admiral then pulled off his reading glasses, rubbed his eyes then asked, "How many we got so far?"

Capt. Wolfson quickly scanned the files and responded, "Seven. Four that we picked this morning and can be made available at a moment notice. And the three that are already here"

"We'll give the files to my assistant and he can start sending out one-page transfer orders. The sooner the better."

"Good. But what about Pentagon approval?" asked Wolfson.

"Oh the Poseidon Project has Priority One over anyone else. If we've got the bodies nearby I want to see them and interview them. Start the process in house so to speak. Besides, it'll give the whinny little bugger of an assistant something to do."

Wolfson laughed and twirled loosely at his moustache. The Admiral did not miss anything.

The small mess hall had been designed to hold fifty people. Wolfson ate his lunch with the Admiral as several of the guards and some of the last minute tenders wandered in and out. Underground like the rest of the facility, it could offer a little better fare than the standard mess hall menu. The head chef had been picked by the Admiral. The chef even went so far as to make take out lunches for Schmitty on the weekends.

The Admiral and Captain decided to take a tour around the submarine after their lunch. The selection process was slow and a walk would do their backs and stomachs some good they decided.

An open hatch at the rear of the submarine caught their attention. From the dock they could see Merrick on his knees talking to someone down below.

"Good afternoon Mr. Merrick. Chief," said the Admiral acknowledging the two men across the small expanse of water.

Gunther Schmidt's head poked up through the hatch. He waved slightly. His head was a stark white contrast to the black interior of the sub. He was a spark plug and packed full of stringy muscle, he felt himself to be the perfect size for a small submarine. But has he had done in the past, he had let his large white handlebar mustache go a little too long between trimming.

"Problems Mr. Merrick?" asked the Admiral.

Don did not really like the Admiral or the Navy for that matter. But he knew where the funding came from and who was in charge. "Nothing really," responded Don standing up. "Last week on our trial run we noticed ballast propulsion was at the middle end of our acceptable percentage and we wanted see if we could find the problem. Or even if there was one. That's all."

The week previously the submarine had actually made its first voyage with no more than four people on board. Captain Wolfson, Merrick, Schmitty and the Wizard had taken her out to open water. She had performed flawlessly, but as usual, Merrick and Schmitty wanted to tweak her one more time.

"And did you?" inquired the Admiral not really concerned.

"Of course."

"Good man. We have selected some crew members and a couple have been invited to join us this evening for supper right here at the facility, if that's all right with you Mr. Merrick?"

Don knew this was not so much a question as a statement of staying for supper. "If we can get them to see what they're up against, the sooner the better."

"And of course, you too, Chief. It seems to me all I ever see of you is a head poking up out of something, or your feet dangling in the air," mentioned the Admiral smiling.

"Just doing my job sir," came the somewhat gruff voice of the Chief. Ranking people made him nervous. He'd rather hug a nuclear reactor than talk to the Rear Admiral.

"And Chief." The Admiral rubbed his chin slightly and smiled. "At least for supper."

"Aye aye SIR!" the Chief responded in obvious reference to his stubbly chin.

The intercom broke in again, over the tones of Frank Sinatra this time. "Admiral Cartwright. Could you come to the guard house? We have a Petty Officer up here that insists he's part of the new crew."

The Admiral bid his farewell's and nodded his head at Wolfson.

Wolfson pulled alongside the rapidly walking man and stated, "Howard never gave the names to the guard house, did he?"

"You'd think I would know better. He is without a doubt the best Gopher I've ever had. But man, you have to explain things to him," smiled the Admiral. Traditionally, Rear Admiral Cartwright went through three Gophers a year. Ensign Howard, however, seemed quite content with his job and as of yet, had not asked for a transfer.

CHAPTER 2

"**P**etty Officer First Class Alex Hernandez asking permission to come aboard sir!" came the enthusiastic voice from the square shoulder man of Mexican descent. Admiral Cartwright snapped a salute right back.

"Welcome aboard," said Captain Wolfson also snapping a crisp salute. However, they were all far from being aboard anything. They were at the last guard station on the main floor of the Administration building of the Poseidon Project. A small set aside room was the access point to the large warehouse complex. Several security personnel with loaded weapons were taking their job seriously and kept the young man from taking a single step.

Hernandez handed Captain Wolfson his one sheet order that he had received less than an hour ago. Dressed in his Navy whites, the seaman's hat perched perfectly on his head, he glanced around appreciatively. He was not the least bit nervous being in the presence of the two men or the loaded M sixteens. He was focused on his surroundings. Only one week into his month-long shore leave, he was dumbfounded at the thought of his time getting cut short. But once he realized where he was being transferred, he suited up.

The Admiral checked him through the guard's station then led the group through the metal door to the warehouse which they crossed to the next guard station. Checking Alex's credential one last time, they continued to the personnel elevator.

Going down for several seconds Petty Officer Hernandez said suddenly, "I must have driven by this place a hundred times. I never knew this was down here."

"That's the idea," mentioned the Admiral.

"I can't wait to see this thing," said the Petty Officer enthusiastically.

"I can't wait to get it out into the ocean," said Wolfson in return. "And don't call it a thing in front of Mr. Merrick. He will hit you."

"Oh, that reminds me, I'm sorry Ralph. I have the packet for naming the vessel on my desk over at headquarters. I'll bring it by," mentioned the Admiral.

"About bloody time. Don's getting upset," responded Wolfson.

They reached the dock floor, turned down a hallway and broke through a set of double doors. At the west end of the dock they came upon the stern of the submarine.

Wolfson watched Hernandez's reaction. In many cases he felt one's attitude was determined by their first impression. He was not disappointed.

"Oh my God! I had heard they were working on a new experimental submarine. Look at her! That thing looks like it could do a hundred knots." Alex started jogging to the retractable gangplank on the front portion of the sub. His eyes never detached from the dizzying display of color that could be seen through the gaps in the tarpaulins. The sub's very hue seemed to change with every step. Sometimes it would mimic the surface water, then the back walls, with a reflection of light dancing merrily throughout the skin that was visible through the tarpaulins. "What kind of paint is that?" he asked suddenly.

"No paint. That's the Liquidmetal surface," responded Wolfson.

"Liquidmetal! Are you serious?" Alex swung around back then bounced onto the gangway, and asked, "Can I go on board?"

A slight swooshing sound then a whirring noise caught the Petty Officer's attention. He was suddenly staring at a nine-inch barrel that had surfaced from the deck of the ship. It was aimed directly at his head and he stopped immediately, his heart leaping to his throat. He gulped appreciatively.

"No." The voice came from Merrick who was looking over the edge of the conning tower. Hernandez finally lifted his eyes from the gun barrel and scrutinized the lack of uniform from the man on the tower. However, he was not stupid, and realized the civilian on board the boat was important. Very bloody important. He quickly backpedaled and said, "I'm so sorry sir. I got excited for just a second."

"That's not a problem Hernandez," said the Admiral. Then he looked up at Merrick and said, "Don, meet our new radar and sonar man. Petty Officer Hernandez."

"Glad to meet you Hernandez. Not to be picky about it, but no one comes on my boat until you read the manuals," said Don matter-of-factly.

"Yes, sir. Of course sir." Hernandez backed down the gangplank.

The Admiral pulled alongside the shaken seaman. He looked up at Merrick and asked, "I've seen every design and modification on this submarine. I thought the cowling was in place for when the gun became operational. I didn't realize it was actually there."

"Oh, good grief Admiral, this thing has been delayed eight times, we've had time several times over." Then Don looking down at the one of kind weapon, said, "Do you like my little toy? Laser targeting, can be fired from up on the conning tower or below. It has kinetic energy penetrators for armor piercing shells, or can be armed with small thermonuclear shells, which could conceivably sink a battleship with enough direct hits. And we've developed an amorphous alloy fragmentation shell that would severally damage anything we aim it at. And we can target and shoot within five seconds. And reload in less than a second." It was obvious he was rather pleased with the large gun.

The Admiral looked up at Don then said distinctly, "Put it away before you shoot someone Don."

"Come now Admiral. You know it's not loaded," Don said. The deck gun muzzle receded back into the turret, sealing itself immediately, then that swung around and quickly plopped itself down on the deck, to form a sleek and tapered six-foot bulb on the front of the sub. The entire process took less than four seconds.

"Cool!" said Hernandez. Suddenly, he wheeled around to face the Admiral and asked, "Am I in?"

"If your clearance checks out; you're in," smiled the Admiral.

"Yes!" the man responded pumping his fist.

Ralph only shook his head with a smile. The man just had a nine-inch wide gun barrel aimed at his chest and he still wanted to play.

Even Don let loose a lopsided grin at the obvious enthusiasm.

"And I make a darned good curry rice and a great cordon bleu," added Alex, kissing his fingers in a typical Italian gesture.

"We know," Wolfson replied smiling.

"We're still gathering crewmen and expect to have supper here at the facility this evening. You are, of course invited," noted the Admiral.

"I'm not going anywhere. I'd like to get going on the manuals, and get my stuff transferred over here if you don't mind," said the wide-eyed Alex.

"Don?" asked Wolfson.

"I'll get the manuals, but don't expect to breeze through them. We don't have sonar as you know it. It's a completely redesigned system," explained Don.

"Cutting edge, I love it!" Hernandez said grinning from ear to ear.

"We'll have Lt. Howard get your gear so you can get cracking," stated the Admiral.

Hernandez stepped off the gangplank onto the moveable dock. He looked back at the submarine, whistled appreciatively and said under his breath, "Liquidmetal. Wow."

Wolfson looked over at the Admiral and said, "I think we have a keeper."

"His record is spotless and he can put up with Merrick. I hope they're all like that."

Three more crew men arrived as the day wore on. They all seemed competent and happy with the small submarine, without the benefit of staring down the barrel of an armor piercing weapon. As with Hernandez, they all had been snagged from some other assignment and had to read the manuals before they would be allowed on board the ship. They took up home in the conference room, with paperwork to fill out, and manuals to read.

Around six o'clock that evening, the men gathered around the gangplank of the submarine.

"Does it have a name yet?" asked Lt. Eddy Faulk. The tallest there at six foot two he reminded everyone of the typical farm boy with a shock of red hair, glasses that never seemed to stay on his nose, an easy manner and a wide grin. But, like the others he had shown superior skills at mastering the weapons systems. And in his case, had long ago mastered the duck through of the typical submarine doorway. But the little sub gave him concern. He had been reassured from Don that the doorways were ample enough for his long frame. Eddy, in this case however, was not very crucial to the ship as they were to set sail unarmed.

"No, not yet." Answered Don sitting on the deck with his laptop beside him.

Hernandez slid up next to Eddy and said, "You ought to see the deck gun. Smooth as a cheerleader's butt cheeks."

Eddy looked over at the man and smiled. "I was looking at the schematic on the thing. Very impressive with the synchronized gears and self-loading cartridges." He pointed then added, "The entire thing seals inside that bubble, with the shells feeding from down below. Absolutely nothing like that on any submarine."

Don looked up and said, "Excuse me. Eddy, right? And you're the weapons officer?"

Eddy smiled and nodded, pushing the glasses back up.

Don nodded back then said, "You are going to have a very boring voyage. This is a dry run. The Bureau of Naval Weapons, in all their stupidity decided we were too experimental to have bullets. No weapons on board this time."

The man nodded his head again and responded, "I understand sir. However, it will need a weapons officer when it goes to permanent duty and the more I know, the better. Even if it is to train a replacement."

Don looked over at the man. All this enthusiasm was almost infectious. He watched as Wolfson and the Admiral walked over to the small group of men. The men asked the Captain and Admiral several questions in each of their perspective fields of expertise.

After several minutes Don heard a question about the amorphous metal which made up the shell of the submarine. He stood up and called out to Wolfson, "Ralph, let's do the metal ball thing."

Wolfson looked over at the Admiral and asked, "Have you seen this yet?"

"No, I can't say that I have," replied the curious Admiral Cartwright.

Wolfson walked back into the main rooms of the facility and after a few minutes returned with a large metal ball, one foot in diameter and hollow. The group of men crowded around as Wolfson held the ball up over his head and dropped it onto the concrete surface of the dock. It bounced four times then rolled a foot and stopped. He then picked it up, walked up the gangplank and handed it to Don.

"I never grow tired of this little trick," said Wolfson as he stepped back.

Don raised the ten-pound ball over his head and dropped it the very way that Wolfson had. However, when it hit the deck of the submarine, it bounced five feet in the air, then continued bouncing for another thirty seconds, glancing off the deck another twenty times, until it finally lost momentum, bounced off the level surface of the sub and rolled off into the water.

"I don't get it," observed an impressed Ensign Bruce Eddington, also with the weapons team. The Admiral too, shook his head in wonderment.

Don sought to explain. "Amorphous metal is a process made with zirconium, titanium, nickel, copper and beryllium. There is no crystallization to destroy. Therefore, it does not dent or fracture the way steel would. The reason the metal ball bounced so well is that the skin of the ship did not absorb any of the energy of the ball. There-fore, it simply bounced until gravity pulled it back to earth."

"So how strong is this stuff?" asked Alvin Allen with a slight Texas drawl. He was to help Willy with the elaborate computer systems on board.

"Alvin Allen right?" Don looked over at Wolfson and said sardonically, "Alvin Allen, Willy Williams. All we need now is a Johnny Johnson and we'll be set. Anyway, Alvin, to answer your question, because it doesn't break down, it is up to six times stronger than titanium steel."

Alvin smiled and asked, "I'm a technical type of guy. How much force can this skin withstand?"

Don shook his head and answered honestly, "We don't know exactly."

Alvin raised his eyebrows dramatically. Wolfson looked over at the man and then attempted to explain. "Alvin, you have to understand, we've done exhaustive tests and there is no doubt this is much stronger than steel. The problem is that even though we've run tests on models and computerized scenarios, no one has ever made anything of this size before. We really don't know what kind of force this amount of Liquidmetal can take at various depths."

Alvin nodded then added, "The ultimate practical test. Battlefield conditions."

"That's why the test drive," finished Wolfson. Then he added, "Our one-month test run includes depth testing and stress relations."

Then Don jumped in and added, "But, using computer models, pressurized stress tests and the typical explosive devices, we think, that it could conceivably, take a direct hit, by the most powerful torpedo the U.S. Navy has. And survive pretty much unscathed."

The group of men murmured between them over the impressive nature when the Admiral injected, "At ten dollars a pound it better take a direct hit."

"Ten dollars a pound? Well, how much is steel?" asked Hernandez.

"About thirty-five cents a pound," replied Wolfson. He heard several whistles of appreciation.

"The skin alone on that little submarine is worth more than a billion dollars," stated the Admiral.

Don started walking off the gangplank and injected, "The nuclear reactor is also made out of amorphous metal, which means that it's much lighter but capable of a lot more power than any other submarine. Cruising speed is well over ninety knots and that's not conjecture gentlemen. That's fact. We've done it."

"And how is it there are no rivets or bolts on the skin on this thing? I mean, it seems to be all one piece except for the conning tower," noted Hernandez as both Alvin and Eddy nodded at the sudden realization that this sub had no plating.

Don smiled then attempted to explain. "There's a reason why it's called Liquidmetal. A couple hundred miles up the coast, in another facility, we built a fiberglass shell, and over a several month time, never stopping mind you, we sprayed the interior of the shell. With Liquidmetal. Its fibrous state makes it stronger, but hard to work with. But absolutely no seams to bust or rivets to bounce radar off of."

Hernandez realized he had been right. There was nothing else in the world like it.

Then Wolfson cut in, "Actually that shouldn't be that much of a problem anyway."

Again the men looked somewhat dumbfounded and finally Alex asked, "And why is that?"

Don answered quickly, "We have plasma-ion stealth technology."

"What the hell is that?" asked Alvin, then realizing the Admiral was still standing there he added, "Sir."

Don smiled, as he had the rapt audience in the palm of his hand. Finally, he attempted to explain. "We have a Plasma Ion generator on board the ship. We found out a long time ago that plasma build up will disturb radio waves, including sonar. We send out a plasma shield around the ship and it bounces sonar off, dissipating it harmlessly. The enemy basically can't get a clear fix of what we look like."

One of the men whistled appreciatively, while Alex simply yelled out, "Shields up Scotty!" Which brought about a small chuckle from the group.

Eddy was looking at the ship riding low in the water, bent over trying to get a grasp of a thought. Finally, he demanded, "But looking at this from this angel, the sub isn't round? Is it?"

Don shook his head once again. "Doesn't have to be. More oval than round because of the amorphous metal. We gain a lot of space that way."

Don looked up and saw the head chef and Schmitty coming up from behind the men and had assumed that supper was about ready. Gunther looked well-manicured with even the ends of his bushy white mustache trimmed smartly, and decked out in a clean uniform.

The head chef tapped the Admiral on the shoulder and said with a smile, "Sir, supper is served."

The Admiral turned, acknowledged the chef then saw Gunther and remarked, "Chief, you do clean up well."

"Yes sir," was all the Senior Petty Officer said in return.

The intercom from above snapped into life and said, "Admiral Cartwright, you have a visitor at the guard station. You told us to tell you when she arrived."

The Admiral took a visible breath of resignation. He grabbed Capt. Wolfson by the elbow and said, "Come with me, we need to talk."

Wolfson looked strangely at the Admiral for a second. He had assumed the woman was the Admiral's wife. As the men slowly ambled toward the mess hall the Admiral and Captain walked briskly to the elevator.

"What's up Admiral? Don't tell me you snuck in a female crew member?" asked Wolfson, grinning, still unsure as to where this was going.

"Worse than that," replied Cartwright, entering the elevator, waited for Wolfson then hit the up button.

Wolfson's brow furrowed deeply. Now he was lost. The Admiral did not speak until they had reached half way up to the guard office. Then he hit the stop button abruptly. He sighed once again then started. "First of all, this was not my doing. As I had said before, this boat belongs to the Navy and they will do with it what they want."

"Why do I get the impression I'm not going to like this?" observed Wolfson, still at a loss.

"There's a woman up their waiting for us. Her name is Beverly Hornacher. Newly commissioned, Captain Beverly Hornacher," said Cartwright.

Wolfson thought for a moment. Then he said, "I know Beverly. Very smart and a good, straight arrow." Ralph shook his head then added, "I sort of wondered why she wasn't brought up as XO. I thought it might have been logistics of still being on the Nautilus Two. The way you're acting, I take it SHE's not the XO."

"No. And I'm really sorry Ralph. I know how much you've been looking forward to this command."

"Anything to do with Admiral Hornacher on the Joint Chiefs of Staff?" asked Wolfson, the realization slowly taking hold.

"I don't know." He looked at Wolfson. Then he said, "All right, the Admiral gave me his assurances that he had nothing to do with her advancement's or assignments, trying his level best to stay out of her career. Vice Admiral Collins was the one that actually promoted her to Captain this sub. But face it, the selection committee is overseen by Admiral Hornacher. And they may have been trying to get on his good side. But, I've never really gotten any confirmation that he had anything to do with this."

Ralph was a calm man but this shook him. He glared at the chiseled features of the Man bestowing this new but disturbing information on him. Finally, he asked, "Why didn't you tell me earlier? God, it's clear you've known for quite a while."

Admiral Cartwright defended himself by saying, "She was still on board the Nautilus Two in the Pacific when the request came down from high command. I thought there was a possibility she wouldn't accept command or her captain would in fact, block the transfer. Or simply, that the transfer wouldn't be made in time. There was a good chance that she wouldn't be here and I didn't want to ruffle feathers before then." He then put a hand on Ralph's shoulder and added, "I had hoped you would maintain command, and sent a letter directly to Defense Secretary Perry on my recommendations. You see how well that went. And so …"

Wolfson ran a large hand over his lower jaw, then brushed his mustache. Finally, he said, "Hoping the problem would simply go away. I appreciate the thought anyway."

"I managed to keep you on the sub Ralph. Just not as Captain."

Wolfson looked down at his hands. If he were the emotional type or the hard edged kind of person, he realized about now would be the time to blow up and throw a temper tantrum. But he was not. He swallowed his feelings and counted the blessings of still being on board. They could have transferred his sorry ass somewhere else.

"Let's go meet the lady," he said finally.

Admiral Cartwright shook his head and said in a friendly voice, "If there was one thing that would raise your hackles and push you over the edge I thought this would be it. You're taking it very well."

Captain Wolfson stopped, his hand hovering over the elevator button, then he wheeled on the Admiral. Suddenly he said, "I'm a Navy man. I do what I'm told. But don't for an instance think I'm happy with this or even okay with it. I'm pissed. This has been my submarine for the last eight months and for the brass to sneak someone in, man or woman, chaps my ass. But, it is my nature to look at the cup as half full. I will be on board that sub and have a guiding hand in its maiden voyage. That's what counts." Wolfson then stuck a finger in the Admiral's chest and added, "Besides, YOU still have to deal with Merrick. He will throw something. I guarantee it."

Before the Admiral could even respond Wolfson smashed the button and folded his arms over his chest. The Admiral sighed heavily. He had pleasantly forgot about Don.

The guard's station to the elevator and to the large freight elevator was nothing more than a large warehouse attached to the administration building. Several guards stood at the large garage doors and walk ways. There were various, covered materials and pallets, parts of the sub not in use, spread out on the concrete floor. At one time it had been filled with parts and manpower. The woman in her dress blues, her service hat and orders tucked securely under her arm, standing in the middle of it all looked strangely out of place.

Wolfson and the Admiral approached the woman as she recognized the Admiral and stiffened to attention. She snapped off a salute and said, "Captain Hornacher reporting for duty sir." She then handed the Admiral a manila envelope with her orders.

The Admiral threw a quick salute back, tucked the envelope under his arm, and said, "Welcome aboard Captain. May I present Captain Wolfson."

Beverly smiled at the familiar face and said happily, "Ralph, glad to see you again." She shook his hand, aware that his palm swallowed her whole hand. Wolfson quickly scanned the woman, letting the memories of several years ago reshape themselves. Statuesque, barely an inch shorter than him, she was cute in a feminine sort of way. She had a round face, a pleasant smile and plucked but dark eyebrows. Her rich brownish red hair, barely shoulder length, pulled into a tight bun. The uniform was immaculate, but her eyes glinted of a steely sharpness that he liked. But even he could tell, she was tired.

The head guard walked up next to the Admiral and said, "Her clearance checked out. We were just waiting for you."

"Of course," replied the Admiral. He turned and started walking back toward the last guard office before the elevators.

"I can't wait to see this ship Admiral. From what I've read there's nothing like it," said Beverly. She then turned to Captain Wolfson and asked, "In what capacity are you linked to this project Ralph?"

"I was in charge," came the curt reply.

The Admiral winced. It would not have been the words he would have chosen to start a conversation with.

"So, you were the Navy liaison man on this project. It must have been quite the endeavor to build the sub," Beverly stated rather innocently.

Wolfson sighed then explained, "I was the Navy overseer on this project, but I was also under the impression that I would command the sub on her first voyage."

The Admiral was holding open the elevator door, aware of the conversation behind him.

Beverly stopped. Then she asked, "Am I to understand this correctly? You didn't know I was coming did you?" Then she turned her gaze at the Admiral.

"No. Not until about five minutes ago," replied Wolfson honestly, he too looking over at the Admiral.

"Admiral Cartwright, you knew. I got the non-secure paperwork and orders for the Poseidon Project two months ago," she said aimed directly at the Admiral.

The Admiral waved everyone into the elevator and closed the door, then sighed. "All right. I knew that the Pentagon had offered the position to you, but I did not know you were actually coming until two weeks ago. And considering you were still out to sea five days ago I thought it best until you actually showed up. I did not receive Naval confirmation that you were on your way until two days ago. This sub was supposed to go to sea almost two weeks ago."

A washed looked crossed Beverly's face. Then she said, "Oh my God. You both think this is political." Then she turned back to the Admiral and stated, "And you were hoping I would go away. Didn't you?"

"No, no, not go away, just, let's say simply miss the boat," responded the Admiral sheepishly. Then he added in his own defense, "Look it. I knew Ralph had been on board for a while and thought it a little unfair."

Beverly gazed down at the floor, chose her words carefully then said, "I'm sorry Captain Wolfson. I put in for this command two years ago. While my father is privy to information and I knew about this, I did not ask my father for any favors. And as far as I know, he had nothing to do with this."

Ralph glanced over at Beverly and said, "I've been here for the last eight months, overseeing the project for the Navy. I've tightened bolts, greased bearings and stayed up until midnight trying to solve problems. I made the fatal error of assuming."

Beverly shook her head and sighed, then responded, "I make no apologies. I am as fit to command this sub as you are. I've done my service as XO on the Nautilus Two. I've read every bit of information that the Navy would supply me. And whether or not it my father had any bearing on the command decision, my name is on the orders to be Captain. And I will not go away nicely."

Wolfson suddenly realized he was arguing with the lady, which was not his intention. Suddenly he said with his mustache turning up into a grin, "And I will be the second in command and help you any way that I can, Captain."

Beverly smiled and gazed up into the softened face of Capt. Wolfson. "The Navy did not see fit to send me certain information. I will need all the assistance I can get in the next two weeks and the coming voyage."

Admiral Cartwright looked at both the Captains and said, "I'm glad you got that resolved."

Beverly said to him as he opened the elevator door and she passed through, "You're not off the hook by any means, Admiral."

The Admiral sighed and followed them out the door. As much as Capt. Hornacher wanted to see the ship she had been reading about for the past two years, she had been told of the first crews supper and she felt that was more in order.

She found the crew's mess to be much nicer than most and definitely an upgrade from the Submarine she had just left. Usually in the course of building the sub, the shifts were every eight hours. It actually had a restaurant styled ambiance as each table had its own hanging lamp. A wood chair rail circled the facility as carpeting soaked up most unwanted noise. Large square tables meant to seat four with comfortable cushioned chairs. Beverly was pleasantly surprised.

Most of the crew members were gathered around Mr. Merrick, Willy Williams, the chief pilot, Warrant Officer Clyde Caldwell and the chief navigator, First Lt Robert Duran. The last two had been on board for the last month as they studied the nuances of the new sub. The nine men had pulled several tables together to discuss the submarine in detail. A group of guards occupied another set of tables in the back of the dining facility.

Merrick had seen the Admiral and the two Captains enter the mess hall. As they lined up to get their steak, which was the specialty of the night, Merrick remarked, "Oh look. It's the floor show. Military style. Loses something in translation."

As the other men turned around to look, several of them guffawing, it did strike all of them that the woman was out of place.

After a few moments the Admiral led the two others to the tables. "May we join you?"

"Pull up a table," said Merrick, still in the dark.

Wolfson pulled up as close as he could to the Admiral and said, "I'm going to go sit down at the other end. I don't want to be in the line of fire."

"Coward," the Admiral said under his breath. Moving a new table onto the end of the three they had already slid together, the Admiral was situated one table away from Merrick with Beverly sitting opposite him. Wolfson sat at the other end.

Before they sat, the Admiral made introductions. Beverly placed her tray next to the Admiral then shook each and every one of the crewman's hands. Until they came to Merrick. He only nodded at the woman in acknowledgement. Don was really not paying attention, but it was obvious that the woman was to be part of something concerning the submarine. A creepy feeling was starting to take hold of him. He could not see her Captain's emblem on her epaulette, but the introductions did not bode well with him.

Beverly stood, at first did not know what to make of Don, as it was clear she was being snubbed. Her intuition was to question him. She was not used to insubordination. Then she thought better as everyone was new and trying to learn their parts. Besides, she thought she could guess Don's importance.

There were a few seconds of awkward silence as everyone gathered their seats. After Beverly had made herself comfortable in front of her food, she decided she needed to break the ice.

Finally, she asked, "So, Mr. Merrick. Are you the DM that I see initialed on all the sub manuals that I've been able to read?"

Merrick in turned ignored the question, glanced wickedly at the Admiral, then asked, "Can I ask what in what capacity you're here? Captain?"

Beverly looked across the table at the Admiral and asked accusingly, "You didn't tell anyone. Did you? These men have no idea, do they?"

"Please don't tell me you're coming on my ship," Don said venomously, his face showing a definite distrust.

"Your ship?" replied Beverly. It was now clear that Don was the mastermind behind the submarine, but no civilian was going to get in the way of doing her job.

The Admiral jumped in quickly. "Now Don. I will not have any heated debates. You know this is not your ship any more than it's my ship."

"Don, meet the new Captain," said Wolfson suddenly, from the safety of several feet away.

Don glared at the woman then turned his hated gaze on the Admiral. Finally, he asked angrily, "Captain my ship? Her? You're kidding right? Ralph's been on this vessel for eight months now! And you bring in a nobody? Are you God-Damned insane?! Or is it just the fucking Navy that screwed up?"

The Admiral was genuinely taken back by the acid blast of words. He charged in, "Don, now calm down. She's a fit commander and there will be no problems in this matter ..." Before the Admiral could continue, Don was raising out of his chair.

Don's face was twisted in rage when he said loudly, "Hornacher. God don't tell me. Your dad's on the Joint Chiefs. Isn't he? That explains why you're here. God I should have known fucking better than to let the Navy have this boat. God I knew they would fuck it up!""

Wolfson could see that Don was going to blow. The Admiral was starting to get out of his chair when Don started in again.

Don slammed his fist down on the table and said, "Cartwright, I will not have some renegade, incompetent politician on my ship!" Then he glared at Beverly and roared, "Especially a female one!" The anger finally vented as Don picked up his tray and flung it at the far wall, clattering to the floor. He glared at the Admiral for several seconds then clenched his fists together and stomped out of the room. A sudden hush fell on the group. All the young seamen stared at each other, an unfounded drama taking them by complete surprise.

"Don't you just hate it when I'm right?" Inserted Wolfson quietly.

The Admiral stood there. He looked down at Capt. Hornacher and said finally, "I'm so sorry. Let me go talk to him."

Beverly, in all her life had never been treated like that in the Navy. There had been times when someone would question her strengths and weaknesses as a woman or her identification with her father. But this outburst went beyond anything she had encountered.

"No. Let me go," said Wolfson raising up out of his chair. "You need to explain to her and the rest of the crew what's going on."

A silence permeated the mess hall as not even the sound of chewing could be heard. Beverly was staring down at the napkin in her lap. Her own exhaustion was keeping the anger from rising up inside. She knew her face was turning red as she was letting her military training kicked in and she realized she still had a job to do. She was the Captain, and she was in charge, no matter what. The Admiral returned to his chair next to her.

Finally, Beverly turned to him and said, "You know, this is not quite the reception I was hoping for on my first command."

The Admiral slowly shook his head. "It's my fault. I'm so sorry. I didn't handle any of this very well."

Beverly shrugged her shoulders and said, "It's not your fault. These men have worked together for almost a year and you didn't want to disappoint any of them. And I can see why you didn't tell Mr. Merrick. As brilliant as the man obviously is, he needs a swift kick in the ass, and the pacifier taken out of his mouth."

This brought about a small chuckle from the group of men. Captain Hornacher turned to them and said, attempting to smile, "Now, introduce yourself properly and tell me what you do."

Ralph had wandered the facility, checking the drawing rooms and conference rooms before he found Don sitting cross legged on top of the deck gun, his feet dangling over the back edge. He had a lit cigar and he was studying the burning ember. Ralph stopped at the entrance to the gangplank and waited a moment. Then he asked, "Permission to come aboard."

"Not my ship, so I've been told. Do what you want," Don responded coldly.

Wolfson walked up the plank and stopped directly in front of Don, then sat down. He spread his arms out and leaned backwards. Ultimately, he said, "Don, it's a minor disappointment to be shrugged off."

"Don't care. I'm not going. The Navy can have the damned thing."

"Of course you are. This ship is to state of the art not to have you on board. The Navy has done what it has done. There is no arguing," responded Wolfson.

Don shook his head. "You know as well as I do just because she's been on a submarine doesn't mean she knows a damned thing about THIS submarine. It's like asking a teenage girl to drive an eighteen wheeler. She may have a license, but she knows nothing."

"Oh, Jesus Don. It's not that simple."

Don shot Ralph an evil look then launched himself. "I've been working on this ship for ten years. Developing the metal, designing the interior, making the technology. All to make this sub run for the Navy. And now they bring in a political stooge, and a woman to boot."

Wolfson let slide the chauvinistic tendency, for he knew Don well enough. There had been several women engineers on the project. Don was a smart man and gleaned his knowledge from anywhere he could. Finally, Ralph responded, "A woman has nothing to do with it, you know that. Look it, initially I was mad too. But it occurred to me that I will still be on the maiden voyage of the most technologically advanced craft on or off the planet. And that's all I really wanted. And you want to see how all your designs work. It really doesn't matter who's in charge. We're the plank owners of this sub and we're all sailing into history."

"Boy, you seem to be taking it well," muttered Don.

"I want to be on this boat. One way or another."

Don then extended himself and said, "That's my point and why I'm so pissed. What gives her the right to be part of this history for what it is when she's done nothing to deserve any part of it? A lot of engineers and builders have put in more sweat and blood then she ever will. She waltzes in here and takes over. Without any real credential to back her up other than political. I don't know Ralph. I just don't like it."

Wolfson shook his head and replied, "Don, you're missing the point. No one remembers who captained the Nautilus or the Triton.

It's the fact that the ship themselves made history. Hell, you built the damned thing and other than a few people around here, no one will probably remember that. But what they will remember is the ship Don. Its radical designs and capabilities make it an important addition to submarine warfare. No one will remember us. But we can tell people and our grandchildren, we were on board the world's first stealth sub." Then Wolfson thought for a moment then continued. "And Don. She's capable. Being XO of the Nautilus Two is rough duty. She's been underwater for periods of six months with a hundred men, telling THEM what to do. She's had to earn her thick skin the hard way. Beverly is a capable leader and seaman, no doubt about it."

Don's hand dropped down and he stroked the glass like finish of the skin of the deck gun. Suddenly he started in. "You know. I grew up with Star Trek. But I realized at a young age that was not how a space ship would be designed. That's when I decided to make my own space ships. Out of paper and cardboard, I sailed around the universe. As I grew older, I realized that I would never get off this rock. That's when I went underwater. Do you know, I actually built a submarine out of a propane tank and went out into the ocean with it at the age of twelve?"

"I didn't know that," replied Wolfson, grateful that Don seemed to be calming down.

Don looked up, smirked slightly and then said, "It sank."

Wolfson looked up at Don, then chuckled slightly. Then he said, "So you built another one I suppose."

"Nope. Taught myself how to dive, then went down and retrieved the damned thing. I wanted to find out what I did wrong," Don said dropping an ash into his hand and crushing it into his trousers. "And then I rebuilt it. Scarred the hell out of a yachting club when I surfaced in the middle of the regatta."

Ralph laughed slightly then said in observance, "This ship sinks Don, and you're not on it they'll never find out what went wrong. They'll be no survivors."

"I know." Don sighed heavily then continued, "I've put everything I've got into this boat. I've questioned everything, turned it around, stared at it through a child's eye and asked what if." Then he stared Wolfson in the eye and said, "I just don't want some nincompoop doing something stupid to her. I trust you. You're about as level headed as they come."

Wolfson directed his stare into Don's eyes and said, "Don, as proud as both of us are with this vessel, if you're not going, I'm not going. I don't have the answers." But then Wolfson thought for a moment and added, "Don, she's not going to do something stupid. She's not a dummy. And quite frankly, between you and me, she's not bad to look at either."

Don continued looking over at Wolfson. Finally, with great purpose and a lopsided smirk he said, "I suppose. We'll have to keep Miss Hornacher from sinking the damned thing."

Ralph extended his hand. "We sail. Together."

Don frowned. He grasped the hand firmly and replied, "We sail. Together." Then he added, "Are we still on for next Wednesday night?"

Wolfson nodded his head, stared blankly at Don, then he too sat on the deck gun and then replied, "More than ever."

For the next twenty minutes they traded tales of their first boats, designs that Don had tried and failed, the shark that pulled Wolfson out into the ocean. Their conversation was finally broken by a voice.

"Mind if I come aboard?"

Don glanced over and without changing expressions he said, "Your ship, do what you want."

Beverly walked up the gangplank, unbuttoning the top of her uniform and loosening the tie. "You don't mind do you? I've had a whole eight hours sleep in the last three days. Helicoptered my way off the Naut Deuce to Newfoundland, grabbed a plane to Maine, grabbed another flight to Chicago, flew into LAX. I'm not even sure where the rest of my clothes are." She sat down on the deck and slipped off her dress shoes. She proceeded to massage her feet.

After a few more moments she looked at the two men, focused on Don and said, "Look it Mr. Merrick. I know my father knew I wanted this command. I honestly don't know if he had anything to do with it. I do know that this ship will sail on time with or without you. And I won't apologize for raining on your parade, Ralph. But Mr. Merrick, from what the Admiral's told me, I'd just as soon you were on board."

Don looked over at the woman and said, "Afraid you're going to get stuck with the Isaac Parel?"

Beverly smiled broadly. "The thought as you might say had occurred to me. This sub is so radical, there is no way our crew is going to know all the answers. And to leave the answers behind would be a shame."

Ralph shook his head and asked, "Isaac Parel? I'm afraid I don't know who that is?"

Beverly looked over at Don then plunged in. "The Isaac Parel is a submarine made by the Spanish. Because of an engineering miscalculation, it was seventy tons overweight. It literally would not surface once it submerged."

"Are you kidding me?" Asked a baffled Ralph.

Don added, "Then to make things worse they decided to fix the problem by making it longer. Unfortunately, at that point it wouldn't fit inside its own dock. They then had to dredge and fix the dock. God only knows how much money they wasted because an engineer screwed up."

"And that's sort of why I would like our engineer on board. In case we can't surface," stated Beverly with a wily grin.

Don thought for the briefest of moments then replied, "I suppose I should be there to make sure the thing functions."

She smiled then said, "I'll buy that I guess." Then she looked over at Wolfson. She asked, "Captain?"

"If Don screwed up, someone's got to help paddle. It will make for interesting sleeping arrangements, however."

Beverly honestly looked perplexed then said, "I've had no information on the actual interior drawings. I hadn't thought of that. A lot more room on the Naut. Deuce." As Don had done minutes before she stroked the deck of the ship. "It's the first time I've seen it. The texture is like glass." She looked up at Merrick and said, "It is a magnificent ship Mr. Merrick. The Admiral has filled me in on all you've done."

Don had come into a melancholy acceptance of the situation. Attempting to avoid a new round of arguments he said suddenly, "Speaking of the Admiral. When in the hell are we going to get a name for this tub?"

Beverly responded, "I believe that's what he went to go find out when I left the mess hall." She muffled a yawn then noted, "I find it curious that the pilot of this boat is nicknamed Crash."

Wolfson laughed. "You mean Caldwell? Did he tell you the story?"

"No, but I'm sure I'll get filled in after we set sail."

They could hear the door opening at the rear of the facility as the Admiral approached, followed by all the crewmen. The Admiral had a piece of paper in his hand. He stopped at the dock end of the gangplank. He took heart in the fact that Don was not strangling Beverly.

Beverly had stifled the act of jumping up and calling attention. She realized the atmosphere was one of mutual cooperation and the fact that Wolfson did not budge made her comfortable. Besides, she was tired.

"We have it gentlemen. And lady," the Admiral acknowledged, correcting himself.

"I just know it. It's going to be the Flounder. Or the Blowfish." Stated Don bringing up snickers from the crew.

"What's with the music?" asked Hernandez cutting in, taking notice of Barbara Streisand singing merrily in the background.

"I like it," mentioned Beverly, taking calm in the excellent voice.

"My contract, my music," said Don. Then he looked up at Alex and asked, "Got a problem with it?"

After witnessing Don throw things in the mess hall and having a gun aimed at him, Alex backtracked and said correctly, "Nope. I like it. Works for me."

"Good answer," observed Don.

Admiral Cartwright shook his head and then glanced down at the single sheet of paper. He grinned slightly then said, "Mr. Merrick, I know how much you wanted the boat to be named Poseidon, but it wasn't to be. But the committee did like one of your other suggestions. Well, lady and gentlemen, you are now sitting on the world's first stealth operating submarine with the designation USS Stealth Sub Number Five-Ought-One. Meet, the USS Specter."

Wolfson smiled, stood up, threw his arms out and said, "Specter." He pivoted a complete turn, keeping his feet on the crystalline deck and then said, "I like it."

"About freaking time," came from Don, who was also smiling.

"The USS Specter," tripped off Beverly's tongue, smiling inward at the slightly creepy title. Then she glanced at the oddly designed conning tower, the odd fins rising up to the conning tower edge, the bubble that Don was sitting on and added, "Now all we have to do is figure out how to get our spooky little ship out into the ocean."

The crew laughed in appreciation.

Willy looked appreciatively at the small group of people then he said, "Oh, Tinkerbelle can do that."

Beverly thought for a moment then stated, "I've read all the specs on the Specter. Nothing code named Tinkerbelle."

"That's not a code name Captain Hornacher. It's my name given to me at my inception." Came a very disembodied voice, distinctly female in nature, echoing throughout the entire chamber.

Captain Hornacher stared into the air; eyes wide in wonder.

"Oh Captain, I'm sorry. Didn't you know? We have a quantum computer; with the neatest AI program you have ever seen." Smiled Willy broadly.

CHAPTER 3

Captain Beverly Hornacher's reflection seemed to splinter away in a million directions. The afternoon sunshine and calm harbor waters would keep her image on the edge of the Specter's conning tower for several seconds, then it would fracture when a cloud rolled by. Looking over the top of the fast-moving ship slicing neatly through the water, there were times she really could not say what color the Specter was. Much more than the muted gray of the interior dock, the ocean let the reflective surface become one with the background. Beverly noted with great satisfaction when the Specter encountered a good-sized wave, it cleaved straight through without even the smallest of shutter. Undoubtedly, the benefit of the many hours Don took to engineer the futuristic machine.

She pulled down on the bill of her red hat, proud of its egg salad on the brim, USS SPECTER stitched on the front. A dark blue windbreaker with an emblem stitched on the left pocket showed a black starry background with a white stitched sub in the middle, the impression being it was a ghost ship. The first of its kind.

Beverly was ever mindful of the radio traffic within the sub. An ear bud and wrap around radio kept everyone in constant communications. A simple tap on the exterior of the bud was the PTT (push to talk) switch. The innovation from Motorola involved a voice recognition system. There was constant radio traffic but nothing geared toward the Captain so it came across low. Until the recognition for Beverly, Hornacher or Captain came through, or mass signal to the entire crew, Beverly took little notice. But she snickered every time Don's voice came across, because he was obviously irritated at something.

Even though the open ocean held a certain excitement, her thoughts were off elsewhere. She mentally reflected on the last two weeks and their intensity. All the crew members had finally been brought on board. First Lieutenant Bobby Smith was brought in to help Lt. Duran in navigation. A stocky African American with a calm demeanor, he was almost thirty years of age with countless abilities under his belt. As with the sonar, navigation was the most redesigned system on the Specter. The plus with Bobby was that he was a trained medic, having had battle experience. Ralph had thought it advantageous to snag the young man.

Three more nuclear engine experts were brought on to help out Schmitty. It was the one consideration where size did matter. Because the engine was available through a crawl space, no one more than a hundred and sixty pounds a person. Admiral Cartwright with the help of Admiral Hornacher, had stolen some of the best. All chiefs, Seniors or Masters, they all looked to be carbon copies. Paul Garibaldi, Denny Kroger, Ray Dicenzo, joined Gunther in taking care of the power plant for the Specter.

Because radar and sonar were separate but compatible, Alex was supplemented by three more trainees. Rory Thayer, Steve Barrington and Henry Hyde, all of which were cross trained in the communications aspect of the Specter. Henry, unfortunately deriving his name by a pair of rather indulgent beatnik parents. But the man with the overly white skin was very proud of his British upbringing and had the typical sense of humor.

Once the stigma of a female crew member was broken, both Wolfson and the Admiral decided that it would be good to have least one more woman on board. Enter Francine Noguchi, a petite woman of Japanese descent. Cute with a round face she quickly let it be known she was just one of the guys. In fact, she hated her name and insisted on being called 'Frank.' Beverly instantly liked her. She would back up Crash in steering. Don, of course was not thrilled with a 'woman' driver. He whimsically relented when she threatened to kick his ass.

It was a good crew that seemed to mesh well together thought Beverly.

She thought of the first time Alex was allowed on board the Specter. He had read the manuals several times, asking Merrick questions time after time. But to actually enable the working system made the young man giddy.

Don had explained to Hernandez the first day on the ship, as Beverly had also listened intently, "Alex, I'm not even going to try to explain how this works. Your job is to simply read the damned thing. We do not have SONAR at all but instead it is PDM's own version of LIDAR. Think laser targeting coming from sixty-four different points on the Specter all flashing at the speed of light ranging out too almost a hundred miles' passive, and ten miles active. Once it pinpoints an object, the computer zeroes in on it and creates a dot matrix of the thing then identifies it and turns it into a Three-D picture for you to read on your monitor. The thing to remember is we don't do any freaking pinging or noises or anything like that. Got it?"

Don had also gone on to explain it was sonar in name only as there was no sound echo locating involved. And no little blipping radar screens, no telltale pinging noises to give away the submarine. Thirty-inch computer monitors gave a detailed picture of any object in the water and another computer was used to track down any information. The LIDAR station was just a few feet away, set up much the same way, with several monitors offering several views. Don insisted they refer to them as Lidar as radar and sonar were now very obsolete.

Letting Alex and the others play with the system; they detected a fish cruising around in the lock with them. Using the computer, it identified the sand shark. As a young male, looking for food and a way out.

Once a day Merrick would throw something in the water and have the guys find it. It took a long while for them all to get a hang of a new system, but the image was ten times anything that they would have had with sonar. A dozen underwater infrared high image cameras' made things even easier.

As Beverly looked into the ocean, she smiled and tenderly touched a bruise on the hairline of her forehead. It was the prize of being allowed to tag along with Schmitty as he took her on an inside tour of the workings of the sub. There was a small tunnel that ran the entire length of the ship. All the electrical and computer feeds, the access to the engine itself, the emergency route to the weapons system, all accessed through the four feet by four feet tunnel.

Gunther was at home cruising through the narrow shaft. And he seemed quite at ease showing the new captain how the ship worked from the inside. Having read most of the schematics on the vessel, she was still surprised that the engineering literally went through a small hatch in the conning tower, another hatch in the control room to the engine room. She crawled through it with Gunther, abruptly looking up when the small blast door to the engine room came open and the magnitude engulfed her. And with much fanfare he showed her the propulsion system, opening another small access panel leading into where the Injector Jets that rocketed the Specter at unprecedented speeds. And the nuclear reactor that generated more power than the one that ran the standard Triton class in less than a third of the space.

There was no shape way or form that Beverly even pretended to understand how all this worked underneath the submarine, but at least she understood what they were talking about when she heard the Jets were running at eighty percent.

Of course, Schmitty chastised her when the tour was done, feeling it was his fault that the woman bumped her head. Beverly thought Gunther treated her more like a daughter than a commander. Like her own father, she felt that Gunther was one man that would be there to the bitter end, and go down swinging.

Beverly was also amazed at how functional the Specter was. Unlike any other sub she had been on, the control room or attack center as Don called it, had no pipes or steam lines or even the millions of dials and levers and large shut off valves. Everything was computerized.

The nerve center to the ship was almost thirty feet long and twenty-two feet wide. With ambient lighting, its dark gray interior was well lit without being direct or garish. Beverly did not know how Don did it but she could not honestly tell what caused the lighting. It had an eight-foot table in the center of the room, meant for mapping. But there were no maps. Even this was computerized with charting done with split second accuracy. They could come within inches of their destination. And the entire sub could be run by three crewmen, who knew what they were doing. The navigation also had access to the computers and could simply, using the mounted swivel chairs could go from the mapping board to the navigation consoles in a matter of seconds. A large hand rail and six chairs made this the most active part of the control center.

The massive computer consoles from the LIDAR station took up almost one entire side of the control room. Enough room for three people to monitor, it could be run by one, very adept person. The communications center was up front of that with its own set of monitors and detection equipment.

The other side of the control room had the ship monitoring system, usually by Willy. An extensive weapon's system, each separate system having its own targeting and information controls.

The piloting for the Specter was probably the only thing that was typical. A large computer monitor gave the pilot a picture to steer by, with two more with actual camera imagery to guide by. The diving planes were still controlled by the feet.

Beverly thought she knew the ship. But when she was given the Classified, Secret, Top Secret and NATO Secret files she had a book more than a thousand pages long. That was why she put in sixteen hour days. That was why she listened to anything that

Merrick, Schmitty, and Wolfson had to say about the ship. That was why she stayed for training lessons on oceanographic monitoring and engineering. That was why she was stiff and sore.

And then there was Tinkerbelle. Willy informed Beverly that the Specter was equipped with a quantum computer. No more than four in the entire world, it could very easily run the Specter without a single soul aboard. But would not because Tinkerbelle was told not to.

"Why the name Tinkerbelle? I mean it's cute, but really?" Beverly had asked Ralph one day. Ralph simply looked into the air of the control room and smiled. "I'll let her answer."

"Don wanted a name that would not come up as a typical name so he gave me my own special name. I like it." That answer had come from Tinkerbelle herself.

Unlike the voices that occupied cars or cell phones, Tinkerbelle sounded just like a 30^{ish} woman would sound, complete with inflections and sarcasm. One evening when Beverly was the only one in the command center, she asked Tinkerbelle a question which she politely answered. Then Tinkerbelle asked her own question. "Captain Hornacher can I tell you a secret?"

"Of course."

"Don, doesn't like being called Donny." Then Bev could have sworn she heard a slight giggle. So Tinkerbelle has a sense of humor. Then Bev asked, "Is it okay if I call you Tink? You do have a long name."

"Wellllll. I guess it would be all right. Don said he was he only one that was given permission. But you ARE the Captain. We'll keep it to just us girls."

Beverly only smiled. She resisted the urge to explore what else Don had told Tinkerbelle. But she was alright with the personality laden AI as long as Tinkerbelle was on their side. She did ask one more question, though. "Would you ever not obey a direct order?"

The answer had been swift. "No. However, I would never destroy this ship or another United States warship or harm a person. Does that suit you?"

Beverly smiled, nodded her head and replied, "That suits me just fine. Thank you." Still, she wondered who would Tinkerbell would follow if it came down to herself or Don? She hoped they would never get to that point.

She smiled when she thought of Wolfson. He had a boyish charm and a devil may care attitude. When the new navigator Lt. Bobby Smith asked where they kept the periscope, Wolfson had answered in distress "Oh my God! Merrick, I knew we forgot something. This damned tub doesn't have a periscope!" Ralph made quite the commotion with Merrick playing along. It almost seemed to Beverly like watching Abbott and Costello. It took Bobby a few moments to realize that the Specter did not have one. It did not need one.

Merrick of course kept his distance from Beverly, doing his job to the utmost but being polite. But on one occasion, in the control room, he rolled up next to Ralph and Beverly and said simply, "Watch this."

Hernandez was at the monitoring control going through specifications on the computers storage. Merrick said very quietly into his lapel microphone, "Willy, now."

The massive underwater monitor went blank. Alex immediately rose up in his seat, and stared dumbly at the blank screen.

"You have no picture. Now what do you do?" asked Merrick creeping in from behind the young man.

"Um, um. Wait, I know this, you go to the computer identifier and initiate the back-up sequence and …"

The computer screen running the diagnostics of the oceanographic systems and the Lidar went blank.

Merrick rolled up directly behind Alex's padded swivel chair and said, "Now what do you do?"

Alex stared down at a smaller monitor that acted as the controls for the system, all by touch screen control. It too was blank. He tapped furiously where the power button should have been. Nothing happened.

"A Chinese Sub has just fired its torpedoes at us. You've got maybe thirty seconds to plot a counter solution. You're looking at a blank screen. What do you do?" Then Don wheeled around quickly and shouted, "And Tinkerbelle you stay out of this."

"Don, I can HELP," replied Tinkerbelle.

"I know you can help but he needs to learn this." Don admonished.

"Got it. Staying out."

Beverly at this point almost stepped in. She thought Merrick might be overstepping his bounds on the young sailor. She had glanced at Ralph, who had put a hand out in front of her and shook his head.

Alex sat, his mind racing. Finally, his swivel chair slid across the floor to the LIDAR station, as he accessed the computers main frame, using those systems touch screens to initiated the sequence to reboot the system. That failed, so he initiated the back-up orders to bring the other computer system on line. Time ticked by too quickly.

"BOOM," said Merrick right behind the young man, slamming his hands over the touch screens. "Captain Hornacher has done everything she could, to outrun the torpedo. She gave you an additional twenty-five seconds. We just took a hit from two-ton bomb that sent the sub into a roll and killed half the crew. But you'll still be alive because you're fastened to this protective chair. I hope you can pick up the pieces, because the Chinese just shot another fish at us. Oops, too late, the crew of the Specter just died. Because you didn't know what to do."

Beverly could actually see a tear form in Petty Officer First Class Hernandez's eye. He stared at Merrick for several moments. She could see the resolve overcome the young man, then he finally responded, "It won't happen again. I can guarantee it."

Merrick smiled, clapped the young man on the back and said, "You've got to know how to FIX things, not just freaking run them. You got to know how to access other systems, how get back what you lost, you've got to know! And damned straight, because if you do blow up my ship with me in it, I'm kicking your ass all the way to hell."

Beverly remembers turning to Wolfson and saying, "Harsh. But very effective."

Wolfson had responded, "Sometimes these kids get caught up in the technology and what the Specter can do. They forget our mission. Alex will remember that more than any other lesson."

Captain Hornacher remembered the lesson well. She went back to the conference room and looked up the solution. All computer diagnostics were run through Willy's monitoring station, with the mapping board as a backup. And of course, Tinkerbell was there to help. But the ship was fraught with these kinds of technological obstacles. Ralph had told her once, "Don't do everyone else's job. That's Merrick's problem. Just be the best at yours as you can."

Her mind bounced back to the present, as the Pacific blue water slid off the bow of the Specter. Somewhere in her ear she could hear Barry White singing. She smiled at the thought of Don's choice of music. He loved good singers. Occasionally he would let someone else slip in a song onto the computers, and listen to something else, or simply let Tinkerbell play disc-jockey. But it seemed to fall back to what Don wanted to hear. Beverly then heard the massive hatch open up and felt a presence on the conning tower with her. She glanced over at Ralph.

"Mind if I intrude?" he asked looking out over the opening ocean, fixing his hat and adjusting his sunglasses.

"Man, this is a fast little boat," she responded, glad for the company, watching the wake neatly slice away from the front of the Specter. The antenna array fins, all tucked neatly against the skin of the Specter. Even though it was a pleasant, sunny day, the wind whipping through the conning tower made Beverly wrap the dark blue windbreaker closer around herself. It was the tiniest bit disquieting. The massive Nautilus Two which rode on the waves feeling a large presence in the massive ocean. The Specter rode so low and was so small, she had the feeling a simple wave would topple them over. And yet as it smacked into each wave, they sliced through with little movement. Glancing at Ralph, the wind even made his mustache bristle.

"A little different from the big Nautilus Two, isn't it?" Ralph mentioned, bringing his binoculars to eyesight. Then he lowered them and looked at Beverly, then asked, "Is this what you imagined when you thought you'd get your first command?"

"No. As a kid I grew up with the Naval Submarine Fleet. But it was always the biggest and boldest that I wanted." Then she looked over at Ralph and said, "But you know, this seems like a good fit. The little girl gets the little submarine."

Ralph ran a hand over the glass like finish of the top edge of the conning tower and said, "Don't sell yourself short. There's nothing like this sub in the world. Nothing as fast, or invisible, or technologically advanced as the Specter."

Beverly then looked up and let the sun warm her face. Then she said, "I was really surprised when Merrick suggested we sail out on the surface."

Ralph shrugged his shoulders and replied, "The guy is always wanting to test something. He wanted to see the picture from space to see how the boat looked to the enemy. I guess from what I saw a few minutes ago, he's pretty happy with it."

Beverly nodded, for she had already known this. Then she said apologetically, "I'm sorry about your demotion."

"Paper demotion only. Can't have two Captains on board." Then he shrugged again and said, "I play Commander for a month."

"What happens after we hit port?" asked Beverly, in obvious reference to the fact that only one would stay as Captain.

"Let's survive the first cruise and Merrick, then figure that out," replied Wolfson. Ralph then said moving onto a different subject, "It was sure nice to see your dad again. I haven't seen him in a couple of years."

"It would have been nice to have a bigger send off, considering the importance of this ship. But at least it got a proper dedication," said Beverly in acknowledgment.

She was referring to the ceremony the evening before, where the bottle of champagne was smashed against the boat and Rear Admiral Hornacher dedicated the submarine. He was the only official invited to the ceremony, as the submarine was still under wraps, at least for the moment. It had almost seemed funny to her as the chaotic assembly of crew members had come to a halt for such a trivial occasion.

"Do you think the Admiral took offense to Merrick?" asked Ralph.

Beverly laughed slightly then said, "I chatted with Dad a little last night. He made no mention of Merrick's disappearance." Changing the subject, she then said, "The Admiral gave me another bottle of Champagne. To toast the completion of our first mission."

"I'll toast the mission if Don doesn't choke someone," replied Ralph with a grin.

Beverly turned and said to Wolfson, "Tell me about him. He won't talk to me."

Ralph shook his head and said, "He's not holding a grudge if that's what you're thinking. I learned a long time ago, he boils, blows, then moves on. I think it's just that he's wrapped up in his boat, and you're simply in the way. It could be that he won't say much to you the entire voyage. He's got a lot more on his mind than what you or I are doing."

Beverly nodded and charged in, "Always the brilliant engineer. And we're just in the way. Actually, I hope it stays that way. I don't tolerate temper tantrums very well."

Just then the small ear bud in Captain Hornacher's ear came to life. "Captain, this is steering, the sounding shows over one hundred fifty meters."

She tapped the small wireless unit in her ear and responded, "Mr. Caldwell, make for periscope depth."

"Excuse me Captain?" came the reply.

Wolfson smiled at Beverly as she smiled back. She glanced around the conning tower, and unlike any other submarine, with antenna and periscope towers, the Specter was a clean as a whistle. The antenna array, spread out before her on the ascent to the deck of the Specter, in a fin like progression.

Beverly then stated, "Just seeing if you were paying attention. Down half bubble, rig for depth of twenty meters."

"Crash, the Captain made a funny," inserted Tinkerbell quickly.

"I noticed Tinkerbell. Very good Captain. Down bubble ten degrees, making for depth of twenty meters."

A claxon horn went off below, on the conning tower and in all the radio's. Ralph stated into his radio, "This is the Commander, secure all hatches, rigging submarine for submersion. Dive, Dive Dive."

"Let's see how well this thing holds water," mentioned Beverly as they scampered below and electronically, secured the hatch.

They came down into the control room at the rear, next to the doorway that lead out of the main room, to the rear of the ship. The doorways had the traditional security latches meant to keep water out. But with a touch of a button, they swung open. Like any other control room of a submarine, it was dark, muted tone, so that monitors and readouts could be seen without a glare. Subdued lighting, completely unseen, radiated through the ceiling, controlled by dimmer switches. Seemingly packed to the gills it reminded Beverly more of the aircraft controllers building at Kennedy Airport than it did a submarine. The chairs were cushioned, high backed with arms and harnesses for wartime situations. They also had electronic lumbar controls and rotation and swivel capabilities. One could easily sleep in the things.

The room was abuzz with activity. Every station had at least one man sitting and another looking over their shoulder. Beverly surmised that every single sailor, other than the engineers were in the control room. Dressed the same, they all wore dark blue shirts and dark blue slacks. Several of them were also wearing the Specter hat. Merrick was chewing on his little cigar, bouncing from one monitor to the next, dressed in a rumpled dark blue sweatshirt with the small Specter emblem.

The Specter took the full brunt of the ocean water as it submerged below the waves, the engines not missing a single beat in the additional pressure.

"Chief, how are we running?" asked Beverly pressing the radio again.

Gunther's prickly voice came back quickly from the engine room and said, "Eighty percent capacity, running at thirty-nine knots. Heat is normal and tell Don our drag coefficient is a half percent better than our first test drive."

Beverly glanced over at Don who was also listening. He nodded, obviously pleased with the fact.

"Captain, the Specter is running at a depth of twenty meters bearing one five zero and holding," said Crash, who had Frank observing every move he made. Crash was already viewing Frank as his sister as she was a constant shadow, having steered the massive Alabama. This was a much more precise system, demanding a better feel for the controls. She was that teenager going from the Semi truck to an Indy car.

Steve Barrington was monitoring the communications system as Alex had control of the LIDAR and OMS surveillance. Henry was monitoring the submarine itself, running the ballast, PSI, depth and displacement.

"Thank you Mister Caldwell. Mr. Merrick, if you would do the honors."

Don looked a little surprised, then he moved over to the chart board. Six feet by four feet, the chart board occupied the front portion of the control room. Unlike other submarines, there was not one map or chart on the surface. The entire thing was one huge computer screen lay on its side. They could move from chart to chart effortlessly, moving directions, rotating charts and transferring data at ease. Six cushioned chairs and a large hand rail were the only things that reminded Beverly it was still on a submarine.

Don went over to the chart table and touched a one-inch square icon in the corner. Suddenly, out of the ceiling swung down a six by three-foot monitor. The two-inch thick liquid crystal monitor could be viewed from anywhere in the room as it snapped into place.

Don walked to the screen which was already coming to life with a watery image. It transformed to crystal clear clarity, showing a clean ocean view, then a set of numbers started bouncing across the bottom of the screen.

Don turned around from the screen and looked at the stoic group staring at him, pulled the cigar from his mouth and said, "The satellite can't see us but it knows our exact position. That be us." Then he looked over to Willy and said, "Let's bring up infrared."

Willy, who was sitting at the main computer console, punched a solitary button. The screen dissolved to a dark blue, and in the center was a dark red, oblong shaped image.

"That be us also. At twenty meters," said Don.

"Excuse me Mr. Merrick. Where in the hell are we getting this picture from?" asked Ensign Bruce Eddington from his position behind the weapons consoles.

Don simply nodded at Beverly and said, "Captain?"

Beverly smiled then answered, "Bruce. We have our own satellite. Ground Positioning Poseidon Project, Sat Com. G, triple P for short."

"Excuse me?"

"One hundred and seven miles up and sixty-five million in cost. It was launched three months ago," replied Beverly. "Like a faithful puppy dog, it follows us wherever we go."

"I have Gypsy on a very secure leash," mentioned Tinkerbell.

Beverly only shook her head. Of course, Tink named her pet satellite.

"What happens when it's cloudy?" asked Henry in typical bland British fashion.

This brought several guffaws from the rest of the men. "Well, no, really. We don't have a proper periscope," he said in defense.

"Don't worry. We've thought of that," responded Willy smiling, adjusting his glasses.

Don walked up to the board and switched the picture back to a pleasant ocean view. Then he punched some more icon buttons on the bottom of the screen and drew the picture back to encompass several nautical miles. On the corner was a small fishing boat. Don wheeled around and commanded, "Alex?"

The young seaman's focus had not fluttered. "Satellite reading puts the boat at twenty-three degrees off port bow. No physical encounter as of yet, but we do have a signature on the wake, which puts the boat displacement at seventy feet in length and the computer reading identifies it as a shrimp boat. Probably out of San Fransisco, Mr. Merrick."

"Willy?" asked Don.

Willy was already working and glanced around quickly at his four twenty-five-inch monitors and replied, "Twenty-three degrees off port, heading south southeast at sixteen knots and using the GP's periscope imagery I found the name being the Justine Queen."

"Accessing San Diego Naval directory her Captain is Jerome Slagg and it is registered as a fishing trawler," inserted Tinkerbelle.

"Eddy?"

Lt. Eddy Faulk looked up from the weapon's console and replied, "Torpedo range within eighteen seconds at current speeds, advising the computer to set to heat-seeking mode since it's using an inefficient diesel engine. Set the torpedo to arm at one thousand meters. One fish would cause total one hundred-percent damage, in roughly forty-three seconds. Sir."

Don crossed his arms like a parent whose kid had just caught the winning touchdown. He was smiling broadly. Beverly looked at the man, when it suddenly occurred to her it was the first time she had ever seen Don smile.

"Damn, he's good." Whispered Ralph to Beverly.

"That was impressive men, but let's not blow up anything just yet," said Captain Hornacher. "Let's try to keep from tangling up their nets, shall we. Lt. Duran, Lt. Smith, let's plot a course to open water. Make a long term plot to our destination, and five degree offsets at the half hour. I want to know ETA at present speed." Then she turned to the communications center and added, "Steve, let USPACFLT at Pearl know our current status and tell them we are on target for our mission. Then we'll see what Mr. Merrick's little boat will really do."

Duran and Smith both smiled as Don took curious note of Beverly. She could have said it any other way. He knew it was an acquiescence, meant to mollify. He paid it little mind, but still, the recognition was there.

Then she said, "Mr. Caldwell, you have the conn for the next fifteen minutes as Commander Wolfson and I figure out our sleeping arrangements."

The entire crew sat in stunned silence. Suddenly Don started chuckling. Then the rest started laughing at the obvious joke from the new Captain. Captain Hornacher just smiled and turned to the hatchway. Wolfson only shook his head and grinned stupidly back at the group.

"Ohhhh, the Captain said another funny," inserted Tinkerbell. "And saucy too."

There were six bunks for the commanders. Don, Beverly, Ralph, Mr. Caldwell, Willy, and Lt. Duran, were the senior members. Captain Hornacher, for obvious reasons, had her own bunk on the bottom, rigged a light weight corrugated bifold door system, that would trap any light within and keep the occupant from rolling out. Beverly had teased Merrick that it was the only thing on the Specter that was not state of the art. Don only responded by saying he would work on it. Beverly had extended an invite to Gunther for more exclusive and slightly bigger accommodations but true to Schmitty's temper, he chose to stay with the guys. Wolfson told her he thought Gunther probably just slept in the engine room.

Enough lockers in the command quarters for eight people, there was also storage underneath each set of bunks for clothing and personals. One large locker was white with a blood red cross on it. The medical locker, it actually contained a small, portable x-ray unit and enough supplies to splint up the entire crew. Bobby really hoped he never needed to use it.

The boat was effectively split into a blue and gold crew, each running twelve hour shifts. Captain Hornacher and Commander Wolfson overlapped time lines with Mr. Merrick overlooking the Specter on his own agenda. The rest of the crew split up their time on duty, engine room or the eight bed-bunk room. Don had managed to design in a fold out treadmill into the wall in with the bunks. But he'd be damned if he was going to use it.

The Specter was equipped with desalination, and could replace its fresh water storage. There were just two showers however, one with each bunk areas. Bathing was reserved to every other day, but sweating was actually kept to a minimum as the Subs temperature stayed at a pleasant sixty-eight degrees. The sleeping and galley were in the center of the small sub with the nuclear reactor in the rear. The engine was actually under the midsection, which was why the tunnel was so important.

The chow hall or galley was the only place other than a shared bunk that one could actually sit down. One six-person table off the small kitchen gave them any leisure time. The crew was allowed to sit and read or write or work on crosswords as long as nobody wanted the spot to eat.

Food was not an overriding concern for Don as he had envisioned the ship. Most meals were personal packaging meant for the microwave. But once a week, they would try to gather up as much of the crew and have a meal together. Alex had already informed the crew that Sunday's dinner was Chicken Alfredo in a four-cheese sauce with a green beans salad, fresh homemade garlic bread and a salad. Don was curious as to how he was going to pull off the baked bread at below sea level.

After returning to the control room and the excitement of the launch was over, Captain Hornacher having shed her jacket and dressed in crisp khakis, identical to Wolfson's, gave instructions that only those on duty were to remain in the center. The crews scheduling had been worked out in advance. She noted with satisfaction that the crewmen off duty slunk out of the room like chastised children. They wanted to stay and play.

Beverly took a chair at the chart board next to Lt. Duran. She noted with satisfaction their present speed and course. Robert expanded the view to show the topographical coast of North America, then their immediate destination. The Aleutian Trench. That's where they would learn how good their Oceanographic Monitoring System really was. Then it was off to even colder climates, past Alaska for another battery of tests.

"I vote we plot a course for Hawaii," said Ralph as he sat down on a chair facing Beverly. She looked up over the brightly lit computer display and smiled.

"Would you believe Don and Admiral Cartwright came up with this plan?" she responded.

"I know. Let's stress the little boat to the extreme's," Ralph said, echoing Don's words.

"Let's hope we don't find a flaw in it," Beverly said off handedly.

"Naw, no problems. In a month, we'll be home sipping that expensive champagne and enjoying the sun."

Beverly flipped the screen back to their current course and said, "Let's hope so. Even as small as we are, with no firepower, we make a tempting target."

Commander Wolfson smiled and glanced over at Don. Don only lifted his eyes for a second, then went back to his laptop.

CHAPTER 4

One week later it was a slate-gray sky and drizzly rain that the guard was looking out into when he saw the headlights of the jet-black Lincoln Continental approaching his guard shack. The smooth suspension bounced effortlessly over the ancient cobblestone street. The guard could see the small, one starred flag waving from the front fenders of the vehicle. He glanced again out the guard shack window. He would have to leave the warmth of his home away from home.

The driver of the car looked out between the sweeping wiper blades. An extensive iron and barbed wire gate stood in front of them, the rest of the wall was concrete with guard towers every two hundred feet. Beyond that, a massive installation with more than a hundred ocean going vessels of various sizes added to the gray landscape. The amazing thing was that this was an installation within an installation. This was merely the dock area. It did not make the driver any safer to see weapons hanging out the towers, even though they were supposedly on the same side.

The vehicle stopped below the canopy as the guard came out, saluted, then stepped down to the driver's window. The driver rolled his window down, handed the guard his paper work and sat back. The guard looked into the back seat and smiled.

Speaking in Russian he stated to the Admiral, "Comrade Admiral Rabinov. I'm surprised to see you so soon. I thought you were on leave for a month," the guard said paging through the driver's authorization. Another guard exited the guard station to check the license number on the car.

"The Volga is a commanding mistress, Andrev. She beckons to me, allowing me no rest," acknowledged the stout Russian Admiral in the backseat.

"Just like a typical Russian woman, isn't she," replied the guard. Then he said into the back seat, "I'm sorry Comrade Admiral, I need your credentials also. The rebels you understand."

"Oh, if you must," responded the Admiral gruffly. He pulled up his brief case off the floor and pulled out a small leather portfolio and handed it to the guard. The guard retreated into the guard hut for several moments. Double checking all the papers and running a computer check, he presently came back out. In his hand was a ten by ten-plate glass scanner, battery operated, and connected by tether to a central computer.

Tapping on the rear window, the Admiral slid down his window to receive his paperwork. The guard then asked, "I'm sorry Admiral, I still need your authorization code, and palm print."

The admiral sighed heavily then said, "Wouldn't it just be easier if they caught the rebels then making me go through all of this?"

"Yes sir," the guard responded taking joy in disrupting the mighty Admiral's day.

Admiral Rabinov pulled a plastic card out of his uniform overcoat and handed it to the guard. The card contained a UPC with Admiral Rabinov's personal authorization.

The Admiral then stated, "The access code is AR eight-one-seven-nine." He then stuck his right hand out the window and pressed it to the scanner. An infrared light made a sweep, taking a picture of the print.

"Thank you, Comrade Admiral. This won't take but a moment."

They waited patiently, the diver turning the car heater down but turning the defrosters up to keep the moisture from settling on the inside windshield.

After a few moments the guard came back out, handed the paper back to the Admiral in the rear seat and said, "Everything checks out Comrade Admiral, have a nice day."

The Admiral simply slid the window back up and waved on the driver.

The massive gate slid open and the car rolled through. Closing the gate, the first guard said, "I wouldn't want his job for all the money in the Ukraine. That Submarine is his wife, mother and mistress. He has no life for all his power."

"When he retires, he will be a rich man," replied the other guard staring out the window, watching the vehicle motor around the dock warehouse, and disappear from sight. He shook some of the rain water off his coat.

"He will never retire. He will die in that sub."

The Lincoln Continental rumbled over the remaining cobblestones, then hit the new asphalt, smoothing out even more. "That went well enough," noted the relieved driver as he drove a familiar path to the Volga.

"I told you. You worry too much," came from the back seat.

"There are a lot of ways this can go wrong before we set sail."

"Yes. But we have done our homework. Such as the guard. I've never met the man and yet he thinks I'm his best friend. And he takes joy in making me dance."

"I must admit, but the transformation is incredible. You could fool Rabinov's mother."

"Fortunately, he had no wife to fool. I draw the line at making me anatomically correct. But the face and voice was easy," noticed the man in the back. Then he reached across with his left hand and peeled a whisker thin layer of polypropylene from his right hand. He balled it up and threw it on the floor.

"I hope, for our sake you have studied all your lines well." Came from the front seat.

"A man had to die to get that simple code for us. For probably that one occasion it will be used. We have shed a lot of blood for this. We will not fail until we have our objective."

"Do you really think the UN will bargain with us?" asked the driver, turning the wheel of the large car, past several large warehouses and aiming for the open water and the extensive docks. The man was in too deep to ever back out. And yet, he was extremely anxious. As if the entire thing was going to fall apart at any moment.

"That, I cannot answer," replied the Admiral, looking out over the gray sky that enveloped them. Then he added, "Considering what we are about to do it would behoove them to do so."

Past the warehouses, the shipyards, the smaller naval fleet, and a few battle cruisers in for repairs. Steam and smoke rose in wisps as diesel fumes hung in the moist air as it followed them through their two-kilometer drive. This was also the dock for part of the Russian Pacific Fleet at one time, the largest in the world. Hard times had fallen on the economy of Russia, and in a cost cutting measure, the fleet was allowed to be decommissioned, one ship at a time.

But at the end of their drive, they arrived at the largest, and most prized submarine of them all. The Volga. It was named after the Volga River where Admiral Andryich Rabinov had made his home. It was his determination, his drive that made the costly submarine a reality. And no matter what politics ran the Kremlin, Rabinov was going to command it until his retirement. Or his death.

The Volga had only been in dock for a week from its latest cruise of the last four months. In dock for a month, it was to be restocked and refitted for battle stations in the North Pacific. During the day the ship was being power blasted and repainted, the interior gone over with a fine edged razor. Engineers were restructuring the sub, replacing needed items and improving the mechanical. On any given day there were approximately sixty men working on the large submarine. The men worked diligently, focused on their work, but happy the Admiral was on vacation.

At almost two football fields in length, the Volga was an immense machine. A Russian class unto itself, the sub was designated a Typhoon Class 2 Project 942 Akula. Unlike most American submarines, this was a catamaran-type design that comprised two separate pressure hulls joined by a single outer layer. Under the conning tower was five different levels. Unlike the Specter where everything was poured into one small room, the sub had separate and individual stations for weapons control, sonar detection and control room. It had enough nuclear fire power to destroy most of China. Including the shores of the American Western Seaboard, from its location at the dock of Vladivostok

Andryich Rabinov had an iron will and determination that made him a welcome ally and a hated foe. A stout man of two hundred pounds and six feet, his face was a map of battles won and lost. There was a small cut on his upper lip, a chunk of skin missing from his eyebrow, a small scar on the chin. His skin was rough and weather worn from salt spray for more than thirty years, but the chiseled features had made him a handsome man, as he aged well.

Admiral Rabinov had bullied the Russian Kremlin into acclimating the money for his grand design, to bolster an aging Russian Submarine Fleet which included five diesel models. The five-year-old submarine was his last grand gesture at an outstanding naval career.

The large naval yard of Vladivostok situated on the Sea of Japan, dangerously close to both China and North Korea, is the permanent home of the Volga. With technological advances coming at light speed, the massive submarine was already showing her age. Still, in the Russian arsenal, it was newer than most but it still did not have all the refinements that Rabinov had wanted. However, it was the largest submarine in the world, five hundred and ninety-one feet in length and capable of striking terror in the world from an underwater position.

The Lincoln pulled onto the dock edge. The Admiral and driver exited the vehicle and looked down the pier as the massive grey submarine. The driver, in reality a naval man named Nicholas Vilnius had been aboard the sub, had been out on duty with the ship two years previously. He was the inside man, himself and several others working to get the crew they could trust on board.

This Admiral Rabinov had never been on board the ship. Two years. Two years he had studied Rabinov's life. Two years he had gone underground, to change his looks, to become another person, to take over another existence. He had studied secret files, had interviewed disreputable men, giving information for money. After two years he had become Admiral Rabinov. And after those two same years, the crew of the Volga had been slowly replaced from well-placed sources in the Naval command. They were inside men, meant for one reason.

The real Admiral Andryich Rabinov was dead. Buried deep into the mud and slime of the very Volga river where he had grown up. His singular devotion to the Russian Navy was to be his undoing. A brilliant loner with few friends but many enemies made him a recluse on the few occasions when he was on leave. This was to be a month-long holiday for the man, then his last cruise on the Great Submarine. Two days into his leave he was murdered. And no one would ever be the wiser.

Nicholas stood on the dock, watching one man working on the exterior of the ship. Standing next to Rabinov he said, "All the crewmen on the ship are loyal to our cause. Either by choice or by a few million well-spread rubles. The workers however, are simple Russians, doing their jobs."

"You have a compassionate nature my friend."

Nicholas had worked hard at getting what they needed on board the submarine. He shook his head and said, "I wish for subterfuge in this matter. If we kill them, they will be missed very quickly."

Admiral Rabinov nodded. "Then let's not kill them, shall we."

They walked forward on the pitted concrete docks, to where a guard was standing. A simple gate kept them from the pier on which the Volga was stationed. The guard shouldered his AK-forty-seven, came to attention, and saluted the Admiral upon his approach. Rabinov saluted back.

"Comrade Admiral, an unexpected pleasure," stated the guard pulling aside the small barricade.

The Admiral snarled slightly in response, "I seem to have caught everyone off guard. I thought the command center had told everyone I was coming back in."

"I have heard nothing Admiral," replied the guard sheepishly.

"That is apparent. I would have thought a formal greeting would have been appropriate. I will have to bring my displeasure to bear to the central command about their lack of organization and information."

"I believe Commander Ushinko is on board Comrade Admiral. Should I contact him?" asked the guard desperately trying to stay out of the dog house with the Admiral.

"That would be wise."

The guard was quick to radio to the submarine about the Admirals arrival. Rabinov only had a two-minute wait as Commander Ushinko came walking quickly to the small guard station. He pulled his dress coat around himself, trying to keep the rain out of his collar, and saluted the Admiral.

The guard nodded and opened the gate without receiving any authority. The three men strolled past and onto the pier. The guard, still in fear, did not even bother to check Rabinov's brief case.

Commander Ushinko then said, "The Volga awaits you, Comrade Admiral."

"She is a mighty submarine, yes," replied Rabinov.

"But not as fast as her torpedoes," answered Ushinko.

"And not as deadly," responded Rabinov.

Ushinko gazed hard to look at Rabinov. Finally, he said, "I really did not know. We've had no word on whether or not everything was still as planned." He looked at the face of Rabinov, who smiled back. "Remarkable. Simply remarkable. The small cut on the upper lip. Even the voice."

"Two years in the making," responded Rabinov. "And everything is definitely a go."

They started walking again when Commander Ushinko mentioned, "We will be sailing with a skeleton crew. But a loyal one. The question is, how do we slip out of here undetected?"

"Let us get out of this drizzle and we will discuss it," replied a knowing Rabinov.

The formidable military top coat kept out the rain, but the Admiral's insignia on his service cap elicited many a salute. Except for the contract workers restocking the ship. They only glanced around, aware that this was someone important.

Viktor Puchinko would have stopped and talked to these men, shaking hands, slapping backs. They were on a serious mission which needed a strong hand and a confident word. Puchinko was a friendly man, a solid six-foot man. As Admiral Rabinov, he merely walked by, saluted or nodded, taking his cue from a man who was only unto himself.

"You play the part well," whispered Nicholas.

Rabinov nodded once again and whispered back, "Rabinov was an arrogant slob. It is an easy fit. I just think distant and angry thoughts and it's Rabinov."

They traveled through the massive submarine, the call to attention coming loud and clear throughout the metal canister. They strolled down several levels to the crews' quarters. They finally reached a small conference room, where Rabinov and eight other officers met and took their meals.

Rabinov removed his coat as did Nicholas and Ushinko. Within a minute a cook from the galley came and took an order of hot drinks. The men said little until the cook had deposited the hot coffee and toast.

Commander Ushinko was a square man with a square, but pleasant face. He had been waiting the past five days in anticipation of the plans going forward, almost hoping they would not. In his heart it was the right thing to do, and yet, he also knew in his heart, a lot could go wrong. And being only one small part of a much larger plan, did not infuse him with confidence. But he took heart in the fact that this man had never set a foot on the Volga, and led them directly to the conference room. He was doing his homework.

Ushinko sat off to Rabinov's right and asked finally, "We have been kept in the dark. What is the plan?"

"That has been the plan so far," replied Rabinov. "The less each one knows the better. No slip ups that way."

If Ushinko felt out of the loop, he did not show it. He merely nodded and waited.

Rabinov smiled then said, "We are embarking on a noble cause my friends. But it will be a misunderstood mission. We will be hunted down and possibly killed. But that is the choice all of us have made."

"You must be careful Viktor."

Rabinov waved a finger at Nicholas and reprimanded him by saying, "No. Never get out of character. No slip ups. I want these men to think Rabinov is in command."

Nicholas nodded and said, "Sorry. I understand. My point was however, that some of these men may be loyal to the cause, but they are more loyal to glory and especially the money they think they will be receiving from the Ukrainian Government. Some of these men are here only for the money and will not take to being bullied. By anyone."

Rabinov sat forward and drew little circles on the table top, deep in thought. Finally he said, "I understand, however the crew does not worry me. No matter our plans, there will be a small amount of luck involved. Even though the ocean is vast, this is a big submarine to hide. And there is our time line. It may not give us any more than a few hours' head start. What I am saying gentlemen, is that we could very well die on this submarine less than a few miles off the coast of Japan."

"I would caution you; I would not tell the men this," stated Ushinko, with Nicholas nodding his head in agreement.

"Of course not," smiled Rabinov.

Pouring himself another cup of coffee from the carafe, Nicholas said, "I would like to know how we are to get this massive submarine out of Vladivostok and the Pacific Fleet, without anybody getting just the little bit upset."

"Come now Nicholas. We would not get this far without a carefully constructed plan. We have people on the inside. The docking authority of the submarine fleet here at Vladivostok has been told of a shakedown cruise of a one-day test period of a new reactor. It is in the computers and has been approved by Admiral Rabinov and the high command that this will happen. We sail tomorrow night. The guards on the dock will turn a blind eye and will conveniently disappear half way into their duty. The next morning the new guards, the REAL guards, will find us gone. And considering these are the lowest of the military, they may think this is quite normal. Notice the guard at the dock gate. He checked nothing."

"I take it this is one of those places where luck needs to be on our side," observed Ushinko.

"Exactly. If there is a surprise check in the middle of the night, we may be found. If we are questioned simply leaving dock, we will be found. If the guards sell us out, we will be found. If the Military docking authority suspects something fishy, we may be found."

"I get the point," replied Ushinko, taking little heart in all the failed scenarios.

Nicholas then inserted, "What about satellites? Won't they see us?"

Rabinov smiled and patted the hand of his comrade. "Excellent point. That is why we sail at the dead of night, for we will be on the surface sailing out of the Amurskiy Bay. That we must do this as quickly as this massive machine can handle. Without a tugboat escort, so we must be not only lucky but good." Then Rabinov stopped to reconfirm his thoughts, then added, "Do not fret my friends. Once we are moving, it will be very hard to slow this submarine down. I would just hope for a little head start, before the Russian and American Navy's hunt us down."

Nicholas' eyes shot open. "American Navy? Why the American Navy?"

Rabinov sighed, then replied, "It would stand to reason. Once we are out to sea, and the Russian Navy has lost us, they will probably not ask for help. Face it, they do not trust the Americans and to admit a blunder of this size will not endear the authorities to anyone. But when the couriers disrupt the UN and the American's figure out that the Russians have let the Volga slip through their fingers there will be an all-out manhunt. Maybe not right away for there is still arrogance in the Russian Navy but IF, they figure out our target, the American Navy will jump in with both feet. No, my friends, all the scenarios point at a world-wide hunt for our little indiscretion."

Nicholas shook his head and said, "I had not thought of that."

"Do we have anybody on the inside in America?" asked Ushinko hopefully.

"The Koreans have graced us with several well-placed people, but not high enough. The timing was not right for our man in the Pentagon." Rabinov then smiled and added, "However, he is high enough to maybe, as the Americans would say, throw a monkey wrench into things. We'll see and hope."

"One of the luck things we're counting on," said Ushinko, acknowledging to Rabinov.

"If something happens, then that will boast our chances. But, my friends, we make our own luck. We have a good chance of succeeding, once we leave dock. That would be our best luck," stated Rabinov firmly.

Suddenly there was a tapping at the door. "Come," said Rabinov.

The door opened slightly and a seaman's voice said, "Sorry to disturb you Comrade Admiral, but an official is out on the dock to see you."

Rabinov sighed visibly, as if he being disturbed while making love. "All right. But this had better be good."

The seaman nodded and closed the door. Rabinov smiled and said, "I love the little act of being nasty. So much fear."

"I don't think it's funny. You've got visitors already and we've only been here fifteen minutes," pointed out Ushinko.

Rabinov stood up and tapped Ushinko on the forehead and said, "Use your head man. It is one man, not an armed guard or garrison of men. It is a dock supervisor double checking our orders I would surmise."

Ushinko nodded. Nicholas smiled as Rabinov's words made him feel better. Viktor was no Rabinov, but he was a very capable man nonetheless.

As predicted Rabinov talked with the man and within a couple of minutes the gentleman walked back to his vehicle and drove off.

Rabinov returned to his state room with Ushinko and Nicholas in tow. Putting his coat in a closet he turned and explained to the two men, "A computer malfunction is making the main office and dock authority nervous. They were just double checking our intentions."

"Let's hope they don't take the initiative and double check with the Pacific Fleet Commander," stated Nicholas, making himself comfortable at the desk chair. Even though Admiral Andryich Rabinov was a powerful man in the Russian military, submarine logistics made his room nothing more than a eight by ten office. Rabinov sat down on his bunk with storage over- head, forcing Ushinko to simply stand.

"This command came from the Russian Fleet Commander. At least according to the main frame computer," said Rabinov. Settling into his bunk he then added, "You worry too much."

"And your over confidence will be the death of us," shot back Nicholas.

Rabinov smiled then said, "My confidence comes from our planning. With inside men everywhere, and us knowing the system as well as the Russians, including all the holes. The Americans took the nine-eleven terrorist wake-up call seriously. They reformatted everything. The Russians simply plod on thinking they are making a foolproof system, adding one ineffective code to another. And yet they are surrounded by their enemies. All looking to attack back. Russians lack foresight. Look at where we sit my friends."

"But powerful. Do not underestimate our adversary. There may be holes that we can take advantage of, but they are not stupid," argued Nicholas.

"I never said that," replied Rabinov, leaning back in his bunk, his head finding the pillow. "I'm just saying that the Russians think that any terrorist attack is going to be a suicide bomber in a Fiat. They are not looking for anything this elaborate. We will never underestimate our nemesis. But we have studied them to the point, we know them better than they know themselves."

Nicholas smiled slightly then said, "I hope you are right Admiral Rabinov."

The Admiral slid his service hat over his eyes, made himself comfortable and said, "Admiral Rabinov is always right. Even when he's dead wrong."

Nicholas and Ushinko laughed. Rabinov mumbled from underneath his hat, "Do I have time for a short nap? It has been a long night."

Commander Ushinko said, "I can cover for you, that is not a problem. However, I would just like a little insight as to what the plan is for the next couple of days."

Rabinov pulled the hat off, tossed it onto the desk, then removed his shoes and loosened his dress tie. Finally, he said, "I'm sorry you've been kept in the dark. You are without a doubt an important part of this. Undoubtedly you and Nicholas have the roster of men that are with us on this endeavor. Tomorrow night, after the engineers leave, these men and we set sail to test out our not so new reactor."

"You realize that a skeleton has more meat than what this crew does. We will be short handed in many areas. This ship is supposed to have a compliment of around one hundred and sixty personnel. We have fifty-two."

Rabinov nodded and asked, "I did not say it was going to be easy. How are we set on supplies?"

"Enough supplies for this crew. We will have a full complement of weapons and will be fully powered. The new reactor is set to be installed next week as is most of the computer and radar systems. This week was mostly cosmetic repairs," responded Ushinko.

Rabinov nodded then said, "A best case scenario, we set sail under the vail of darkness, the new guards come on, notice we are gone, but make no effort to double check that this is abnormal. We then have a weekend head start; in which case we are five hundred kilometers out to sea. If the guards decide to do their duties, then we have a twelve-hour jump on the Russian Navy. Even if the Dock Command finds out something, it has been determined that all we need is an hour jump to get far enough out to submerge. The key is, the second we are out to sea, we become scarce. All GPS positioning will be disabled and a communications black out will be in effect. We will explain this to our crew to a man."

"That shouldn't take long." Stated Ushinko.

"Then what?" asked Nicholas.

"Then we counter course our way north and come down the American Western seaboard."

"America has nothing to fear from us if we can't fire our missiles," observed Ushinko, bringing up the last obstacle to overcome.

"Ah, you are referring to the fail-safe system for nuclear missile deployment." Rabinov gathered his thought then continued, "It takes three men with the proper magnetic keys and codes to fire the missiles. Then we also need a confirmation code from Pacific Fleet command, so that what we are about to do, does not happen. Correct?"

"Exactly."

Rabinov shrugged his shoulders and said, "We have all that."

"And how exactly did you manage to pull all of that off?" Asked Ushinko quickly.

Rabinov smiled back, then pulled out a small key out his breast pocket. "This key is to the safe behind that little ocean front picture on the wall."

Ushinko wheeled around and looked at the picture for the first time. He had been on the ship for over a year and had never once paid attention to the bland little portrait.

"In that safe is my magnetic key and the authorization code to duplicate to fire the missiles, of which we don't need verification."

"And the imbedded verification code from Fleet command?" asked Nicholas, believing full well that Rabinov had an answer for this.

He did. "The five-year-old computers on this submarine have never been updated, unlike all the older subs which have been."

"Which means?" inquired Ushinko.

"In my brief case is a lap top computer with a small transmitter. It has one function. It will lock onto the Central Commands Russian radio frequency to authorize us to fire, and simply turn on the authorization. At that point we will override the Russians and enable the first missile prompt."

Ushinko nodded quickly in understanding. "Of course, the Black Box. And of course, for the record we are to confirm the verification order, of which we will not. Once your computer gets the code, no matter where it comes from, we can safely punch it in and it will enable the missile command." Ushinko nodded his head and uttered, "Genius."

Rabinov smiled. "Correct. Rabinov's arrogance in this case is the Russian undoing. As I said, we have planned well." He looked to both men, slid back down in his bunk and asked finally, "Now, may I catch my nap?"

Nicholas and Ushinko nodded and left the Admiral. Nicholas said under his breath in the hallway, "Do you share his confidence?"

Commander Ushinko thought for a moment, then replied, "I believe Yashangov and the Resistance have thought this out. I believe the North Koreans have given us an edge. All these men on this boat will fight hard for they think they are going to be rich after the outcome. But I also believe that we have to keep our guard up. Anything can go wrong."

Nicholas nodded. The future was going to be very anxious, no matter the outcome.

CHAPTER 5

The thick folds of flesh refused to move. Try as it might, the eye would not open. It felt pain throughout its ancient body, as a long sleep would make one stiff. But this was beyond stiffness and the mind did not understand.

Again, it tried to open its eye. It felt the skin around his eyeball was puffy and still unwilling to move. There was something there, as if gluing his eye shut. A cold shiver radiated through the long body, quivering the skin. At least there was a sensation.

Its mouth could open and it forced water through its gills. The huge gill slits only opened slightly, as if the top half were still pinned shut. And still, it could not move. It swished its tail, which only moved a small amount. The brain did not acknowledge whether it was from his inability or something trapping him. It just could not move the way it wanted to.

It had no reasoning behind its existence. The small brain could not fathom the thought that it in fact should be very dead. It had no concept of time. It had simply awakened from a long sleep with muscle cramps, huge sores covering its body, and a deep, rumbling hunger.

But it was still having trouble moving, of which it could not understand. It could feel its huge muscles contract, so it knew they functioned to some degree. It was trapped.

After a time, the nostrils picked up a different scent. It had already detected the typical oceanic smells. Salt water, dead fish, icy oxygen. But this was new. It was the smell of dirt, or better yet, mud. Frozen mud. The oval slits flexed massively, and it snorted. As it did, something moved off the head. Suddenly, an eye ball slid open. The eyelid felt heavy but the creature felt a surge of defiance. It was still alive and was starting to reassume its importance in the matter of its universe.

Its long body, full of nerve receptors could detect the massive cold on the top, but the bottom side of its body was feeling a warmth it had not felt in some time. The warmth felt good, but it did not know why.

Had the animal had any idea of what had happened to it, it would have been very grateful to be alive. Cruising too far north in search of food, it found itself in a massive ice storm complete with devastating lightning strikes. This only served to confuse its normally clear senses. Maybe in a fit of panic or simply looking for refuge, it went down a fjord. It would not know it was on the coast of Chukotka Peninsula, the north eastern tip of Siberia. It could not know of an intense lightning strike which forced part of the huge glacier to split and fall off into the Chukchi Sea.

The huge creature had never been in such distress before in its life. The wall of ice, hundreds of millions of tons, forced the animal into the icy mud. There was something in the air, or rather, the lightning strikes which infused the water. It thrashed, trying desperately to escape its icy prison. Its mind did not understand death, only the mindless entrapment that its body could not move. After many hours of struggling, it gave up in utter exhaustion and closed its huge eyes.

It did not understand its awakening. It could not know of mankinds warming of the world. It did not understand the drifting current which slowly and timelessly took it south to ever so slowly warm its huge body. But there was something else. The random chances of man and nature to build up a soup of methane and volcanic disturbances. And the ice flows, trapping the heat, causing the seas to boil. The animal had been on the cusp of everlasting death and decomposition when a natural stew warmed the creature. It was slow process, but it felt its intensity.

It knew nothing of its odyssey through time and the changing world. It only knew it was alive and hungry. And still trapped. The mind registered the fact that if it did not break free soon, it would starve to death.

Ever so slowly, the warmer salt water washed over it, bathing the sore and infected body. The warm water was also causing erosions in the massive ice chunk still clinging to its head and back. Locked around the upper tail and huge dorsal fin the ice was being shaved away layer by layer.

The lone eyeball looked around its world. It was an incredibly familiar sight. The open ocean. The cold climate did not maintain an overabundance of marine life, but it knew it could swim fast enough to catch about anything. Just given the chance.

After a time, it felt something slide off the other side of its head. The ice had taken a massive amount of skin with it and the creature could smell its own blood, which only fed its growing hunger. But the other eye was now open, the folds of flesh grudgingly retracting.

The solid black oval looked around. Its vision was not as clear as it was accustomed to, but it could make out shapes. Something small, about four feet long swam by. It was tantalizingly close, but the creature could still not move. Frustration and madness infused the creature. Food! Ever so close. It could smell the tuna as it took no thought at the iceberg floating by.

It thrashed suddenly, using the massive muscle. Something broke, and the tail moved several feet each direction.

The tuna darted; suddenly aware the icebergs bottom section was coming undone. Still, it did not worry. Icebergs do nott eat tuna.

The creature regained its strength for another attempt. It convulsed, contracting and thrashing. Its mind registered that the tip of its huge fin had broken off, but feeling no real pain it ignored the sensation. However, the massive muscles had done their job. He was free!

The tuna did not stand a chance. The huge maw opened and swallowed it whole, taking all four feet in. The jaws were stiff as it tried to chew as several of its huge teeth broke off. Through all the pain though, it felt satisfied that its hunger was being taken care of. Not all of it, but at least the hundred pounds of tuna was a good start.

The creature could not know it was the last of its kind. It had been the ruler of the ocean, the most feared animal on the planet, as much as the Tyrannosaurus Rex ruled and roamed where it pleased on land, this creature did so in the sea. There was no natural predator or enemy. It died of disease, old age and in some cases, starvation.

The demise of the dinosaurs did not affect this creature like it had so many others. It was a fish, much like the tuna or swordfish. And its kind could adapt, like the crocodile or the kimono dragon, it survived. He was alive again, after twelve thousand years of sleep. All eighty-seven feet of him. Sleeping for the past twelve thousand years, he had some serious feeding to catch up with.

The orca kept an eye on his pod and the other, scanning the ocean. He was not looking for trouble; he was not concerned about the safety of his pod. He too was looking for food. A seal, walrus, a small whale, he was even tempted with a large turtle.

He was the apex predator. Twenty-five feet of muscle, sensory receptors that rivaled any animal on the planet, and a brain that could reason and learn. It was not afraid. Of anything.

It had once encountered a 17-foot great white shark. While the shark was the epitome of an eating machine, it could not reason. While the shark in essence had bigger teeth and as many sensory armors as any animal, it could not rationalize the camouflaged animal that was in fact turning the tables on it and hunting it.

They had circled, the orca more concerned with identification and leading this monster away from his pod, which had several pups. The great white was simply trying to figure out if the orca was edible. They kept the dance for several minutes, the orca clicking wildly, the shark unfamiliar with the noise. Then, the shark decided it was simply a whale and could be taken advantage of. It would take a bite. But it would be careful. The killer whale was still bigger than the shark.

The shark went in for a preemptive strike. Suddenly it was blindsided. The clicks had in fact called in for reinforcements. The orca that hit the shark was not interested in eating or even doing damaged, it just hit the shark at twenty knots and pushing it through the water, almost folding the shark in half.

It was over before it started. Even the shark, top of the food chain predator, knew these fish were hunters, possessed no fear, and there was more. The female shark swam off, in a hurry.

But this time the senses were different. The orca knew it was a shark but the figure that moved very slowly through the water distorted the senses. It should have been a whale shark, but it did not move like one. The keen eyes of the orca were trying to rationalize the immense torpedo shape moving through the frigid water at the great distance. Its memory did a quick search and pieced together the definite analysis. It was indeed a shark, but not a pleasant whale shark, this was a great white. A bloody big one.

Like a cat that spies a mouse, the killer whale went into a stalking mode. It stopped all movement staying perpendicular to the immense shape swimming in the distance, to make as small a target as possible. It did not even start its ritual clicking as it did not want to attract attention. This may be a shark but it was beyond its realm of rational. The pods safety was foremost, so it would stay and watch. And protect if necessary.

And yet it never occurred to the orca that it should be afraid. It had never once had its life threatened. It's mind however, acknowledged a threat that was beyond anything it encountered before. It was on edge. As was the ocean around it. Any fish that had seen the pair of huge predators were hiding or being as damned still as they could be. Way too many teeth for any comfort.

The prehistoric shark paid little mind to the orca, one eye still not functioning. Still, it was hungry. And the orca was a big morsel. Almost too big. Almost.

It sliced slowly in the orca's direction. Like a great white it only saw a food source. It could not know that even smaller, it was too being a formidable predator, and in fact swifter and more agile. The huge scythe type tail swished to make up the distance to the orca.

The black and white mammal realized it was now a target. It began its high-pitched clicking noise, realizing this had gone beyond a simple observation. Its brain rationalized two quick thoughts. One, that it was processing its own defensive maneuver. And two, this was a shark beyond what hell could imagine. And it had a big mouth.

The eighty-seven-foot eating machine simply kept swimming until it made up the distance to the orca. It did not rationalize the immoveable posture of the black and white mammal; it just knew that it was an easy target. It opened it huge maw, its one good eye losing sight of the animal for the last second before it bit its head off.

It got nothing but water. Through the swirling mass of bubbles, it had just made, it saw nothing.

The orca dove at the last second, getting a glimpse of the huge seven-inch teeth. Moving swiftly through the water under the huge shark, it put some distance between itself and the shark, then spun around quickly to once again spy the shark. Now behind the beast it knew that it could safely track it and alert the pod of the impending danger.

The warning system had done its job. Several more male orcas were now coming in. They had separated at various depths. The table had now suddenly turned. The prehistoric shark had now become the hunted by much smarter animals than itself.

The black and white flashes were coming at the prehistoric shark, very rapidly. It lashed out with its huge mouth, close but never finding an end to its huge teeth. The vast bottle shaped snouts of the orcas pummeled the soft sides of the shark, literally pushing it in a new direction. And doing soft tissue damage upon each strike.

The enormous shark tried to swim one direction, suddenly realized the orcas were blocking that way, so it turned away and started swimming in a straight line. It did not know it but it was being forced away from the pod. Several orcas trailed the huge predator for several minutes.

It swam a couple of miles when it realized it was yet again, alone. At least in its mind. Behind its flank was the first orca. Keeping a wary eye.

The immense sharks first real encounter with an intelligent animal would prove fruitless. It would do much better at killing the animals that did not belong on, or in, the water.

CHAPTER 6

It was an unlikely type of ship for a research vessel. The one hundred and fourteen-foot Ring Andersen two-masted schooner, was much more at home drifting lazily off the shores of Bermuda with several scantily dressed ladies sunning themselves on deck, with a pompous millionaire at the helm. Oddly enough, it had started out being used that way at one time, but the wife of the pompous millionaire, found out about his dalliances and took him for every penny.

The National Geographic Society contacted the woman with hope that she would sell them the boat for considerably less than what it was worth. However, in a fit of rage, she simply gave the boat to the National Geographic, knowing it would extremely piss off her ex-husband. Which, in every sense of the word, it did.

Not exactly maneuverable enough for ice flows and several months on oceanic voyages, it was being used for just that. Gutted for storage and research, and an engine for extra speed and dexterity it found itself permanently moored in Nome, Alaska. Stationed there for just such emergencies, it had just been called back into service. With a crew of eight it had been dispatched to cover an amazing new find.

The Iceland Venture was a stable enough ship, but even fully loaded rode the waves rather high. Captain Garth Drummond, had a hand in refitting the wooden yacht and loved its very nature. The beautiful wooden accommodations of the lounge had been removed to make room for a laboratory. The three luxurious state rooms had been gutted and turned into a very small kitchen and plain Jane folding bunks for people to sleep. The head was barely four feet by five feet. Drummond had made sure the wood had been taken out in complete pieces and resold. Still, it made him cry. It had been a beautiful ship.

It was his baby. But he would have liked something larger and less predisposed to failing around in stormy weather. As with any research vessel, it was outfitted for a specific mission. This team was there for samples and studies. No large submersible, no whale captures or tagging, no large rocks or sunken treasures. Just water samples, take pictures, take measurements and observations. He could handle that, even on a ship that bounced like a bobber.

He was in fact one of only two on board that was intended, to strictly take care of the Venture itself. Everyone else doubled as hired hands, sailors and crewmen. But they were scientists.

Sailing out of Nome, with instructions to sail to the Aleutian Islands specifically Attu Island the western most Aleutian attributed to the Alaskan chain. Captain Drummond was to assist the sort of dysfunctional science team. He had caught enough of the Alaskan current to make up time. Even though Drummond was not one of the scientists, he was very much aware of what was going on and was involved in every study and find. His booted six-foot four-inch height and broad shoulders made him a good digger and pack mule. His large brownish red beard and mustache made him easy to spot in any crowd.

Monroe Ruff, his first mate and friend, was the opposite. Clean shaven, almost a foot shorter than Drummond, and with an easygoing manner could get lost in a group of three. But his two hundred pounds made anyone feel like he was a tempest just getting ready to let lose. Bumping into the man was like bumping into a large rock.

Two days out of Attu, Drummond was at the helm, watching the choppy waves, using the engine to weather the rolling ocean, not wanting to do battle with the sails in the heavy wind. He could have the boat on an autopilot, but still loved the thrill of steering the ocean-going vessel, loving the feel of the enormous wooden wheel. He was waiting for Monroe to relieve him, all the while watching Scott on the upper deck. Doctor Scott Pierson was bent over the sturdy wooden railing, throwing up, again. A few more moments went by and as if on a cue, Monroe came out of the deck house and to the helm. Drummond gave him a few instructions and then went over to Scott, Drummond's sure-footed steps taking him over the wet deck of the boat.

The thirty-five-year-old researcher looked up, swiped some spittle from his lips and said, "Man, I really liked that ham sandwich too. I just didn't want to see it again."

Drummond knew better than to give the man a rough time. During the trip to Attu, it had been a daily ritual, and Scott had not complained once. Unlike several others on board that seemed to voice their opinions every time someone passed gas.

"I restocked with Dramamine. It should be below," mentioned Garth, laying a large hand on the man's shoulder.

"I know. I just keep hoping I'd get over this." Scott said, raking his sleeve across his mouth. Then he smiled and added, "The first really good chance we've had to look at what we've found and I have to come up and upchuck." Then he turned and went below deck with Drummond directly behind him.

Drummond had captained National Geographic Society adventures before. But this crew seemed a little off to him. One was a marine biologist, one was a geophysicist, and yet another of the crew was a Herpetologist, or reptile expert. There was of course the ever-present photographer, one that he had never worked with before, and did not really like. But it was Scott, along with Gary, being a paleontologist, that struck Drummond as the oddity. He knew that some fisherman had found something in the waters off the Attu Island that should not have been there. They had managed to pull the remains to the unhabituated island. And there had been disturbances on the ice flows on the western coast of the Kamchatka

Peninsula. But why the paleontologist? Drummond had thought as he followed Scott down below.

The schooner had been divided up into four compartments. The engine room, sleeping quarters, galley, and laboratory area. The deck house was the only real entrance to the below decks and was home to the radio and signal equipment as well as the GPS, flotation devices, and emergency supplies. Just large enough to have a table for charts and maps it was Drummond's space for supplies. The bathroom was nothing more than a closet with a camping commode. Of which the two women on board still found rather distasteful. They had insisted on coming with, without knowing of the accommodations. And one seemed to complain constantly, which was starting to irritate Drummond.

Connie looked up from her microscope and saw Scott returning. The other four people were all busy at their little stations, examining or spraying some God-awful chemical on something. Drummond thought that might be part of Scott's problem. The place smelled like a morgue. With the closeness of the bodies, it was rather warm, moist and most of all; stinky.

Connie finally said to Scott, "Scott, I just can't match this skin sample to anything I know. Our computers don't have all the data necessary and until I get a proper satellite feed to Seattle, I can't access the data there." Connie stood, in her lab coat, with one hand on her hip. Twenty-pounds overweight, she could muscle anything with the best of the men. A large tattoo of an octopus on the arch of her back had been a source of amusement for the whole crew. Usually, under her lab coat was a midriff baring top. Normally black.

Drummond answered quickly and said, "No computer signals or anything like that this far out to sea. It will take us a few days just to get close to Juneau to maybe bounce off a signal."

Scott went over and looked through the microscope. "Octopus?" he said looking over at Connie. Then he smirked.

"No. No suckers to speak of and if it were somehow, part of the head, it'd be a different texture," replied Connie, taking no notice of the implication.

"Mola Mola maybe? They're not supposed to go this far north. Could be a fisherman caught one in its net and didn't know what it was?" offered Drummond, speaking of the big ugly flat fish.

Connie smiled and responded, "That, I can cross reference and no, it's not a Mola Mola

fish, but that did occur to me."

"It's a mosasaur." This came from the tall, forty-year-old Gary, looking over the top of his small, rectangular glasses, his dark skin shinny with a layer of the stinky moisture Drummond did not like.

Scott looked over at Anthony, who was the photographer. He had taken more than a hundred pictures of the thing the fisherman had hauled aboard their tiny boat. "Digital pictures are loaded into the computer, but the thing doesn't look like anything to me," said Anthony. "I have a portfolio of eight by ten prints over there if you want to look at them, but it all just looks like a big slimy mess to me. Hard to make out anything."

Scott went over and pulled the file on the creature and handed them to Drummond. All the time Scott and the other scientists had been dealing with the creature, Drummond had been supplying the ship. This was his first view of the thing.

Drummond thought like everyone else had upon seeing the pictures. It had been hacked to pieces and parts were missing. It was hard to tell what the critter might have been. After several moments of scanning the prints, he handed them back to Scott and said, "Sorry, it doesn't really look like much to me either."

Scott sighed as he ran a hand over his close shaved head. They had all viewed the pictures. It had been mostly body and little else left of the creature the poor fisherman had brought to the surface. "But how could a live mosasaur be running around in this day and age?"

"Are we talking about what I think we're talking about?" asked Drummond, running a perplexed hand through his beard.

"Mosasauria, a group of EXTINCT marine reptiles from the Cretaceous period," replied Scott. "The best-known one is the plesiosaur. There have been fossil finds on just about every continent."

"Can grow as large as fifty feet long. Some people believe there is one trapped in the Loch Ness Lake in Scotland," explained Gary, taking his glasses off and wiping them on his shirt.

"I wish we could have taken the carcass on board with us," offered Brice, the reptile expert.

"This place smells bad enough without something rotting on board. Could it have been a crocodile or something that got too far out to sea?" asked Drummond. "Heard of one swimming out into the Mediterranean and scarring the hell out of some bathers," he recounted with a chuckle.

The entire group seemed to shake their heads at the same time. Scott then explained, "A croc wouldn't survive the intense cold and salt water, and the skin samples not a match. The carcass just didn't fit the bill." Then Scott looked over at Gary, smiled and said, "Not even a Super Croc."

"Like I said. A mosasaur," said Gary putting on his glasses and smiling.

"Look it, this isn't the movie Jurassic Park," retorted Scott.

Gary launched in, "Hey, I'm looking at the facts. Connie can't determine anything known from the skin, Brice tells me there's no known fifty-foot reptiles out in the open ocean, and we just had a major earthquake in an area of solid bedrock in Siberia. The carcass, for what it's worth was in terrible shape. But even the carcass, hacked to bits was still over thirty-five feet long. I'm just saying that when we remove the possible, no matter what's left, no matter how improbable, if it fits the facts, that's our conclusion."

"What about the carcass?" Asked Connie, putting a hand on her hip.

"A sea plane is being dispatched from the University to gather up the remains. Hopefully, the fisherman gives it up without realizing it might be worth something," stated Scott.

"Or haven't cooked the damned thing for lunch," offered Anthony.

"So, what your saying is this fisherman caught this animal, which was still alive and nobody knows what it is?" asked Drummond incredulously.

"It died in his nets, or it would have taken his boat down. Unfortunately, they sliced it up pretty bad untangling it from the nets," responded Scott. "The nets apparently are worth their weight in gold."

"It was in really bad shape. Tell him about the organisms," said Gary, thoroughly enjoying the give and take of a live and spirited debate.

Drummond looked over at Scott with a concerned frown.

Scott smiled and said, "Nothing to be afraid of. It just had some plant life and single celled bacteria growing on its skin. The kind that, well, like, we've never seen before."

"We've never seen before seems to be coming up a lot," observed Drummond, shaking his big burley head.

"It would have been nice to get into the belly of the thing," mentioned Brice.

"Sort of like if its last meal was prehistoric, then you would have an idea?" asked Drummond smiling at the idea of some rotting and partially digested fern being vomited on the deck.

"Very much like that," returned Brice grinning. The squat little man was the quietist of the bunch. He was the thinker, would not talk until the right idea struck him.

"We need a bigger boat," observed Barb, sitting on a stool in the back corner of the small room. She was studying one of the organisms in a petri dish. More than fifty years old she had maintained her physical conditioning and was wearing her age well. Without knowing what she was in for she talked Scott into letting her come with. She was not used to the dregs of laboratory life. Barb had quickly nicknamed the boat the Floating Museum.

"No offense Captain Drummond, but I hate having to make do with what little research we have on this boat. It would have been nice to have the ship the Artic Commander or something like that. Then we'd have every research tool available and the carcass of that beast." It was only the second trip for Barbara Rolland and she was not weathering it well. She had barely muddled through a one-month cruise on the Artic Commander two years previously. However, the Commander was moored in Liverpool.

Drummond smiled and stroked his bushy beard. He said in return, "None taken but the Commander was already on a mission and this was all they had for a spur of the moment. Sorry we're just not big enough for a fifty-foot carcass."

Scott jumped in to defend Drummond by saying, "And our wonderful university labeled this mission a boondoggle and barely paid for our air fare. We're lucky the Society helped us out."

Barb turned her attention to Scott and said, "I'm not a microbiologist, but it seems to me the bacteria and organisms we took off the beast were very much like the chimneys in the Black Sea. And there was mold, but and this is important, it was not from decomposition materials."

"Is that what caused the earthquakes off the coast of Siberia?" Scott asked realizing the geophysicists could only manage a guess.

"Could be. A massive buildup of methane gas, like we've never seen before and it suddenly blows. As if someone put a cork in it then lit the match."

Drummond shook his head and said, "There's that term again." Then he asked, "Are you saying that the earthquake in Siberia was not actually an earthquake but more of an explosion?"

Barb patently explained, "One third of all life on this planet resides in microbes below the ocean surface, moreover, in the sediment on the ocean floor. They have lifted off areas of the ocean floor and not found mud, but several solid feet of bacteria and organisms. What they produce, very much like the cows that chew on grass worldwide, is methane. Now if all the cows in the world expelled at once …"

"It would be really stinky," finished Gary, drawing a laugh from the group.

Barb nodded and even allowed her usually cantankerous side a smile and responded, "Yes Gary, it would stink. But it would also pollute the air to such a degree that life as we know it would be altered. Now under the ocean, we have the same problem. So much rotting decay that if it all developed into methane and blew at the same time, it would wipe out the world."

"Sort of like an extreme case of a compost pile that actually gets too hot, and starts itself on fire," observed Drummond. He noticed several people looking at him then he acknowledged, "Seen one once in England. An unseasonably hot day, a lot of cow manure and someone threw on some straw bales. The entire thing burst into flames."

"A very good observation. But put it on a global scale, altering the entire ocean's temperatures by as much as ten degrees, and tectonic repositioning causing untold pressure," replied Barb.

"Wow. But, unlikely to happen," observed Drummond hopefully.

"I'd have a better chance at the lottery. But we think something did happen, or something like that off the coast of Siberia."

Drummond shook his head. He had seen a lot of weird things in the ocean, but all that could be explained to some degree. This was all beyond him. Finally, he said, "Well, I have a job to do and how it is that I am no help to you on yours. I will leave you to toil on unknown phenomenon, and prehistoric beasties."

Barb watched the man walk out then said, "We still need a bigger boat." But her mind drifted. Drummond was the only one on board that was remotely her age, and she had a pleasant appreciation for the ruddy, seafaring man. Even though his cheerfulness was sometimes irritating to her.

Drummond however, was happy to leave the mad scientists and their methane, organisms, and bloated beasts. He preferred to watch the ocean, especially with its three-foot swells. There was something about choppy water that excited, and hypnotized him. It reminded him of how human he was. The sheer force and magnitude, and being such a small speck in the scope of things.

He had sat down on the huge cushioned bench behind the wheel and chatted with Monroe for a few minutes, getting the buzz on which bars were the best in Nome the port they were coursing for. He hated to say it but he had more in common with Monroe than with the scientist down below, even though he considered himself an educated man. Having sailed around the world several time, he had a small apartment that he called home and no family to speak of. He liked it that way. As did Monroe.

After a half hour chat Drummond turned his eyes to the open water. As he had predicted, they were finally sailing out of the choppiness. His eye caught something off in the distance. Going over to the wooden railing that circled the edge of the boat deck, he reached in his breast pocket and pulled out a pair of glasses. The image was still too far to ascertain so he went into the deck cabin and pulled out a large pair of Bushnell binoculars.

It took a few moments for the moving boat and the image to come together, but he found it. It was an odd sight as he focused the eyeglasses. It had the right color for an old sailing vessel sail, but there did not seem to be a boat attached. He looked again and noticed the tip of the sail seemed to be missing.

"Monroe, what do you make of that?" he asked, fully aware that Monroe was one of those curious people that actually had 20-15 eyesight.

Monroe glanced out over the waves and formed the words 'sail' in his mind. Then he looked again and thought better of it.

"Well?" asked Drummond realizing the man was also having a hard time with the image.

"Shark?" he answered questioningly. Then he added from a seaman's perspective, "The horizon and size seem out of whack." He was still squinting across the water at the odd shape slicing through the water. He knew in his mind they were wrestling with three-foot swells and the shark fin never disappeared.

Drummond's mind bounced back to the strange conversation below deck. Suddenly his mind sounded an alarm, a sense that something was amiss. "Damn," said Drummond, then he flung open the deck cabin door and bolted down the short steps into the research area. Somewhat breathless he located Scott quickly and said quietly, "I need to see you up top."

Scott looked up from his skin sample and responded simply, "Sure." He had learned the first day to take the captain seriously.

Drummond and Scott climbed up to the upper deck and looked out over the water. Scott wrapped his arms around himself for the air was starting to get colder. "What?" He asked finally.

Drummond scanned the horizon one more time and noticed his anomaly was missing. "Monroe?"

"It went down about five seconds ago. I didn't get any better look at it though."

Drummond looked over at Scott who was looking out over the water. "What did you see?" asked Scott growing more curious.

Captain Drummond chose his words carefully and asked, "Is there such a thing as a prehistoric shark?"

Scott nodded, then glanced out over the water again, then answered, "Yes of course. Several different varieties. Why?"

"How about a rather big one?" asked Drummond.

Scott shrugged his shoulders and answered, "Sure. Carcharodon Megalodon. Big nasty thing."

Drummond nodded his head slowly then asked, "How big?"

"Reports of up to a hundred feet long, though I don't quite believe that. Teeth seven-eight inches in length. A person could walk into its mouth. Ate its way into extinction, about two million years ago. Why?" Scott looked over at Drummond and scrutinized the man.

Drummond pointed out over the water and said, "I think we're being hunted."

Scott looked to the end of the finger and blinked several times. Then he said breathlessly, "Oh my God."

It had just surfaced, less than three hundred feet off the port bow. Drummond did not need the binoculars to see the large fin parting the waves. "That's a seven-foot dorsal fin," he said in reverence. "Nothing that big alive in our day and age." He also noticed the tail fin was now visible. Like the dorsal fin, it was mangled at the tip, like it had been frozen off.

Monroe had spotted it too and he added, "Space between the tail and fin puts that thing at over eighty-feet long."

"I got to get my camera and Anthony to get some pictures!" shouted Scott turning to race down the deck.

Drummond pulled him up short with a large, beefy hand. "Doctor Pierson. I was dead serious."

Scott's face contorted in thought, his mind a blank. Then he looked again at the fin, slicing neatly, ever closer. "Oh shit," was all he said when the reality sank in.

"Monroe, evasive measures, if you would," Drummond commanded.

Monroe said nothing as he swung the Iceland Venture to the starboard, away from the gray mottled fin. Thankful they were on the engine, Monroe slammed the throttle on the helm console to the breech, to full steam. However, he knew the big diesel engines were no match for the speed of the shark. Drummond and Scott watched the fin slip neatly beneath the waves.

Drummond and Scott made their way to the stern of the ship, keeping a watchful eye on anything popping up out of the waves.

Within a minute Gary came up and yelled from the deck house, "Hey, what's the big idea? I'm a little tall to be doing cartwheels on this boat."

Scott ran to him and explained very quickly. Gary pulled away and looked Scott in the eye and asked, "You're kidding? Right?"

The answer however, came from below. The Iceland Venture lurched from the rear and rolled over several feet. Scott and Gary hung onto the top of the deck house as Drummond looked over the edge of the railing. What he saw made his stomach churn, almost as much as the froth below. The fish had literally tried to take a bite out of the rear of the ship! He could see the flashing of white beneath the waves as the great fish gnawed on the wood.

"Sweet Jesus," Drummond said. Then he wheeled around and ran toward the deck house. Seeing Scott and Gary he yelled, "Get your wet weather gear on boys. It's going to be a bumpy ride."

Scott disappeared below deck to alert the others. Gary ran to the stern railing and looked down, seeing the huge dorsal fin slip below the water. Drummond was in the cabin searching for the only two weapons they had. His Smith and Wesson 44 magnum hand gun, and a spear gun.

The boat got hit again, actually lifting out of the water and bouncing sideways, to a twenty-degree angle on its port side. It righted itself, but not without several people being tossed around. Monroe, swung the wheel to the starboard side, trying desperately to get away from the fish, but it was clear to him that the thing under the waves was much faster. Drummond came up and handed the hand gun to Monroe who tucked it in his belt. Drummond went to the side with the spear gun loaded and ready for action.

"You're not going to kill him with that thing!" Gary yelled.

Drummond flashed him a nasty look and said, "You got a better idea I'd surely like to hear it about now." Drummond glanced fervently around the water for any sign from the great fish then added, "If I can hit him in the brain, we might stand a chance."

Scott and the rest of the research team came up, all wearing their bright yellow slickers and rubber clogs.

"I can't believe this," said Barb unwilling to accept the fact they were being hunted by an eighty-foot shark. "Where is this big fish anyway?"

Drummond looked around at the water. Then he said, "I sincerely hope we've seen the last of the thing. Hopefully, it didn't like the taste of us."

"Had to be an over friendly whale shark," Connie said coming to the only really logical conclusion.

"Hang on, I'm turning again," said Monroe, steering the boat back to the left.

The rudder had barely acknowledged control, when the boat lurched again. Scott just managed to grab onto the railing as his feet slid from underneath him, hitting the deck hard and extremely grateful the wooden railing was solid. Connie ran to his rescue when it became clear that the shark was not letting off. It was pushing the boat sideway through the water.

Pulling Scott back up to his feet, Scott smiled in appreciation and murmured, "Thanks." Connie smiled back. Then they both backed away from the edge, trying gamely to see where the monster was now headed.

Drummond was racing around the stern of the boat desperately searching the water. He could not make out his target through the churning waves.

Anthony was bent over the starboard railing taking pictures of the foaming water. He could make out a great white form coming up through the foam and he grinned as he continued to snap picture after picture.

The massive shark came up out of the water and smashed into the boat at the height of the railing. The snout of the great beast hit the boat, splintering the wood and tearing off a chunk of the upper deck, rocking the boat sideways from its weight.

Anthony had fortunately lurched backwards and slid across the deck, grabbing onto the hatch edge of the deck cabin to keep from slipping off the port side of the ship and into the water. His camera however, was not so lucky, slipping out of his hand, and bouncing off the top for the wooden railing, and bouncing out of the boat.

"Son-of-a-bitch!" he yelled. "My camera!"

Drummond had managed to get off a quick shot, the spear piercing the shark in the left side of its body. But he felt like he was trying to take down a moose with a BB gun. Either he was going to irritate the great beast enough to make it go away. Or piss it off worse.

"Hang onto something, this thing hits again it's not going to be pretty," yelled Drummond loading another spear into the gun. All the researchers grabbed onto the upper part of the deck housing, and waited. Barb was literally shaking, as Connie put a firm arm around her.

"It'll be okay," said Connie soothingly.

"Did you see that thing? How is it going to be okay?" asked Barb, convinced this was the end.

Gary looked over at Scott and asked, "Why do you think it's attacking us? We've done nothing to irritate it, we don't smell or look like a fish in distress, do we?"

Scott shook his head when the glimmer of a light went on. He replied, "Think of how big that thing is and think of what the bottom of this white boat looks like."

Gary nodded quickly and said, "Oh shit. It thinks we're a whale."

Everyone seemingly held their breath to see if the shark was coming back for another attack. They searched the water for signs, glancing at each other for signs of encouragement, or signs of weakness. Several breathless minutes ticked by, with Drummond going from side to side looking for the great beast.

Monroe had abandoned the helm and gone to the rear of the boat. With the toe of his shoe, he deftly flipped open the hasp on the engine hatch. Then he flipped up the hatch and peered down into the darkness. He could see enough.

"Captain, we're taking on water," Monroe announced.

Drummond came over quickly and looked down into the hole. "The engine?"

"Full of water. We've stopped."

Drummond swung around to take stock of the situation. "Hit the pumps," he said to Monroe as he quickly moved into the deck cabin, got on the radio and called a mayday, giving their last coordinates, leaving out the fact that it was a monster trying to eat them. He made sure the GPS was transmitting then he went down to see what the damage was.

Scott could tell the boat was listing to the starboard side, but there seemed to be little movement. He scrambled to where Monroe was kneeling over the engine hatch, shining a flashlight down into the water.

"How are we doing?" he asked putting a hand on the man's shoulder.

"Pumps are holding their own." Then Monroe looked up and said, "But the batteries won't keep them going forever, and we have no way of patching that hole."

Scott knelt and asked in a whisper, "We're going to sink, aren't we?"

Monroe nodded, then said solemnly, "Sooner or later. Yes."

Scott stood up and, like everyone else was doing, looked out over the frigid water. "It's going to be sooner," he said suddenly.

The large fin was making a bee line for the starboard side of the boat.

"Hang on!" yelled Monroe, pulling the Smith and Wesson from his pants and taking aim.

Drummond was on the steps to the upper deck, when the boat suddenly lurched sideways and he could make out the repeats of his hand gun. He hung on desperately, realizing he could hear the cracking of the hull, and the splintering of the wood. He crawled up the steps and stayed on the deck floor. The boat was listing terribly, as he made his way to the cabin port hole and looked out. He grimaced as he saw a huge tail thrashing about, he knew, doing damage to the Iceland Venture with every stroke.

Scott had managed to latch onto the top of the rail as Monroe had moved closer to the wooden railing. He was shooting straight down into the water when the creature struck. There was a great spray of water and he heard Monroe swear. Scott blinked. Then never saw the man again.

"He fell in!" Scott shouted as Drummond finally made his way top side. Drummond noticed that everyone else was still holding onto something, as Barb had now taken to crying. He lurched over to the railing and looked desperately into the water. But neither Monroe, nor the shark, were there.

It took a few moments for the reality to make itself evident to Drummond. In one blinding moment, Monroe was gone. With the ship listing, he was dangerously close to the water, but at the moment, he did not care. Monroe, his friend and shipmate, was gone. Just like that.

"Captain, what do we do now?" Asked Scott. He waited a few moments, then asked, again, "Captain?"

"Get ready to abandoned ship!" Drummond yelled as it was clear to him, the ship was not going to right itself, and was slowly sliding onto its starboard side.

"Abandoned ship? We can't abandon ship, we're out in the middle of the freaking ocean with a monster shark! We can't abandon ship!" stated Gary loudly.

"Wood floats. Wouldn't it be better to stay with the boat?" asked Connie, hanging onto the port side wooden railing, and onto the hand of Barb, who was now sobbing uncontrollably.

"Not with a five-ton engine in it, it doesn't," replied Drummond angrily, pulling himself up toward the cabin. Climbing inside he pulled out a huge, five-foot-long canvas duffle that contained a ten-man life raft. Scott pulled himself over the ever-precarious deck to lend a hand. Untying the draw ropes, they pulled it out and laid it on the port side of the cabin, as the boat continued its starboard journey into the water. Drummond then reached into the canvas duffle and pulled out another large sack and handed it to Scott.

Drummond pulled the raft up to the bow, where the boat was already sinking into the water. He pulled the cord then placed it on the edge of the boat. In a few seconds, the raft started unfurling, inflating itself.

Drummond motioned everyone over. "Everyone get in. Try to keep yourself dry. I'll push you off."

Climbing into the raft was treacherous, as the ship bobbed and the raft, plunged around. Barb and Connie were the first ones to scramble aboard and fell in doing so. Anthony followed behind and Gary pulled up next.

Scott looked at Drummond, could see something forebodings in the man's eyes, and asked desperately, "You're coming too, aren't you?"

Drummond looked at the man and slowly shook his head. "No. There's a GPS on the raft and a satellite transmitter and phone, turn it on when you get away from the boat. Water and provisions in that sack to last several days and also, there's shark repellent on board, use it as soon as you get a couple hundred feet from the boat."

Scott looked at the man, then motioned at the raft and said, "If that shark attacks this thing, we won't stand a chance."

Drummond sighed heavily, then said, "I know. I'm going to try and attract his attention while you slip off. Hopefully, the raft doesn't look like anything to him."

Scott nodded sorrowfully. This turn of events was striking him to the core. Monroe was dead and the thought of being out on the open ocean without Drummond made him scared to death, even without the shark.

Scott stuck out his hand and Drummond smiled and shook it warmly. Finally, Scott turned, tossed the emergency kit into the center then crawled over the edge of the huge, yellow raft. It took little for Drummond to push for the water was rising up under the raft. It floated off, bobbing mildly in the calming ocean.

Drummond quickly turned, for he had a plan in the back of his mind. And he did not want to look at the only way of escape, leaving the boat. In addition, he felt like they were probably no better off than he was at the moment.

Scott watched the man scurry away. Then he shouted stupidly, "We'll send help!"

"Who's going to help us?" asked Barb through the tears.

"Oh, shut up Barbara," said Scott irritably. Barb stopped for a second at the sudden words, then she started in crying harder.

"Scott!" reprimanded Connie cradling Barb in closer.

"She's being a pain and she's been a pain in the ass since we've started this voyage," said Scott heatedly.

Gary and Anthony exchanged looks then Gary asked, "What do we do now?"

Scott looked at the man, shrugged his shoulders then said simply, "We survive. And stay close by to see if we can pick up the pieces."

Drummond was scampering over the side of the deck house, the boat, now almost perpendicular to the water. Sliding into the water, the frigid shock electrifying his legs from the waist down, he moved through the deck house door, grabbed the flair gun where it was mounted to the deck wall, and pulled it off. Getting back out he climbed back up on the cabin.

Using the hand railing, which was now over his head he made his way back to the helm, sliding hand over hand. He dropped down onto the helm and fishing in his wet trousers, pulled out a round, barrel shaped key. Kneeling down he slipped it into the key hole on the helm console and turned, hoping the batteries were still providing juice, even in their precarious position. He heard with satisfaction the small pump start up.

Using the edge of the engine cover to move to the stern, he looked out over the water. The diesel fuel was starting to rise, and its oily gleam bringing a smile to Drummond's face.

"Come on you son-of-a-bitch. I've got a present for you," he murmured to himself.

It did not take long. Even in the growing dark, Drummond could make out the massive fin slicing through the water, the sun glinting off the large wake. It was coming from the port this time, which Drummond took heart in. It had looked over at the raft and decided it was not anything it should waste its time with. Nothing in its prehistoric past looked like a large, yellow donut. It was coming back to the thing that looked like a whale, but sure did not taste like one.

Drummond had taken position on the railing, standing on one and pulling his arms through another one, using it to steady his cold fingers. He took delight when the huge fin sliced neatly into the floating diesel fuel. He took aim with the flair gun and said, "Smile you son-of-a-bitch." Then he pulled the trigger.

The research team saw it before they heard it. A massive fireball mushroomed into the air, then the sound of the blast echoed through their ears. From his position in the raft, Scott had to turn to view the fire. Then a second smaller blast rocked the air.

"Oh, my God. Drummond blew up the boat," said Gary in awe.

Scott looked transfixed at the spectacle, then realized what actually happened. "No, he didn't. He blew up the shark, using the boat," said Scott in a respectful tone.

Anthony balled up his fist and pounded the edge of the raft. Finally, he said, "The only thing in this world that I'm good at and have no God-damned camera!"

Scott continued to look at the flames, the oily smoke rising, but quickly being smothered by the ocean. He continued to stare until they died down. Then he turned back to face Anthony and said, "I hope you're good at surviving. For Captain Drummond bought us some time with his life."

Anthony pulled his slicker in around him, but said nothing. There was nothing left to say.

Scott finally allowed his body to relax. In less than fifteen minutes their lives had changed forever. A slow, shallow sobbing came from Barbara as she nestled into Connie's arms. The cold was already seeping its way through the open zipper of Scott's jacket. Their chance of survival was not good, for none of them knew what to expect. At least the shark was gone.

In the depths of the ocean, several thousand feet below them, finding its final resting place in the muck and mud, was a Canon EOS 80-D, with a telephoto lens. In it was the only known picture of a Carcharodon Megalodon, with its black, dinner plate sized eyes, mouth wide enough to walk into, and row upon row of replaceable teeth.

CHAPTER 7

Commander Wolfson poured himself a hot cup of coffee and was preparing to seat himself down with Merrick. It had been a rewarding voyage so far, of constant alerts, situations and fabricated scenarios, filling up the first week of the voyage. And the small ship with the knowledgeable but an untried crew handled it all well. As in all emergency situations, they had found glitches, and remedied them.

Even though Don and Ralph had been on the submarine much longer, Captain Hornacher never once backed down from her role as supreme leader, commanding the submarine efficiently and without delay. It did not take the men long to learn that she was an even-tempered leader, with sixteen years of knowledge in the Submarine Corp., and very capable of dishing it out to the men. Some had even gone so far as to simply forget she was a woman, by swearing profusely in front of her, especially when they screwed up under Don's watchful eye, or talking about their latest female conquests. It was when she added her own experiences and two cents was when they realized who they were talking too. She had definitely heard worse in her travels and on the other submarines. In fact, that was the way she preferred it. Just to be one of the crew.

Merrick's scenarios for disaster were in some occasions just to see what the ship would do, and others to test a system or the handling of it. Twice he woke the split shift in the middle of the night for some purpose. One was even a surprise to Wolfson who had helped design the Emergency Test Operating Procedure. Merrick had told him afterwards that it was no fair he knew all the answers. Wolfson had to agree.

They had also succeeded in taking the Specter to the crushing depth of twenty-four hundred feet below sea level. Taking the submarine almost six hundred feet further than a standard sub. Other than the crew breaking out in a sweat, the Specter handled it flawlessly. It's sensors barely acknowledging the crushing pressure on its hull.

But late in the evening on Friday, the ship had finally settled into somewhat of a routine. Alex was promising something good for supper Sunday, as Beverly's sleeping arrangement had finally molded itself into a pleasing situation in the commanders' quarters. She had her own bottom bunk and her down time managed opposite the men. After a time there had still been no chance encounters in this department. Things were handled in the utmost respect and civility in this area. One would not tamper with the captain.

The mess quarters were cramped with every available inch used for storage. The one table was not even capable of holding half the crew as it folded down from the wall. Wolfson came into the mess, guided his large frame around easily, one who was used to a small ship and limited access. Lightweight Kevlar, the bench seat unfolded with the table. Wolfson carried his cup to the boat styled bolted down coffee maker, positioned his cup and pushed the upper button until he filled his cup. He then went to where Merrick was sitting at the mess table. He was on his notebook computer and had a large pad of paper next to him. Ralph glanced at the paper and noticed it was completely filled with numbers, small scribbles, and several small drawings.

"What's with the music?" asked Wolfson finally coming across a singer he had not heard of before. The music was coming out of Don's notebook as he had set up to two portable Bose Cubes. Wolfson noticed there was no wiring to the cubes.

Don shrugged, turned down the volume and responded, "Harry Connick Junior. Felt like some jazz today."

"What are you working on?" Wolfson asked sitting alongside, and trying to crane his neck to catch a glimpse. In his mind he thought Don probably played games on the thing.

"An anti-matter engine," Don replied matter-of-factly.

Ralph's eyebrows shot up, then he smiled. "You're serious, aren't you?" He finally noted.

Merrick responded without once looking up from his computer, "It's the one thing on this ship that really needs improving. Even though we have the smallest working nuclear-powered engine in the world, with an anti-matter engine we could save some space."

Ralph smiled again and asked, "So you're working on an anti-matter engine just to save some space?"

Don stopped for a moment, looked up and grinned, then said, "Well, not just that, but if we ever want to get off this rock and into outer space, we're not going to do it with rocket fuel. This is the next step in the evolution of man's thinking."

Ralph nodded without really knowing why then observed, "I bet you were a lonely child and bullied by the jocks."

The statement caught Don off guard for a second. He sat back against the bench back, put his hands behind his head, as an ever-widening grin spread along his face. Then he said finally, "I went to a small high school. I was the starting tailback on the High School football team. I was the SMART jock that everyone was afraid of. I was also president of the student council, and even though I had a scholarship, to finance my hobbies and living arrangements, I sold naked pictures of cheerleaders."

Ralph settled in then said, "Oh, you've got to tell me about that one."

Merrick just shrugged his shoulders with a slight grin, letting his mind wander off to more pleasant and simpler times. Finally, he explained, "Nothing much to tell. I bought a Nikon camera and sort of set up shop as a photographer. Took a lot of senior pictures, but because I didn't have a studio we would find outside locations, wildlife pictures or all natural. Made pretty good money because I had no overhead and I didn't charge professional prices. Had a homemade one trig computer just for picture taking. Pretty darned good at it if I do say so myself."

"So where did the cheerleaders come in?" asked Ralph.

Don grew thoughtful for a moment then he explained. "That's sort of funny. It was one girl's idea actually. Like I said, I was making pretty good money in those days. A couple hundred dollars a session. Well, I had a photo shoot with a gal named Mary Lou who loved horses. So naturally, we went to her farm, found a pretty grove of trees and she rides around on her horse. I take a hundred pictures and I'm about to wrap it up when she casually mentions she'd like one special one. One of her on the horse, totally nude. I make sure no one is watching and I shoot another round, on a completely different card. Well, she pays me a little extra and I blow one of them up. And being the nice guy that I am I give her all the SD cards."

Ralph smirked upon the words 'nice guy.' "So, where did the cheerleaders come in?" asked Ralph finally, trying to cut to the interesting part.

"Mary Lou let some of the girls in school know. I get approached by several girls liking the idea. As much as the idea exhilarated the mind of a sixteen-year-old in the throes of hormones, I figured though it was one of those things that would get me into trouble. A lot of Daddies with shotguns if you get my meaning. So, I resisted."

"So where did the cheerleaders come in?" Ralph asked for the last time.

"They approached me as a group. I told them my dilemma, not wanting to get kicked out of school or punched out, or shot by someone's big old Daddy. We came to a compromise. We waited until after graduation. I paid off the janitor of the school and we shot the whole cheerleading squad. In their uniforms for personal keepsakes. And in the buff, for whatever reason. Anyway, they got a copy of the prints when I left for college to protect my ass. They got free pictures and I got one hell of a Calendar to sell at MIT to finance my first year through college."

"Do you still have the pictures?" asked Ralph, intrigued with the entire story.

Merrick shrugged his shoulders. "Na. I didn't keep them; I still had too much fear of having the shit kicked out of me. But it is funny. At my last reunion I actually had some of the old cheerleaders tell me they still had the pictures. Proof to their kids they were really something to look at one time I guess."

"How come I got this feeling in college; you came up with more inventive ventures?" Ralph mentioned smiling.

Merrick smiled back and replied, "Actually, you have to remember the time. I had biggest and most powerful computer on campus, including the school itself. I and another guy built it, put it in the steam tunnels under the dormitory. Where it just so happened most of the cables ran. It did the job rather well."

"Term paper time I take it," observed Ralph.

Merrick just looked at him with a wry grin and said, "Yeah, something like that."

Ralph just nodded, aware that Merrick did not seem to want to go into details. So, he took a gulp of his coffee then changed directions. "So, this anti-matter-engine. Just sort of tinkering with some science fiction. Right?"

Merrick looked up and glared at Ralph. "Oh, come on Ralphie, you know me better than that. I don't tinker." He flipped the notebook computer around and showed Commander Wolfson a three-dimensional graphic of a massive display of tubes and chambers to the point that Ralph could not understand it. Wolfson was both intrigued with the graphics and paper-thin expanding computer screen. The silicon wafer tri-fold design unfolded out to almost thirty inches. Finally, Ralph said, "I thought anti-matter was just a pipe dream."

"Oh no, it's never been a pipe dream. NASA been working on an anti-matter engine since two thousand. There's three different ways this can work and there are several models already in production. Including PDM's version."

Ralph looked across at the man then asked, "Um, okay. So why don't we have an anti-matter engine?"

"Anti-matter. Producing it isn't easy. Or cheap."

Ralph took the next step. "So why are we building anti-matter engines?"

Merrick responded, "A new six miles in diameter collider in Nebraska can produce enough to actually see. In a couple years' time, the Valentine facility could produce enough to generate a space craft out of our solar system. Or blow the whole of earth to hell if they don't capture it right." He then spread out a huge grin.

Ralph glared at him for a second then said, "Now come on just a cotton-picking minute. I know enough about anti-matter to know its instability is the very reason we haven't been able to conquer it. Once in contact with matter, which is all other atomic structure by the way, you would have a terrible result."

"Cataclysmic," replied Don off the cuff.

"Exactly."

"So? What's your point?" Merrick asked smirking a bit knowing where Ralph was leading.

"SOOO. You can't exactly make a blob of this stuff and carry it around in your hand then slide it into your gas tank," Ralph said letting a little frustration edge into his voice.

"Oh," Merrick nodded. "Okay, let's use your example. What is gasoline made of?"

Ralph was taken aback for a second then responded, "Oil?"

"Exactly. But we don't dump straight oil into the car, in fact we use oil to protect the running parts from burn out."

Ralph nodded sensing the line of thinking. "All right. So, we have to refine the anti-matter. How do you refine something that doesn't like matter?"

"What we do is introduce a microscopic anti-matter magnetic isotope into the entire process, tricking the anti-matter into thinking it's also anti-matter. Atomic level tinkering you might say. And since anti-matter is so unstable, we can manipulate it and put the anti-matter into a magnetic vacuum canister. It may be as simple as an x-ray scanner."

"That will work?" asked Ralph incredulously, not quite understanding the whole process.

"In theory and by every computer scenario. The problem, as you've noticed is, you can't exactly pump it into a gas tank. However, Professor Norm Finnegan at MIT has already designed a working transfer system, or magnetic ring anti-matter pump as it was. We just need a working engine to enable that massive amount of power. We can take a pin point of anti-matter, introduce it to a stable but opposing matter to create a reliable implosion that we can harness. Actually, for the submarine, it's easier because all we have to do is make bubbles and the sub moves. A space ship has to move in a completely different way. What we're attempting to do is harness the power of the Big Bang and make a tiny little speck of a ship move."

Ralph sat back. Sometimes Merrick scared him, and yet he sat in the safe confines of a submarine with a glass like surface, stronger than anything else known to man. Finally, he asked, "I suppose next you'll be telling me you're also working on Nano-technology."

Don looked over at Ralph, his eyes wide acknowledgment. "This notebook could run this ship. A hundred trig bytes, with an expanding liquid silicone screen. And Tinkerbell, well, Tinkerbell with the help of Gypsy could fend off every naval ship on the planet."

"Oh, that WOULD be fun!" Exclaimed Tinkerbell into Ralph's ear piece.

Ralph looked somewhat distressful, then asked Don, "Do you believe in God?"

Merrick again sat back and smiled. He thought for a moment, more amused at Ralph's question than his answer. Ultimately, he responded, "Sure. Whom do you think caused the Big Bang in the first place?"

Ralph nodded then said, "Leave it to you to break it down in a scientific way."

Sitting there in their own thoughts they both felt the sensation at once. Ralph looked across the table at Merrick. "I think we're surfacing," Ralph mentioned finally.

Don nodded and added, "Something is up."

Just then Captain Hornacher popped her head in the galley door and asked, "You gentlemen want to be in on this? We just intercepted a distress signal."

Merrick shut down his computer as Ralph and his coffee cup followed Beverly to the control room. Beverly explained the situation as they walked over to the communication's console where Ensign Barrington was monitoring the static filled communiques.

Barrington looked up when the three people entered the control room and said, "We've locked onto a GPS distress signal dead center of the Bering Sea."

Don had already walked to the front of the room and initiated the satellite system. He brought down the liquid crystal screen, using the controls on the map board, walking around Lt. Smith who took up a lot of space. Immediately, the satellite pinpointed the signal as the telescoping camera closed in on the target.

"Too dark," Don said as he switched to heat-seeking mode. A round red blob came up in the corner. He honed in on the image, projecting it to a quarter of the screen. He turned back to Beverly and said, "It appears to be life raft out in the middle of nowhere. Six bodies by my calculations."

"Captain, our position is three hundred ninety-six kilos' away," inserted Henry, running the monitoring equipment and taking his calculations from the satellite.

Surely, there's a fishing boat or a freighter closer than we are to intercept?" noted Wolfson.

"When we first got the signal, I alerted the Coast Guard at Juneau. They had already found the signal and are aware of the situation. They're going to gear up a sea plane for a rescue mission. Get there faster than anything else close by," replied the Ensign.

Beverly nodded, then turned to Lt. Smith and said, "I want a course plotted for intercept."

The big man nodded then said, "Done." He pushed a button on his computer board that sent the coordinates to Frankie who was the pilot on duty.

Don furrowed his brow and asked, "Why?"

"A squall is starting to creep toward Attu, Mr. Merrick. We just became the backup plan."

"And Don, the Specter is faster than anything on the ocean." Stated Tinkerbelle.

"The last time I checked we were still on a secret mission. I can't see us blowing our cover on helping some lost lunatics out in the middle of the ocean," Don retorted arguing with the captain and thoroughly ignoring Tinkerbell.

Beverly turned back to him with a concerned look on her face and responded, "And the last time I checked Mr. Merrick, you were not in charge of this ship. This is Naval procedure. I'm following regulations on open water rescue. That sea plane turns back for any reason we become the primary search and rescue." She glared at him for a moment, then turned back to the satellite screen. Beverly then turned to the communications console and asked, "Anyone have an idea where these people came from?"

"The signal frequency can be traced back to the ship, Iceland Venture, out of Nome." answered Barrington. Suddenly he pressed a hand over his ear piece and listened intently.

"What do you have, Ensign?" asked Beverly.

"Once Mr. Merrick initiated the satellite I started getting a scratchy signal."

"Satellite phone?" asked Don walking behind the man, looking over his shoulder. Being chastised had already lost its feelings as he concentrated on his work. Besides, this was a good test of his systems.

"Possible. I'm trying to clean it up and boast the power. A lot of magnetism this far north." Steve adjusted the frequencies and had the computer adjust for densities, until he had a recognizable human voice.

"Mayday, Mayday, this is the remainder of the crew of the Iceland Venture. Can anyone hear me? Over." Came out over the communications headset.

Don could hear the muffled voice. "Put it on control speakers," he said.

Barrington adjusted the volume then pressed and button and the whole control room heard the crackle of the distant satellite phone.

"Survivors of the Iceland Venture, this is Captain Hornacher of the United States Navy. Can you hear me?" Beverly said loudly into her clipped-on radio.

"Oh my God, we've got somebody." They could hear as the man with the phone was talking to the rest of the survivors. "Captain, this is Doctor Scott Pierson with the National Geographic Society. Are we glad to hear you!"

Don looked at the satellite picture of the six bodies floating in the cold water and said loudly, "Scott this is Don Merrick. What the hell you doing in the middle of the ocean?"

Beverly turned to Don and asked quickly, "You know him?" Don nodded in response.

"Oh man am I glad to hear your voice, Don. And I might ask the same question. What are you doing on a Navy ship and how did you pick up our call?"

Don responded, "Let's just say I got taken for a ride and we have the best wireless plan in the world. Scott, there's a US Coast Guard sea plane leaving Juneau in a few minutes. They should be there in about two and half hours."

Everyone in the control room of the Specter could hear Scott tell the others the good news. Then Scott got back on the satellite phone and said, "It's already pitch dark out here and more than a little scary. Tell them to hurry."

"The Iceland Venture is Captained by Garth Drummond. It is a two masted schooner one hundred fourteen feet long. Awfully small to be in the Bering Sea," inserted Tinkerbelle.

"Thanks Tinkerbelle." Don answered then asked, "I will. Where's the captain Scott, and what happened to the boat?"

There was a small pause, then Scott answered, "The Captain and the first mate gave their lives to give us a chance for escape. You're not going to believe this Don but we were attacked by a Carcharodon Megalodon. Anthony, our camera man says that it was as long as the ship."

Don turned and said, "Tinkerbelle?"

"That's a shark of some kind if I don't miss my guess. It would have to be a big son of a bitch to sink a boat," remarked Wolfson, listening to the conversation intently.

Don looking up at the screen watched as Tinkerbelle displayed a large computer model of the shark come up on the screen. "Up to a ninety feet long Ralph." He noted finally.

"No such thing," said Beverly scanning the shark.

"Correct. But there used to be." Don responded, then said into the air, "Scott, are you sure you saw one of these? You are aware they have been extinct for a few million years?"

"I know, I know. We all saw it. Hell, it ate the freaking ship. Beat the poor thing to death. Captain Drummond didn't stand a chance."

"He must be mistaken," observed Beverly again.

Don turned and addressed Beverly, "You know, normally I would agree with you but Scott's a Doctor of Paleontology. Sort of knows his prehistoric monsters." Then he turned back to the screen and said forcefully, "Scott, is it roaming around you anywhere?"

"No Don, it's left us alone. We sort of have this theory that it thought the ship was a whale. We're sort of hoping Captain Drummond blew the damned thing up. Don, we think it has to do with that under sea tremors that have been happening off the coast of Siberia."

Just then they all heard a loud beep. "Don, we've been trying to raise someone for over an hour. We're down to less than fifty percent power."

Don glanced at Beverly who nodded then he said, "Scott you're going to need to disconnect. We'll monitor the situation and if for any reason the sea plane doesn't make it, we'll come get you. I'll call back if there's any change. You got that?" Don then glanced at Barrington to confirm a lock on the signal. The Ensign simply nodded.

"Got it, Don. And thanks."

Don could plainly hear the click, then he said to himself, "Don't mention it."

Captain Hornacher walked up to Don, looked into the blue eyes and said, "So. Full speed ahead Mr. Merrick?"

Don searched her eyes for a second, realized for the first time since they had started the voyage that she had pretty green eyes. Then he said finally, "Yes. If you please Captain."

Beverly could have rubbed in the decision, or mentioned the fact that when a lunatic is a friend, it makes a difference. But she was not that type of woman. She had done it by the book and it paid off.

"You heard the man Commandeer. Adjust to a new heading, bring us up to twenty meters and set cruise at seventy-five knots," Beverly said.

Commander Wolfson then stated to Frankie, "Mr. Niguchi, proceed to new heading at the depth of twenty meters and crank out seventy-five knots for the rescue."

"Aye commander, setting new heading locking in on moving GPS signal of Iceland Venture up bubble to twenty meters at seventy-five knots." Frankie smiled broadly at the commander. It had been the first real command at steering she had received, and was extremely proud of the fact she was the one piloting the most complex vessel on the planet.

Beverly smiled and nodded at Merrick and turned to Ralph. "Commander Wolfson, that cup of coffee looks good. Would you be so kind as to assume command until I return?"

Ralph nodded, then said, "Done Captain. My shift starts soon anyway."

"I'm sure Mr. Merrick will agree with me that we need to keep an eye on this situation. I'm going to stick around until the rescue."

Ralph and Don watched her leave the control room. Ralph could not help himself as he walked over to Don, nudged him in the ribs and chortled, "Chalk one up for the captain."

"You like that don't you?"

"My question is why do we even have a picture of a prehistoric fish in our computers?" Ralph said changing the touchy subject.

"There are four different encyclopedias downloaded into the mainframe, Commander Wolfson. Don does like knowing stuff." Explained Tinkerbelle.

Don smiled and said, "What she said."

Ralph grew quiet for a second then asked, "Do you think this shark really sank that ship?"

Don thought for a second then answered, "I have no doubt about it. Scotts in his mid-thirties, and not one to fantasize. Besides, it sounded like everyone on board saw the shark."

Ralph stood quietly for a moment then smiled and asked, "So, when you designed this ship, did you account for defense against a big shark?"

Don answered quickly. "One torpedo down the gullet and she's toast. I wouldn't worry about it too much Ralphie old boy."

Ralph closed in on Merrick and looked him in the eyes and mentioned, "Don, we don't have a torpedo. Remember?"

Don looked at Ralph, smirked and retorted, "We're still the biggest indestructible chew toy in the world. Not to worry."

The personnel in the control room all watched as Don popped around different views of the Atlantic. Beverly had returned when the Coast Guard sea plane had finally departed for its rescue mission.

Ensign Barrington motioned for Captain Hornacher. "Ma'am? I have a coded transmission from the Attack Submarine USS Seattle on Com. They've been monitoring some of the transmissions out of Juneau. They'd like our position."

Beverly shook her head. "Why?"

The Ensign talked briefly into his headset. He listened intently then turned and said, "Captain, they are to the north of the rescue position and just want to know if they can help."

"Tell them we appreciate their help and they should continue to monitor the situation and send them our USS designation. But they don't get our position. Understand?" Beverly responded.

Barrington nodded quickly as he had already thought that would be the response. After a brief exchange he smiled and turned to the captain and said, "Captain Urlacher of the Seattle says he appreciates our discretion since he's never heard of the Specter."

Beverly smiled back and asked, "What's so funny?"

Steve smiled back again and said, "Well, it's what he said at the end. He was anxious to see the new Super Sub the Navy's been working on. 'It must be huge' he said."

Beverly grinned back. "Let's keep it that way."

Don looked over at Wolfson with disgust and asked, "Why is it all military people think bigger is better?"

"Started in World War One. The guy with the biggest gun usually won," Ralph responded with a sly grin.

Beverly then asked Alvin, "Who else is on point in the North Pacific?"

Alvin, anticipating the question swiveled around and replied, "Both the submarines, Seattle and Cheyanne are in the Bering Sea. The North Carolina is on a rogue mission in the North Pacific. And the CVBG with the Gerald Ford."

Beverly walked over to the mapping board where a current ship locator identified the heading of the two subs in question. Glancing at several other ships in the area she shook her head and said off handedly, "At their slow speed they're still too far away. We're still on point."

They continued late into the evening to monitor the situation. Following the path of the sea plane, on the huge satellite screen they watched the two signals get closer.

Beverly noticed that Don was working with Alvin Allan at the main computer terminal. Her curiosity finally got the best of her and she strolled over to look over Merrick's shoulder. "What's so interesting?" She finally asked.

"Oh, just something Scott said. We've been doing some cross referencing out of the naval computers at San Diego and we found some interesting stuff," replied Don.

"Like what?"

"About two weeks ago there were tremors off the coast of Siberia. Since that stretch of rock is about as stable as they come, it's been a buzz with scientific activity. Following the path of the Iceland Venture, they apparently were originally commissioned to look at a reported catch of a plesiosaur."

Beverly blinked several times then asked, "A plesiosaur? As in a dinosaur?"

Merrick turned and looked at the captain and replied, "Pretty much."

"So, what you're saying is that our shark might not be alone?"

"Two survivors of the Ice Age. There just might be more."

Beverly swung around and said to Wolfson, "How long until the sea plane has rescue?"

"About twenty-eight minutes," he replied swiftly.

Beverly nodded then said to Steve, "Ensign, get the survivors back on the phone."

"Yes Ma'am." It took Barrington a few seconds but he soon had tone, and the phone was responded to on the first ring.

"This is Scott." Came the voice over the loud speaker.

"Doctor Pierson, this is Captain Hornacher. You should have contact within twenty-five minutes. Do you have a flair gun on board?"

"Yes, Captain. Anthony's been clutching it as if his life depended on it."

"Well, it does. I would start signaling in about twenty minutes so that the plane may find you. Black water landing is going to be tough, so don't panic if the plane doesn't set down exactly in your local. They well maneuver over to your position."

"That's nice to know Captain. Thank you."

Beverly stopped for a second, then asked, "Has there been any troubles?"

"The only thing is we're cold Captain. We have emergency heat sticks but they only last for a half hour or so."

All the warm crew of the Specter could hear the tension in Scott's voice. It was plain even with the Specter plunging quickly in their direction that time was of the essence. Beverly was glad no more prehistoric beasts had shown up.

"We'll continue to monitor. Save the rest of your battery for any emergencies. We're out," Beverly said finally, aware that those people holding tenuously to life probably felt like the loneliest people on the planet. All she could give them was hope.

Merrick stared up at the satellite image of the sea plane crawling ever closer. He walked over where Ralph was seated next to Lt. Smith. He asked simply, "Time?"

"Twenty-three minutes by current air speed."

Beverly pulled up next to Don and she too looked up at the screen. "A billion-dollar submarine and all we can do is give words of encouragement." She offered to him.

"Yeah," he nodded. Then he inserted, "Three billion. The skin alone is worth a billion."

Beverly glanced over at Don then snickered. "You're priceless."

Even though the rescue mission seemed to tick slowly by, as each agonizing moment brought a new peril, the US Coast Guard sea plane landed safely on the inky water, found their target, and propelled itself to their position. The infrared showed the plane and the bodies slowly being loaded. One mishap with a female falling into the water made for a mad dash as a frogman, at the ready, had to dive in and pull the woman out. From the Specter's point of view, they would not know it was Barb, but she would live another day. And very probably never set foot on a boat again.

The Specter intercepted the communications with the Coast Guard sea plane that everyone was safely aboard and they were heading back. Finally, able to relax when the plane was in the air, Captain Hornacher instructed Lt. Smith to plot a course south of the Aleutian Islands, and head for deeper water.

Wolfson looked at the woman with nothing but admiration in his heart. She was doing well, considering she had been a square peg shoved into a round hole. Finally, he said to her, "Captain, why don't you sleep in this morning? Merrick and I can steer this tub for the night."

She nodded her head, yawned ungraciously, then said in return, "I might just do that. Commander, you have the conn."

Beverly was no doubt tired. But as she made her way back to her bunk she smiled inwardly. It had been the most consistent conversation with Merrick since the entire voyage had started. To that point most conversations had been two or three words. For the first time she had seen a part of the brilliant engineer that was not calculating. There was care in the man after all.

Don and Wolfson watched the woman exit the control room. Then Don turned to Wolfson and said, "She won't."

"I know she won't. She has too much of her old man's blood in her."

The two men and the midnight crew monitored the sea plane. Commander Wolfson still had Lt. Smith maintain a constant upgrade on an emergency course change, in case the sea plane had to ditch in the cold and dark ocean.

They received confirmation from the Coast Guard station on Juneau at two-forty-eight in the morning. Six survivors, safe and sound. There would be no rescue mission for the Iceland Venture as six confirmed testimonies confirmed her sunk and destroyed.

When the mission seemed to be all over, Wolfson turned to Don and said, "I met Captain Drummond once. A twenty-year man in the Navy, he took to captaining vessels for the National Geographic. He was on the mission that located Amelia Earhart's Lockheed off Howland Island." Wolfson stopped and let his thoughts gather themselves. Then he continued. "He would have made a great pirate. Red beard and big bushy mustache, larger than life. He probably arm-wrestled that damned shark all the way to its grave."

Don sat at the mapping board in a solemn state. However, his thoughts were not on the good Captain. They were on the shark. He wondered as had Captain Hornacher, whether there were more.

The nightly silence of the small ship's efficient running was broken by Barrington. "Mr. Merrick, you have a call on open radio frequency, from Juneau."

Don looked up and said "Put it on speaker." He was aware that it was undoubtedly the Coast Guard connection out of Juneau, but wondered exactly who would be calling.

"This is Mr. Merrick." Don said into the air.

"Don, this is Scott. The communications guy managed to hook me up. I thought I would give you a thank you call, before we all passed out."

"No problem, Scott. Is everyone all right? We saw somebody fall into the water."

"She's fine. The cold dip calmed her down a bit if you know what I mean." Don could hear Scott hesitate for second then, "You're on that submarine that you wanted to build, aren't you? That's why you know so much. That's why you're out in the middle of the ocean. That's why you can see everything we're doing."

Don smiled and replied, "Scott, it's supposed to be a secret, at least as long as we can keep it."

"Hey, my lips are sealed. I'm just glad you guys were out there to help us."

"What about the shark Scott?" Don asked changing the conversation.

"I'm pretty sure Captain Drummond managed to blow it up. He had a darned good plan and we saw the ship explode."

"That would have been a hell of a find."

"You know, I don't even care. That prehistoric thing killed two people and almost killed six more people. I really hope Captain Drummond sent the damned thing back to hell."

"Roger that Scott. I understand. Do you think there are any more?"

"It's possible Don. We've now got two reports so maybe something else survived."

"Well, I tell you what, if we run into anything, we'll drag it back to San Diego for you to study."

Scott chuckled briefly then responded, "It's a deal Don. And thanks again. They tell me here I've got to go."

"Stay warm Scott."

"Doctor Pierson, this is Tinkerbelle and I've got a question. Your university is set to go to the island Attu to pick up the carcass of whatever that fisherman found. If it is a Plesiosaur, can your scientific team create a clone?"

For a moment there was dead silence. Then Scott answered finally, "That's not really my field of expertise but I do believe it's really not on our agenda. But, there's always that possibility."

"Thanks Doctor Pierson. I was just curious."

"Don? Was that ...?

"Tinkerbelle is a very good friend of mine Scott. Let's leave it at that."

"Got it. Hey Don, one last thing. That Captain of yours sounds kind of cute, but I can't see you taking orders from a woman." Scott did not honestly know if Beverly was listening or not, either way he was looking to get Don in a little hot water.

Don glanced around with a sinister grin as everyone in the control room looked at him in anticipation of his answer. Finally, he said, "Just because I'm prehistoric doesn't mean I can't adapt."

CHAPTER 8

There was no common sense to rationalize what was happening. Its body was an amazing assortment of senses and rapid firing neurons. The animal was the most perfect and largest eating machine ever devised. However, his recent reincarnation was a ragged mess of sores and peeled skin from thousands of years of sleep. Its eyesight was not as keen as it used to be with one cloudy lens, dinner plate in size, looking blankly out into the ocean it once ruled. There was nothing in its world it was afraid of, even if it had a reasoning brain.

And yet, this was not the world it had been born into, this was not the world he once ruled as Poseidon would reign over. It hungered, but other than the occasional small fish it was not finding the bounty it had once knew.

He had found the whale but found it to be a bitter disappointment. It could not fathom why it could not eat the dead and floating carcass. Its sense detected a whale in distress and its own distressed body hungered. With little thought its feeble mind went into attack mode. But it could not eat. The whale was not edible, no matter how the great shark tried. It in fact brought pain into its mouth instead of the salivating salvation of hunger. After several attacks it did find one small mouthful of edible meat, but that was not enough.

In its old world there was plenty of food. Some fought back but most just became lunch. It did not understand. It could not comprehend. After a frigid sleep it had awakened to a world it did not know.

The explosion had caused a pain it had never known before. Heat. Concussion. Splintered wood penetrating its sore body. All new and unknown. Its reactions were not fast enough, its mind incapable of coming to grips with the incredible force.

It had drifted for several hours under the water, its mind shut down from the concussion. But slowly, like it had done before, the massive tonnage that was its body had slowly reawakened. It had drifted with the current, sliding unknown and unseen underneath the life raft of the survivors of the Iceland Venture. The raft had drifted one direction while the shark had been pulled into an undersea current and drifted another. It was long since gone when the rescue plane landed and retrieved the freezing people. Lucky, for the shark would have most assuredly gone over to investigate this new phenomenon and the things splashing around in it. All Captain Drummond had done in the end, was buy the survivors some time.

In its day it was the most fearsome thing in the ocean and quite possibly, on the face of the earth. The only thing it could not fathom was one of its own that was bigger. And that never happened. Now was a new set of rules. But its mind did not comprehend. These were all things that just happened. Like the ice flow that buried it or the giant squid that fought back, they just happened and the huge fish with the massive mouth and an appetite for everything just went along.

At the moment it only knew pain and hunger. It could not do anything about the pain, but it could quell the hunger. And that was its quest.

Groggy and half blind it swam, filling its flailing gills. Slowly the brain that grabbed hold of what little function it offered and it sped forward. It needed to hunt again. And find a large amount of food. For the massive fish was starving to death.

It knew no direction, just an instinct, or a hint in the water. It started swimming toward the south. The Aleutian Trench had a very tantalizing smell to him.

The Aleutian Queen had a fancy name for a very plain looking vessel. It had started its life as a mine sweeper, working the Atlantic, Mediterranean, the Strait of Suez. For over 40 years it patrolled and only once had it found a mine. It had been decommissioned and swiftly bought up by Billionaire adventurer Clive Montgomery. He literally did not know what for until Ethan Baxter approached him. He had a Carbon Fiber Composite submersible that took up every penny he owned. Could they join forces?

The two-hundred-and-twenty-foot ship was very capable and quite set up for the six- person submersible. However, it took two years for the ship to be retrofitted and the final modifications for the deep-sea sub.

They had tested the submersible named the Beatle. Baxter loved the Beatles and the name stuck. But submerging to 12,000 feet became an everyday occurrence as they tested in the Aleutian Trench just to see what they could see.

But as luck would have it, they were in Nome when the earth quakes struck the very solid bedrock. The earthquake had radiated through the Long Strait, the Bering Strait, the Gulf of Anadyr and the Bering Sea. And the Queen was right there. Within hours of the massive sea quake, they were being contacted by The Woods Hole Oceanographic Research Center. The deal was struck. They were going to creep as close to Russia as they could, and try to see exactly had happened to the sea bed.

Doctor Mort Exter was looking out over the very frigid water, white foam lapping incessantly against the metal hull of the Queen. The Beatle was securely strapped down on the stern, still connected to its grappling hooks and crane. The Queen was very capable to taking on the choppy North Pacific. But disconnecting the Beatle and reattaching it in the swelling wakes was a problem. So, Mort stared into the water.

The ship contained a compliment of forty personnel on board, including Clive and Ethan. There were only five researchers as that was all Woods Hole could scramble together on the spur of the moment. When they would finally get to go down.

Doctor Exter rubbed a hand through his frozen gray beard then over his bald head. His skull should be freezing and it probably was but he did not seem to notice. The Aleutian Queen was creeping in as close as it could dare to the Komandorski Islands or better known as the Commander Islands, the very edge of the Aleutians but belonging to Russia. However, they were having to maintain the two-hundred nautical miles limit as regulated by international compliance. They had asked, then begged the Russian government to let them simply investigate the sea floor. Something had happened there. Of course, the answer was no. Doctor Exter had agreed to work with any Russian Government official or entity that they wanted to bring onto the Queen. Again no. Could they assist any Russian Oceanographic team looking into the sea floor? This time the answer was different. There was none.

"Damned stupid people. Their sea floor blows up and they don't care. I hope their country falls into the ocean," Doctor Exter mumbled to no one.

Except Clive had come up behind him and put a hand on his shoulder. "I get it. A real pain in the ass."

"Hi Clive. You got good news I hope?" Asked Doctor Exter shooting a slight glance at the man.

Clive stretched out his long frame and bent over the metal railing. "I do. Our weatherman says this shit should clear up in an hour or so. And we got word that the Iceland Venture crew is very safe and sound. Got picked up last night."

"That's good on both counts." The Coast Guard out of Nome had contacted them to see if they could assist with the rescue, then called them off when they realized the US Navy was hunting them down.

"I was wondering where you guys were at."

Both Mort and Clive turned to face Ethan Baxter, his squat frame and bald head blending into the setting sun. Coming along side of Clive he too propped his body against the metal railing.

"What's the word?" Asked Clive.

Ethan rubbed his chin then replied, "Well, it's sort of up to you all."

"What do you mean?" asked Mort.

"Weather's clearing. How do you feel about diving in the dark?"

Clive jumped in. "Pitch black down there anyway. What does it mean to the ship and loading?"

Ethan responded, "You have a well-lit ship, it really makes no difference if we go now or in the morning. I've had enough coffee to stay awake a few more hours."

"Oh God. Could we?" Asked Mort getting excited for the first time while on the ship.

Ethan smiled. "Get the Beatle ready and by that time the water should have calmed down to make it smooth sailing."

Clive grinned then looked over at Dr. Exter. "Well, what do you say?"

Mort's grin could have lit up the night. "I've got a team to assemble."

By the time Dr. Exter returned with his three men one-woman team they had unclamped all the safety harnesses to the Beatle and was out of its docking blocks. The small crane, just capable of hauling the Beatle fully loaded had already been clamped on. All that was needed was the occupants.

The Occupants stood by and watched as an engineer had started coming out, having checked out all the operations of the Beatle. He came down the very small ladder strapped to the exterior. They had all been in it once knowing where they were to sit what they were to do and what they might see. Still, that was different than actually going down to a crushing depth with God only knows what was going on, on the sea floor.

They were not the cream of the crop of researchers, they were in fact what was available at Woods Hole, the people that could drop what they were doing, catching four different planes and make it to Nome.

Rex was a little blob of a man with a vast fuzzy head, a vast fuzzy face, and the only one at Woods Hole that had any knowledge of plate tectonics and undersea tremors. Evie Sinclaire was a tall, good looking blonde woman who hated Rex, hated the dark and hated small places. But she was absolutely the only one the Woods Hole institute that knew anything of ancient sea creatures. THAT was the only reason she was there. Theodor or of course Theo, was an old curmudgeon of a man who simply knew the ocean and its currents. But being a daily runner, he was in amazingly good shape, for an old fart with a trimmed grey beard. Then there was Hailey. At barely five foot and less than a hundred fifteen pounds and not quite thirty, she was literally an afterthought, with nobody on board with really any idea, other than Dr. Exter as to why she was there. She was somewhat of an anomaly, having caramel skin and bright blue eyes that twinkled constantly. A thatch of black hair in a constant pony tail could be seen swinging around the ship on many occasions. Rex speculated she was a writer and was chronicling their misadventures. Or to keep Mort warm, Rex could not decide.

And for some odd reason she had sought out Theo early on, and on several occasions. Theo thought merely he maybe, reminded her of her father and he was damned good at playing chess, of which she was a master. He liked her well enough, as she was well spoken and bright. But she was a little quirky, as she would grab his hand at odd times, asked constantly if he wanted to share her food, or on one occasion, simply sat in his lap. By accident of course, or so she said. Theo, unmarried, really did not mind.

"We're going in the dark?" asked Evie. "We've already heard of an eighty-foot Carcharodon Megalodon down there and we're going down in the dark? What the fuck?"

Theo slid up next to her and other than speculating what it would be like to get in her pants, really did not like the woman. He said, "At four hundred feet we're entirely in the dark anyway. This ship has twenty, two hundred watt lights off the bottom, should see it a quarter mile away, and the Beatle has massive search lights and a state-of-the-art radar system. We're going to see the same thing as if it were noon."

Evie looked up at the twinkling stars then at the velvet black ink that was North Pacific.

"You may be right, but I don't feel any better."

Theo replied, "Oh I never said we were coming back alive. It just doesn't get any better, that's all." Then he smiled broadly at her.

Rex then inserted himself and said to Evie, "I wouldn't mind getting stuck down there with you."

"I would do the old man before I would touch you." She stated down at the little fat man.

"Hey, sloppy seconds works for me." Rex then broadly smiled also.

Doctor Exter had heard it all, and decided to ignore it. He then noisily cleared his throat. "All your equipment should be on board, but there are no bathroom's people. If you have to go, go now, I would like to stay down there a few hours. This is only dive one of several."

"The only one tonight, right?" Demanded Evie.

Dr. Exter looked at her stupidly then responded. "Yes, just one dive tonight."

"How is the heat on board the Beatle? I mean should we stay in our coats?"

Asked Theo

Dr. Exter looked over at Ethan. Ethan finally responded, "I'll be honest, we've never had this many dive, don't know how the temperature will modulate with the body heat. The Beatle should maintain at least sixty-five degrees. I guess I would keep the coats on then take it from there."

Theo wasted no time and started climbing the very small ladder bolted to the exterior of the Beatle. He got to the top and waited, probably the only one on board with any social graces and waited to help the women on board. He stood waiting next to the massive hatch. Evie looked up completely uncomfortable with the whole situation.

Hailey strolled past her and climbed the ladder, latching onto Theo's hand. Hailey smiling broadly. He helped lower her through the hatch and she disappeared into the Beatle.

"Rex?" Requested Dr. Exter making it plain that Evie was not moving. Rex shrugged then he too climbed the ladder, and had Theo's help get lowered into the Beatle.

They all then turned to look at Evie who had not yet moved. "Oh, come on blondie. First dive, we're not going that deep. Times a ticking." Inserted Theo getting slightly perturbed.

"Really Miss Sinclaire, we've submerged to almost twelve thousand feet. Our depth now is just five hundred feet. No danger what so ever." Stated Ethan. He then smiled hoping to disarm her insecurities. It did not work.

"There is an eighty-foot prehistoric shark down there somewhere and that thing is only fifty foot long. You still guarantee no danger?" She replied nastily.

By that time Clive had pulled up next to her. "Seriously? It was a fishing boat that sank Miss Sinclaire. Nothing to worry about, really." He was simply amazed that this gorgeous woman was such a pain in the ass.

She ultimately realized she was the hold up. She wrapped her coat tight then went to the ladder and gingerly climbed up. Theo very politely grabbed her hand but found she did not want to let go. Finally, she whispered in his ear, "I die down there I'm coming back to haunt ALL their asses." Then she dropped down the open hatch.

Theo did not know if that was meant to be funny or not, so said nothing.

Theo assisted Dr. Exter then waited for Ethan. Ethan smiled then said "You first, I'll get the hatch."

"Deal."

Ethan lowered himself in then pushed the small ladder into a folding position on the wall. It was cramped quarters at best as he sincerely hoped everyone had taken a shower that day. The occupants sat smushed together in little plastic swivel chairs, each one trying to get their own computer stations built into the curved wall, the chairs leaving a bare two-foot-wide isle.

Theo got the position behind the driver as Evie sat opposite. Rex and Hailey were in the rear, hugging the back wall. Hailey did not seem to mind. Dr Exter had a chair of honor, as the navigator, sitting directly next to and to the right of Ethan's pilot's chair. However, Dr Exter was in fact the least likely of any of them to have command of electronic equipment.

Ethan had seen Dr. Exter's hesitation then said, "Just read what's in front of you, I do all the steering."

Dr. Exter smiled then glanced back at Hailey who grinned back at him and nodded heartedly.

Ethan moved through to the pilot position which has a much more comfortable chair and all the controls. He explained things the entire time he was checking out his controls. "There are seat belts I suggest you use them. Once you turn your systems on you will see an exploded overview of the Beatle, you can access any sensor or camera that the Beatle has." He turned slightly and said to Dr. Exter, "Except you have two monitors and have access to the ships computer."

Ethan then continued, "Put on your headsets and you can talk to me there and to the Queen." Then he sated loudly, "DO NOT TOUCH ANYTHING ON BOARD THIS VESSEL THAT YOU DO NOT KNOW HOW TO RUN. Any questions?"

As he sat forward of everybody and heard nothing, he assumed there was none. He said into his headset radio, "Communications,

Aleutian Queen, this is Ethan on board the Beatle. How do you read me?"

"Loud and clear Beatle."

"Thank you, Clive. Everyone on board and ready to go. Waiting for transport." At that point Ethan flipped on the heating with a dehumidifier to keep the moisture down. Then he hit a rather large switch and with that came a whirring noise. The large glass dome came into view at the large metal corrugated gate slid up and out of the way. He looked down, turned on the exterior lights and watched the crew untethering the Beatle. He felt a small lurch.

"OH MY GOD! This thing has WINDOWS? Why the fuck would this thing have windows? We can't go down with windows. What if they leak?" This shrill exclamation came from Evie who was now looking out the huge glass dome in front of Ethan.

Then came Rex's voice from the back, "God, I love it when women talk dirty."

A voice came on suddenly through all the headsets, "The Beatle has been down to twelve thousand feet with the observation dome open. Don't worry about it. If you have a problem Mrs. Sinclaire we can stop and drop you off." The voice was distinctly from Clive who had little tolerance for ignorance. He meant to nip it in the bud and as a rebuff. Evie shut up predictably.

Ethan glanced at every instrument he had and said into his headset, "Thanks Clive. ETA?"

"Less than a minute and you should be in the water. Just hang on till then."

"Clive was being honest. Hang on people, sometimes this gets choppy."

However, with little whimpering the Beatle hit the bitter North Pacific with a small splash. It quickly began to sink. Evie bit her bottom lip as she watched the froth hit the glass dome then slowly turn the interior a dull green. At that point she seemed to come grips with the fact they were going under and were perfectly safe.

"Beatle you are now free to roam around the cabin." Came through the headsets.

"Roger that Queenie. Are you getting video feeds?" Responded Ethan. At that point there was a small lurch in the Beatle as the huge rear propeller kicked in and drove the small submersible forward into the North Pacific. Ethan flipped every exterior light switch as the aquatic membrane was bathed with iridescence for almost a hundred feet around the Beatle.

"That's a big ten-four Beatle. We've got you on sonar and we got a constant array of all your vitals and a good video feed. If you see a big prehistoric beastie, send us a good picture."

Evie did not need that what so ever. However, her fear and flight senses had been taken over by the pure adrenaline of the situation and found herself glaring out the domed front window. That's when she realized everyone else was accessing the exterior camera systems and gazing at the views under the submersible through their station monitors. She had not even turned to face hers or even turn it on. But first she unzipped her jacket as it was warming up inside the submersible.

"All right folks. Our first run of the sea bed is only going to take us down about five hundred feet. We're still a few miles from the deep and a few miles off of Russian waters but it should give you a good idea of what's going on down here and how to access all the tech that the Beatle can give you," Ethan explained. He was watching a small fish swim across his window. At that moment he felt more like a bus driver than a state-of-the-art Oceanographer. But he was grateful for it was the paying the bills rather well.

"Son of a bitch." This came from Theo, who was staring at his computer in disbelief. He too unzipped his old leather coat.

"Theo, what you got over there?" Asked Rex

"Oh. Um. This reading I got. The water is getting warmer."

Rex acknowledged, "That's not right. That's not right at all."

Evie then again got anxious and asked, "Is that not good?"

Theo just shrugged. "It's obviously because of the sea floor exploding, from the methane of which there is more than usual. Not bad just unusual. Considering the sea quakes were over two hundred miles from here, very unusual."

"Passing one hundred feet people. Glad to see we got unusual readings for you already." Mentioned Ethan glad the Beatle was finally earning her keep.

They passed two hundred feet without another word being spoken, each person engrossed in looking out the large window, or their monitors. Even Evie had figured out how to access all the camera's and was busy popping around. If there was a beastie, she did not want it sneaking up on her.

Ethan had been watching something out the window and finally asked, "Um Evie? Any idea what the hell that thing is?"

Evie looked up and immediately gasped.

Theo swiveled in his chair and looked out. "Whatthefuck?"

Staring at them through the glass was the ugliest looking critter that had ever swam in the ocean. It had a dangling thing in front of his massive teeth that looked as if it's jaws would never close. Its little fins were keeping it a clear distance from the Beatle. Ethan could tell this was important and piloted the ship to keep it a safe distance from the creature, his hands and feet controlling the rudder and speed, and stopping its rate of descent.

Evie unbuckled herself from her seat and crawled behind Ethan. Then she said in a quivering voice, "Doctor Exter. That's a Humpbacked Anglerfish. I've never been this close to one before."

Dr. Exter then said over to Ethan, "Please tell me we're getting video of this."

"About five different views. Can I ask why though?"

"Anglerfish are EXTREMELY rare. And are ONLY found in the deepest part of the ocean," explained Evie.

"And very freaking ugly. Wow," mentioned Rex, having slid in behind Evie. He was so engrossed in the ugly fish that he did not even take advantage of hugging Evie's backside.

Ethan was just a word away from reminding everyone to buckle up back into their seats. They watched the gangly fish swim away from the lights which clearly irritated it. Since the Beatle had stopped moving, it cleared its way from the range of their lights and disappeared into the inky blackness.

Ethan then said, "If everyone would take their seats, we'll continue our tour of the bizarre."

Dr. Exter asked, "Evie, what do you make of that?"

Evie stood and turned around directly into Rex, who smiled broadly at her. She growled at him, shoved him backward, and Rex back peddled in the narrow lane to land into his chair. She made her way back to her station and plopped into her seat. "Definitely out of its comfort zone. It does not like the warm water, it does not like the light. All I can think of it's confused, because of the underwater earthquakes and trying to make sense of its warmer world."

"But isn't it like way off where it would normally be? It isn't even close to deep enough here, it's like a hundred miles off." Asked Theo.

She swiveled around abruptly, poked Theo on the shoulder and exclaimed, "I KNOW. It makes no sense."

"Man, I really hate that," observed Rex.

Theo then added, "There's no current that could have dragged it here. It swam here on purpose."

"Passing three hundred feet. Aleutian Queen you still in contact.?"

"We got you Ethan. Nice pictures of very ugly fish." Came the reply from Clive.

"Ten four Clive. Those long teeth keep giving me the willies."

"I'm seeing something sort of gray on one of our camera's. Down below I think." It was the first thing Hailey had said since entering the Beatle.

"I see it also, I think it's heading the opposite direction, can you turn around Ethan?" Asked Dr, Exter.

Ethan glanced at his two sonar screens to make sure that an about face was not going to run them into an outcropping. Seeing his path was clear he stated, "Initiating thrusters and doing a one eighty, Doc. Keep me informed on which way I should go. I can't pilot, watch sonar and the cameras."

"Well do Ethan," answered Dr. Exter, realizing he had to take his navigation duties seriously.

The thruster quickly brought the Beatle to the port side as Ethan initiated a slow descent. He fined tuned one of the sonar apparatuses to zero in on any moving object. It quickly pinpointed on something two hundred feet in front of him.

"I have something about ten feet long out in front of the lights. Anyone have a sighting on cameras?" Every monitor had the multiple camera angles playing. Dr. Exter had both his monitors playing on the bow and directly beneath. Ethan took by the silence that no one had. But it did not take long.

"Sea serpent directly in front of us," yelled Rex excitedly.

Ethan also saw it, glancing at his sonar to make sure it had not grown in size. Still just ten feet. He looked out the glass, right at the edge of the strong lights was a long narrow tail whipping back and forth. The Beatle edged up closer so that the whole thing was in view but still they were getting the rear end as it was attempting to swim away them.

Rex finally mentioned, "Can we grab Cecil to get a better look at whatever that is?"

Ethan knew Rex was referring to the claws. They had two manipulating arms on the front of the Beatle. They could extend out twelve feet from the Beatle and moved just about any direction Ethan wanted them too.

Ethan glanced back at the Doctor then asked, "It's something we could do but do we really want to do that? I don't want to harm Cecil just because we're curious."

Dr, Exter nodded then asked, "Evie, do have any guesses as to what that creature is?"

"I do but you're not going to like it."

"Try us," said Theo.

"A Frilled Shark."

"If I don't miss my guess that's another beastie we shouldn't be seeing," inserted Theo. "A shark doesn't sound so bad." Observed Ethan.

"If you don't mind three hundred teeth on a grin that will scare the hell out of you,"

replied Evie.

"You mean like that?" Ethan asked. The creature had turned and sure enough Evie was two for two on her ugly fish. It had a broad head with its open mouth showing off those three hundred teeth. They started at the end of the jaw like every other creature, but they continued through the back of its mouth to its throat, uppers and lowers. It did not have dorsal fin like a normal shark but merely a raised hump and its swim fins were small. It had large frilled gills which were blood red. It apparently did not like the Beatle following it and had decided to confront the submersible.

"Good God that's ugly," Came through the headsets. It was Clive from the queen.

"Doesn't matter what it looks like. It's simply not supposed to be here." Stated Dr. Exter emphatically.

"Um it's getting closer and that is one very ugly fish," mentioned Ethan looking at the fish that seemed to take a dislike to them.

"It can't hurt us, can it?" asked Evie rather loudly.

"Na." Ethan then hit a front thruster just to scare the fish that was now within fifteen feet of the Beatle. It did the trick as the sudden blast frightened the strange creature. Like an animal that had been spooked by the unknown it dived to the left and swim down out the reach of the lights, it's long whip like tail flashing through the fading light. All the while Ethan motored the Beatle into a safe holding pattern three hundred forty feet below the ocean waves.

Finally, he spun around in his chair and addressed his observers. "I need an explanation here people. As Evie keeps saying, there is a prehistoric shark out there, we just ran into two old and very ugly fish that I keep getting told shouldn't be here. Now I'm not a worry wart, but I would really like to know what we're up against here and what the hell is happening."

Dr. Exter took off his glasses and wiped at his brow. It was not hot in the Beatle but all this was starting to make him nervous. "I guess I'm the best one to explain. About nine days ago, the Alaskan Earthquake Center out of the University of Fairbanks detected a quake centering out of Kamchatka. But …

"It wasn't an earthquake," continued Rex. "What happened was a methane build up along the entire coast of Kamchatka. Normally that's not a problem. Methane usually just dissipates into the water off of the sludge on the ocean floor. But the Russians did something stupid."

"Noooo. That never happens. So, what could have the Russians done to explode the bedrock off of Kamchatka?" asked Ethan.

Dr Exter continued. "An Industrial company in Russia called LuvoDoybvat was building a refinery. They were trying to figure out how to harness the methane off of the seafloor. Without knowing EXACTLY what they did, there's been some confirmation that they did something with their machinery that caused the methane to explode."

Rex then jumped in and finished, "Probably tried to thaw out a big area of ice that had six to eight feet of sludge underneath of it and having it trapped then heating it up set off a cataclysmic chain reaction."

"So instead of capturing it, they exploded it? And other than unleashing our prehistoric fish, did it cause any damage to the coastline?" asked Ethan.

"Well, you have to understand it wasn't two hundred and fifty miles of constant explosions, it was a lot of little explosions all over the place. Russia won't tell us where or if there was any damage to any villages or more importantly, any off shore pipelines. And no idea what it did to the bedrock." Explained Dr. Exter.

"The Russians really don't know either do they?"

Dr. Exter shrugged his shoulders and added, "Rumor has it they've got some kind of exploration vessel coming but they don't seem very worried about it all."

"They're waiting for something catastrophic to happen and then they'll have some idea what to respond too," inserted Evie. Like the rest of them, she was miffed that the Russians were keeping this so close to the vest and not sharing any data. All of it was an important scientific discovery and they were hiding the info.

Ethan swiveled back around to face the huge glass, checked over his controls, his eyes stopping on the radar unit. "What the hell?"

"What the hell?" Asked Evie excitedly.

Ethan ignored her and asked into his microphone, "Clive, you showing anything on your radar up there?"

The response was instant. "I'm showing two different things both being very slow moving. The Queen is too far away and we're getting to much interference at that depth. What do you have?"

Ethan double checked his radar scope. Then he responded, "I've got five things out there moving, all of which are over ten feet long. One of them is damned close and closing in fast. I'm going to try and maneuver around to see what it is."

"We've got one smaller item barely moving and something else much larger. Nothing on cameras?" Was more of a question than an observation.

"Guys we seeing anything on camera's?" asked Ethan of his wayward observers.

"I've got a Goblin Shark," stated Rex excitedly.

"What the hell is that? Oop never mind." Ethan was suddenly staring at it through the glass dome. A left over from prehistoric times, it was absolutely ugly as the mouth protruded out from underneath a flattened snout. The rows of needle-sharp teeth were hanging out as if they actually did not fit the mouth. The blood vessels so close to the surface it gave the ugly beast a pink hue, giving the twelve-foot body the image as if it was going to pop out of its skin. The grotesque animal was in a hurry as it swam across the window.

Following quickly behind it was a pair of large almost normal looking fish.

"Coelacanth. I've never seen a pair before. Or that freaking big." Inserted Evie, almost giving the impression that this trip through the Cretaceous era was getting mundane. Almost.

"Aren't those things supposed to be dead?" Asked Theo, never taking his eyes off his monitor. In the back of his mind he remembered, 'something larger.' He was flipping through the camera's as fast as his fingers would let him. Evie could only respond with a shake of the head.

"Son of a bitch, whatever that was it was fucking ugly. You still got something big coming at you Ethan." Came from Clive. He was starting to get distressed from the massive amount of abnormality.

"Clive, I'm not waiting to see what it is, I'm starting evasive maneuvers and getting the hell out of here," Stated Ethan. He was even more distressed than Clive as he was watching a parade of ludicrous and grotesque animals swim by the huge window, themselves apparently afraid of something. Ethan started up the throttles of the Beatle and brought the planes to bring the submersible to the surface. He swung the sub starboard, hitting the thrusters to bring the nose up.

"Ethan, it picked up speed. It's headed your direction."

"Shit."

Evie started breathing hard as Theo extended a hand and grabbed her elbow. He was watching her face to see if she would hyperventilate. Then she screamed.

It hit the huge glass windows, bouncing off as Ethan threw the Beatle into reverse. He had no idea what the hell the thing was but it hit hard, sending a lumbering thud through the entire submersible.

"That was a big fucking turtle!" Yelled Rex watching the eight-foot turtle shell bounce repeatedly off the glass and finally fall past.

Evie managed to gather enough breath to utter, "That's an Archelon. A prehistoric turtle. It … it looked dead."

"Yeah. Yeah. It didn't look to lively, did it?" Observed Ethan.

What slid by the glass just fifty feet away, in the middle of the massive flood lights, was very lively. And very long. The huge fins stroking the water as the huge body extended back to an immense moon shaped tail that stroked a good twenty-foot arch. Nobody spoke, as stunned silence permeated the submersible, as wide eyes could not comprehend the white ghostly image smearing its way across the glass. Clive came alive in Ethan's headset.

"What the hell was that?"

It took a moment for Ethan to answer, his heart racing at the size of the thing. "That was your large blip on the sonar," Ethan responded, willing the Beatle to go faster in reverse. What went by the glass was bigger than the Beatle, more maneuverable than the Beatle and definitely better armed. Ethan was then aware of a slow rising screaming, enveloping the air. And Theo's failed attempts to quiet Evie down.

"I've lost it, I've lost it," yelled Rex staring at his monitor, showing the bottom camera's. "The damned thing grabbed the Archelon and dove underneath us."

Dr. Exter swung around, still vaguely aware of the smothered screaming coming from Evie. "Do we have any weapons on board this vessel?"

Ethan glanced back at him and shook his head vehemently. "NOOOO! Why the hell would we have weapons?"

"That … that thing whatever it is, is at the bow, Ethan, but we can't tell how deep it is. It seems to be moving forward, can you swing to the port and make your way upward? WE'VE got weapons."

Ethan heard Clive and understood. The Queen did come supplied with a cache of automatic weapons and if Ethan did not miss his guess a couple of old LAWS. (Light Anti-Tank Weapons) Ethan reset the throttle to full speed ahead and moved the dive planes up forty degrees.

The massive propeller churned at the cold North Pacific as the Beatle reversed course. Seemingly to take minutes it actually took less than fifteen seconds to pull it out of its reverse mode and to send it forward. Even in the dense water, inertia sent Dr. Exter swinging around in his chair awkwardly. Evie had been pressing against Theo so hard she now went sprawling onto the floor between the seats. Even the normally docile Hailey grabbed onto Rex to steady herself. Rex glanced at her appreciatively, his normally droll humor had escaped him. He could only smile. "This isn't going to end well," she merely responded. His smile faded.

Nobody was watching the cameras except Clive. "ETHAN! It's coming up your direction." Came over Ethan's headset. There was nothing Ethan could do.

It took less than eight seconds as the Beatle was just finding its feet in the water. It hit the aft hard, sending the bow deeply into impenetrable darkness, and twisting the Beatle to the port side. Ethan, Dr. Exter and Hailey were the only three still strapped into their chairs. Theo let go of Evie and slid down to the floor. Rex slammed into Evie's chair, and flipping over the back, then came at Evie's back side head first. Except Evie was not there. She was summersaulting into Ethan's control console; the pitch was that great it had upset all the equilibrium. Ethan tried to anticipate incoming and managed to turn in his swivel chair. The wrong direction. Evie crashed into the bottom of the console shoulder first. She remained awake just enough to realize she was in pain and could hardly move.

Ethan realized he could do nothing about the carnage going on behind him, so stuck to trying to gain control of the submersible. He pulled at the plane controls to bring the vessel level, extremely happy everything was still responding. Until he glanced at his sonar control. He had none, as the screen was entirely blank.

"Clive, I've got no more sonar, you got a bead on this damned fish?" He asked pleadingly, hoping he still had communication.

"Ethan, after it hit you, it went over the top and past you. But I think it's turning back. Do you have injuries?"

"Ummm." Ethan swiveled quickly and Dr. Exter was out of his chair trying to help Evie and Theo had crawled back over to Rex.

The eyes were open but his head was bleeding. "Yeah, we got injuries but no casualties. Yet."

"Okay. That thing is turning your way. What are you guys doing to piss this thing off?" Clive understood animals just do not generally attack for any reason, especially when there is no food involved.

Ethan said to himself as he found the control for the manipulator arms, "I don't know but there is one thing I can do."

Theo had managed to get Rex into a chair and stem the bleeding using Rex's jacket sleeve. Leaving Rex to hold on to his head, Theo pulled up behind Ethan's chair grabbing onto it as the Beatle still was not completely level. "There it is," Theo said pointing out the glass through the end of the flood lights.

"Good God." Was all Ethan could say.

It was huge. It looked like a prehistoric submarine, its wide fins keeping its ancient body level, Theo seeing the massive tail swishing behind that humongous mouth. It was getting close enough that it was smiling at them, pulling its gigantic mouth open, showing the dismal remains of a prehistoric turtle. It hung in brown shreds off the eight-inch teeth.

Theo was oddly complacent as the shark closed in. "I hope you design good ships," he mentioned to Ethan.

"Fuckin A. So, do I. HANG ON!"

It obvious that the shark was going to try to take an enormous bite out of the Beatle. Or try to swallow it whole. Its mouth had widened to its maximum opening as the men in the cockpit looked down that gigantic gullet. Dr. Exter slammed the rag doll that was Evie into the front set of seats. He then flung himself back into his chair, realizing he had no time to find his straps, merely hung on to the consoles as best as possible. The collision was not going to be happy.

But Ethan's timing was perfect. He brought the highly responsive extended manipulator's up hard, smashing into the bottom jaw as the shark rammed its immense weight into the glass of the Beatle. The glass held the force of the million-year-old fish, but the Beatle was sent sprawling to the rear, with an abrupt downward twist.

Theo grabbed onto the back of Ethan's chair as Dr. Exter flung sideways in his chair. The Beatle swung sideways and descended to an almost ninety degrees angle. Everyone was trying to hang onto their chair to keep from being part of the front glass. Except Rex. He flung upwards against the ceiling, like a catapult, bounced off then rammed into Evie, the huge thud echoing through the submersible. He then crumpled to the floor, which was now the wall and wedged himself between the front row chair and the wall. Rex was now dead, his head hanging abruptly sideways, his neck taking the brunt of all the hits.

Ethan had quickly switched back to the dual controls and was pulling with all his might trying to right the submersible, working the throttle to back out of the deep dive and working the dive planes to get them back to level. "Dr Exter, any sight of that monster?" he yelled.

Dr. Exter was scanning his controls painfully aware his hip was shoved into the arm of his chair. Finally, he located the large blip on his remaining sonar. "I think he's behind us!" He replied excitedly.

Theo was busy scanning all corners of the glass, the penetrating lights showing nothing but a swirling water as the churning of the propellers going backwards was washing over the Beatle.

"Theodore? Can you give me a hand with Rex?" Came a voice of Hailey from the rear. Theo turned around and saw the small woman trying to keep upright and manhandle the very limp body of Rex. Ethan was doing a good job righting the vessel, making it possible for Theo to let go and make his way the few feet to help Hailey.

Holding onto a chair Theo bent down and asked the obvious question. "He's dead, isn't he?"

"Very. Can we move him into a rear chair and strap him in to keep him from being a ping pong ball?" Stated Hailey simply, looking up at Theo with a sad look in her eye.

"Poor Rex. Yeah, let's get him strapped in. The tighter the better." Replied Theo.

While they unceremoniously dumped Rex in a rear chair and started pulling in all the straps, Ethan was scanning the glass for anything that moved. Having quickly righting the submersible, he decided, without having any idea where the Queen was, that he had more speed and maneuverability going forward. He shifted the dual controls back to the bow position and reached the breach. He punched as much power as the Beatle could afford. It was not enough.

"I think it's coming from behind us!" Exclaimed Dr. Exter.

"Get seated Hailey, it's going to be a bumpy ride." Said Theo as he quickly sat down in his original chair. To his surprise she plopped down in his lap.

She turned just enough to catch his eyes and said, "I hope you don't mind; it was the quickest chair." Theo's mouth opened as if he was going to argue then he closed it and merely pulled the shoulder harness around both of them. He made no bones or excuses when he shoved the clasp down between her legs and shoved it into the connector. Her right hand quickly found his and she wrapped her fingers around his hand. And grasped hard.

Ethan had no idea as to the top speed of a prehistoric shark but he surmised it was probably faster than the Beatles twelve knots. He was willing his vessel to move faster.

"Here it comes!" Informed an excited Dr. Exter, staring at his sonar scope.

It was quick. Ethan had no idea what the damned shark was going to do, but was totally unprepared for the next move. He saw an immense flash of mottled flesh out of the right side of the vessel. Then the huge jaws clamped around the forward manipulator arm. The jarring motion shocked the vessel with an enormous shaking gesticulation. Ethan grunted noticeably as the Beatle was thrown sideways. Theo wrapped his arms around Hailey as the Beatle suddenly went into a steep downward pitch. It was suddenly clear to everyone that the shark was dragging the Beatle down. It was an odd situation as Ethan could plainly see the immense fish actually mushed up against the glass driving the Beatle ever lower.

Theo pulled his head around Hailey's and asked, "What the hell is it trying to do?"

Ethan replied desperately, "I don't know but the sea floor is coming up quickly then we'll find out." Sure enough, the edges of the flood lights found the sea floor rushing at them at over twenty-five knots. "Hang on!" Yelled Ethan, coming to the conclusion that the shark was going to ram them into the sea floor muck. Why? He had no idea.

Even though it is six feet of biological ooze, the Beatle rammed in hard to the muck, twisting the left-hand manipulator arm against the portside of the vessel. The glass viewing bubble suddenly filled with greenish brown mud. Ethan should have been proud with the amount of assault the Beatle was taking. He was just damned happy the ooze was still on the outside of the vessel.

The sideways abrupt crashing of the Beatle caused both Theo and Hailey to fling forward hard in the straps. Theo grunted viciously as all the air expelled from his lungs. Still, he hung on to Hailey as she got compressed by the twin belts with Theo's weight adding to her pain. She was not sure she would ever have to wear a bra again.

Dr. Exter had flung his head against the headrest on impact, then just as quickly his torso was flung forward, his head coming into contact with the overhead monitor, sending blood and sparks flying. Losing all control of his hand holds, he flung hard against the outer wall and bounced hard against the rear console. He was dead on impact.

Ethan bounced heavily in his chair trying gamely to make sense of things. The last shove into the muck, stood the Beatle straight up on end. His buckle broke. Head first he smashed into the domed glass window. He was followed quickly by Evie, who had awakened and was screaming at the top of her lungs.

Ethan was vaguely aware of someone tapping his face. He could smell the acrid odor of burning electronics. His name was floating in and out of his consciousness, as if coming from the inside of a coffee can. Then, there was the pain.

"Ethan? Ethan? I think he's coming too."

Ethan's eyesight was fringed in red as he could see the face of Hailey. His hand reached up to touch his hairline. Hailey grabbed his hand.

"You have a nice cut on your head but it's your arm. We think it's broken."

"It hurts." Responded Ethan, flashing the briefest smile.

"Does the Beatle have a medic kit? We've searched everywhere."

"No. no. My coat jacket has aspirins in it though, inside pocket."

Hailey quickly rifled through the jacket, found the aspirins shook out four into her hand and placed them in his good right arm, then handed him a bottle of water. He swallowed them wincing from the pain from just that meager head and arm movement.

Finally, Ethan asked, "How long was I out?"

"Just a few minutes, just long enough for Theo and I to get you into the chair." They had placed him in the chair directly behind the pilot's chair. Theo realized that Ethan was no longer going to drive the Beatle.

"How many other people are hurt?"

Hailey looked back at Theo who had been buckling in the other people. He came up to peer over her shoulder. Finally, Theo said, "Mrs. Sinclaire has a very nasty bump on the front of her head, I'm guessing a concussion. And. And Doctor Exter is dead."

"Oh crap." Ethan sighed heavily then asked, "How is the Beatle?" He knew they were not in too bad of shape as he could not detect any alarms,

Theo responded, "It seems to be holding together pretty well. We ARE about half way buried in the mud. But the good news is the shark seems to have left the area."

Ethan looked up dejectedly. "I can't pilot this thing with a broken wing and I do believe there something wrong with my knee as it's also throbbing. Get a hold of Clive."

Theo nodded solemnly then turned and sat heavily in the pilot's seat. He found the head set wrapped around the throttle control, unwound it and placed it on his head. "Aleutian Queen, can you hear me? Over."

"Oh God, we've been trying to contact you for the past five minutes. Who is this?" Asked Clive desperately.

"Theodore." He quickly brought Clive up to speed with the head count and the predicament of the Beatle.

"Theo, we've got all the vitals on the Beatle and I show only one real problem. It seems like your oxygen units are not functioning right, as in only fifty five percent."

"Which means what?"

"You're going to run out of air quicker. You had ten hours when you went down, you now have less than five hours of useable air left."

Theo nodded as if he had already guessed as much. Then he glanced out the front glass, at a wall of mud. "We're really buried in the sea floor, unless we get out it really doesn't matter how much air we have."

"Don't throw in the towel just yet. We're developing a plan. The Beatle may not have the power to pull you out but we do."

Theo thought about it for a second then turned back to Ethan, and inquired, "Can they do that?"

Ethan quickly ran the entire scenario through his mind. Yeah. Yeah, it was doable. They had an old but very useable Newt suit, or Atmospheric diving suit, and spools of spun cable that could be welded together to reach them. Yeap it could be done. But before they ran out of air? They may be simply bringing up a submersible full of corpses. Finally, Ethan responded, "Yeah, they have a Newt suit. Just depends on how much cable they have."

"So, they lasso us and winch us up. So just wait them out?"

"Theo, at the moment that's the plan. So, hang on for a little while and save your air and batteries. I'll be in touch." Came over Theo's headset.

"What's our depth?" asked a weary Ethan, clenching his teeth as a wave of pain streaked through his arm. The four aspirins were tearing up his stomach but they were taking the edge off.

Theo looked around at the two monitors, found the altimeter reading and responded, "Four hundred sixty feet. Why?"

"Trying to remember how much cable was hanging around the Queen."

"And?"

Ethan shook his head. "I remember one spool of a hundred feet. But that means nothing."

Hailey cleared her throat, sat down in the navigator's chair, took her glasses off and wiped them on the edge of her white blouse. Returning them to her face, she turned to Theo and asked, "Am I being a simple girl here or can't we just try to back out of the mud?"

Theo gave a lopsided grin then asked in turn. "Have you ever had a pair of boots on and go play in a mud puddle? And lose your boots when they get stuck?"

"No," she responded, "I was a book worm. Didn't play in mud. Or rain. Or snow."

Theo smiled back. "Well, there is a certain amount of vacuum action with the mud, which means we just don't slip out. But you know what, we could give it try."

Ethan quickly gave Theo a rundown of the controls, which he found to be very similar to a skid steer machine he used to run. The thrusters were on stocks on the end of the dual joystick controls. He wiggled the controls for a moment to get the hang of what they did. Satisfied, he took a deep breath. "Here goes nothing,' he muttered.

He jammed the controls forward.

"Where you going?" asked Ethan.

Jamming the controls to the aft, sending the propeller and thrusters into a frenetic reversal, Theo quickly explained, "Trying to shock the mud loose. Sort of like tightening a bolt to untighten it."

Ethan had no response. Pain had overtaken him, and he eased into unconsciousness.

"Ethan's out." Hailey said into Theo's right ear, which took him by surprise. It was not so much the voice tickling his ear drums, it was the arms around his neck. Her head was right there at his right, peering out the glass, willing the Beatle to move.

For ten minutes Theo, jockeyed the Beatle, back and forth, side to side and in fact made head way in pulling the beleaguered submersible free, leaving the top third of the front glass open as the mud had slid off.

"Theo, you may want to back off that for a while." Came from Clive in the headphones.

Theo quickly glanced at the displays and saw it. The rear motor was overheating. It was not so much the work as it was the constant shifting and the muddy resistance. He ran the controls back to neutral and peeled his fingers off the stalks. He flexed his fingers a few times, finally aware that Hailey was no longer hanging on him. She was safely in the navigator's chair.

"Theo, we got eyes on you guys and it looks like you may eventually bust free, but how do you feel about your chances.?"

It was a loaded question. He honestly had no idea. Would they get lucky and pop the Beatle loose before the batteries die, or simply run out of air? And he did not want to sound negative in front of Hailey as he genuinely liked her and really did not want to disappoint her in any shape or form. Or watch her die a slow death.

Theo chose not to answer instead, asked his own question. "Ethan mentioned you had a Newt Suit?"

"Yes, we do, Theo. But, not nearly enough cable."

Hailey's heart sank. She had always thought that would be plan B. They would lasso an arm and drag the Beatle to the surface. And now, there was no chance of that. But as she gazed over at Theo, she did not see the face of foreboding. She saw a man deep in thought.

Finally, Theo responded, "Understand that Clive. How much gasoline do we have?"

Hailey could not see it but Clive was smiling. "Got you Theo. A couple of Molotov cocktails positioned around the Beatle should break the suction. Let me see what the guys can concoct from our assortment of armaments. Hang on, give me a few minutes."

"Roger Clive, we'll be right here." He pulled the ear phones off and turned to face a smiling Hailey. "What?"

"When were you going to tell me, you had a plan C?" Hailey asked smiling.

"Learned that from an old plumber friend of mine. Start looking for other plans even before you initiate the first plan, because nothing is ever simple."

Hailey merely shook her head, tussling her black pony tail and stated firmly, "Everything has gone wrong so far, it's time for something to go right." She suddenly jumped up, spun around and plopped directly into Theo's lap, making him visibly grunt.

"You are an excitable young thing, aren't you?" He managed to shove out of his mouth as her face came within a whisker of his.

"Right now, I'm just happy to be alive." Then she was within a bare second of laying a big wet sloppy kiss on him when he quickly brought a hand up and pressed a finger against her lips. She sat there with a deer in the headlights look as she was puckered against his finger.

"Noooooo." He stated firmly. His sensibilities told him that he was just about old enough to be her father. His mind told him that he should push her away and tell her to behave herself. His hands came up to grab her shoulders to do that very thing. But the pit of his stomach told him that, well, this could very well be the last real thing he did in his life. So, his hands did the only thing he could think of. He very firmly returned her back to her chair.

The big blue eyes blinked several times and Hailey continued smiling. Theo then said in a low voice. "I think we need to concentrate on the problem at hand."

Hailey glanced down at her hands then back up at him, her face turning crimson and demur. "Okay." Was all she responded.

"If you guys are done, I think we've got a plan going here." Clive inserted, coming over the Beatles intercom.

"They have camera's, remember?" Stated Theo with a lopsided grin.

Hailey glanced back at the small camera in the rear of the cabin, then her eyebrows shot up and her hand went to her mouth.

"Yes, we have cameras. The guys have figured out four little explosives with makeshift timers and detonators. We hope that will be enough. John, our best diver is suiting up in the newt suit. In about fifteen minutes we should be ready to rock and roll. At that time, we'll be asking you to turn on every exterior light that the Beatle has. That's if you can keep your hands off each other."

Theo pointed at Hailey and said in the sternest whisper he could muster, "Behave yourself."

Hailey crossed her heart and raised her hand.

Theo glared at her then grabbed the head set with mic and said into it, "Clive we're standing by until we hear John is on his way."

"Okay Theo. It's going to take us a few minutes to program these things so we don't blow John up."

"Roger, Clive. We'll hold our breathe."

"Do you think it will work?" asked Hailey. She wanted an honest answer and she got it.

"I don't know. I don't see why not? I just hope that damned shark has gotten his fill of us and has left the area. I really don't want anyone else hurt."

Hailey nodded briefly. Every monster movie she had ever seen replayed it out in her mind. The cavalry or squad meant to save the stupid people in danger, get more killed than what they went to rescue. Suddenly she had this terrible image of the Carcharodon Megalodon swooping in, eating John then sinking the Aleutian Queen. They would watch it sink from their cameras as the reality of their own death wrapped its icy fingers around them, slowly running out of air and dying a horrible death. It would not be quick, though. They would suffer, gasping for air, their eyes bulging out of their heads, their lungs filling with carbon dioxide. More than likely Theo would watch Hailey die grizzly first as his own mind was shutting down from lack of oxygen. It would not be pretty.

Hailey shuddered, shaking the image out of her mind. Still, she understood Theo. No one else should die and she knew in her heart that Theo would chase John away if there was any danger. As it should be. But sealing their demise.

Theo flipped the switch to the mic and asked, "You Okay?"

Hailey smiled back quickly. "Yeah. Just thinking. I'm not good at waiting."

"I get that. Relax, all we got is time." Theo grabbed her petite hand and clutched it tight. They both stared down at the hand hold, each lost in their own thoughts, wishing time would go by quicker.

Finally, Theo asked her, "Why exactly are you here? I mean, everyone else here is an expert in some way. You just seemed to be with Dr. Exter. What do you do?"

Hailey smiled. "Dr. Exter in all his brilliance has absolutely no idea how to run a computer. I'm Girl Friday and his eyes when computers came up which was quite often. He didn't have so much as a cell phone, as was also his operator." Then as an afterthought she added, "And no, despite what Rex thought the Good Doctor never got frisky. I do have SOME respect. Not much but some. But hanging out with the Doctor ALL the time did make for a lonely girl."

Theo swung around to glance at the radar, forgetting the pilots' controls were dead, and responded, "I sort of get that." Flipping the switch back on He asked, "Clive, how are we doing?"

"Good," came back the immediate answer. "John should be ready any minute. All we could come up with in the spur of the moment was four detonator devices. We would have rather had detonate by signal but couldn't rig that so they all have timers. And since John really doesn't have hands, they are already preset."

"How long?" It was meant to be an opened ended question from Theo.

"The dive shouldn't be long as he's got a thruster pack. Take about five minutes to get there. The bombs have a twenty-minute fuse."

Hailey touched Theo's hand and asked, "How will we know exactly when?"

"I heard that Theo," came back Clive. "Go to the 'C' screen and you should see what John see's. He has a helmet cam."

As Theo glanced around the controls, Hailey quickly moved in, pulled out the little keyboard under the console, glanced at the main screen, saw the right application and quickly initiated the 'C' screen. She blushed slightly then pushed the small keyboard back.

"Thank you." Theo said as he looked at the screen. He could see nothing but the black water lapping away, a sliver of a moon glancing off the water, dancing rays through the swells. And then the picture went bubbly. Harsh lights blasted through the water, fastened to the side of the helmet, reflecting back into the camera. After a few moments, it cleared and Theo could see the start of the decent.

A loud noise crackled through the Beatle, then John's voice came over the intercom, the thrum of the thruster pack reverberating in the background. "Theo, Hailey. I'm a coming for you all and I'm a packing. Keep a look out for that fucking shark. I make a lousy snack." Came the voice with the slightest tinge of a Jamaican accent.

Theo smiled and suddenly realized why John was picked to come rescue them. He was crazy. Carrying a package of bombs and dodging a prehistoric shark in the pitch-black north Pacific. Got to be crazy.

"Absolutely John." Theo watched screen 'C' as small fish and particles floated in the front of the camera. Then suddenly he could see the lights of the Beatle bursting through the dark.

"That's us," Hailey said serenely. Theo just nodded. They watched in rapt fascination as the light blot grew larger on the monitor. In what seemed just a couple minutes, they could hear a thump on the outside hull. It was hard to tell where John had landed as far as the Beatle's hull was concerned. It was all lights, water particles and gray hull. They could see him looking down at his grappling hooks at the end of his arms. Now Theo understood why John could not set any of the bombs. Between the two massive hooks he could grasp the bombs and place it but there was no dexterity. Theo was simply glad to see it working.

It was taking longer for John to manipulate his way around the Beatle than it did to actually travel to the sight. He had stopped once to wave through the viewing window and Hailey waved back enthusiastically. Theo waved half-heartedly, watching intently the 'C' screen as there was now a countdown timer on the lower corner. John had 11minutes and 27 seconds to do his job. Theo thought John should get going.

"Shit," came over Theo's headset. Theo sat up a little straighter and replied, "What."

"I got something on sonar. Hurry up John." The voice was clearly Clive's.

"Bitch. Okay. Keep an eye on the fucking thing."

Hailey quickly swung in her chair at the navigator's control, aware Theo's sonar was not working, looked at her sonar scope. Sure enough, she could see a rather big image slowly moving in an erratic fashion. "May I?"

Theo propelled himself back and said simply, "Go."

She brought up the keyboard, brought up the computer controls, then suddenly there was a meter monitor on the sonar. Still several hundred meters off and seemingly not in any hurry.

Theo glanced over Hailey's shoulder. 8 minutes 31seconds. "John, how are you doing?"

A few second delay and then, "Planting the third one now, heading to the last one."

Theo thought that was cutting it close. For some reason he felt, the explosions would attract the shark. And the motors of the Beatle. "We can't see from our view but are you on a tether or just on the thrusters?"

"Both. Communications tether. If they don't pull too hard, they can yank me up in a hurry."

"Good." Nodded Theo, happy with that idea.

Less than three minutes later, keeping an eye on the shark monitor, John informed them it was a "GO."

"The shark is less than two hundred meters away. It might even see our lights thru the mirk."

"Come on up John, get your butt out of there." Came across Clive with a desperation ring to his voice.

"No. I don't think so. I'm going to stay on the upside of the Beatle and ride her up. I feel I stand a better chance that way."

"All right John you got three and half minutes to go." Stated Theo glancing at the controls. He was not sure if the engines needed warming up or what the procedures were.

As if reading his mind Clive came on and said, "Theo, not much you have to do. Just make sure all your operational switches are to the on position, the motors are all electric. When the detonators start firing, giver her full throttle and see if you can back the Beatle out of there."

"Got it Clive. Thanks."

Hailey could hear the slight scrapping as John was making himself comfortable on the small metal enclosure that was around the hatch. Hardly a shark cage it would at least give him something to hang onto.

"Two minutes John." Hailey buckled herself in as she looked over at the sonar scope. The huge creature was not making a clear beeline for the Beatle, but it was creeping ever closer. Maybe it was the lights or the sound from John's thrusters. It seemed to be an ever-curious animal.

Time is a strange commodity. In a gridiron football game going into the last quarter, one team is running out the clock, the other fighting the clock. To a marathon runner, they are fighting the clock, their opponents, and the conditions. For the entire race it is a constant battle, measured in a footfall and a millisecond. In space where everything is measured in lightyears, years are an expanding commodity.

To Hailey two minutes was one hundred twenty seconds until they were free to meet whatever fate was meant for them. And she prayed Clive and Theo and John were as good as she hoped. To Theo, it was an intense stress meter for that one acknowledging second when he had to act. For John it was simply waiting until … well until only God knew what. But it had to be better than hanging onto the submersible waiting for a giant assed shark. Time, was moving too slowly.

"Three hundred fifty feet on the port side," stated Hailey, staring at the sonar scope. And then the first bomb went off in the front left side.

It was early. Just two seconds. But it scared the shit out of Theo who thought he was ready for it but obviously not. Actually, it worked to his benefit. The Beatle was already engaged in reverse when the three other detonators blew.

The Beatle shuddered violently from each shock wave, as Theo flexed his muscles pulling on the control stalks. Because of the port side being off kilter in timing, the Beatle rocked severely to the left. Theo merely hung onto the stalks and kept willing the Beatle to move. Hailey got flung against her seatbelt once again.

"Didn't count on a blizzard of muck," said John through the headsets. Theo glanced forward and sure enough there was no visibility but, he had bigger problems. There was an alarm going off for some reason. Did they breach the hull?

"I'm doing a remote shut down Theo of your alarm, nothing to be afraid of. Beatle doesn't like getting rocked like that and just letting you know." Mentioned Clive also through the headset.

"Copy." But Theo said it with a wide grin. They were going in reverse. "Hang on John!"

"Got it. I can feel us moving even in my murky blizzard."

"Keep the tether out of the way," said Clive.

"It's starting to loop down in front of the sub. I'm just hoping that big assed fish doesn't grab it by mistake."

"Copy that." Theo finally glanced over at Hailey who was vigorously massaging her left breast. "How you doing?" he asked.

"I just know I'm going to need a boob job when this is all done. Second time today they've been crushed. For all the wrong reasons." She stated with a lopsided grin.

"Sorry?" Was all Theo had in return.

Clive broken in. "Four hundred feet. Theo, maintain reverse throttle at about five percent incline. That should bring you up behind the Queen."

"Ummm, Right Clive. Thanks." Theo had forgotten about the Aleutian Queen as Clive had simply turned into a disembodied voice directing him.

Hailey had managed to untangle her breasts from the shoulder straps and finally went back to all her instruments. "Right on cue." She said tapping the sonar. Sure enough, the shark was now making a bee line for the Beatle.

"I could really use a torpedo about now." If he had a button, it would not have made a difference. The shark hit the Beatle with a direct port side blow that shook the sub to its core, John using his clamping hook hands to lock onto the grid on the top side. Hailey reactively latched one hand onto Theo's shoulder, hanging on with every fiber to keep from being flung against the left wall. Another alarm went off in the interior of the ship.

Hailey noticed on the screen the shark had swam away from the Beatle. With the Beatle still quaking and listing to the port, she started punching camera buttons until she found a bank of port side cameras. She saw a swishing tail whisking away from the Beatle. A top side camera still saw John hanging onto the conning gate.

"John?" yelled Theo into the headset mic, even as the Beatle was just settling down.

"Can't get rid of me that easily."

"JOHN!" Yelled Hailey not realizing she had no transmitter hook up. The topside camera caught a glimpse of what Hailey really had hoped not see. And it was coming in fast.

The sonar scope showed the shark coming in from the rear of the Beatle.

John saw it too, through the dust cloud that had followed them upward. He saw a lot more than he ever wanted too. Instinctively he ducked under the handrail, knowing full well, it was absolutely no protection.

The massive shark did not judge the retreating Beatle well and glanced off the rear end and bounced high over John. But not before he got a mouth full of transmitter cable.

And just like that John was gone from the view of the camera Hailey had been watching. "JOHNNNN!" she yelled again. She turned to Theo and screamed "The sharks got him!"

Theo glanced at the sonar, seeing the shark streaming away from the bow, he shifted the stalks forward, and slammed them to full speed. "Come on," he willed the Beatle.

"Theo, a little help. Hate the sleigh ride I'm getting. Any time n …"

"Hailey, any visual?"

"NO! the mud is still coming off the sub! I can't see much," she responded quickly running through each camera view.

Theo, could just make the immense swishing tail bouncing a stray light pattern. But he could not see John.

"Theo, we've lost comm with John. You still got him?" Asked Clive desperately.

"NOOO. I think the shark snagged the transmitting cable. But I think he chewed through it," responded Theo still focusing on closing the gap to the tail, that at least seemed to him to be getting closer.

"I'VE GOT HIM!" Ummm, Camera view is straight ahead Theo!" yelled Hailey one more time, thrilled she had a small image of John ahead of the Beatle.

"Hailey? I can make out the tail. Can you see John?"

"He's alive, he's turning back to the sub." Both Hailey and Theo heard the clunking around on the Beatles top side. Hailey watched John pull himself into the conning gate, then turned and waved at the camera. "He's on. He's back on," blubbered Hailey.

"Thank God," stated Theo as his heart dropped out of his throat. And then, much to Hailey's chagrin, Theo shut down the engines of the Beatle. She sat there stunned but guessed he had a plan in mind. He did.

"Clive, for some Goddamned reason that Shark doesn't like the whine of our ship. Is there any way we can just blow some ballast to make us go up slow?" asked Theo. His thought was to simply and slowly rise to the surface without the engines.

"Of course," responded Clive following the thought, "Bank of rocker switches to the left under the first screen, hit one of those and it will start to pump you out. If you look at the center screen, that should tell you exactly what is going on."

"Got it." Theo glanced at the center screen and sure enough it stated what was happening with the latest alarm. They lost the left manipulator arm, and the port side sensors were reporting structural damage but no breech. As Theo read the dancing images, he realized he had completely ignored the alarm still sounding through the vessel. He glanced around until he saw a red light going off and he hit the switch next to it. It shut off the claxon.

Theo popped one of the ballast switches and sure enough the screen flashed to ballast levels and pumping speeds and rate of ascent. Theo noticed there was knobs with marks under the switch and turned it down slightly. They were going up about thirty feet a minute. He liked that rate. Surely the damned shark did not have a problem with a few bubbles he thought.

The sonar scope showed the shark receding off into the dark, blue Pacific.

Hailey looked back at Ethan still safely strapped into his chair, except his head had lolled around and instead of laying on his chest it was now hanging back completely. She got up and went to him and still detected a strong pulse. Then she turned back to Theo, moved up and wrapped her arms tightly around his neck once again. This time it really did not bother him.

To John, simply wrapped up in a small metal cage on top of the Beatle was worth its weight in gold. His clamping hand hold had been ripped away in a blinding thirty MPH. He had swung around the under belly of the beast, bouncing off the huge hardened and aged body, looking very much like a bobber hanging onto a big fish. Slapped around repeatedly by the huge switching tail. Unfortunately, he had no pole to hope he was going to be reeled in. Just about the time he thought his Newt suit would not take another blow and swing him around like a top, it stopped. He watched as the huge shark swam away. He prayed the Beatle would find him, for now he knew had had no contact with the Queen. Down one light off his helmet, he tried his thrusters to find limited use. just enough juice to turn around. And there it was. The Beatle, lit up like a Christmas tree bearing down on him. He did not know Hailey was manning the camera's and thought it absolutely fluke like he had found the top of the Beatle so easily. He managed to scramble into his little cage. And then, found it distressful the Beatle had lost power. But after a few minutes he realized. They were simply going up. Foot by foot.

The lighting of the Aleutian queen was scanning the water with every candle powered it possessed. They had communications with Theo. They prayed they had five survivors, for they had no knowledge of Johns situation. After around twelve minutes the bubbles and radar showed the Beatle a good quarter mile to the west. Theo refused to turn the motors back on so the Queen made a bee line for the crippled sub. Their first image was a helmetless John waving from his little station a top. The arm he was waving had a broken clamping hook, courtesy of a million-year-old animal.

They had literally pulled enough alongside the Beatle that they jumped onto the top and secured the harness. Within a few minutes it was stationed on the foredeck of the Aleutian Queen. John helped down still in his mangled newt suit. There was not an extremity that did not have a dent in it, including the helmet. John wanted to know who built it because he wanted to send them a thank you note and a couple million dollars.

The bodies were brought out, one at a time. It brought a solemnness to the entire boat and every single crew member was on deck, doing anything they could do to help. Then Ethan was pulled out. An oxygen mask and bottle attached to his face, as he was gingerly lowered down to a small gurney. Evie was the last body, as even though nobody really liked her, she was treated with the utmost care for the bruises were multiple and deep. She would not be doing any screaming for a while.

Finally, Hailey climbed out. She was not sure who's coat she had on but it was too big. She climbed down the ladder then quickly latched onto Clive, and started sobbing. Clive had no words. It had been a simple exploratory mission gone horribly wrong. All he could do was lend a strong shoulder.

Theo, beleaguered and tired, crawled down the ladder. Surrounded by the crew he looked back at the Beatle. Unarmed, it had survived multiple attacks by the biggest prehistoric menace ever known to man. The port side had a huge dent in its hull from the last attack, the port manipulator arms dangling in pieces. He could only shake his head, thanking God, and Ethan who built damned good machines. His eyes darted around for the Newt suit as he really did not know what John looked like. A small black man with a huge smile found him, his hands finally set free as all he could take in the newt suit was the huge hug from Theo.

And then. There were the ever-present arms around his neck. He managed to turn around to face Hailey. She was smiling with tears running down her face. She managed to mumble, "Now?"

He nodded slightly and muttered, "Now." The huge kiss planted on his lips. And he responded, picking her up, wrapping her in his strong arms. Then he suddenly he put her back down, conscious of her maligned breasts.

Hailey knew exactly what he was thinking and responded, "They're just a little bruised."

This brought a huge laugh from Theo. Then suddenly Clive was in his face. "Good driving. You looking for a job?" Then his hand went out and Theo shook it warmly.

Then Theo aptly responded, "You outfit the Beatle with some torpedo's and damned straight. I'm going hunting."

"Not tonight you're not," chastised Hailey. Clive merely started laughing as Theo smiled.

CHAPTER 9

Don glanced at his watch and noticed the split time on his digital watch. One time carried the Pacific time zone, of which they departed from, and the other was the current time zone which was several hours earlier. Since they hailed from San Diego, they maintained Pacific time so as not confuse everyone.

Then Don yawned heavily. He figured he had been awake just about twenty-four hours. He just received a message from Hornacher that she wanted to see him. The strange fact was that he was to meet her in the crew's quarters.

With his notebook computer under his arm, Don opened the door to the crew quarters to see all the bunks folded up against the bulkheads, and Beverly being the only person in the room. She was making use of the treadmill, running along steadily on its smooth surface. All that action sort of made Don nauseous. He glanced up at the large screen on the wall and saw a lot of green. It was moving around and he decided not to focus on the image.

Don went over to the treadmill, pulled down the bunk closest to the machine and sat down gingerly, directly across the treadmill, giving Beverly a couple of inches in clearance. "You wanted to see me?" he asked finally. He thought he knew why. He figured he was about to get chewed out for questioning her authority in front of the crew.

She ran along briskly, sensing Don's presence, putting up one finger and saying breathlessly, "One more minute."

Don nodded, unzipped the leather case, pulled out his computer, expanded the screen and laid it out in his lap. Turning it on he stared at for a second as if to focus then started to type in some new specifications on something he was working on. He glanced up once at the taut body running along smoothly. He focused enough for a moment to be aware that there was a pleasant bounce to her figure. He might have enjoyed Beverly's athleticism if he had been less tired, but all that movement just made him feel exhausted, then he went back to his computer. However, after a moment, he chanced to look back up and noted the running shorts she was wearing had a nice flip to them as he could see the stitched in underpants. He glanced back up and admired the view from the rear, plugging the swinging derriere into his memory, then shrugged his shoulders and went back to his computer.

The minute ran by as she finally punched the button to stop the treadmill. Her white athletic bra was soaked in sweat. Her green, three quarter split running shorts were wet all the way around the waist band. She punched another button that brought the treadmill to three miles an hour as she walked for another minute, taking the time to calm down her heart and relax her muscles. She then grabbed the towel hanging from the right arm of the treadmill and mopped her face, her knotted hair wet around the edges. Finally, she stopped.

Looking over at Don she mentioned, "Man, that is a heck of a gizmo you have here." She then stepped back and folded up the large screen that had been occupying her senses while running, and slid it up into the ceiling. Then she folded up the deck, the entire thing now only taking up two feet at the end of the quarters.

Don smiled then replied, "Wish I could take credit but it was only an idea. The treadmill company did the computerization for me. I told them to spare no expense. I believe it has more than a hundred courses that you can follow."

Beverly nodded and said, "Yeah. Last time I ran part of the Boston Marathon course. Today I ran a very scenic Cascades route by myself. I love the idea that the front of the treadmill goes up and down with the terrain on the screen. That's quite the innovation."

Don mentioned lazily, "Yeah, and you don't even have to worry about turfing it on an exposed root."

"But you're working on it, right?" Beverly smiled, draping the towel around her neck and the top of her chest.

Don grinned back, glancing quickly at the wet spandex under the towel and then said, "I'm still trying to figure out what you did with the day crew."

She shrugged her shoulders and said casually, "I really didn't do anything with them. I came in here the first day and started running and by the time I was done they were all gone. I guess they grew tired of watching my backside bouncing around and would immediately leave when I showed up. I believe they're all in the galley."

Don simply nodded and suppressed another yawn, thinking correctly the day crew did not want to be caught ogling the captain. Then he asked, "You wanted to talk to me?"

"Yeah, I've got some questions about the Kamchatka earthquakes and I figured you're the guy to explain this to me." Then she turned and said, "But you're going to have to keep up because I've got less than fifteen minutes to get ready for the Conn." She walked out of the crew's quarters with Don in tow.

"I thought it would be about my objections last night," Don said to the bobbing pony tail of Beverly as she walked down the corridor and into the Command quarters. Even though Don did not mean to bring up old wounds, it was the only thing his mind was working on and he definitely was not afraid of confrontations. In addition, his bed looked awfully inviting and he wanted to get the ass chewing out of the way.

"I think we settled that last night. At least I thought we did," She replied as she held the door open for Don.

Don only responded, "Okay."

The Command Quarters was probably the only room on board with any kind of amenities. The six bunks were stationary with every kind of storage space available including underneath and over-head. Although narrow, there was room for a bank of plastic lockers, enough for ten occupants. A chair was up against the wall, its function being twofold. As with the other chairs on board it was fastened to the floor, however, this padded chair tripped a switch that, when pulled out it brought down a large desk top and pulled out a bank of drawers. The chair locked into place as a computer monitor opened up. The computer itself was integrated into the Specter's mainframe, giving instant access to whatever the situation on board the ship.

The head, or bathroom was full sized, with a full range of medical supplies as the quarters also doubled as the sickbay. But, like any other submarine, things were light weight plastic or Kevlar, and bolted down. When Ralph asked Don about the quarters he only answered, "I knew it was where I was staying, so I made it comfy."

Beverly closed the quarter's door then moved across the room toward her locker, all the time saying, "I mean I understand, you're not military and you're most certainly one to express your opinions. And I respect your judgement. But I make the decisions on board this naval vessel, based on naval protocol." She pulled out a complete khaki uniform, fully pressed and draped on a hanger. She walked over to her bunk, opened the slide doors then opened a lower storage drawer, pulled out a crisply folded bra, a set of old-fashioned men's boxer shorts, and her ditty bag full of personals, then headed to the bathroom.

Don pulled out the chair to bring the desk open. He made use of the desk top by propping his elbow on the surface and popping his chin into his hand. He realized that she had not fully closed the door, when he heard the sound of the water saver shower. Then he heard through the water and echo of the bathroom, "So explain this anomaly to me."

Don sighed, having to get out of his comfortable position, stood up and walked over to the ajar door, and said, "Well, Geophysics is not exactly my forte, but I did do some research last night."

He heard a laugh then she said, "Funny, I thought you would. You just seem to have this knack for wanting to know everything."

Don leaned against the wall still speaking at the partially open the door. "Yeah, well, sometimes that gets in the way. Anyway. The Kamchatka earthquake. As you probably already know, Kamchatka is as about as stable as it can be, but like any other surface on this planet, it's subject to plate tectonics, or the shifting of the continents."

"Okay," was Beverly's watery response.

Don continued to explain. "Just discovered a few years back is the fact that some part of the ocean floor is not actually the ocean floor. It's actually a bacterial goo, more prevalent in warm climates. It's been thought that the ocean floor makes up almost one third of all the life on the planet."

"I had read something about that a few years back. The article I read was about the Red Sea."

"Exactly. Now going back to the earthquake, Geologists think that underneath the glaciers of the northern Kamchatka, a geothermal anomaly occurred. Bear in mind that the peninsula is a hot bed of volcanic activity. They think about three weeks ago that the bacterial soup under the ice built up to a boiling point and that a small volcanic fissure, hardly noticeable in the scope of things, set off a chain reaction."

Don listened as the shower turned off then he heard, "They think the bacteria exploded?"

Don leaned against the wall, staring at the floor, the gentlemen in him showed discretion as it was that Beverly did not seem to mind walking around in the bathroom with the door open. "Methane gas build up. Think of that proverbial pile of oily rags in the garage that self-ignites. Then percolate that for a million years with the added pressure of ice flows, then add a hot catalyst. Thinking outside the box, if all the bacteria on the ocean floor found a catalyst, with the perfect blend of methane, the Earth would be blown off its axis."

Through the rummaging around in the bathroom Don heard, "But in this case it was secluded to a portion directly under an ice flow because it was trapped."

Don muffled a yawn, then replied, "Now you've got it. Usually, the methane expels itself harmlessly into the water, but in this case, it was allowed to build below the ice." Then Don let out a huge sigh and continued. "That's the official version according to the United Nations, scientific community and the Russian Politburo."

"Okay. I'm sensing there's a big but coming up," came Beverly's voice just inside the doorway.

"Buuuuut. That's not what happened. I made a little phone call to a friend of mind in the Pentagon and he said that in fact the continental shelf off of Kamchatka was blown up by a Russian mining outfit."

"Are you kidding? What the hell for?"

"Well, do you remember a few years back there was a big push to harness the expelling natural gas from the fracking wells? Well, that was what a Russian mining company was trying to do. With the methane build up. A mining company called LuvoDoyByat, was attempting to harness the methane. A completely renewable source of gas."

"But something went wrong?"

"Yeap. They failed miserably. Not sure exactly since the Kremlin is still in complete denial, something their machinery did that blew up the edge of the peninsula."

There was a brief pause as Don could hear very little, then he heard her ask, "All right. So, what about Carcharodon Megalodon and our Plesiosaur. What explains them?"

Don shook his head and replied, "I'm sure Scott could probably explain this better. Basically, at some time in the not-so-distant past, say a few hundred thousand years, or even sooner, our present shark, probably ran across some kind of cataclysmic event that caused massive earthquakes. Enough to trap the beast, by a glacier falling on it. Probably drug along our plesiosaur as well. We know this can happen under the right circumstances because they have found frogs buried in the ice in Iceland and brought them successfully back to life. One, they figured had been buried three thousand years. Anyhow, in a rapid warming then freezing period our shark got freeze dried, then a few weeks ago, its glacier melted in rapid fashion as the bacteria effectively burped. Methane heated up its frozen world."

He heard Beverly laugh, then felt the door swing open slightly. Don looked up and over to see her head pop out the bathroom door, to come within a foot of his face. "I think that explains it rather well," she acknowledged. Then she asked simply, "You said sooner?"

The face-to-face contact rattled Don for a second as his eyes shot open, then quickly looked down back down at the floor, aware that Beverly's shoulders were very bare, then he looked back at the now empty doorway. Then he explained, "Yeah, sooner. There's a theory that might hold true in this case. Not all dinosaurs, especially the ocean-going ones were wiped out in one fell swoop. Speculation has it that a lot survived into what we might say the age of men. In our sharks' case, the Megalodon might have simply become extinct through natural selection. Its ferocious appetite being its undoing. Sort of like the Sabre-toothed Tiger. His demise might have been less than ten thousand years ago."

"Or his entrapment?" came a muffled voice as Beverly was struggling with something.

"Close enough. There's a lot to old stories about sea monsters and unknown beasts of the deep. The Chinese were some of the earliest ocean goers and they described prehistoric dinosaurs, or what they thought of dragons, to a tee. Anyway, that sort of explains why our Plesiosaur, if it was in fact one, was in such bad shape. Between being boiled back alive and having a bad case of freezer burn, it did not survive, instead, becoming tangled in a fisherman's net. Another version of a Globster."

"Globster? You've got to explain that one to me," replied Beverly intrigued with the word.

"Globster. A name given to beasts that wash up on shore that can't be identified. It happens a lot more than you think. The monster of Sakhalin Island, in two thousand and six. Trunko monster in South America had fur like a polar bear, took on two orcas. Then of course there are a lot of fishes that have survived better than the dinosaurs. Hag fish deemed to be over five hundred million years old and even the Coelacanth once thought to be extinct still being pulled out of the water just a few years ago."

"I understand that, there are still areas of the ocean we haven't seen," said a muffled Beverly. A blow dryer came on and stopped the conversation for a few moments. Then Don heard some more rustling, then the light turned off and Beverly came out, dressed in a very white full figured type bra that did little for her bust. Complete with the large boxer underwear, she padded across the floor, aware that Don was taken aback.

"Sorry," she explained, "forgot my uniform." She grabbed her khakis and walked back to her bunk. Don thought she would hightail it back to the head to dress, but she started putting on her pants, careful to pull the boxers in so that they did not bunch up, then slipped on her shirt and buttoned it up, and tucked it in. She quickly went back to the bathroom, retrieved her gear then came back out and stored it away.

Sitting back down she slipped on her black socks and found her shoes and slipped these on she glanced up at Don with a questioning look and asked simply, "What?"

Don suddenly realized he had been staring at the behavior and shook his head instantly and responded, "Nothing. Nothing at all."

Finally standing up she looked at a bleary-eyed Don and asked, "Any idea how big of a glacier that dropped on our shark was?" Turning her back on Don she retrieved her hat from an interior hook, slipped her hair through just enough to make a proper pony tail, then turned back to him.

He shook his head slowly and responded, "No way of knowing. You have to take into account that this happened at least one ice age ago. It has more than likely gotten smaller as the planet is heating up."

"Okay. How big of an area was this so-called little mining disaster?"

"Over a thousand square miles," replied Don empathically.

Beverly arched her eyebrows and said, "So, there could very easily be more out there."

"Possible." Then Don searched Beverly's eyes then asked, "Why? Why the concern?"

Beverly shrugged her shoulders and responded, "My job is to protect people, whether from another country, or nature. It already sank one boat and killed people. Considering we're not armed to do battle; I don't like surprises."

Don watched Beverly walk to the quarter's door. She stopped, turned, became thoughtful for a moment then asked, "Why is it I've never heard of this shark before?"

"One simple word. Cartilage. A shark is made mostly of cartilage. No bones to fossilize, except the teeth. Which have been found to be over seven inches long, and as far inland as the Dakota's and Canada," Don responded muffling another yawn.

She smiled and said, "Thanks Don." Then she was gone.

Don thought for a moment, then sat down on his own bunk and slipped off his shoes. He laid back and stared at the bunk above him. He was tired to the bone and yet his mind wandered. He was still deep in thought when Wolfson walked in.

Ralph crossed the floor in a hurry, hit the head, then came out. He too sat on his bunk and slipped off his shoes. It had been a long night for both and Ralph was tired.

"Ralphie, can I ask a question?"

"You're asking me a question? That's a new one. Okay, as long as it only takes a one-word answer," Ralph responded leaning back on his bunk

"Has Beverly always had those?" Don asked indelicately.

Ralph sat for a moment, totally perplexed. Then he realized that Don had been talking to her while she had been on the treadmill. He grinned, then replied, "Oh, you mean the thirty-six B's."

"Yeah. That's what I mean."

"Yeah man. She's always had those."

"Where have I been?"

Ralph chuckled slightly then said, "You're not dead if that's what you mean. She had her uniform custom made to be a tailored fit, and she probably wears a minimizer bra. Today's probably the first day you've seen her out of uniform. She actually has a nice figure once you get past the military regimen."

Don thought for a moment then asked, "I take it you've seen her out of uniform. You had run into her before, didn't you?"

"Annapolis at around the same time. Ran into her more than once. Had a couple classes with her. Actually, a lot of the women tailored down their figures, to be taken a little more seriously, I suppose."

Don shifted out of his bunk, pulled a clean pair of boxers and T-shirt from his storage under the bunk and headed for the bathroom. Today was not his day to shower, so he sponged bathed as best as possible and came back out to his bunk, sitting heavily on its foam mattress. He sat back, his head finding the pillow, but again, his mind was full of thought.

Finally, Don asked, "I don't see any connection between you two so you never got into her pants. Was she always this anal?"

Ralph let out a chuckle, then he replied, "Man, you do cut to the chase, don't you?" Ralph thought for a second then added, "Naw, I never even tried to. She's not my type. She's too career minded and plain old too smart for me." Ralph thought for another moment then continued, "You know. She wasn't to begin with."

"What do you mean?"

"She was actually somewhat of a party girl. Made the circuit pretty regularly. Bumped into her a few times late at night. Seemed to have a different guy on her arm every time I did run into her."

"Oh man, if you're telling me that she got by on her old man's name I'm going to jump ship," said Don with a hint of bitterness. An old anxiety rose in him, then he dismissed it. Everyone had skeletons in their closet. He was damned sure no exception.

"No Don. Quite the contrary. Her name got her ostracized more than once. Hell, there was even one instructor that was always on her case. Some personal vendetta he had against the old man. I sort of felt sorry for her." Ralph sighed, fluffed his pillow and continued. "Nope. She got by the same way you did, I'm sure."

Don's forehead furrowed deep in thought. Ultimately, he asked, "And how exactly, was that?"

Ralph smirked then said, "Pure brains. She'd party all week, come in on Friday and ace her test, then party through the weekend. Carried a three-point eight or nine if I remember correctly. One of those irritating types. Just like you."

Don smirked back. He had graduated High School at the age of sixteen, bouncing past two grades. And even MIT was no real challenge as he carried more classes then necessary, and won the Rube Goldberg Award. Twice. Finally, he asked, "Okay. You said to begin with though?"

Don could not see it but Ralph closed his eyes deep in thought then he answered simply, "She got kidnapped. Supposedly raped."

"Are you kidding me?" was Don's immediate response. Even at a college like MIT it happened to girls he knew and he always wondered what would make a man reduce himself to an animal. The stupid idiots always got caught and sacrificed a life of learning for a set of jail bars. In Beverly's case he could readily guess.

Ralph continued. "Yeah, and it wasn't pretty. Some pot head who got kicked out of school, resented Beverly and her grades and especially her name, took it upon himself. I guess she refused him once for a date, making it pretty clear to the guy he was a loser. I never got the details, and I'm not that insensitive to ask, but I guess it ended up being really nasty, if you know what I mean. Locked her away in some cabin out in the boonies and would not let her go for like a couple of days or something like that. I had heard he kept her blind folded and feed her. Sort of psychological terrorizing so I've been told. Luckily, she managed to escape. They tried to hush up the entire thing, but it came out. And when it did the shit really hit the fan. Jack had just become Rear Admiral, and he came stomping through Annapolis like the place was on fire. Of course, the crummy kid did time in the stockade, but Jack did not stop there. He got several other students expelled that had ties, and one or two teachers if I remember right."

"What about Beverly?" Don asked with more concern than Ralph would have thought.

"Jack took her out for a few weeks, or maybe even a month or two. I really don't remember. Anyhow. I think she did some extensive counseling. I heard they did a lot of medical tests on her. I even heard once through the grapevine she had an abortion, but I never really believed that one. Anyway, she comes back to classes, and she's still bubbly, you know, she seems all right. But after a while we notice she won't leave her room much at night. Turns her three point eight into four-point. I guess she just didn't want to be in that position again."

Don turned deep into thought. Then he said in observance, "She was looking for the power that was just taken from her."

"Say again?" came from the bunk next to Don.

"Power. Her brains gave her power, and her name gave her power and some asshole very simply and violently, took that away from her. Turned her into a piece of meat." Don shut his eyes putting himself in her place, as best as he could. Then he said, "Up till that point she was going to have an all right naval career and retire safe and sound. Then this happens and she realizes, for her to have any power over having this happening again, she needs grades and promotions and to make it as aggressively as possible."

"She's definitely smart. And your right, I think she had to redevelop her attitude," said Ralph in finality.

Don nodded into his pillow then observed, "But you have to wonder how much something like that scars a person."

"It's been quite a few years Don. It really seems like she's put it behind her. It takes a lot of freaking guts to be XO on a sub with a hundred other men. Given her name, she had to do her job better than average. Sort of in the hot seat. I had heard from Cartwright that the Captain of the Nautilus Two tried to talk her out of the transfer to the Specter. The guys on the sub felt that if a woman could do it, so could they. Heard one story on the first day out to sea, a seaman pinched her butt. She decked him. Laid him out cold. And then she dared the crew to try anything stupid again, they would get the same. The seaman never got brought up on charges, but man did he get ribbed the rest of the tour. And he kept his God-Damned distance."

Don mumbled as if talking to himself, "She's seems to exude confidence. She took a shower with the door open, walked around in her BVD's and it didn't seem to faze her a bit."

Ralph sort of snorted then said, "Don, you may have an arrogant air about you, but you're quite harmless. But you know, in hindsight though, it's probably why I've never seen or heard of her with a boyfriend."

Don thought for several moments, then replied, "Yeah. Between that kind of stigma and her old man, a guy wouldn't stand a chance." The words fell on deaf ears, however. Ralph was fast asleep. Don drifted off a few moments later, his mind recalling delicately, a creamy white shoulder and a smiling face.

Don woke with a start. He glanced at his digital watch, saw the time of one-thirty-six PM and flung back the bed covers. Six hours was a good sleep for him and he felt refreshed. But grumpy. He was not a morning person. He reached for his pants, climbed into them and put on his socks and shoes. Still only in a T-shirt, he glanced at Ralph's bunk to see it empty.

He wandered down to the galley, retrieved a cup of coffee, then headed for the control room. Sealing the water tight door behind him he glanced around. Beverly was at the mapping board going over directions with Lt. Duran. Don noticed that there seemed to be some kind of buzz in the air. He walked over to Ralph who was looking over Barrington's shoulder at the communications console.

"What's up?" Don asked as he put a hand on Ralph's shoulder.

"Your shark's back," Wolfson replied without turning around.

Don looked shocked for a second then asked, "How?"

"We've been in communications with the Coast Guard in Nome. They gave us some details of an incident from a ship called the Aleutian Queen with a very expensive DRSV that got the crap beat out of it. Several died in the confrontation."

"And how do they know it's our shark?"

Ralph turned around and looked at Don and said, "They have thirty minutes of video of the entire fight. No doubt in any ones mind it's a megalodon. 'Big sucker' the guy at Nome kept saying. Drug the submersible around like a bath tub toy."

Don's quick mind put together the scenario. Then he asked, "Why the hell would our Meg attack a DRSV? What did it do?"

Ralph shrugged his shoulders and responded, "They sort of have this idea that it's the high-pitched whine of the electric motors."

"Damn shark was freeze dried, and then blown up. No telling what the hell that did to its senses."

Ralph only shook his head slightly.

Hornacher broke in, "We have their exact location. We've been tasked with a search of the area to see if we can find the shark before it finds something else."

"So, we're going shark hunting," Don said with a slight irritation.

"Two people just lost their lives. I don't think it's very funny," shot Beverly looking over at Don with her hands on her hips.

Don glared back at her and said argumentatively, "And, if you recall, the Navy in all its wisdom, deemed we should be unarmed. Just what do you plan on doing? Bashing it to death? The Seattle or the Cheyenne, has a much better chance of dealing with a hundred-foot shark than we do."

Hornacher took a step forward and said, "The Seattle has been redirected from their mission to assist. But they don't have the technology like we do. We can pinpoint this thing to the exact foot for the Seattle and they can shoot it out of the water."

Don's eyes shot open. "We're going to play tag with a live torpedo? And some Navy guy is pulling the trigger? I don't like that idea …" Suddenly his mind shot to an image of Beverly, helpless and vulnerable in some dark and dank room. And he felt the beefy hand of Ralph grabbing his elbow.

Ralph explained quickly, "Don, we've contacted Fleet Command and they concur with Captain Hornacher's plan. We're to assist the Seattle in any way possible."

Don had managed to settle himself down. He nodded his head and said, "To protect people. All right. Let's go do that. And hope the Seattle can shoot straight."

At forty-seven knots an hour the Specter crisscrossed the Bering Sea. Petty-officer Hernandez located seventy-two fish of ten feet or longer, but nothing near the size of their Carcharodon Megalodon.

After four hours Beverly came up to Don at the auxiliary monitoring console next to Willy. Don had been so focused, the hand on his shoulder brought a shock and he wheeled around, took a deep breath then turned back to the computer screen. He had developed a three-dimensional grid of the entire Bering Sea, the last location of the shark and an ever-increasing wheel of supposed traveling area. He had access to the satellite images, infrared underwater cameras, and all the monitoring equipment.

"Any luck?" Beverly finally asked, a little surprised at feeling the knotted muscles beneath Don's T-shirt. For some reason, she had always assumed the somewhat baggy shirts beheld a skinny man.

Don leaned back in his chair and waved a dejected hand at the screen. "With an average cruising speed of twenty miles an hour, this thing expands by a mile in every direction every three minutes. And we can only guess at the shark's destination. We're coming up from the south, he might have cruised north. Hell, we could have actually cruised over the damned thing and not known about it."

"I doubt that." Came from Alex across the control room.

Don nodded and replied to Alex, "All right. As long as you can see the bottom, we can see the damned fish. But still, we're only guessing at its direction."

Beverly nodded slowly. It had been a crap shoot. "All right Don. I get it. One degree off and we miss it." Then she turned back to Duran and asked, "Navigation, how far to the approximate location of the battle with the Aleutian Queen?"

Duran glanced quickly at the map board, hit an icon which brought up his original triangulation and then replied, "We passed close to it about an hour ago. We do a one-seventy to port now we should be on it in about forty-five minutes."

"Commander, plot an intercept course, best possible speed please." Stated Beverly.

Commander Wolfson nodded then said, "Navigation, plot a course to the last location of the Meg, sending to steering and let's do eighty knots' please."

"Aye Captain," replied the senior pilot, getting the new course setting from the mapping board and changing his mark.

Beverly then turned to the communications board and said, "Comm, let's tell the Seattle they can return to station and the search is off. Tell them we're going to search to make sure there's no shark carcass down there."

"Yes Ma'am," came the quick response from Barrington.

Beverly stood in the middle of the control room, trying hard to think of a better plan of action. Ralph came up next to her. She glanced up at him then said simply, "Damn."

Forty-four minutes to cover the distance, and another seventeen to find a very large, very old turtle shell. It took some deft computer maneuvering by Don and Willy to make sense of the upside down, monstrous shell, but finally, they got the image they wanted. Don had the imagery transferred to the six-foot screen at the front of control.

Beverly crossed her arms as the outboard cameras scanned the shell, the swirling of the sea floor still floating around the battle scene. Don, Beverly and Ralph watched as the camera scanned back and forth.

Suddenly, Don saw something and said back to Willy, "Can you zero in on that?"

Willy said nothing, deftly operating the computer and the camera. The camera zoomed in then focused.

Beverly gazed at in awe. Finally, she asked, "Tinkerbell, what the heck is that?"

"Glad you asked Captain," Tinkerbell replied quickly. "That is the remains of a prehistoric turtle called an Archelon. I'm guessing it bubbled forth from the undersea earthquakes."

"Thank you, Tinkerbell. But … is guessing in your nature?" Beverly asked smiling.

"When the possibilities do not meet the facts. The turtle is extinct, and yet, there it is."

"Willy, zero in on that." Stated Don pointing at the section of the shell where the head should have been.

"Going back," responded Willy.

Don looked carefully, searching through the drifting the soot. Finally, he found it and said, "Willy hold. Zoom in."

Trapped in the edge of the shell was a tooth. Gazing at the size of the shell and white and pink splotch on the screen, Don finally asked Tinkerbell, "How big is that tooth Tink?"

"It is exactly six inches and nine sixteenth of an inch. Wow Don. That's big."

"Man, look at the size of that thing," observed Ralph.

"Can you imagine the thoughts on the DRSV when that thing attacked?" questioned Beverly.

"The problem is, it's still out there," observed Don, looking away from the computer screen back at Beverly.

"I see that." She sighed heavily then turned and instructed Barrington, "Communications, let the Coast Guard at Nome know about this and express to them that they need to keep the fishing fleet in dock."

"They won't listen, you know," observed Ralph.

Beverly nodded, then said dejectedly, "I know. And when the next ship goes down, we'll do this all over again."

Don stretched, walked over to his computer console, and reached for his empty coffee cup; aware he was still in his T-shirt. He stood for a second, deep in thought.

"I see the wheels whirling frantically Don. What's up?" asked Beverly, starting to get an insight to how the man worked.

He shook his head then said, "Two thoughts actually. One being all the technology I stuffed in this sub and we can't find the world's biggest shark."

Beverly understood the frustration then asked, "The second?"

"What's to say this isn't a different shark?"

Don left the control room, Ralph and Beverly looking stunned.

Little did Captain Hornacher and the crew of the Specter know that in a few hours they would be hunting a much bigger, and much deadlier fish.

CHAPTER 10

Beverly felt the body on top of her tense excitedly. An excited breath buried itself in her neck and groaned, a hand firmly stoking her flesh. After a few moments, the face presented itself and they smiled at each other. Finally, she asked, "You done big boy?"

Hernandez smiled sweetly then kissed her on the cheek. There seemed to be more muscles to the man than Beverly remembered, but it was time to move on. Hernandez slipped out of Beverly, crawled out of her bunk and walked across the Command Quarters naked. Beverly got out of the bunk and followed, also completely nude, the cool air of the submarine raising goose flesh upon her chest.

Hernandez opened the quarter's door and walked out into the hallway. He yelled like a carnival barker, "Step right up! Who's next?"

Beverly opened the door wider and looked into the hallway. Ralph and Willy were leaning against the wall, waiting patiently, dressed in their uniforms.

Ralph whistled seductively at Beverly who was now dressed in a solid black merry widow bone crushing corset, with fishnet stockings, a red silk tie straining the cleavage together. The push up padding and boning, chiseling her bust upwards as her waist tapered into a perfect hour glass shape. Underneath was a pair of red ribbon crotch less panties and five-inch stiletto heels inching her taller.

Long reddish-brown hair draped around her smooth shoulders as her full painted lips kissed at the two men. She ran a tongue around her luscious lips with a wicked smile. "Oh, I can't decide. Why don't you both come in?" she said with a long fingernail waving in the two men, a firm leg caressing the door.

Ralph was naked as he pressed in from the front, his firm chest muscles pushing her bosom even more upwards. Willy had also suddenly become nude as he came in from behind, circling his hands around her and pushing gently from behind. All her seductive clothing was stripped off in a second as she let the two men lead her to her bunk. Hands were groping at every curve.

"No, no, no, the bunk is too small. Let's use the floor," she uttered as Willy was instantly on his knees, and starting to probe delicately. She moaned loudly, then closed her eyes to let the sensation infuse her.

"Captain? Captain? Wake up Captain."

The voice cut through the fog and brought Beverly to reality with an eye-opening start. She could see through the tiny gaps around the top of the accordion divider, the main lights on in the command quarters were on. She glanced at her watch which read twelve eighteen AM. She wiped at the puffiness in her eyes, punched a button on an overhead light fixture and responded thickly, "Yes? What's the problem?"

"This is Lieutenant Smith. Commander Wolfson told me to wake you and tell you we have a situation in control." The big seaman felt decidedly out of place trying to wake the lady Captain in the middle of the night. He had been raised by a strict Baptist mother who had taught him the sanctities of women and to respect the opposite sex. Sneaking into a sleeping woman's quarters raised a lump in his stomach. Then on top of it all, she was moaning and he did not really like what he heard.

Beverly cleared her throat, thought of opening the bifold doors, to talk face to face, thought better of it, then responded, "All right Bobby. Tell him I'll be there in a minute. And thanks."

She could hear the audible sigh as he responded, "Yes Ma'am." Bobby then turned quickly to get his butt out of the captain's quarters.

Beverly usually could jump straight out of bed, ready to go with her day. But she had been sleeping lightly and she did not feel the least bit rested. It took her several attempts to find the latch on the accordion door, but finally she managed to unlatch it and slapped it open. She swung her feet out onto the floor, flexing her feet as she did so. She rubbed at her eyes as if they were trying to droop down to her chin, glancing at the glaring white light of the quarters.

She sat for a few more seconds, a creepy feeling coming over her as the dream suddenly rushed at her senses. She rubbed hard at her eyes as if to rub away the sensations and the images. Suddenly, she lashed out at the wall with the fleshy part of her fist, slamming the surface three times in rapid succession, all the while muttering "Damn, damn, damn. Go away!"

The pain caused her mind to focus for a second as the safe reality struck her. "God, I hate dreams like that. Christ, it's a good thing Bobby woke me up or I would have done the entire crew," Beverly muttered to herself. Then the shocking force of the all too real dream hit her and brought back a million old and terrorizing memories. She closed her eyes to force the images away, and take hold of the reality of being safe and sound. Then the feelings subsided as she took a deep and comforting breath. Her mind, knew how to mend and come quickly to grips with reality.

She had endured two years of psychiatric counseling, probing her deepest and darkest memories. The Military had a term for her condition, but it was used usually for war time applications. PTSD or Post Traumatic Stress Disorder. After her incarceration and timely escape, a long and lengthy trial for her captor, which brought out every nasty thing Beverly had ever done in her life, all aimed at discrediting her, all trying to blame her for the vicious attack. And the asshole that terrorized her had a nice cozy bed courtesy of the government for a whooping five years, while she labored with a horrific, lifelong stigma.

For two years afterward, she would have the most disgusting dreams. She would wake up screaming or worse, in the middle of the night. There were times Beverly would fight it with everything she had, then she would succumb and hide in a hole and live in it for extended periods of time. To get away from people. To get away from prying eyes, and as time had the ability to do, she slowly worked her way out of the horrific events of the past, to become stronger. But they were always there. It ate at her soul. And the dreams were as real as they could be, remembering every detail upon awakening. There were times she struggled to separate reality with what her mind played before her. But that was long ago.

She had thought she had left it all behind. No more dreams, no more stares, no more questions. Military psychiatrists, three of them had probed and prodded at her sanity, exposing every nerve, every nuance that was in her mental capabilities. They would not let her on a submarine if there was one ripple in her sanity. They could find no effects, no cataclysms of left over hostilities. She was eventually cleared for sailing, finding a stable woman in charge of her feeling.

Finally, when women were granted permission to be assigned submarine duty, she was among the first. Even on the Nautilus Two, surrounded by more than a hundred men she had not succumbed to any more thoughts or nightmares. She was now Captain. And now again, out of nowhere, suddenly, it surfaced. It had been a solid four years since the last vivid nightmare. She knew it was the pressure and anxiety, working at the feverish little corners of her brain.

But there was a trigger. As with most war situations it was known as Shell Shock. The bombs falling all around followed the soldiers home, and became the back blast of car exhaust or a solid door slamming. The ex-soldiers would jump and even hide or worse at the sharp noise, triggering their subconscious.

With Beverly, it was the simple infusion of light, or in her case the complete lack of it. The bifold screen, meant for solitude, let very little light into her little bunk area. While stationed on the Nautilus Two, three women shared a small eight by eight cube and had a security light on at all time for emergency reasons. Even on the Specter, nothing was completely in the dark. Except her bunk.

It went back to her imprisonment so many years ago. Her eyes had been duct taped until her captor had dumped her in that cabin. The windows were boarded over and filled with insulation. Entirely in the black even on the sunniest of days. The only thing was the light that would come through the bedroom door. When it was opened, she was terrified beyond belief. When it was left open, albeit a crack, she thanked God for she knew she was not yet dead. A little stream of light was her salvation.

For two years after, she could not force herself to sleep in the dark. Every light in her room was on, and her sleep was fitful at best. She needed to know what creepy, crawly monster, childish or human was coming out of the dark at her. Even if she could not sleep, it was better than not knowing and being frightened out of her wits. But she had eventually outgrown the lights, and finally found peace with a simple night light. Even the military doctors knew this and questioned it. No, she would answer, she did not need a light. And she did not, at least not in the safety of her own bed, for even there a light bled in through the curtains, from some distant street lamp. She was never really in the dark, was she? Until now.

Beverly had decided when coming on board the Specter that the captain of the ship did not need a night light on in her bunk. She thought she was now beyond that. Her disgusting morning nightmare proved her wrong.

But she would have to deal with it, the way it was. She would not let her past or emotional stigma's creep in on the way she managed herself, or the crew. Not now. Not ever.

Going to slide off her bunk she suddenly became aware of a wetness in her crotch. "God Damned," she thought out loud. That was the part she hated the worst. The stark, utter realism.

She thought to change her boxers, when the emergency of the situation grabbed her. This must be serious for Wolfson to wake her she decided. Pulling her khaki pants from their hook, she crawled out of her bunk and slipped them on. The T-shirt would have to do, she thought quickly. When she found the problem in the control room, then she would change. Or maybe go back to sleep, and have nice dreams for a change, she thought. She quickly massaged her fist, content she had not broken anything. She had done worse in her life time, to blot out the terror.

Slipping into white deck shoes she brushed back her hair into a semblance of shape with her fingers, crossed the room quickly and was out the door. She took no notice of this as she had been dressed in less under emergency conditions on the Nautilus Two. Getting some stares from the crewmen, but getting high marks from the captain. She was there to do a job, decorum be damned, he had noted.

Lt. Robert Duran peeked out from his covers. He had the bunk above Captain Hornacher and up until now then had never been any 'accidents' or unexpected sightings of the fleshy kind. But her moaning had awakened him. He had heard every groan, every word, the bunk shaking climax. Then Bobby entered. And he heard Beverly talking to herself. Then there was the fist against the wall, an exclamation of control. It was more than he wanted to hear from his Captain.

Lt. Duran had heard rumors from his older brother, also in the US Naval Submarine fleet. He had heard that Beverly Hornacher was no longer allowed on submarines. His brother had told him of a problem on the USS Stingray, where Beverly had been the weapons officer. The Captain of the Stingray could not wait to get her off his boat, Duran's brother had heard through the grapevine

And now Robert heard her with his own ears. And it made him wonder also, the sanity of his Captain.

When Hornacher entered the control room, there was no sense of an emergency. Petty Officer Hyde was at the Oceanographic Monitors, Bobby was at the mapping board, and Frankie was piloting the ship. However, Wolfson and Don were staring at the satellite image at the front of the control room. She walked the narrow passage between the electronics of the control center and reached the two men, standing on Ralph's side away from Don

"What's up Commander?" she asked quickly, folding her arms across her chest.

Ralph glanced quickly at her, said nothing about her dress and replied, "We were doing a satellite scan, and Tinkerbell alerted us something disturbing from the Russian Naval Base at Vladivostok." He waved at the image on the huge six by three-foot screen. "As you know the security mode of the satellite alerts us to any disturbance it deems unusual. Twenty minutes ago, we saw this."

Beverly studied the screen. What she saw were the naval docks at Vladivostok. There seemed to be sixteen different ships or subs, all leaving port at the same time. Two thoughts quickly crossed her mind and she asked, "I didn't realize we monitored the Naval base in Russia.?"

Wolfson replied, "Umh, well we don't."

"Sooo, where did we get these pictures?"

"Well … just so happens there was a satellite monitoring so we piggybacked." Replied Don, as if it were an everyday occurrence. "Tinkerbelle keeps an eye on the skies."

"Oh, all right. A US satellite is keeping an eye on them. Got it."

"Um no. Chinese." Stated Don.

She smiled for s second and shook her head. "And how is it we got a streaming video from a Chinese satellite?"

"I speak fluent Mandarin." Stated Tinkerbell. Beverly could have sworn she heard a smirk.

Don shrugged and added, "I asked Tinkerbell to hack it." Then added, "We imbedded our code into a dozen satellites. When one pings, we see what it sees."

Her eyes widened and she asked, "Uhm, you aren't worried about getting caught? I just as soon not get a nasty call from the Pentagon wondering why we're on a Chinese satellite?"

Don glanced over as if dealing with a dull child. "Oh, come on. We use a randomizer circuit that picks IP addresses out and changes them constantly. Hell, they probably think it's the ghost of Mao viewing the videos."

"Oh yeah, that's lots better." Beverly then refocused on the screen.

Don had not paid Beverly's dress any attention until he reached across Ralph and handed her a list of Russian ships they had identified. She looked down at the list as Don stayed in his extended position looking across at her.

Beverly, glanced at the list, then suddenly realized he was staring at her. "What?"

Don only smiled and said "An unusually casual look for you. Captain."

She knew her hair was falling around her shoulders and in her way. But she glanced down at her shirt which was nothing more than a T-shirt. It was a thick military style and there was little to see but still, she was braless in the control room. She was thirty-six years old and had certainly gone without a bra before, and thought nothing of it, given the situation. For a briefest of moment's, she got mad at Don for bringing it up, then she thought to mollify the situation and responded with a grin, "You wear a T-shirt in the control room and no one says anything, why can't I?"

"Oh, no reason, no reason whatsoever." Don responded with a devilish grin.

Beverly looked back up at the screen, handed the list to Ralph, and said in all seriousness, "Where's the Volga?"

"The Volga?" asked Don.

"Big Russian Sub," explained Ralph scrunching his eyes together to peer at the screen. Then he turned to Beverly and asked, "You know it's supposed to be in dock?"

Beverly rationalized, "While on the Nautilus Two we played tag with the Volga, Admiral Rabinov, loving nothing more than to playing games in the middle of the Pacific. We got very familiar with it. It was supposed to be going into dock for a month-long refit. That should have been a couple weeks ago."

"It's not there," Don observed, recalling every ship name off the list.

Beverly studied the screen for a few seconds then asked, "You said we monitor Vladivostok on a regular basis?"

"Right," replied Don.

She looked over at Don and asked, "We wouldn't happen to record that in some way, would we?"

Don looked over, glanced down at the T-shirt once then looked back up into Beverly's green eyes and said, "Possible." He wheeled around, noticed that Alvin Alann had returned to his post from fetching a cup of coffee and said to him, "Al, we need the back up for satellite imagery for the past few days."

It took Alvin several minutes to retrieve the information, then he said, "Don, to the screen, starting last week."

Don, Beverly and Ralph stared up at the huge monitor. Vladivostok popped onto the screen, the date one week previous. Beverly walked up to the image and pointed at a large, black, cigar-shaped image on the largest dock.

She tapped the image and said, "That's it. I'd bet my bottom dollar. It was definitely there."

Don turned and said to Alvin, "Can you enhance that?"

The screen changed as the submarine shape encompassed the entire image. Then Alvin

sharpened the image enhancing the details.

Ralph nodded, "The thing is full of activity, like it's being worked on. Why isn't it still there?"

"Al, forward." Don commanded.

They watched in rapid fashion small boats come and go, the various exhaust plumes casting a humorous image in the high-speed video. Suddenly, the Volga disappeared.

"Back up," said Don.

The screen bounced an image one hour at a time in reverse. The night vision picked up the departure. Midnight, Russian time, on Friday the Volga left port.

"I don't know Russian Naval protocol but setting sail in the middle of the night is suspicious as hell," mentioned Don.

"Some kind of Russian exercise maybe? The Volga is the point?" Mentioned Ralph to Beverly.

Beverly shook her head and responded, "In the middle of a retrofit? From what I remember, they were due to get all new computerization and a new power plant. Besides, knowing Admiral Rabinov, he'd never be the point. He'd much rather be the hunter."

"Admiral? That's a little unusual, isn't it?" observed Don.

Beverly inserted, "Rabinov is a genius. But Rabinov does what Rabinov wants to do. And he loves his ship. He had it built for his own purpose, to be the biggest and nastiest in the Russian Navy. And nobody's going to take it away from him."

"None of which explains what's going on," observed Ralph stroking his mustache, deep in thought.

Beverly turned to Ralph and asked, "Have you been in contact with Command?"

"Not yet."

Beverly turned back to the screen and watched for several moments. Then she said, "Well, it's certainly curious. It's obvious something's up, but I'll be damned if I know what it is." She turned to the communications console, saw it vacant and asked, "Who's on the com.?"

"I am," replied Don sheepishly.

"And why?" Beverly asked gazing across at Don.

"Rory said he didn't feel that great, so I sent him to bed and I said I would cover. I didn't actually think I would have to do anything," explained Don.

"Well. Okay, we need to send a message to Command, and make damned sure it's encrypted Mr. Merrick," said Beverly, in mocking tone treating the smart engineer like a pion.

"And what should I tell them, Captain?" Responded Don like the dutiful little secretary.

Beverly thought seriously and responded, "Tell them the Russian Ballistic Missile Submarine Volga has left port unexpectedly on Friday night, and there seems to be a mass exodus from Vladivostok. Tell them we think it's related." Then she thought for a few moments and said, "Is there any way we can send them an encrypted picture of this?"

Don smiled and said simply, "Possible."

She nodded and said simply, "Do it."

Don walked to the rear of the room, first to talk to Alvin about an encrypted video transfer, then over to the communications console to send the entire thing back to the states, via the GPPP. The two men worked together to get this done.

Beverly continued to stare at the image on the screen. She was trying desperately to put the two facts together.

Ralph stood next to her and finally observed, "It seems the game is a foot and we don't know what we're playing."

"The good thing is the Russian Navy doesn't know we're playing. And they won't know if Don's as good as he thinks he is," she responded with a grin. She continued to stare then said off handedly, "I wonder if any other satellites have picked this up?"

Ralph looked over at the woman and said politely, "You look a little rough. I just wanted you to be aware of the situation, even if there is one. If you want, you can go back to your bunk and we'll alert you if something comes up again."

Beverly blinked several times, thought for a moment then said, "From anyone else I would take that remark as an insult." Then she smiled and continued, "But I have a different plan. I'm going to go back and snooze a bit, but I need you and Don to grab some shut eye also."

Ralph just looked at her with a concerned and confused look. She replied back, "I think there's a lot to this. The Volga does not simply set sail for absolutely no reason. I have this gut feeling that our day is going to turn hectic and I'm going to need you and Don to be at your best."

Ralph smiled at the woman's insight. "You know; you might just be right. Don and I will catch a nap. We'll wake you at six hundred hours."

Beverly stole one last look at the image on the big screen then turned and started walking out of the control room. But first she stopped and strolled in behind Don and looked over his shoulder. Then she laid a hand on his shoulder and squeezed. Again, she found muscle and took pleasure in the fact that the man was not a boney little computer nerd. Somewhere, she theorized, he had worked out with weights.

He looked up and said, "Naval Command has confirmation they've received our message and picture. And to answer your question, no. No one else has seen this yet."

She nodded then said loud enough for all in control to hear, "All right. Now I'm going to go do something about my hair."

Don swiveled around in his chair and looked up at her, making sure to look her straight into the face. He replied, "Hair?"

"Yes. My hair. Well, you keep staring at me and I figure it's my dreadful bed head. Right?" This brought several giggles from the other men, especially Alvin who snorted through his nose.

Don smiled, without missing a beat and responded, "That's it. It's that atrocious hairdo you have going."

Beverly only nodded, swung around and left the control room.

"But I thought Captain Hornacher looked rather fetching myself," observed Tinkerbell.

"A little jealous Tinkerbell?" Asked Don with a lopsided grin.

"Nope, not at all. I appreciate the human form but prefer my low maintenance lifestyle."

Don smiled at the thought, then quickly rubbed his eyes and stood up and yawned. He walked over to Ralph who, although heard the entire conversation, never moved. Don pulled up next to him and said, "Man, I'll never figure her out."

Ralph smiled back and responded, "Why is that?"

Don glared at Ralph for a second then said, "I don't know." Don continued to think for a while. Then he said noncommittal like, "I guess it's just women I'll never understand."

"Which explains at the age of forty-three why you're not married. But what does Beverly do that confuses you so much?" asked Ralph, taking joy in the one little thing that perplexes the very smart engineer.

Don shrugged and said, "Well, she wants to be taken seriously as a captain. To be noticed for her brains."

Ralph shrugged his shoulders and said, "She's teasing you, Don. She's being one of the boys while being a woman. She's a good Captain who's bringing a little bit of her own levity to the control room. Besides, you're the one that keeps staring."

"I do not. Okay, maybe I do, but it just part of this whole I'm captain, treat me like one, and oh, by the way, here's my boobs."

"Donnnn." Chastised Tinkerbell.

Ralph smirked for a second, then he said quietly, "Don, you're the only one looking at it this way. I had a co-ed dorm at Annapolis. You should have seen the various modes of dress during midnight inspections, from both the men and women. I remember one time, well, never mind, let's just say there was a few times when someone forgot to even throw on their jammies. And this is the US Navy, where exotic ports are the norm. You would not believe what goes on in Singapore."

Ralph stopped for a moment to gather his thoughts then continued, "Like I said, it's just her way of goading you, because you're just like her and you're the easiest mark, because you're not military. Besides, she's a woman and she has breasts. There's no way of getting around that. The rest of us practice military decorum, and uniforms be damned, higher echelon rules. They're ingrained into the military standards. You obviously, don't have those standards."

Don thought for a moment then said grudgingly, "Hey, I went to College and we had our own version of girls gone wild. I guess I just put Bev on a different playing field, that's all. So, now I know.

She knows she has money makers and knows how to use them. I'll play along then."

Ralph looked back up at the screen and said disheartened, "Besides, I think she's right. I think we have a much bigger problem to worry about."

Don's mind always ran on full steam. Which meant that when he slept, he liked his full eight hours. His notebook computer alarm went off at five-thirty AM as he caught a three-hour cat nap. Crawling out of his bunk, he chanced to look over at Beverly's quarters. The slide door was still drawn which meant she was still asleep. He took his gear to the bathroom, cleaned up, dressed in his blue sweatshirt, khaki pants and headed to the galley to fetch a cup of coffee. He thought to maybe throw it on himself, it would probably do better that way.

Don finally wandered into the control center. Ralph was still studying the screen, as it was clear all the ships had departed the immediate area of the Vladivostok Naval Base. They were after something and making great time in catching it.

"Anything new?" Don asked, sipping a burning mouthful of Columbia's worst.

Ralph merely shook his head then responded, "They've all left the hive. However, we did receive a message from command."

"And what did it say?"

"Keep on top of the situation."

"Oh, THAT'S profound." Don replied dejectedly. Then he asked, "You get any sleep?"

"Crashed in a chair for a while. You design good furniture, extended the damned thing out, fell asleep pretty easily."

"Navy fought me on the lounging feature. I guess I was right. As usual." Don said with a big smirk running along his face.

They only had to wait another twenty minutes for Beverly to join them in the control room. This time she was in a proper uniform, with her Specter hat and pony tail. She was informed by Ralph of the things that had happened since her departure.

"And no sighting of the Volga?" She asked finally.

"None. It's clear she dove the second she got out of the La Perouse Strait into deeper water."

Beverly nodded and said, "It's clear she's hiding. Any word from the Seattle?"

"We initiated communications with them around four o'clock and they're aware of the situation, but they're in the same boat that we are. All we can do is sit and watch to see what's going on," replied Ralph, letting the tension show in his voice.

"Well, hopefully, it's nothing. It's not like we can do anything anyway. With no weapons, all we can do is run interference," said Beverly stoically. Then she turned around from the screen and had Bobby run probable coordinates of the Volga's estimated speed and range.

Finally, Beverly, with acceptance of the situation said, "Well, at least this gives us a good training voyage and a chance to test out our equipment. Right Don?"

"Yeah, that it does," acknowledged Don.

"Too bad about the weapons though. That would have been nice to run the situations also," Beverly said despondently.

"Yeah, too bad," responded Don weakly.

"Yeah, too bad," echoed Ralph, looking over at Don.

CHAPTER 11

Fleet Admiral Jack Hornacher and Rear Admiral Cartwright walked down the narrow halls in bowels of the Pentagon. Decked out in Navy blues with a multitude of ribbons and medals glittering from the lighting overhead, they marched steadfastly. They both carried their naval service hats under one arm while carrying briefcases in the other. Both were very distinguished looking, Admiral Hornacher with less hair, grey or otherwise than Cartwright, and slightly taller. In step and in unison, they turned a corner and headed down one last long corridor, to a meeting room. Their footsteps echoing off the spotless beige walls and the highly polished, brown speckled tile floor. Both knew this was a meeting of dire circumstances.

They were on the "M" level or Mezzanine level, one of the two basement levels of the Pentagon. They had come down in the "E" ring to find one of three such rooms built for nothing more than military strategy. Cartwright had asked for the room specifically.

They finally came to a stop as a diligent and dutiful Pentagon guard stood up from the desk. Wearing a two-toned grey uniform, he was part of the Pentagon Force Protection Agency. A retired Army Sargent, Joseph Pierce was a big man. He nodded and smiled at the two admirals.

"Could I see proper ID and if you would scan your cards, please?" the Sergeant asked, holding a wand that connected to a lap top computer sitting on a small table, on a small podium next to his desk.

Admiral Hornacher nodded, opened his brief case on the small desk and withdrew his military identification. As did Cartwright. The Sergeant nodded knowingly. Then the Admiral stood patiently as the Sergeant scanned the ID. As he did, he asked, "Everything set up with what I asked, Joe?""

"All stocked and turned on sir."

"Anyone here yet?"

"Yes sir, Army, Air Force, CIA And they don't look happy to be here sir."

Admiral Hornacher nodded then replied, "I had a four o'clock tee time myself. I understand completely."

"Hold on!" came a voice and a clattering of a woman's heels on the hard tile, as she too turned the corner of the hallway. Georgiana Wannaker was a stout woman of African heritage. Standing at five foot ten without her heels, she gave little to the men in her life, and there was a great deal. A form fitting slack suit of chocolate brown graced her body as she jogged down the hallway. She brushed the streaked grey and black hair out of the way.

"Don't let the President see you that way," admonished Admiral Hornacher, poking fun at the woman, as dignity had definitely left the woman.

"Oh, phooey on him. I'll sit on him and crush the little man." A large smile lined her face as she came on the two men, somewhat out of breath. She was allowed to talk about the President of the United States that way. She was one of the few that could and get away with it.

"I hate to disturb you on this beautiful Sunday, but I felt it was important," apologized the Admiral.

"At least I didn't miss my morning nap," Georgiana said while also taking out her credentials and brushing the hair from her face once again.

"Come again?"

Georgiana snorted then explained, "I go to church with the President, but the minister lets me sit in the back so I can take a quick snooze. I leave a hefty tip for this indiscretion." Again, a broad smile lit up her face. Admiral Hornacher loved the lady's smile. But he knew that behind it was a lethal mind of a very successful lawyer and hardened politician. She was also the Secretary of the State for the United States.

Both men smiled, then Admiral Cartwright waved a hand and said politely, "After you Madam Secretary."

As Georgiana walked past the men she said quietly, "This has something to do with the business with the UN, doesn't it?"

"Yes, George, it does," replied Admiral Hornacher. The business with the UN was less than nine hours old and George had heard already. There were times he could have sworn the woman was psychic.

"Well, let's get it out in the open then and we can deal with it by the light of day," she declared.

Opening the massive oak, double doors, Admiral Hornacher took rapid stock of the staff taking their seats. Even though he was part of the Chiefs of Staff, he had only been in the room four times in the past two years. Not once, had it been a pleasant experience.

The room itself was sixty feet long and thirty feet wide and buried underground in the Pentagon. It had fake windows on the walls, complete with glass and draperies. An all-wood decor, built in the sixties, it contained a massive, cherry stained twenty seat table in the center. On the left side was a sideboard with a fifty-cup pot of coffee, and already brewing was a pot of tea for the Secretary of State. That was where she headed immediately, after she had dropped off her briefcase on an empty spot on the table. There were also donuts, pastries, bagels and a toaster. At the end of the room were an old projector, an old overhead paper projector and a state-of-the-art tape and compressed disk machines, and of course a massive computer console. Large pendant lights hung every eight feet.

The men greeted each other. Five-star General Blanchett from the US Army was the Chairman of the Joint Chiefs of Staff. To his right sat his able assistant Colonel Rebecca Mayfield. General Tolliver represented the US Air Force with General Prescott decked out in his olive uniform of the Marines. The man that looked out of place was Kirk Billingham, in charge of the CIA. He wore a crumpled green suit, which did nothing for his spreading midriff. The goatee, peppered gray, was also out of place. Even the UN ambassador from the USA, Jonathon Peeper looked like he belonged, with a straight lace black suit and red tie. His round glasses gave him a bookish look.

Service hats and brief cases or portfolios were positioned either on the floor or in front of them on the large table. Admiral Hornacher and Admiral Cartwright took their position at the head of the table, where they could access the various screens. Besides, it was Admiral Hornacher's show. Admiral Cartwright had been there earlier that morning setting up the briefing. As the large double doors were closed, two Marine guards stood on the outside of the room.

After five minutes of pleasantries, making comfortable and quick feeding, Admiral Hornacher took his position at the head of the table, with General Blanchett immediately to his right and Cartwright to his left. The President and Vice President were missing, but they had a conversation with him less than an hour ago, and they were headed back to Washington, courtesy of Air Force One. The Secretary of the Navy was in fact in San Diego with his own problems as something had come up since the launch of the Specter. The Secretary of Defense was in-route but exactly where was any ones' guess.

"Good afternoon, we're missing a few people but I think we need to get started," Admiral Hornacher stated, taking several sheets of paper out of his brief case.

"Admiral Cartwright, not to put too fine a spin on it, is there a good reason why you are here?" asked General Tolliver.

"He's here at my request because he is privy to information that is important to this matter," answered Admiral Hornacher succinctly.

He knew where the General was going. These meetings were on a need-to-know basis.

Colonel Mayfield, quickly jumped in and asked, "Do you have a problem with me being here General?"

General Tolliver glanced over at General Blanchett and replied, "No. No problem."

The Colonel looked at General Blanchett and shook her head. It was going to be that kind of meeting she decided.

"This better be good." This came from Billingham. The man's brilliance was constantly overshadowed by his brusque manner. Blanchett shot the man a curious look.

"Actually, it's not good. That's why we're here. I've already conferred with some of you on various matters earlier and General Blanchett I think is up to speed on most of this," replied Hornacher. Cartwright started handing out a single sheet of paper to each person seated.

"What you have in front of you is a paper that was handed to the UN Secretary General Amini Bekela at one o'clock this afternoon." Several pairs of glasses were brought out to view the paper.

Georgiana was a speed reader and took her less than a few seconds to scan the paper. She asked, "Was the courier detained?"

"No. He killed himself, on the spot."

Her eyebrows went up as Billingham responded, "Paramedics couldn't revive the bastard. I would have liked to torture the guy first. Maybe learn a few things. Then kill him."

Georgiana reached across the table and touched Billingham's hand, telling the man, "And if you did that, you would be in jail. I would make sure." Kirk only smiled in return.

Hornacher glanced around then continued. "The paper says briefly that the People's Resistance of the Ukraine wants their Ex-President back. And their government. According to the threatening nature of the statement, they have the means to do massive destruction and demand a response of Kuznotzhov's release. The means by which will extend to another courier, to arrive precisely at seven o'clock PM Eastern time."

"Why is this just now coming to light?" asked General Prescott. A stout man of wide and muscular build with a typical marine buzz cut, the four-star General was smart and no nonsense. He was not a man who loved throwing the military into the mix without a good reason. His men generally died first.

"Unfortunately, the UN didn't take the threat seriously," replied Hornacher.

"The courier kills himself and they don't take it seriously?" observed Georgiana incredulously.

"Happens a lot in New York," explained Billingham quickly with a touch of wit.

The Admiral cut in and added, "As you can read there is to be another courier with more explicit instructions. We assume it's to tell us exactly what they want and what they can do."

"And why should we take it seriously?" asked General Tolliver. Tall and perfectly bald, of African American descent, he was a man who felt the Air Force was the backbone of any military exercise, and did not always share his experience or knowledge with the other men. He was one who crossed swords with the others quite often. He felt that was part of his charm.

Admiral Hornacher nodded to Admiral Cartwright who walked to the back of the room and dimmed the lights. A notebook computer sitting on the table in front of the Admiral, was pulled up and he tapped one button. A large twelve-foot screen crackled to life.

"We received this early this morning," injected Admiral Hornacher. It was the satellite image of Vladivostok, the very same the Specter had seen earlier, with ships secured to the docks. He watched the image for a few moments then, tapping another button.

He walked up to the large screen and tapped the massive submarine in the center and explained, "That ladies and Gentlemen, is the Russian Ballistic Missile Submarine Volga." Going back, he tapped the start button once more on high speed, coming to the point where the submarine disappears. The Admiral then added, "Then, almost twenty-four hours later, this happens." The assembly then viewed the rest of the Russian Navy scramble in a seeming search mode.

"Where did it go?" asked Prescott.

"Jonathon?" Hornacher referred to the U.N Ambassador.

"We contacted the UN Russian Ambassador. He says it's nothing more than an unscheduled exercise and we shouldn't worry," Jonathon responded adjusting his glasses. Then he added, "At least, that's his official statement." Pausing a second Jonathon added, "He was a little miffed that we had better videos of his precocious naval yards then they do. He really wanted to know where we got the videos."

"Surely we didn't tell him," stated Georgiana.

"Oh of course not," Jonathon glancing at her.

General Prescott jumped in and asked, "But we have knowledge to the contrary, otherwise we wouldn't be here. Don't we?"

"What I want to know is where did you get a bird's eye view like that?" asked Billingham, knowing full well where all of the US spy satellites were located and none had a picture like this. He was a little more than miffed.

Hornacher glanced at Billingham then turned to Prescott and said, "That will be explained shortly. And yes, we indeed think it's something more. The Volga, by our intelligence community, is supposed to be in dock, going over a massive retrofit. A new computer system, new electrical, a nuclear systems upgrade. Suppose to be in dock for two weeks then taken to a sub bunker for more upgrades. But as you can see by these images, none of this was done, and by closer examination, there's not much of a staff on board. And then there's the rest of the Russian Navy seeming to give chase. We used this information to access our other spy satellites and sure enough, we have over half the Russian Navy, changing course and heading for the North Pacific. Forty-two combat ships in all at this moment."

"Good Christ Jack! You think the Volga is in the hands of the Freedom Fighters?" blurted out Georgiana, as the rest of the room grew somber. Colonel Mayfield's mind was already racing, as she scribbled notes on her yellow pad of paper. She knew exactly where her friend Beverly Hornacher was at.

Finally, General Tolliver asked, "Does any of this have anything to do with the sinking of the Iceland Venture?"

"No. I've been in contact with the Coast Guard at Nome. It's an unfortunate event and not to be taken lightly, but it is a completely separate incident." Hornacher had talked to Dr. Pierson and there was no way he was going to pass on the idea of a prehistoric shark terrorizing shipping, no matter how traumatic it was. And at this point in time, there was bigger fish to fry.

"And the satellite feed?" asked Billingham again.

Hornacher sighed heavily. He motioned at Cartwright. "Admiral Cartwright has been on this project from the beginning. Better him to explain."

Cartwright walked up to the front of the table and said, "It's part of a new project that the US Navy has integrated called the Poseidon Project. The reason most of you don't know about it, it had been approved more than six years ago, by the previous administration."

"I had information on it but I don't remember any updates on its progress. I take it the ship itself has set sail?" asked Georgiana, rummaging through her brief case for the file on the sub. Somehow she knew it was pertinent.

Billingham looked at her then asked angrily, "And when were the rest of us going to find this out?"

Cartwright looked down quickly, chose his words then responded, "When a full test has been done. It's strictly a military operation, which didn't lend to yours, or the FBI, or the NIA, expertise, or knowledge Mr. Billingham. Only by chance did we get lucky to get these pictures." Cartwright then rethought some words and added, "This was strictly naval, with advanced approval, and extremely experimental. We wanted complete success before we tell anyone of the technology."

"The Navy has its own satellite?" observed Billingham growing more agitated at being left out of the loop.

Cartwright continued to explain. "The satellite is in fact in a part of a new Submarine, called the Specter. The sub design does not include a periscope. The satellite transcends that feature."

"Wait a minute. The Navy has a sub that doesn't have a periscope?" asked Billingham.

Georgiana jumped in and said, "Christ Billingham. What part of this aren't you getting?"

Rebecca smirked as Kirk shot her a sinister look. She then jotted down a line on her yellow pad and pointed at it for General Blanchett. He nodded in understanding.

The Admiral in turned sighed heavily, and responded, "It set sail earlier this week. It's being tested in exercise mode under real conditions."

"Vladivostok is on the Northern Sea board of Russia, if I remember my geography. I take it the Specter is somewhere near by?" asked General Prescott, wanting to get back to the problem at hand.

Cartwright nodded, and replied, "Yes General, that's affirmative. The Attack Submarine Cheyenne is on point closer to Russia."

The massive doors swung open as a large man entered the room. He stated apologetically, "I'm sorry I'm late. I was on the phone to San Diego and lost track of the time." He was a hundred pounds' overweight, but he carried himself well. White hair parted on the side, he could have easily played Santa Claus, or someone's grandfather, which he was. But he was a sharp man with a quick wit and a stickler for knowing the numbers. But he was always late which drove the President insane. Lucius Perry was the Secretary of the Defense.

"Lucius, if you don't mind," stated Hornacher, waving to a chair. He suddenly felt better, for up to that point he had felt that the room was divided. Lucius and he saw most things the same.

"Of course. Oh, Sec. Nav. sends his apologies. I'll keep him informed."

"Donut?" Asked Billingham trying to antagonize the man.

Lucius pulled his pants up and said with a smile, "Nope. Watching my weight."

Admiral Hornacher lost no time in bringing Lucius up to speed. The Specter he already knew about. Earlier that morning he had already conferred with Lucius about the UN incident.

"Do the Russians know if Rabinov is on board the Volga?" Lucius asked finally.

"Rabinov? Why is that name familiar?" asked General Prescott.

While Admiral Hornacher explained, Cartwright punched up the information and sent it to the screen. "Admiral Andryich Rabinov. He designed the Volga to be his pride and joy. General Prescott, you and I once met him at a state function in Berlin. A brilliant tactician, but very full of himself. He referred to the Russian Government as short sighted and petty."

Hornacher then turned to the screen and viewed the Russian Military vehicle entering the picture, and two men boarding the Volga. He turned back and continued, "This is a picture of whom we think is Rabinov. The car was his and the stature is the same, but without actually seeing the face, we can only assume. But as far as Rabinov actually being in command, I honestly don't know."

"According to the Russian consulate, Rabinov is always in command of the Volga. It would not leave port without him," inserted Jonathon, adjusting his glasses.

"So, this is all conjecture based off an experimental submarine. It's merely an exercise," observed General Tolliver, thinking it was all a show by the Admiral to expound his new war toy.

General Blanchett ignored Tolliver and inserted, "Rabinov's a lot of things Jack, but he's no traitor. If he's on board there's something else going on, but nothing to do with these Ukrainian freedom fighters. He'd sooner cut off his arm then deal with them. Could it be he's after somebody?"

"That thought had occurred to us, but satellite reconnaissance doesn't show us anything. At least not until the very moment the Volga departs," countered Hornacher.

"Besides the fact that Kuznotzhov is dead. In the bloody battle with Russia, he died while in office. Everyone knows that," stated General Tolliver with certainty, growing weary with the meeting, starting to drum his fingers on the table top.

Georgiana looked down into her brief case and brought out another file, opening it up and glancing at the information.

Billingham smiled knowingly at Tolliver, then said, "Finally. I know something you don't."

"Oh, don't tell me he's alive?" asked Tolliver incredulously.

"In a maximum security on Coats Island. An agreement brought about by our Secretary of State here." Billingham turned in her direction with a devilish grin. She in turned glanced up from her file, smiled warmly, then looked back down.

"Coats Island? Where in the hell is that?" Asked Blanchett.

"After Gitmo was closed the UN still needed a place for world terrorists, and the upper part of the Hudson Bay looked as good as any place. The Canadians get a hefty contract fee for the place. Anyway, the UN stepped in and took control of the situation, and had a very quick, very secret trial of Kuznotzhov, after his terrorist take over of the democratic government. In an agreement that the President made, Kuznotzhov's name was changed and he was sent to Coats, to spend the rest of his days," explained Billingham, having updated this information on a monthly basis at the CIA. Then Kirk looked at the Admiral and asked, "That's why I'm here, isn't it?"

"I wasn't even aware of this." Stated Jonathon sitting up in his chair and looking around at the rest of the group, adjusting his glasses.

"If you weren't aware, then how in the hell did this Ukrainian Resistance find out?" asked Lucius.

"Somebody from the inside. Obviously." Said Billingham as if it were an everyday event.

"And if they can pull off something like that, then I believe in taking the Volga seriously," said Hornacher earnestly.

They all stopped to think for a moment. Then General Blanchett cut in, "If I remember correctly, a Russian Ballistic Submarine has a range of around seven thousand miles by missile, and twenty missiles with multiple warheads at her disposal. But even Rabinov can't shoot a warhead at us or anyone else, without the Russian armament code."

"Seventy-five-hundred miles and the Volga, actually has twenty-four missiles with multiple war heads. It is the biggest submarine in the world General," Hornacher replied succinctly. Then he thought of the coding and added, "That should be correct about the codes. But you have to wonder."

Georgiana nodded then said, "If, for some Ungodly reason, the Volga is in the hands of the freedoms fighters, with the Specter and the Cheyenne and the Russian Navy bringing up the rear, once we get conformation that it is in fact a danger, we should be able to out shoot the Volga before she ever fires anything, shouldn't we?" Then she smiled at Kirk and added, "Or am I being a simple politician in this regard?"

Hornacher again sighed then said, "First of all, it's not that simple to find a submarine, being the pure reasoning of the ship. It's underwater, and not wanting to be found. No American ship has managed to tag it and it does not appear that the Russians have any idea of its location as they are all over the Pacific searching. Secondly, we still have no real idea if it is in fact part of the resistance. It looks like it, it makes sense but no proof. And yes. All things being equal, yes, that kind of fire power can most certainly out shoot the Volga. But it's not that simple. George, you're thinking the Specter is a conventional submarine."

Billingham glanced around at the group with a frown on his face then he narrowed his gazed at Cartwright and asked, "What kind of Sub is it? A bath tub toy? Powered by baking soda and vinegar?"

Cartwright felt the verbal slap, but stared right back at the man. Then he explained. "It's a new type, we've designated as a Stealth Sub. Everything on this submarine is experimental. Technology we can share and use in other areas."

"That explains the spooky name I guess," mentioned Kirk.

"But the damned thing does have torpedoes, doesn't it?" asked General Tolliver.

Admiral Hornacher cut in and replied, "Normally yes, it does have weapons. But its design is to get into places other submarines can't. And on its first experimental voyage ..."

Cartwright cut back in suddenly, "What the Admiral is trying to say is that the Sub is only two hundred feet long and has a crew of only nineteen members. This is not a sub designed to send against a behemoth like the Volga. Besides, we allowed the civilian engineer responsible for the design and function of the Specter to stay on board during its maiden voyage."

General Tolliver rocked back in his chair and shook his head in disdain. Then he uttered, "Oh God. Leave it up to the Navy to make something unusable and put a civilian in harm's way."

Lucius barged in with both barrels aim at the Air Force General. "Excuse me? I don't see the Air Force coming up with pictures of a potential raid from Vladivostok. Your reconnaissance pictures don't show us shit." He turned quickly to Georgiana, smiled and said, "Pardon my French."

"I would have given it to him in both French and German," she said without batting an eyelash. She turned to Hornacher and asked, "Jack, you said normally yes, when it came to the weapons. What did you mean?" Georgiana was letting Tolliver stew without response.

"You don't miss a trick, do you George?" Hornacher took a deep breath then started in. "Normally, the Specter is as equipped in warfare as any other submarine, but the Naval Bureau of Weapons had thought it more prudent ..." The Admiral felt a hard pull at his elbow, as Cartwright pulled himself close to him. Cartwright whispered quickly. Hornacher turned to look at the man, then whispered back. Cartwright softly nodded.

Hornacher thought for a moment, then said, "As I said, the Specter is equipped as any submarine, but the weapons system is completely state of the art and untried. It is not the type of thing we want to experiment with. Especially in combat mode."

Lucius nodded slowly, as if reality had dawned on him, but he said nothing.

Colonel Mayfield suddenly felt a tightening in her throat, and her stomach churned. Was the Admiral saying what she thought he was saying? She had a chance to visit Beverly one night, a few months previously, before she set sail on the Nautilus Two. Rebecca had been filled in on Beverly's potential promotion and some details of the new sub. She had been told the entire voyage was experimental. So experimental, they were not allowing any weapons. Or so she thought.

General Prescott, however stumbled in and asked, "But the crew is experienced, isn't it? I mean, they got us the pictures of Vladivostok, it must be a seasoned crew. Who's the Captain? Is he a capable one?"

Cartwright answered before Hornacher could and he replied, "General, there's no such thing as a bad Captain, whether it is the Navy or Marines. And it's a crew that's been picked from the best of the best. But it's a crew that is learning a whole new machine. This submarine can do things others can't and the crew, no matter how seasoned, is still finding its feet. The lack of a periscope being just one thing. That's why we have the engineer on board."

"Admiral Cartwright is being diplomatic," came quickly from Hornacher.

Colonel Mayfield quickly slid over and whispered into Blanchett's ear as the man

suddenly sat straight up and looked across at Hornacher. He whispered something back, then Rebecca whispered something back him. He nodded his head.

"I don't understand?" asked General Tolliver, aware of all the whispering. Lucius Perry cringed noticeably. General Blanchett surveyed Admiral Hornacher closely

Admiral Hornacher finally took the plunge and said, "The Captain is Beverly. Um, Captain Hornacher as it was."

"Oh God," said Billingham with distaste.

Georgiana glared at the man from across the table then stated angrily, "And there's a problem with that, spy boy?"

Billingham suddenly realized he had crossed the line. He was getting no support from anyone else in this matter as he could see General Blanchett actually grin. "Georgiana calm down. I didn't mean it THAT way," he explained finally.

Georgiana was leaning across the table to try and get as close as possible. "And how else am I to interpret it? If you did what you're supposed to do, we wouldn't be in this position, to relay on a WOMAN to sit out in the middle of the ocean to save our ass."

Admiral Hornacher may not have been on a life-long friendship with Kirk, but he had been to the man's house and shared a bar-b-que. He knew better and jumped in. "George, that's not fair. Kirk has three daughters himself. I think I understand the sentiment."

Billingham softened a little and said to Madam Secretary, "Georgiana, I didn't mean anything by it. It was just a gut reaction. One of a father."

Georgiana Wannaker looked over at Hornacher, then her features sagged as she thought of Beverly. She of course knew Beverly as did most of the men in the room. There was not a father or mother among them that did not share the Admiral's trepidation. Georgiana finally calmed down, but continued to glare at Billingham.

Colonel Mayfield finally inserted, "If I remember your engineer, Mr. Merrick correctly, even though he is a civilian, he would in fact be an asset in this case with the Specter." She looked up at Cartwright and asked, "Am I correct in assuming this?"

"Yes Ma'am. That's why he's on board. As the chief architect and engineer in this project, he has more interior functional knowledge than any other person alive. He is the key troubleshooter on board," inserted Admiral Cartwright hopefully.

Hornacher gathered his thoughts then said finally, "My concerns for my daughter not with-standing, we still have bigger problems."

"Kirk, what do we know about the Ukrainian Resistance?" asked Lucius.

Billingham sighed for a second, then replied, "When Kuznotzhov was forcibly removed from power by the Russian military, they put in their own puppet government, which all of you know. The resistance sprang up immediately, with Vlad Yashangov gaining quick control. Flamboyant, he's in fact a great organizer, capable of crippling the new Russian government, given enough time and money."

"The Kiev Air Port," mentioned Georgiana, already putting her anger behind her.

"Exactly. As you may remember, no one was ever caught and laid to blame for that massacre, even though the Resistance and Yashangov took full responsibility."

Lucius pondered the Air Port incident. It was the second most deadly terrorist attack, behind the 9/11 fatalities. Almost half of the new Ukrainian congress, all put into power by Russia, were headed home for spring vacation. They never made it as airplane upon airplane started blowing up on the tarmac. Over a thousand dead and forty-two members of the congress. Since then, it had been hard for the Ukrainian congress to even staff itself, everyone afraid of being the next target.

"That we know Kirk. Is there anything we don't?" asked Georgiana.

Billingham pulled his brief case closer, opened it and pulled out a sheaf of papers. Finally, he said," We have current information that states, he has been seen romancing the new dictatorship in Libya. And trust me, it's not about grain."

Georgiana blanched for a second then said, "Wait a minute. I'm set to go to Libya next week to open talks. And one of the things on the agenda is the installation of an American owned Solar power plant, which Libya so desperately wants"

Lucius asked quickly, "Does the President know this?"

"I'm supposed to have a meeting with him this afternoon," Billingham disposed.

"What else?" asked Lucius. He may not have liked Billingham very much, but the man was a good weasel.

"The Moscow train derailment."

"That was determined to be purely accidental," stated Georgiana.

"Yeah. Sure. The Russian authorities. By pure happenstance, the Russian Premier's wife, daughter and her future husband were supposed to be on that train. They never made their connections and missed it by minutes. They held tickets to the very first car that went off the tracks. Accident? Not hardly."

The group as a whole nodded. Finally, Lucius asked, "And what about Yashangov? Anything new on him?"

"He's a busy man. But I'm sorry, I wish I had concrete evidence. The only thing we have is people in the underground that are only telling me that Yashangov is planning something big and very secret. His network has gained spider web proportions. To the point that we think he has high-ranking plants in several other countries. Including ours."

"Could the Volga be it?" asked Hornacher finally.

"The time line doesn't fit by my sources, but if you're talking conjecture, yes, this might be something Yashangov could pull off," Billingham answered honestly.

Colonel Mayfield glared down at her hands. The joy she had felt when Beverly had told her of her promotion and the possibilities of the new sub were turning horribly wrong.

Georgiana looked over at Billingham dumbfounded and observed, "Even if Rabinov is behind the wheel of that sub, wouldn't the Russian Military like, stop him before he ever left port? Wouldn't his second in command question his actions? I mean, am I stupid in this, or shouldn't it be harder than that to just waltz in and drive away a big nuclear submarine?"

Billingham thought for a moment, then returned, "Madam Secretary, every nuclear and military system has a certain number of checks and rechecks. The Russians haven't updated theirs since the nineteen-nineties. A few months ago, one of our operatives, who works in a little hole in this building hacked into the Russian Military Computer system. When he did, he alerted our staff. With a push of a send button, he could have scrambled their Air Force situated in Moscow, for some unknown alert that he made up. Now, I know that doesn't sound like much, the situation could have been brought to a halt before one single MIG left the ground. But the point is, if our guys can do it, imagine someone working from the inside."

"Kirk, what you're telling me is then that you believe the Volga is a threat?" asked Hornacher.

Billingham sighed noticeably then responded, "I don't know how, or even if Rabinov is on board, but looking over the satellite imagery of the departure and what you said, that skeleton crew might be a handful of well-trained resistance fighters. Yashangov is a brilliant tactician. Yeah, I think, in retrospective, that the threat with the Volga is real."

Georgiana jumped in and said to Jonathon, "We need to contact the Russian consulate." And while she was saying that General Tolliver was saying to Prescott, "I want better consultation on projects even though preapproval," as Prescott was saying back, "I don't think that's our responsibility to question every …" Just as Lucius was inserting, "Kirk, we need to set up a better counter intelligence or we're going to fall behind."

After a few moments, Admiral Hornacher trying to make a point glanced over at General Blanchett. He had rose, fetched himself a cup of coffee then came back to the table and tapped Lucius and Rebecca. They both rose and the three people walked to the end of the room. They conferred briefly for several moments, the conversation being very animated. It seemed Rebecca was doing most of the talking. Finally, they came back.

Hornacher waved his hand excitedly and finally managed to quiet everyone down. Then he turned to the General and asked, simply, "You've made a decision sir?"

General Blanchett looked over at Secretary of Defense Perry. The man looked outwardly somber as he responded, "Lucius and

I agree on this. Jonathon, you need to contact the UN, very quietly mind you, and tell them we believe the Volga means business in this regard. We need to know the truth. Billingham, contact the Coats prison, get Kuznotzhov moved quickly and quietly, and no reasons why. Understand? Then I want maximum security at the UN and I don't care whose toes you step on. You need to snag the next courier. Alive. Got it?"

"Got it," Billingham replied already pulling out his cell phone and a directory of important numbers from his brief case.

Lucius then charged in and said, "Georgiana, contact the Russian Premier. Shake some booty make some bedroom promises, I don't care, I want answers to what the hell is going on. This is no exercise and be damned if the United States Military is going to sit and watch. And find out what kind of protocol for nuclear deployment they have on that damned sub."

"Right," answered Georgiana decisively, pulling all her files back together.

As if on cue Blanchett inserted, "And the US Military, just went to Def. Con Three. I want planes in the air and all military leave canceled. Treat this as if we are under nuclear threat, and damned seriously. Got it?" He stated glaring at General Tolliver who looked back up and nodded succinctly.

"Yes sir," he got as a response from General Prescott.

General Blanchett then looked up at Hornacher and he said, "You and I have the most important business to attend to. The US Navy is now under alert and hunting the Volga. Until I am convinced otherwise, I'm treating this as a war maneuver. Lucius and I are going to contact the National, and Homeland Security Advisors and the President and bring them up to speed. Then I will meet you downstairs."

"What if the President doesn't really like this battle plan?" Asked the Admiral. It was well known; the current President was somewhat of a Dove. He had in fact sought to shut down the Poseidon Project.

Until he had a two-hour conversation with Don Merrick. And Tinkerbell.

Lucius cut in and responded, "He's not a fool. There is something going on out there and he has to acknowledge we need to be ready. And if he doesn't, well … we'll have Georgiana sit on him." Then he smiled broadly.

Fleet Admiral Hornacher smiled back then started gathering up his papers and stuffing them in his brief case. "I'll be there in a few minutes. I have a phone call to make from my secure line."

"Give the Misses my best, Okay? And tell her not to worry," Lucius said with a twinkle in his eye.

Colonel Mayfield cut in and added, "Beverly's smart Admiral. She'll know what to do."

Hornacher grinned sideways and replied, "Mom is still not going to be happy."

Georgianna had a sudden thought then asked Jonathon, "You said you talked to the Russian Consulate. What about the Chinese? Has anyone been in contact with them? They're not going to like it any more than we are that the Volga might have gone rogue, and that the Russian Navy is buzzing the Pacific."

He responded quickly, "We've contracted the UN Consulates but he knows nothing. However, our intelligence community has stated that there is a lot more activity at the North Sea Fleet Headquarters. My guess they are indeed very nervous."

Georgianna gathered up her papers and replied simply "Great. Everyone's nervous."

The assemblage of men and the ladies all stood up and started walking out of the room. Everyone was talking or thinking about their positions and what they needed to do. Just as they reached the massive oak doors, it opened to reveal a Navy Lieutenant. He saluted, obviously nervous with all the brass and waited patiently for Admiral Hornacher.

The Lieutenant handed the Admiral a single note and said, "For you sir. It just came in from upstairs and they said it was very urgent,"

Hornacher scanned the message quickly just as Lucius pulled him aside. Lucius said softly, "Look it, Jack. General Blanchett and I can get Beverly out of there. I'll take the responsibility of pulling the plug on the Specter by calling her home. I'll make up a story about a malfunction on our experimental sub, or something. The Cheyenne and the rest of the Navy can take care of the Volga."

Hornacher folded the note back up and handed it to Lucius and said simply, "You can't. Not now."

Lucius opened the slip of paper and read quickly, TO COMMANDER OF US FLEET FROM USS SPECTER. HAVE LOST CONTACT WITH THE SEATTLE. FEAR THE WORST. PLEASE ADVISE, CAPTAIN HORNACHER.

"Oh Christ," mumbled Lucius under his breath.

Admiral Hornacher shook his head dejectedly. "It's started. And the Specter stays."

CHAPTER 12

On board the Specter, things were not as chaotic. Don, Ralph, and Beverly were watching a satellite transmission of the last known location of the USS Seattle. Satellite imagery had recorded the instant the sub, or something very big in that location had blown up. A plum of water more than two hundred feet in the air, and a massive disturbance of the water surface over a mile wide was a good indication something had gone tragically wrong.

Present imagery was sweeping the area and about four nautical miles from the spot the Seattle should have been, they located floating debris. The first item had been a seaman's wooden lock box. A life jacket, torn and ripped floating unmanned in the midst of a spreading oil slick. A debris field scattered over a mile wide. Using the infrared signal on the satellite, the boat still showed the last heated remains of its explosion.

They stood stunned, none believing what they were seeing as a complete destruction. Ralph finally turned around and said solemnly to Williams, "Willy, let's do a hundred-mile scan of the area. I want to rule out a surface vessel."

"Yes sir," responded Willy, realizing something was out there hunting down American submarines. And he was on the smallest one in the US Navy, with the biggest weapon on board being a hand gun.

Ralph only shook his head and said finally, "It has to be the Volga."

"Captain?" Duran got Beverly's attention. She moved over to the mapping board and looked at the projections that Lt. Duran had drawn up. He pointed out, "If the Volga continued her known speed, based on her departure, and the Seattle had maintained her speed and direction." He stopped and pointed to the black circle on the big lighted board.

"Damn. They very well could have intersected."

"Yes Ma'am. The Seattle, because of all the emergencies situations had abandoned her post and could have conceivably run straight into the Volga."

"And the Russian Navy has a good idea as to our sub coordinates. But they couldn't have guessed as to the exact location of the Seattle. Damn," mentioned Beverly.

Don turned to Ralph and asked, "Why wouldn't the Seattle have notified us of contact?"

Ralph responded, "You know as well as I do, we're running a peacetime navy. The Volga, most probably, is not. As Beverly had stated before with the Volga, Russian Captains like to play chess games. The skipper of the Seattle probably thought the same. Probably thought he was going to sneak in on Volga's baffles and play tag. Until the Volga opened fire. Probably full bore."

Beverly shook her head then said in understanding, "First contact, and the Volga just started shooting. The Seattle probably saw it coming but had little recourse and was not in any kind of mode to respond. But you have to wonder, even Rabinov knows that would be suicide in the end. With half the Russian Navy after him, and now the US Navy, he won't get very far."

Ralph glanced over at Beverly and stated, "Yeah, but you have to understand what the Volga is doing. It can't afford to have a shadow and that's what the Seattle would have done. So, the US Navy is looking for him? So what? Until accidental contact is made, it's pretty safe."

Don pulled up beside Beverly and asked, "What's the range on a Russian sub missile?"

She thought for the briefest moments then replied, "About seven thousand to seventy-five hundred. Why?"

"Maybe that's all the further he wants to get."

Beverly's eyes again stared at the huge image of the few and scattered remains of the Seattle. Ultimately, she stated, "This makes no sense. Rabinov would not do this. Something has gone terribly wrong with the Russian Navy." Then she turned to the communications officer Barrington and said, "Open up communications with Pacific Naval Command. Send them this image and tell them we believe this is the Seattle. Then tell them, we think the Volga is responsible."

"Yes Ma'am," Steve responded, also taking no heart in being on the small submarine.

Don then observed, "If it is the Volga, she's gone deep because we can't pick up any heat traces underwater within a hundred miles of that location."

Ralph then speculated, "What I'm afraid of is not only the Volga, but the rest of the Russian Navy. They're less than a day and a half behind. Then there's the Pacific Fleet coming up from Pearl. The Cheyenne and the Sandshark are already changing course from the Barents Sea. We start running into a head long fleet trying to hunt a renegade Russian sub, we just might be in the way."

"A twitchy trigger finger," mentioned Don raising his eyebrows.

Ralph stroked his mustache then lamented, "Exactly. Especially when they find out about the Seattle. They are going to shoot first, then ask questions later."

Don then smiled and mentioned, "Well, then it's fortunate we don't sound like a regular submarine. We can't out shoot them, then we'll baffle them."

Beverly, her arms still crossed in dejection piped in and said, "This is all for naught anyway. All we can do is try to find the Volga, then get the hell out of the way and let the big boys duke it out."

Don glanced at Ralph. Ralph frowned noticeably.

Lt. Eddy Faulk flinched nervously in his chair. He did not like where this was going.

"Ma'am? We have a coded, incoming audio message from Naval Command, direct from the Pentagon?" announced Steve.

Beverly glanced around at her crew and asked, "Ask them if it's okay if we put it on control speaker."

"Yes Ma'am." Steve talked for a second, then pressed a button on his touch screen for internal control room communications. He turned to Beverly and said, "Admiral Hornacher on the Com. Ma'am."

"Admiral. I take it you see what we see," Beverly said completely at ease with her father being in charge.

Admiral Hornacher had made his way to the Pentagon communications center, to gather his wits and more importantly, talk to his daughter. "Yes Captain. Let me bring you up to speed. We think that the Volga has been taken over by a Ukrainian group. The purpose of which is speculation, but we think it has to do with the ex-president of the Ukraine. The Ukrainian Resistance wants to set him free and install their own free government, and we feel they are going to use the Volga to do it, but as of yet, we're not sure how."

"Mr. Merrick made mention of simply using the nukes as a threat to keep the navies out of the way until it's all done," mentioned Beverly gravely.

There was a slight pause, the Admiral asked, "Can I ask Mr. Merrick a question?"

"Yes, sure. Go ahead," replied Don a little baffled.

"Mr. Merrick. How conceivable is it that a renegade crew could shoot off an ICBM?"

Don replied instantly, "I really don't know what the Russian system is Admiral, but if all the crewmen are on the same page, and all the computer systems are still intact, before they left port, there's a good chance, that's exactly why they have the sub. And if not, given an old system, all codes can be broken given enough time. The Specter itself is capable of running a billion computations a second, using Fibonacci randomizer code finder software. Which we have installed. Even a thirty-four And gate code, it wouldn't take too long. If they are black-box capable, then a small homing transmitter would be very capable of sending the right signal to engage. And conferring with Tinkerbell, our AI program, she has confirmed that they do not need Russian assistance to fire an ICBM."

There was an audible sigh on the other end of the connection. "That's what I was afraid of. Thank you, Mr. Merrick. Anyhow, the US Navy is at Def. Con three and we are actively searching the Volga. We have not yet received any reasoning from the Russian government, and in view of the Seattle, we're not waiting."

Beverly responded, "Yes Sir. What is the Specter's mission in all of this sir?"

There was a long pause. Everyone in the control room of the Specter held their breath. Finally, Admiral Hornacher responded, "Unfortunately Captain, you are in the best position to target the Volga. I realize this is not fair considering the status of the Specter but ..."

Beverly cut him off suddenly, confusion racing through her. "Excuse me sir. You ARE aware of our status? Our entire mission is one of exercise and experimentation. We are unarmed."

Don shook his head as Ralph looked over at him. Eddy flinched noticeably.

Again, the air was full of tension as they waited for a response. Suddenly, "Captain, I'm fully aware of your status and from what Admiral Cartwright tells me you are expected to get a full briefing from Commander Wolfson and Mr. Merrick. Captain, as in all of the US Navy at the moment and until further notice, your mission is to detain the Volga in any way possible."

Beverly responded quickly, "Yes sir. As you know sir on that type of commands, we need encrypted written verification."

"Yes Captain, we're assembling a detailed strategy to the North Pacific fleet with yours attached. Commence with intercept as the orders should take a half hour to assemble."

"Anything else Admiral?" Beverly asked stoically, holding in her emotion.

"Yes. We have absolutely no idea what the Chinese may do, in what capacity they are viewing this situation. They are refusing to collaborate anything with the United States Military at this moment. But they have to be as fearful of a Rogue Russian Submarine as we are. And of course, there is the Russian Navy. Not all are giving chase as there is a Russian fleet just a few hundred miles from Pearl, that we believe maybe be simply looking to cut off the Volga. They don't even know who the Volga's target maybe and no one in the Russian military is giving us any indication of what the exact situation is. So be mindful." There was a short pause when a soulful voice came over the speaker and added, "And. Be careful Captain."

"Captain Hornacher out sir." She wheeled around with ferocity in her features and glared at Ralph. Then said, "Mr. Caldwell, you have the conn. Commander. Mr. Merrick. Follow me."

They both watched the woman tromp out of the control room. "Time to go to the principal's office," said Don stepping up behind Ralph. Wolfson frowned appreciatively, then glanced at Eddy, who was shaking his head. They both knew this was not going to be good.

They followed her into the galley where she went to the end of the table and wheeled around. Don stopped and fetched himself a cup of coffee. He felt oddly sublime. Ralph sat down at the edge of the bench and studied his hands.

Finally, Beverly jumped in angrily, "I guess I need a briefing from you two. There's something which I don't know about our little submarine, concerning our weapons systems. Anyone care to elaborate?"

Don strolled up to the table, pulled his leg up on a chair, sipped his coffee then said casually, "Contrary to popular opinion, we're packing."

"Oh, Jesus Christ Don, even I gathered that much!" Beverly said as she slammed a fist down on the rigid plastic table. Ralph flinched noticeably at the sound.

"It's not Don's fault Beverly," finally offered Ralph.

Beverly glared down at Ralph. She yelled back at him, "Why? That's all I want to know. Why didn't anyone feel the need to inform the captain? The last time I checked I was supposed to be in charge of this vessel!"

Don sipped at his coffee again then responded, "It was actually Cartwright's decision. Your dad, or, some stupid idiot higher up was the one that didn't want us to be armed. Too experimental he kept saying. Take it out for a little test spin he kept saying."

"Don, why in the hell are you so smug?" Beverly yelled at him.

Don smiled and returned simply, "Not my fault this time. The decision was made by Ralph and Cartwright. It was one of those Naval things you like to tell me."

Beverly looked at the man. His calm demeanor only made her the more confused and angrier. Getting no pleasure out of dealing with Don, she turned back to Ralph and asked, "But why?"

Ralph sighed heavily then started in. "Cartwright and I felt uneasy about sending the sub out unarmed. The Pentagon, including your father determined the sub to be too experimental to allow it to be armed. Especially with all the weapons being experimental and completely untried. But both the Admiral and I thought, that: well, no Naval combat vessel had ever set sail without being fully functional. Don agreed to have a proper systems check we needed to be armed. And we did not want this ship to be any different. With all the delays, Don progressed with the weapons and managed to get them done in time."

Beverly hung her head and rubbed her face with her hands. Finally, she looked up and said, "That's not what I meant Ralph. Why did not anyone bother to fill me in? I mean, is it that I'm incompetent to command a ship with real bullets? Or is it that as a woman I'm too soft to want to shoot someone? Or is it the fact I'm the Admiral's daughter? I mean, what is it? Why am I the last to know?"

Ralph was shaking his head and said quickly and apologetically, "Oh God no Beverly! It … it was that we broke a direct command from the Pentagon. From your dad. It wasn't something we wanted to spread around. We just thought, in case, we wanted to be ready."

"And now this happens! And I look like a fool arguing with my dad," she stopped, shook her head, and said instead, "Admiral Hornacher. Who else knows?"

Ralph merely twirled his finger around in the air, meaning the three of them, then he said, "And Lieutenant Faulk of course so that he has the proper skills and didn't accidently shoot something off going through the drills. And now, probably the crew knows or has at least guessed."

Beverly was running out of steam. Ralph's explanations did not really make her feel any better. It was like they were all letting her play at being the captain, but they were really running the ship around her. She wanted desperately to cry, lash out or at least kick something. Cartwright had not told the crew of her command and now he held another secret over her head. What did she have to do? Arm wrestle all the men? Kill someone to gain their respect? Every step of her life she was being questioned. She knew she was not the old man and there was no way to step into his shoes. But could not they accept her for her capabilities, let her prove herself? And now this. And now Ralph.

Beverly gathered her thoughts. She touched the microphone on her ear piece and said into it solemnly, "Mr. Caldwell, come to the galley please."

Don looked at Beverly totally confused. He could not figure out what she was doing. Surely, she was not going to try and lock them up, would she? He thought.

It took a few moments for Crash to show up, but when he did, he could feel the immense awkward silence. He asked, "Captain? You called?"

"Beverly, you don't have to do this," stated Ralph. Don glanced at him, still completely clueless. It was another one of those naval things he surmised, gazing into the features of Ralph.

"Mr. Caldwell, as next in command, I want you to witness this," instructed Beverly somberly.

Crash was just as confused as Don. He glanced around then said, "Yes Ma'am?"

"Mr. Caldwell, as third in command, I'm transferring Command of the USS Specter to Commander Wolfson."

"Oh, good Christ Beverly," said Ralph rubbing his forehead aggressively.

Don furrowed his brows and almost dropped his cup. He looked at Beverly cocking his head and asked, "But why? Ralph told you he didn't want to get into trouble. It had nothing to do with you."

Beverly glared at Don then replied, "Mr. Merrick, I'm incompetent to run this ship."

"Ung? Say again?"

Ralph stood up, looked down at her and said, "Oh, of course you're competent Beverly."

Crash looked completely uneasy as he stood there, for what reason he was still unsure of.

"Commander." Beverly flung herself in Ralph's face, started poking herself in the upper chest and growled, "I know nothing of the weapons systems on this boat. Stupid me, someone told me there were no weapons and I never bothered to study them. I have not so much as opened the manuals, as thick as they are on what the weapons might be on this submarine."

Don looked relieved and said, "Oh, is that all. Well, heck, you're a quick learner, we can teach you that."

She turned and launched herself verbally at him. "Mr. Merrick, this boat is supposed to go to combat mode with a Captain that doesn't even know how many torpedoes we have on board." She started clicking off items on her fingers as she walked toward him backing him into a corner and said, "I know nothing about launch sequences, I know nothing about seeking capabilities, I know nothing about range, I know nothing about any kind of deterrence that we may have." She stopped her tirade then said simply, "I know nothing and I'm not going to jeopardize the lives of the crewmen on board this ship with my lack of knowledge!"

The dead silence was cut by the tiniest of voices. "I will help you Captain Hornacher."

"See, even Tinkerbell will help, no problems." Added Don. Beverly only glared at him.

"Yes, you are. Because I will refuse command." Stated Ralph decisively, crossing his arms across his chest in defiance. Don had never seen that look before and felt slightly odd.

Then Don looked at Beverly square in the eye, his heart aching a little at her upturned face and determined chin. He decided she was sort of cute when she was mad. Finally, he too attempted to explain. "Look it, Beverly. This was never about you. This decision was made before you were ever on board."

Beverly stood there, almost quivering. Then she said softly, "Yeah, but I am on board and you still decided not to tell me Don. At any time, you two could have let me know, and you know what? I would have kept it secret. But no. I know nothing."

Don finally blew. The coffee cup went sailing at the floor. The dregs off the bottom slashing against the wall and the bottom of her slacks. Her eyes bugged out of her head as Ralph grimaced noticeably. Crash backed up, resisting the urge to run from the room.

Don's anger boiled up suddenly as he yelled, "Oh, screw you, Beverly. You know you're really getting on my nerves at the moment because you're beginning to sound like a whipped little puppy. Oh, woes me. Poor little girl, no one takes me seriously. I can't fill my daddies' shoes so everyone is picking on me" Don let his tirade settle in then yelled, "We didn't know what you would do Beverly! Do you fucking understand?"

Before Beverly had a chance to reply Don walked up to her, aware that he was a bare two inches shorter, poked her hard on the upper chest on her T-shirt, hard enough for her to take a step backward, and launched at her, "It's called deniability Beverly. Think of someone but yourself for once. Someone in the Pentagon finds out we broke orders;

I get my hand slapped which is an everyday occurrence. But Ralph and Cartwright get brought up on charges for disobeying orders. Especially if something goes wrong. And what about the crew, unh? They were protecting you, Beverly. Do you understand? And in this case, we're going out to sea to find out how this ship runs. Some idiot in the Navy decided; not me, not the builders, but some desk jockey decides that we don't need weapons because of the nature of this sub. And guess what? He was dead, God-damned wrong! Especially now. We're staring down the asshole of the Russian Navy and all you can do is whine!"

Beverly stood there stunned. She had not been brought up short like that in several years. Her emotions all bubbled forth. Anger, frustration and tears all ran together as she attempted to keep herself controlled. Don had turned around, his right-hand quivering as if he was going to strike. He walked back to the coffee machine and got himself another cup. To calm himself.

"Beverly?" asked Ralph softly.

"What?" she responded even softer.

"You refuse command now that goes on your record. Nobody wants that. I was willing to take the heat for disobeying an order. We didn't want to drag you, or, whoever was the captain on this vessel, with that decision. All the weapons were loaded except the Bird of Prey, before you even came aboard Captain. That's all. Plain and simple."

She allowed it all to sink in. The logic. The realization, that Don and Ralph were simply covering for her. She had come on board late. Don had the weaponry ready to go months in advance. Ralph and Cartwright had already made that decision, in spite of possible retribution and charges. And she had to agree, she would have done the same thing. They had made the right decision.

Beverly needed to confront her doubts. She gathered up her thoughts and observed finally, "My Father, in all his wisdom, might have known I was coming on board, in one capacity or another. So, he might have wanted the sub to find its feet first, before being armed for battle, especially with everything being extremely experimental. Before his daughter shoots herself. You guys put your asses on the line and the less that knew the better." She turned to look at Don and added, "I just wish I had found out in a different way. I just wished you had trusted me. To tell me. I would have confirmed with Cartwright about the weapons and let him decide the future of the mission. And now this happens." She screwed up her mouth then said slowly, "That's all."

Don stared down into his muddy coffee. He was out of words. He could only mumble, "We didn't know what you would do Bev. And we damned sure didn't know this shit was going to happen. We never meant, for you, I mean. To get in trouble."

"Captain, if I may?" This came from Crash, who was starting to figure everything out.

Beverly nodded slowly and said, "Go ahead Mr. Caldwell."

"Ma'am, it's true we were all sort of used to Captain Wolfson and didn't know what kind of Captain you would be. All of us crewmen are experienced submariners and even though there are a lot of good female Naval officers, we've never had the pleasure of working under one. Until now Ma'am. You've asked no special treatment, you've given no quarter to the men, even standing in line to use the head. And if Mr. Merrick here and Commander Wolfson has confidence in you, then I think I stand with the rest of the men in saying we're behind you Ma'am. I'm willing to go to combat with you and this crew at the ready."

Beverly smiled slightly. She looked down at the red marks on her knuckles where they had met the plastic table. She looked up then said, "Thank you Mr. Caldwell." She stood and thought for several moments.

Ralph injected, "Beverly, this is still just a submarine. You have all the working knowledge of the weapons systems from the Nautilus Two. We just apply that knowledge to the Specter, together with Don's expertise and you'll have full grasp in no time. Now is your time, Beverly. You want to show the world what kind of Captain you are, then it's time to take command. We will go to combat with you. There's no doubt in my mind, you can do this. Regardless of what your father's motives were, this sub and this crew, is suited for battle. And hell Captain, YOU know more about the Volga than the rest of us. That's a big plus for us."

She nodded. There were several moments of uncomfortable silence. Finally, she replied, "You're dismissed Mr. Caldwell. Crash. And thank you."

Crash smiled and left the galley in a hurry.

She looked first at Ralph then at Don. Finally, a hint of a smile etched her lips as she said, "You all are willing to go to war with a temperamental female in charge. I think you're crazy. But I'll tell you something. There's no way I'm going to go through that big ass manual Don wrote up on the weapons on board this boat. You two are going to have to give me a crash course and in a hurry."

"You know, I know the weapons systems on this boat pretty well too," stated Tinkerbelle.

"I'm sure you do Tinkerbelle," smiled Beverly.

Don looked over at her, his face softened, his voice lighter, and he remarked, "You know I don't really know what this was all about. It isn't like we're going to actually try to take on the Volga. I mean that we're not going to actually get into a firing battle with a submarine in the Russian fleet. I mean, this ship is designed to slip in undetected, strike quickly and get the hell out. Not go toe to toe with big and ugly."

Ralph glanced at Beverly who only smiled. Ralph was happy to see that smile, even though he knew it was not going to last long.

"Um Don?" said Ralph shaking his head.

"You guys aren't serious, are you?" asked Don incredulously, not getting the affirmative response he had hoped for.

Ralph walked over to him, put an arm around Don's shoulder and said, "You ever play dodge ball in school Don?"

Don looked at Ralph as if he was off his rocker then responded, "Of course, what does that have to do with it?"

"Well. We had this kid in high school. You know the kind, never picked for basketball or volley ball or those kinds of games."

"Yeah?"

"But he was always picked for dodge ball. And do you want to know why? Because he could dodge the ball. Had a real knack for it. We nicknamed him Spiderman. He just plain old didn't like getting hit." Ralph then smiled broadly.

"What does that have to do with us?" asked Don still not getting the gist.

Beverly came up from behind him and said in his ear, "Don, because you and Ralph saw fit to load us up, we're going to go play dodge ball. We're in the game to win or lose. With the biggest asshole in the entire world." She stopped and walked around the front to look at him in the eye, poked him in the chest and added, "I sure hope this sub is light on its feet. Because I have a feeling, they have more balls than we do."

Beverly walked out of the galley with Ralph a few steps behind. Don stood in the middle of the room, his coffee cup tipping just enough to dribble on his shoes. Finally, he yelled, "I always got hit in the head playing dodge ball!"

CHAPTER 13

Beverly and Wolfson entered the control room with Merrick bringing up the rear, the man still muttering to himself about dodge balls.

Lt. Barrington caught a glimpse of the captain and grabbed her attention quickly. "Captain? We've still received no written verification for orders to engage the Volga. All I keep getting is a garbled mess."

Captain Hornacher glanced at him briefly then said to Wolfson, "Commander, bring the Specter to a depth of thirty meters, set at sixty-five knots and plot an intersect course with the last known location Volga."

The Commander nodded then said to the control room, "You heard the captain, depth of thirty meters, speed to sixty-five knots and navigation, send coordinates to steering to last location of the Volga."

Then the Captain of the Specter glanced around the control room, grabbed everyone's attention, then asked Steve, "Put me on ship com." He nodded at her then she went on to explain, "Crew of the Specter, this is Captain Hornacher. If you haven't already guessed, this vessel which was supposed to be under experimental training and unarmed, is in fact, fully battle ready. So much the better for us. North Pacific Fleet Command has decided we are to engage a very big Russian submarine called the Volga, controlled by renegade forces. Considering what has happened to the crew of the Seattle, I expect everyone to be on their toes. This is not an exercise." Then Beverly stopped, chose her next words carefully, then added, "In view of the inexperience with both the technology, and the leadership of this boat, I expect everyone to learn quickly, and adapt quickly. We are all going to have to grow up while on the run. Carry on."

Mr. Caldwell looked up from his massive steering console and replied simply, "Already done Captain." Then he turned and smiled.

Beverly looked over and let a slight grin break her face. Then she turned her attention back to Barrington. "Are we getting anything?"

"All encrypted communications are coming across as garble, whether written or spoken Ma'am. On the other hand, we can send and receive on open frequencies."

"Diagnostic check Wiz," mentioned Don pulling up behind Williams.

Willy wheeled around in his chair, adjusted his specs and responded, "Already done Don. Our system is five by, our code is fine. The satellite has full communications capability. The problem is at the other end."

Ralph pulled up next to Beverly and said, "Captain. Technically, we don't fire a cap gun until we have coded verification for any type of counter action. Technically, that is."

Don jumped in, "This is one of those Naval things again, isn't it? We all heard the Admiral give the go ahead, but we have to have orders. Don't we?" Then the sudden realization sunk in and he muttered, "What the hell am I arguing for?"

Barrington inserted, "Captain, can we get open signal verification? I've been trying on code but I could signal them through normal channels? We could get it through standard radio signal?"

She shook her head vehemently. "No. No open communications. This has to be scrambled. Or at least some kind of a secure line." Then she turned to Ralph as if to confer and said, "Besides, even if there's a remote chance someone else is listening, I don't want to tip them off. And I'm not going to be the one to tell the Russians the American Navy is hunting one of their own."

Don again leaned over Willy's chair and asked, "It was working fifteen minutes ago, when the Admiral signaled the first time. Does command know of this problem?"

Willy shook his head and guessed, "I don't think so."

Ralph looked over at Beverly and said, "If our message is coming in garbled, and the mess up is at the source, then chances are everyone else's is too. Then the rest of the Navy is blind to even the little we know."

Beverly thought for a moment. It was as if a night light went on in her mind. Suddenly she asked, "Don?" She nodded at his ever-present notebook computer and asked, "Can your little toy make a phone call?"

Don thought immediately of the satellite link ups and shrugged his shoulders and replied, "Possible. We can encrypt our own satellite link up but we have to have a secure line at the other end."

Beverly nodded, thought a moment then said, "If we can communicate with Admiral Hornacher directly and go around naval communications, we can keep from other people listening, and from open com. with the rest of the Navy." Then Beverly thought again and added, "My father has a secure line into the Pentagon. I just happen to know the number. Can we use that?"

Don instantly followed this line of thought and added, "And keep whoever is bugging the communications from suspecting there's a problem. Got it. But we need a way for him to call us back." He turned over to Barrington and said, "I've got just the thing. We need a satellite link to the Prime Star Sat Com. That's over Alaska."

Barrington nodded, typed into the computer possible satellite links, the screen exploding in a map of known communications satellites. He located coordinates for the communications satellite Don wanted, ran the GPPP satellite to search for telephone signaling, found the one he wanted, then made frequency connections, the process taking all of thirty seconds. He then turned and said in his best whinny voice "Telephone number if you please." Then he mentioned quickly, "It's a tenuous connection Captain. Make it short."

Beverly smiled and answered clicking off the ten digits. Steve transferred the process to control communications. Within a few moments they heard the familiar ringing of a telephone.

Admiral Hornacher was in the 'basement' of the Pentagon. Its official name was Emergency Response Operations Center for the Defense of the United States. As the government's penchant for anachronisms, EROC was what it was labeled. What it was referred to however, was simply the War Room. Or as some liked to call it 'The Fortress of Solitude.' A massive facility, it could run the entire defense system of the United States. Sixteen banks of four each communication and systems gathering equipment were clustered near the rear. Four banks each for each major branch of the military. Several more near the front gathered basic information and set up the coding systems for each day of use. Civilians with military supervision monitored most of the equipment. A huge thirty by sixty-foot screen showed worldwide activity while four screens flanking either side of the main screen showed various activities, depending on what was happening in the world. One, at the moment was showing the satellite imagery courtesy of the Poseidon Project, the scattered and dismal remains of the USS Seattle.

A large glassed in room, overlooked the main floor, usually the domain of the various Joint Chiefs of Staff. Both General Blanchett and Admiral Hornacher had abandoned the conference room and chose to be on the main floor, taking positions at a raised console overseeing the entire floor. Telephones and computers at their disposal. General Tolliver, and General Prescott were on their way to meet the President and oversee efforts directly from the White House.

They were trying to trace down a dilemma. The communications console, responsible for directing Naval affairs, had, for no apparent reasoning, suddenly gone dead. The Admiral had directed various backups to no conclusion.

Thomas Chang, a small Oriental man with a pencil thin gray mustache in charge of the systems for the War Room was at a loss, as he spirited himself around the center. He had already conferred with Blanchett about the communications problem.

Colonel Devlin, a straightforward African American Army man with a Master's degree in Computer Sciences was the liaison in charge of the military aspect of the EROC itself. He had attempted to send out a worldwide command of One A Pentagon, which meant that this Center was where the ultimate decisions for the United States Military in this current situation, was coming from. Very much like any plane the President would fly on would have the designation Air Force One. Colonel Devlin was not a happy man as he was not getting the confirmations he sorely needed to continue.

Admiral Hornacher was on the console phone to CIA Director Billingham. The Colonel had informed him that he suspected a saboteur. Billingham was on his way back, which really did not make the Admiral feel any better.

Less than a moment after he had punched the disconnect button, a plain black phone in the midst of the Naval consoles lit up and a computer operator answered it. The man looked completely perplexed then turned and said, "Admiral Hornacher, you have a call coming in on your secure line and it's being transferred down here."

"Who is it?"

"Um? A Captain Hornacher?" the man replied timidly.

The Admiral glanced at the man, then walked briskly to the out stretched receiver. He latched onto the phone; his intention was to berate whoever was playing jokes on the other line. "This is Admiral Hornacher, this is a secure … " he responded, getting cut off.

Beverly inserted quickly, "Captain Hornacher here Admiral. We seem to be having a problem with the crypto unit. All our incoming is garbled. And as you know Admiral, we cannot continue until coded verification. My people here are positive the problem lies with the sending station."

Blanchett was also on a phone, but stopped his animated conversation when he saw the perplexed look cross Hornacher's face. Admiral Hornacher waved at the General to pick the extension and the General cut off his phone call and got on the line. Finally, Hornacher cut back in and said, "Captain, we're aware of the problem and we are attempting to try and correct it from this end." He stopped and thought for a moment and asked, "You've gotten this far. What's your idea Captain?"

Beverly had been watching Don land line his notebook computer to the incoming port at Barrington's computer station, integrating the computer printer. After a moment, she understood and responded, "Admiral, if you can send a coded fax communique to this number, we will have the verification we need to continue." She was being very careful not to express any actual information.

At the EROC the senior Naval man looked up from his computer screen to the Admiral and said, "Sir, I have an incoming phone number for you. It's … from the USS Specter from a Mr. Merrick?" Sure enough, on the screen of the operator's computer monitor was Don's notebook computer phone number. Both Colonel Devlin and Chang were looking at the screen. Chang understood completely and quickly left to coordinate the process as the Colonel gave his approval for the somewhat unorthodox procedure.

The whole thing took two minutes as the Admiral watched the two men at the front consoles. Chang waved when he thought they had tone. After a time, the Admiral asked into the phone, "Got it?"

"Coming through now Sir." Ultimately Beverly answered. "Process completed; orders received."

Suddenly Admiral Hornacher had an idea and said, "Is there any way you can communicate with the rest of the North Pacific Fleet and pass on the orders?"

He could hear Beverly conferring with Commander Wolfson and Don. Finally, she responded, "Believability Admiral. They will know the communique is coming from this vessel and not command. They may or may not believe the orders, Admiral."

The Admiral sighed heavily. "Understood Captain." He thought for a moment then asked, on a whim, "Captain, if you had not received orders, would you have continued anyway?"

It took a bare second then, "Yes sir. I do believe we would have. We did have a verbal command we could have used under emergency procedure. And for the families of the good crew of the Seattle. Plus considering we've already broken about a half dozen orders. And Admiral, tell Admiral Cartwright he's on my shit list. Again."

The Admiral smiled as General Blanchett gave him a very confused look. The Admiral then nodded then said, "Understood Captain. And Captain. Good show of initiative."

"Yes sir, I know how much you love computers. Captain Hornacher out."

The Admiral hung up the phone. General Blanchett looked over at him and asked, "Did you understand what Merrick and Chang just did?"

"No. Not in the least. I just know they got secure operating orders."

General Blanchett, normally a focused man nodded, and said, "Good. I thought it was just me."

The Admiral looked up at the various screens. Finally, he observed, "Unfortunately, we still have some major problems. And because of the Specter's initiative, they're the only ones out there trying to hunt down the Volga."

Colonel Devlin slid up next to General Blanchett and said, "We've narrowed down the problem. We found out the crypto code that we used has a built-in virus, that when, after the first initiations involving the Naval units, attacks the system. Our software picked it up immediately, but now, our coding for this day have been compromised."

"How?"

"At midnight, this facility, like the rest of the Defense Centers around the nation, all switch to a new crypto code. As do all the military facilities."

"Yes Colonel. I understand that. How would a military facility such as this have a virus?" The General asked losing his patience.

The Colonel, looking a little bit embarrassed said simply, "It was planted. That's how."

General Blanchett studied his hands for a moment then asked, "Why can't we just enter the right code and continue?"

The Colonel held up two fingers and explained, "One, is that our man, Captain Witherspoon, who is supposed to enter the new codes at midnight, has been reported missing. Which means compromise. And two is that with the compromise of the code, we have to scrap not only this code, but the Marine code, the Air Force code, the Army code. Not only to this facility, but to every facility worldwide. The good news is that the man who does the codes, does not have access to the backup code. That responsibility lies with Chang and myself."

The enormity of the situation grasped Blanchett. Quickly he responded, "How long to switch to a backup?"

"To get the word out to scrap this code and go to back up will take only about an hour. But General. We are talking a worldwide conversion. Somebody, somewhere will not get the word."

The General nodded his understanding. Someone was not going to do the new code right, someone was not going to believe the orders and ignore the switch, someone will not have the emergency backup coding at all. "Damn." He glared at the Colonel and said simply, "The sooner the better."

Colonel Devlin nodded quickly and walked away with long, purposeful strides.

Admiral Hornacher observed, "Someone with a top secret, NATO and NORAD clearance waltzes in here and screws us up, if only for a few hours."

"Just enough time for the noon hour courier to come in and create more hell," observed the dejected General.

"Billingham is a busy man this morning."

"That's not the half of it. How far does this stretch? If the Ukrainian Resistance can get to our communications system how much more can they do?"

The Admiral only shook his head in understatement, as to how complicated this was all getting. Then his thoughts turned to his daughter, out in the middle of the big pond, in a little submarine. Every cell in his body had confidence in the high-tech little boat and its crew. But the Volga was a big and mean son-of-a-bitch. And had proven that it was out there to shoot to kill. He prayed his daughter could pull the trigger when the time came. And that the experimental guns worked the way they were supposed to.

"Beverly did good Jack. She took charge of the situation." This observation coming from the General.

"Thanks. I wish she were here right now. I'd feel better."

A hand clapped his shoulder as the General said, "I'm sure you do my friend. I can't even imagine."

Both men heard the raucous voice of Lucius Perry enter the big double doors and head their way. He came up quickly moving his bulk with surprising ease. Suddenly he nodded at the screen and asked, "Is that what's left of the Seattle?"

Blanchett nodded and replied, "As near as we can figure."

"What are the Russians saying?" asked Hornacher. The thought that his daughter was hunting a rogue ballistic submarine was not doing his indigestion any good. He desperately wanted some verification.

"Madam Secretary is on the phone right now trying to get them to come clean. We've informed the President, but he's still in route."

"What about Jonathon?" asked Blanchett.

Lucius shook his head and responded, "The Russian state department is not even playing gentlemen. They have no knowledge. The Russians are keeping this close to their vest."

"Close to their vest? Their sub blew one of our boats out of the water!" Yelled Hornacher, loud enough that several people stopped and turned around to gawk.

Lucius could forgive his friend for being agitated. He put a large hand on Hornacher's shoulder and gave a little squeeze and said, "The problem is we know that. The Russians are also being held hostage by the threat of a nuclear strike. They don't really care about our problems. Believe me George is yelling louder than you are right now."

Blanchett then filled the Secretary of Defense in on the communications problem.

"But why? They had to know we had a backup plan? All they gain from this is a few hours?" asked Lucius finally.

Blanchett nodded, then explained, "Worked differently, this might have given them several more hours, or simply the hour or two might have been enough. In this case however, the Russian Navy was so slow to respond that it wasn't really necessary, but the subterfuge was already in place."

Lucius nodded then inserted, "Makes you wonder what else they have in store for us."

"That has crossed our minds," Blanchett answered as the phone in front of him on the console started blinking. Answering it they heard a distinct one-sided conversation with Billingham. It was then that Admiral Cartwright joined the group and informed Admiral Hornacher that the new codes were installed and that the secure dialogue would be forth coming within the half hour.

Blanchett finally disconnected and looked over at his group of the Nation's finest. "That was Kirk. He says that Captain Witherspoon's apartment is vacant. Like the man didn't exist."

"Jesus. He has firsthand knowledge to our coding system and he was never found out," remarked a mumbling Lucius.

"The UN is staked out. Every single minor character has been replaced by the CIA and the FBI."

"And wouldn't they expect that?" asked Lucius. The man always had a knack for grasping the whole picture.

Blanchett nodded, then said, "Kirk mentioned the worst-case scenarios. They think that the man maybe wired with explosives. Touch him and they all die. Or an exterior vehicle shuttling the man maybe loaded and they may try an end run into the building. They even have a doomsday scenario involving an airplane, as the Air Force is coordinating and monitoring."

"Jesus. This will get out of control and people are going to die. God Damned," Lucius uttered in resignation. His thoughts bounced around randomly until he turned to Admiral Cartwright and asked, "Admiral? The Specter. You're the resident expert. What kind of chance does it have one on one against the Volga?"

Admiral Cartwright glanced at Hornacher.

"Forget my daughter Dan. Give it to him straight," commanded Admiral Hornacher.

Cartwright glanced down at his hands then over at Lucius, noticing that Blanchett was also taking very careful attention. Finally, he started in. "You have to understand we're talking oranges and apples. Other than a submersible, these two boats have nothing in common. The Volga can undoubtedly out shoot the Specter, her fire power is immense and more dangerous than anything under the water. However, the maneuverability and speed of the Specter can do laps around the Volga. And gentlemen, you've seen the technology involved with our sub. She will spot the Volga well before Rabinov can even determine what he's looking at, for the skin and power plant of the Specter are completely unconventional."

Then Cartwright looked over at Hornacher and continued, "And as you've seen, her crew is as knowledgeable and as creative as any in the service. Unfortunately, we deal with one major unknown, and that is the skin. The Specter was designed to take a hit, but so too is the Volga, with a triple sealed titanium wafer shell. I pray they don't, but if things escalate to open warfare, it will be a sea battle that will not be won in the first or second round. It will be a chess match, make no doubt about that."

Lucius nodded, content with the explanation, but in his mind, he acknowledged an inexperienced Captain at the helm of the Specter, and a ruthless killer piloting the Volga. With both ships designed to take a hit, it was a chess match of attrition. Then he sighed heavily, afraid of the death that was assuredly to follow.

Glancing up at the dismal remains of the Seattle, Hornacher sided up next to Cartwright and muttered in a low voice, "Beverly's not happy with either of us right now. I tried to manipulate things and you disobeyed a written order. But didn't bother to tell the captain."

Cartwright sighed heavily. Presently he mentioned, "Beverly has all the right in the world to be mad at me. It just never occurred to me, that something cataclysmic like this would happen. I suppose they'll be an investigation?"

A hand laid upon Cartwright's shoulder and Hornacher said, "You did the right thing my friend. I'll take the heat for this one. Especially if we all live."

Captain Beverly Hornacher looked at the verification carefully then folded it up and tucked in her breast pocket. She looked over at Don and said, "Thanks Don."

Don had pulled the plug on his computer and was tucking it away. "No problem. Now it's official. Now we can hunt down the Volga. All by our lonesome."

Wolfson was scrutinizing the screen and said, "It does appear that way."

"It should take only about an hour for War Rooms to go to back up codes and everyone to be on the same page," inserted Steve.

Beverly turned and looked at the young man. Steve looked up and explained, "I spent time at the Center at Omaha. That's how it's done."

She nodded, happy for Steve's previous experience, then turned to Don and asked, "Feel better?"

"No. I hate dodge ball."

Beverly smirked slightly. Then her thoughts turned elsewhere. Finally, she said, "Commander, we need best speed to the last location of the Seattle and plot a best-case scenario of the Volga's location."

"Aye Captain." He turned and said to the mapping board, "Navigation best guess to the Volga's location and send to steering. Steering, let's crank it up, do eighty knots to the last location of the Seattle."

"Aye Commander," responded Crash looking at his monitors, shifting to one five zero and demanding more from the Liquid metal reactor.

Beverly nodded at Wolfson for a moment and said, "Commander, if I could have a word."

Wolfson honestly did not know what it was about so he followed dutifully behind Beverly as she exited the control room and into cramped conning tower area. Ralph stopped, leaned against the aluminum ladder and waited for Beverly.

She turned on him and asked sincerely. "I want to know about Don."

Wolfson shrugged his shoulders and responded, "What about him?"

"How is he going to react to a fight? The crew has had a mind set their entire naval careers that this might happen. They are psychologically tested. How is Merrick, under these conditions?"

Ralph smiled. "Oh. I get it." He searched for the right words then began. "This isn't quite the scenario he had intended, but he also didn't intend for this tight little ship for pleasure sailing either."

Beverly shook her head. "This isn't funny Ralph. I don't want a loose cannon on board worried about his precious submarine getting scratched. He's already made it known what he's thought of Naval protocol."

Ralph studied her solemnly. As Captain, it was her job to be concerned about every little facet of the operation. He however, had given Don little thought. Giving the entire situation more thought, he then replied, "Don knows what this sub is for Bev. He knows that it's for hunting other men. He was the one that was adamant that we have weaponry on board. That's what this vessel is for. I wouldn't worry about him Captain. He'll come through in the end."

"How about-facing death Ralph? How will he handle facing death face to face?"

Wolfson looked at her with concern in his eyes as he responded, "He will handle it as all human beings. In his own way. But I tell you what Beverly. The skin of this sub is designed to take a lot of God-Damned punishment. I'm not ready to die, and I sure hope the hell you aren't either. And I've played Don at poker. Don is as calculating and as cutthroat as they come. He doesn't like to lose."

Beverly stared at Wolfson for a few seconds, then let a slight grin flex her face, "I'm not ready to go quite yet either Ralph. I just want everyone on the same page. And he's the only one I have no knowledge of."

"Believe me. Don has opinions, but he will follow orders. And Don will pull the trigger when the time comes." Ralph then smiled warmly. In his mind Don was not an issue and he hoped he got that across to Beverly.

She nodded then simply said, "Good."

Wolfson straightened up for a second, then realized Beverly was hesitating. "Something else Captain?" He asked.

"Yes. The Volga is a nasty submarine, Ralph."

He nodded then said, "I'm aware of that. Go on."

Beverly seemed to want to choose her words then finally said, "When Schmitty ran me through the engine systems he mentioned where the torpedoes of the Specter would be. I of course did not realize they were already loaded or I would have asked a lot of questions."

"And your question now is?"

"There's so little room for our fish to occupy."

"Right." Suddenly Ralph seemed to understand and inserted, "And you don't think our little fish are going to do much against the hull of Volga."

"No, I don't. I don't know their fire power, but even a regular torpedo doesn't mean an automatic kill."

Ralph seemed to understand the thought process. Finally, he said, "Knowing that a simple hit is not going to be a kill, what did you have in mind as a strategy?"

Beverly smiled then returned, "Not much of a strategy. My thoughts actually are to try and deplete the Volga as much as possible."

Ralph stroked his mustache, deep in thought. He acknowledged, "A shoot out." Then he looked into Beverly's eyes and said honestly, "I like it. The element of surprise is on our side, but once we start firing, they are going to establish some kind of firing range. However, they are going to be much more a sitting duck than we are." He nodded again and mentioned, "It could work."

Beverly then said, "Hopefully our invisibility will keep us out of range and we can dance around, go in, strike and retreat."

"And hopefully keep the Volga in sight long enough for the Cheyenne to engage with us," added Ralph

Beverly relaxed for a moment then said, "And maybe, if we get lucky, we might cripple her. Before any other Russian subs want to get involved."

Ralph thought for a moment then added, "There's a lot of ways this can work. If we can keep them engaged long enough to get help, or they simply turn to run or dive to the point of being unable to launch or if we get lucky. But if they get happy feet and decide to launch, it becomes a whole new ball game."

"They would compromise their exact position to the world. If we find them, then we have their exact position, and there's nothing they can do to keep us from shadowing them. They have to know that at that point, someone is going to shoot them out of the water."

"Let's pray it doesn't get to that point. Shall we?"

Beverly merely nodded.

They walked over to the control room door, opened it and Wolfson stepped in. Beverly stood outside and said, "Commander, you have the conn. Don and I are going back so that he can brief me on a few things."

Wolfson stuttered for a second as he said, "I thought I was supposed to help?"

Beverly smiled at him as she turned, showing the man her bobbing pony tail and replied, "Don has nothing to lose. You, on the other hand, are afraid of getting caught."

Man, she can twist things to her advantage and make you feel little, Wolfson thought to himself. However, he smiled as he watched Beverly leave the room with Don in tow, his ever-present computer tucked under his arm.

CHAPTER 14

Petty Officer Hyde and Lt. Smith were sitting in the galley, sharing a cup of coffee after breakfast, and chatting amiably about the best London bistros. When Captain Hornacher stepped in, she looked at the two men and found them to be the oddest pair, Hyde's English white and skinny frame and Bobbie's bulk and chocolate skin. They both looked up when the door opened and cut their conversation short.

"Gentlemen, if you don't mind, Mr. Merrick and I need to have a conversation about upcoming events," said Beverly easily.

Both men understood completely, Smith draining his coffee cup. They both rose and moved around Beverly and Don to make their way out. Suddenly Smith stopped and asked, "Captain, is it true? We're hunting the Volga by ourselves?"

"News travels quickly on a little boat. Yes, Lieutenant, we're hunting the Volga. At the moment by ourselves," replied Beverly as confidently as possible.

"Can I have permission to help Lt. Duran in control? He may need some help. You know," asked Lt Smith, somewhat hesitantly.

"As our one and only Medic on board this vessel, I think that would be a damned good idea. If it's all right with Duran, then it's good by me," responded Beverly taking pleasure in the man trying to assist in any way possible.

A broad smile flexed Bobby's face. "Yes Ma'am."

The two men left the galley. Don placed his notebook computer on the table then walked over and poured himself another cup of coffee. Beverly noted with satisfaction that the one he had thrown at her had been cleaned up.

He sat down at the end of the table and flipped open his computer, pressing the power button, "You want to know about the weapons systems," he mentioned finally.

"Yeah." Beverly let Don direct for the time being as this was definitely his show.

"Sit," he said patting the bench next to him. "I'll give you a three-dimensional tour."

She made herself as comfortable on the solid plastic bench seat and looked at the computer. She had never noticed it before as it was unlike any other, she had ever seen. The top half, or screen was twice as wide as the keyboard, the three sections locking in together, the screens locking together the divides virtually invisible, expanding out and swiveling in her direction for easier viewing. With a simple five key command the screen produced a fully three-dimensional rotating torpedo gracing its crystal-clear confines. Numbers danced along the bottom with initials and meanings only Don and Tinkerbell knew.

"Looks like a torpedo," she said, still in awe of Don's little toy.

"Man, you're quick," he said back sarcastically. He typed in a command as numbers danced along the bottom of the screen. Then he started in. "Our torpedo however, is smaller for obvious reasons. The one the Navy uses is roughly twenty feet long. This one is eight-feet long."

"Firepower?"

Don shook his head in disappointment. "We're designing one that will, in time have the fire power of a normal sub at one-third the size, and in fact creating one that's nuclear tipped. However, with all the time constraints we were under, we manufactured what we could. Our current fish have about seventy-five percent the explosive punch as a normal torpedo. The Specter's current compliment is sixteen, but we're working on bolstering that number. There is a plus side, however."

"Speed and range?" Beverly asked.

Don smiled. "The plus side. Like everything else on this boat, they're almost twice as fast. The Nautilus Two's torpedoes are around sixty knots, good enough to track down any ocean-going ship. This one stands at one hundred ten. Range is about forty-thousand meters, give or take a few feet. Three interesting points on these fish. First of all, we have only two tubes in the port but we also have two tubes in the aft."

"How does that work?" asked Beverly thinking of normal loading procedures, on board the Nautilus Two and all other submarines. She understood that the engines on the Specter were actually underneath, but the power plant was in the rear. She wondered how can there be 2 different torpedo rooms?

"Point number two. They're already loaded. We don't have to go through the standard loading the torpedo, flooding the tubes, and what not. No manpower needed whatsoever. The interior chamber where the fish are located is already flooded. We just open the outer door and by a tether, these are automatically fired. Like a clip in a side arm, the next torpedo is brought up and made ready."

"So, the time line on firing procession is much quicker," noted Beverly appreciatively. "How quickly can we shoot these?"

"Every four point eight seconds."

"Whoa. All right. So, every five seconds we can rapid fire these. So, in a matter of fifteen seconds we could have twelve fish in the water." Beverly nodded in understanding then asked, "Safeties?"

"One automatic safety. A million ones we can preset."

"Don't shoot the shooter," Beverly inserted quickly.

Don smiled and replied, "Exactly. These will not detonate on us in any way, shape or form. Especially since we are the only ship in existence with a plasma generator. After that, its Captain's discretion."

"Meaning ... we can do anything?"

"Point number three. We control the fish from the outset. Of course, on your previous scenario it will be a little difficult to track twelve fish, but it can be done. And none of those cumbersome tethers. Direct satellite control. Our monitors will show their exact location, with an on-camera view,"

"How much control?"

"We can preprogram to hit a certain object, say, oh, I don't know, a nasty Russian sub perhaps. Or set to heat seeking or simply have the weapons control, hit whatever it desires, by self-control, like a remote control. And in that function, we can take over a preset and turn it around."

Beverly nodded in complete understanding. Like everything else in the little boat, this was highly technical and superior in every way. As long as they worked. "All right. I think I understand," she mentioned finally. "So, what happens if we have a malfunction? The loading conveyor or the torpedoes malfunction?

"Oh, hell, that's simple. We give Schmitty an eight-pound mall and he goes and beats on the damned things."

Beverly looked at the man as if he were serious, then she said, "You're kidding right?"

Don grinned devilishly and responded, "We can get to them but it's not going to be easy. Like an Indianapolis racing car, everything is jammed in tight. In case of a problem, a default mechanism keeps them from loading and detonating. Let's just hope that never happens."

"All right then. Tell me about our one Nuke."

Don rotated the screen back to himself, punched up the data on the missile and rotated it back. It showed Beverly an outline of where it sat on the deck of the Specter. Don then started the lesson. "Thirty-five feet long, it's obviously not a Polaris or a Tomahawk, but one modified to ride piggyback on the Specter. Upon initiation, it will rise up to a forty-degree angle, and fire from there, so that it in effect the Specter should hardly even feel its launch. I nicknamed the thing the Bird of Prey and the Navy liked it, so, it stuck."

"And like the torpedoes, it's faster and more maneuverable. And I'll bet you we can control it to shoot down anything we want to," observed Beverly.

"You do catch on quick," smiled Don.

"What makes it faster than regular missile?" asked Beverly.

"Simple. No rocket fuel. It's a Nuclear Fusion rocket. Only one of three in existence." Then he cocked his head and smiled and added, "Much faster."

"Wow. Okay, the next question I want to know is why do we have one at all?"

"Original design did not call for one. The brass, and actually I had to agree, that to be a deterrent to war and for the Specter to be taken seriously in any kind of battle, we had to have the firepower. And to be included in any naval battle, we needed nuclear firepower."

Beverly nodded rather sadly. "So in conclusion, we had to be able to destroy a city so that we wouldn't be labeled the little Yellow submarine."

Don nodded and sat back in his chair. "That's about it."

Beverly thought for another moment then asked, "I've gone through the missile firing commands on the Nautilus Two. Is there anything I should know on this?"

Don shook his head and ran the facts through his mind. Then he said, "After we get verified EAM coding from Fleet command, you have the firing key, Wolfson has the startup key and Steve has the control panel code. Thumb prints preset in the computer for physical verification of all three of you, with Crash being the back up. There is a large red abort button on the console in case you change your mind. The GPPP will automatically send a distress signal to command, informing them of a launch. Command, has the option of self-destruct. In theory at least."

"In theory?" questioned Beverly.

Don looked over into the green eyes and asked back, "When was the last time you had a live, untested launch of a nuclear missile?"

"Good point. Anything else I should know?"

"It actually has a longer range than any other nuclear submarine missile. About twelve- thousand miles. We could hit anything, anywhere in the world."

"And why exactly is that?" asked Beverly incredulously.

Don shrugged his shoulders then said, "When I built it, we built it as a one of a kind to fit this submarine. The skin of course, amorphous metal, it's actually smaller than most missiles, and nuclear fusion core is smaller which allowed us a lot less weight in the payload."

"Oh, okay, that makes sense. And the detonation factor?"

"Multiple warheads can separate and drop in a hundred-mile pattern to the tune of five explosions. Or one complete detonation would be enough to level a city."

Beverly pondered this for several moments digested the consequences of such action, then asked, "Startup time?"

Don merely shook his head and explained, "No fueling, nothing to initiate. There is nothing in this world that would ever ignite that rocket or warhead by accident. It takes a special mixture of chemicals to even initiate the startup engine."

"We can fire immediately," Beverly noted nodding her head.

"Exactly."

"Anything else?"

"It's not a launch I would take lightly. Other than that, no."

Beverly thought for a moment, then asked with a Cheshire grin, "You mentioned just the officers for fail safe on the nuke. How hard for you and your little computer to override?"

Don glanced down at his hands as if he had just been caught with his hand in the cookie jar. "If you really want to know, not hard at all."

"Captain Hornacher, I can also override the system if I detect any abnormalities," inserted Tinkerbell quickly.

Beverly nodded and said, "Thanks Tinkerbell." Then she asked, "Counter measures? It's obvious we don't have the room for the large mines, or acoustic counter measures. But I'll bet you thought of something smaller and more deadly."

Don almost laughed. Then he said, "You're getting to know me pretty well." He started punching on the computer's keyboard. It brought up a Three-D picture of the Specter, with two massive panels that separated themselves from the side of the Specter's conning tower. He then swiveled the screen to Beverly.

She stared at the picture for several seconds then wrinkled up her nose and said, "I really have no idea what that is."

Don smiled and started explaining. "Something we've been experimenting with for a while. We refer to it as the Ultrasonic Acoustical Canon. USAC for short."

"I'm sorry, I'm still sort of lost."

Don nodded then explained, "Okay. We found out that some sub-Commanders used the conventional Sonar pinging on high intensity to actually throw off the capabilities of a torpedo. Even a standard torpedo has to have sensors and aggressive sonar array to find its target and pinging could confuse the torpedo if they hit it right. So, we intensified that idea with a sonic sound burst that would literally throw a torpedo into a tail spin."

Beverly's eyes widened in understanding then she stated, "Oh my God. We have Mister Limpet?"

Don started laughing at the thought of the old Don Knotts movie. "Yesssss. Complete with the thrumming noise. I had never heard of the movie, until Ralph found it on a streaming service and showed it to me. Ours is a little more sophisticated but very much the same idea."

"Okay," Beverly smiled. "Explain to me OUR version."

Pointing at rotating pictures on his note book computer he stopped it when it reached a head on image of two parabolic dishes sprouting out from either side of the conning tower. Don then explained, "We have two directional dishes that fire an intense sound burst that can be used for several purposes. Redirect a torpedo, screw up the sonar of a sub, ignite depth charges to name a couple."

"I've always wondered why the conning tower was separate from the rest of the ship. It has a lot of its own electronics between the antenna array and the USAC. So, what kind of limitations does our ear drum buster have?" Asked Beverly, genuinely in wonder at a totally new toy never seen on a sub before.

"The ultrasonic burst is about twenty times stronger than a standard pinging. However, it does have limitations. Like a single shot gun that has to reload, it takes time to fire a second shot. The generator that charges the system can only fire after a complete recharge. It will take a couple minutes for it to build up enough power. The parabolic dishes can only fire to the front or to the side, cannot fire behind us. But they can fire independently actually disrupting two different sources. And one last thing, it will slow the Specter down, acting like a brake. We really don't want to initiate them while running a hundred knots, good chance they will simply fold up."

Beverly nodded and inserted, "Good to know. It's not going to be something on the forefront of my consciousness, so I expect you and Eddie and of course Tinkerbell to remind me. Got that?"

"Absolutely," responded Tinkerbell.

Beverly nodded, then looked over at the man and grinned then asked, "And I heard this story about our deck gun which you aimed at one of our crewmen? You didn't, did you?"

"Oh, sure I did. Alex had to go clean his pants."

Beverly shook her head.

"Oh, don't worry Captain, I wouldn't let Don arm the weapon." Inserted Tinkerbelle quickly.

Don sighed and pulled his computer back to himself. He punched on the keyboard and up popped the program for the deck gun. He rotated the computer back to Beverly. "Synchronize Laser targeting Armored Weapon. SLAW for short. The SLAW was a late edition. Self-contained below the deck it has laser targeting with an eight-round compliment of kinetic energy shells, thermonuclear shells, and amorphous alloy fragmentation shells."

"Good grief. That sounds about as deadly as anything on the Specter," observed Beverly.

Don shrugged his shoulders and said, "I felt that our speed made us a good version of a PT boat. On the boat such as the Specter, we put enough water in the main tanks, we would only have about ten feet of the conning tower showing. I doubt if it's a weapon we would ever use, but going into thermonuclear mode, with enough direct hits, we could melt a battleship. From two miles away. And not give them much to shoot back at."

She nodded in appreciation at the little guns' firepower. Then she asked, "I understand the nuclear shell, having fired a hand-held nuke at Quantico, and the fragmentation shell I understand. Explain the kinetic energy shell."

Don nodded then said, "Delayed detonation. Very simply put, it penetrates, the armor of a ship and once it stops penetrating, it then explodes doing much more damage to the interior of the ship."

Beverly nodded immediately, then noted, "And it's loaded like the torpedoes and it's difficult to fix. Right?"

"Impossible to fix from the inside. We have to go through the deck. Targeting and firing for the gun can be done from below or from the conning tower."

Beverly looked up in sudden realization. "The flip out console on the conning tower. I wondered what that was for. Man. That does sound like you've stuffed this little sub full. Is there anything else?"

Don rotated the computer back to him and punched out some letters in rapid succession. Then he swiveled it back. It showed the weapons control on board the Specter. Don then started in. "Eddy has six large monitors, and four smaller ones. One large one for each weapon system, one that monitors his target, and one that integrates all the components. The smaller ones give him speed, range, and count. The console controls are also split up that way and, each having their own method of firing the weapons." He allowed Beverly to study the picture.

Finally, Beverly said, with a nod, "I've glanced over at the controls enough times that I think I understand how they work."

Don said in agreement, "They're not hard. The hard part is to shoot several items and control them all." Then he flopped down the screen of his computer, looked Beverly in the eyes and said, "That's it."

Beverly unknowingly crept closer and put a hand on top of Don's hand still holding his computer. Searching his eyes, she finally said, "You know. You yelled at me pretty hard this morning."

He shrugged, just a tiniest bit uncomfortable, but his nostrils picking up the smallest of feminine scents. Then he said, "That's me. I simmer, then I blow, then I forget about it and move on. No hard feelings Bev. I just felt I had to insert the right facts into it. No one was out to get you. And you weren't listening very well."

Beverly sat back then said, "I know. I've seen that. You know, I hate to admit it, I deserved it this morning. My first gut instinct was that I was out of the loop. It brought back all those times, even on the Naut. Two, when I felt because I was a woman, I was out of the chain. Usually, I was wrong, but the feelings still surfaced, just the same."

Don shrugged again. Then he explained, "Cartwright, Wolfson and I all agreed that the day you came on board, we didn't want to jeopardize your commission with our action. Besides, we figured you would argue or, well, you know …"

"Run to Daddy and tattletale?" finished Beverly with a lopsided grin.

Don chuckled and said, "Unfortunately yeah. Something like that."

Beverly thought for a moment then said, "Like I mentioned earlier, I would have contacted the Pentagon and take it from there. Arming the ship was undoubtedly the right thing to do. But it was against Pentagon orders. In hindsight, it was probably my father all along."

Don shrugged again, a little embarrassed and remarked, "We made that decision for you."

Beverly smiled. She wanted to linger, enjoy a cup of coffee and talk with Don. She knew there was a lot more to the man then technology and specifications. She had seen his extensive bio. But the enormity of the situation was getting in the way. She sighed heavily then rose and said, "I need to get back to the control room."

"Not yet. I have a question for you."

As in Wolfson's case, Don asking questions was an oxymoron. Beverly steeled herself for a moment, unsure where this was going. She felt heat rise to her cheeks for she had opened up to him, albeit the tiniest bit. And somehow, someone had probably told him about her momentary imprisonment. It seemed to come out at the strangest times. She was unsure what he was going to ask.

"I've been watching you and Ralph closely. Every time someone mentions the Volga, there's a concern in your eyes. What's so special about this sub, Bev?"

Beverly was actually relieved. He did not want to delve into her feelings or examine her soul. He wanted to talk warfare. Finally, she gathered her thoughts and said, "You have to understand Rabinov and the sub for they go hand and hand. Rabinov is a genius. The Seattle found out the hard way. And there's the sub itself. It's a Russian sub class Delta Type Five. Comparable to the older Typhon class or the new Centurion. But it's bigger. It's a catamaran-type design that makes two separate pressure hulls joined by an outer layer. CIA speculation and our relations with the Russian military have told us, that the side walls of the Volga are triple sealed, wafer core Titanium. Basically, where the side walls are located. And as you know, that is a lot of the exterior of the ship. Which accounts for the fact that the boat has the biggest nuclear power plant ever put on a submersible, and it's still pretty damned slow. But, rumor has it, it can go deeper and withstand more pressure than any other Sub on the planet. It can literally, dive out of sight."

Don looked up at Beverly for a few moments, his mind calculating the ratio of explosives to the armor of the Volga. "The Submariner Group experimented with the wafer core design on several levels and found the stuff just too bulky to work with. The Russians apparently didn't care they were giving up speed for the additional weight." Don thought for the barest of moments then added, "One of our torpedoes is not going to sink her, is it?"

Beverly shook her head grimly and stated, "Don, a regular torpedo wouldn't sink her unless it hit the right spot. The Seattle might have found that out. Too late."

"My records show that the Volga has a Magneto Hydroelectric Drive unit." Inserted Tinkerbell.

"That it does," agreed Beverly.

"That's not a big concern with me, slower than mud our monitoring system was designed around any actual sonar. We don't rely on noise to identify a ship. We can find it before we'll ever hear it. But it does mean the rest of the Russian Navy won't find their own ship. And they use a standard propeller which cavitates and makes plenty of noise," stated Don

"And the Nautilus Two has given me all Drive resonances that I need to identify the Volga with whatever drive unit it's using," added an eager Tinkerbell. Then she continued, "And they have never heard anything like our Fusion Jet Technology. They will never find us."

Beverly nodded then said, "Rabinov was never one to relay on tech to run his ship so rarely went into Magneto Drive but he did on one occasion when our Captain decided to surprise him by crawling up his baffles then letting out a stream of pinging, just to let him know he had gotten a little close to the Ford for comfort. The Naut Deuce was running it's Magneto drive and the Volga had no idea we were there."

"PDM knew how the Russian Magneto Drive was developed and came up with a slightly better unit, little quieter and quicker. I think it had a top speed of 13 knots if I'm not mistaken," inserted Don, with obvious insider information.

"You are correct as usual. But it was the Pump Jet propulsion that scared the Russians the most. We could catch up with them in a blink of an eye. But you knew that already, didn't you?" She asked with a smile.

Don smiled back, then he asked, "Do you know anything about the Volga's missile launch sequence?"

This struck Beverly as an odd question for a moment. Then she thought and responded, "A little, yes. They, like us have three officers to fire. And they, like us have the Black Box, embedded deep in the computer system, that verifies a correct signal from the correct source. Basically, tells the computer to go ahead with the code. Without the right frequency, they can enter all the right codes they want to and nothing will happen. Very uncomplicated, but enough of a deterrent to keep even Petrov from firing haphazardly. Except, if your theory is true, holds out."

"I see," said Don in obvious thought.

"You're afraid he's going to launch, aren't you?" Beverly finally said coming to the reality.

"If he can launch, then he has nothing in the world to lose by doing so, and everything to gain by simply threatening to do so. The simple threat is his hole card."

The two people caught in a game of underwater chess stared at each other for a moment. In Don's mind the chess match had just gotten more even, for he had always given the Specter the edge in any battle. Highly maneuverable, impenetrable, the Specter was going to give out more than it received. For Beverly, it was one of survival. Especially the crew. She would never forgive herself if they did not make it.

Finally, Beverly had to ask the million-dollar question. "I think I know you and how you work. You think you can stop it, don't you?"

Don slowly shook his head. "I think so, but it won't be easy. We have to lock onto the right Russian frequency, then hopefully initiate the right coding in the Russian computer. Basically, override their Black Box. That's a lot of ifs and I'm not that great at Russian." Then he looked up into the hopeful green eyes and said, "But, yeah, I think Willy and I can. The Specter has the technology. And our hole card, the GPPP satellite run by our favorite lady, Tinkerbell. That's another thing no other sub in the world has."

"I see." Beverly simply nodded.

Don glanced at his watch. "By my calculations, we should be getting awfully close to the Volga." Then he looked up and said, "Don't worry Bev. The Volga may have been the deepest water sub on the planet, but we can go deeper and do it faster than the Volga can. And they don't know that."

Beverly dropped her hand to the table, then moved it over his. She clutched his hand hard and said, "I'm not worried about me Don. I've been given up for dead once before." Then she rose from her seat and walked quickly out of the room.

On board the Russian submarine Volga, things were almost celebratory. Rabinov and the handful of men on the ship had nothing to lose. When they first encountered the Seattle, the US Skipper still had no indication that they were in a hostile environment. The second the Volga was in range she opened fire with four torpedoes. The Seattle quickly used the counter measures and managed to get off one torpedo before their own demise. The fish missed its mark, for the Volga had turned and the Acoustic Counter Measures detonated the fish prematurely.

Even though the crew rejoiced at the quick demise of the United States Submarine, Commander Ushinko did not share in the joy. He thought stealth and secrecy a much better plan. Of course, Rabinov disagreed. Ushinko followed Rabinov through the massive submarine, down the narrow hallways that seemed to lead nowhere, until they came to the officer's deck.

In Rabinov's quarters they squared off. "Come my friend. Why the long face?" asked Rabinov, making his himself comfortable on his bunk.

"I do not think announcing to the world we are a renegade submarine is the right strategy," said Ushinko angrily, refusing to take the chair at the desk, preferring to stare down the man.

"Oh, come now!" Rabinov smiled. "We are being hunted by the Russian Navy and sooner or later, by the Americans. And has you have heard through the radio traffic; the Russians are still not confessing to their blunder. Hell, they haven't even switched to back up coding yet, allowing us to listen in. And the submarine we just destroyed did not take heed and send a message before their destruction. We could not afford a shadow, even a dull-witted one. And now, with any luck we will have the US Navy squaring off against the Russian Navy. They won't know who's the bad guy. Still, the world breathes tenuously my friend. The Americans still know little." He threw his service hat onto the desk then leaned back folding his arms behind his head and said, "And we have sent a crystal-clear signal to the UN, that by God we mean business. And the Americans, as you have heard, are listening to garble. Their codes are botched. No, my friend, this action accomplished much."

"And we are nowhere near our destination. Anything can happen." Pointed out Ushinko.

"We don't have to be near anything. We have a clear firing solution to the US mainland. The only reason we are on the move at all is to maintain a moving target. In addition, I want to get to deeper water at the Chinook Trough and dive deep."

Ushinko searched the eyes of Rabinov then asked, "And we have not yet tried to fire. If it does not work, we are finished."

Rabinov shook his head in disdain at the man and stated finally, "Every single thing has been planned out. Nothing, as of yet has gone wrong. Besides, even if we can't fire, they will assume we can, and that simply is good enough for now."

Ushinko thought for a moment. "Blackmail? Anyone tampers with our objective and we threaten to blow up San Diego or Vladivostok?" He continued to think for a moment, then he grinned. "I like that. It gives us more leverage."

"Hopefully, in our next encounter we will have a clear sailing path, for anyone to get into our way would cause nuclear destruction. You are a good man Ushinko. But you don't always use the gray matter in your head," mentioned Rabinov, tapping a finger on the side of his skull. Rabinov stretched out even further and added, "Besides. We gave our small crew a chance to find out how well they work under duress and pressure. They came through in the pinch, not one man backing off from our objective. That, to me anyway, was worth the exposure, for now I have the fullest confidence in this crew."

All Ushinko could do was nod his head in agreement. The men did behave exemplarily and now they knew firsthand how to kill and destroy. It was a good lesson, to be sure.

Ushinko finally looked at his watch. "The second courier should be arriving shortly."

"Yes. Then the world will know what we want. Or else."

Ushinko silently closed the small door and strode down the corridor. Why was he there his mind wondered? Unlike most of the crew members he was not waiting for glory or a massive Russian pay off. The resistance had approached him two years ago, and having a young wife who liked baubles, had bought him out of rather large debt. At the time it was good idea, Ushinko even liking the idea of sticking it to the Russian Politburo. They had done little for him even though he was a good member.

But they had just killed a boat full of people who had no idea why. He was not a fool; he knew things could go wrong. But in no scenario had the resistance mentioned going out of their way to kill innocent people. He hated what they had done. But now he was into it up to his neck and unfortunately, regardless of the outcome, must see it to the end. He had the feeling something else nasty was going to go wrong.

Lt. Robert Duran had been sitting at the mapping board, wrestling with his feelings. Until Bobby walked into the control room and sat down opposite him at the large table. He glanced around as Wolfson was over Alex's shoulder, watching the oceanographic equipment. Robert then made his decision and slowly strolled around the board, and found a seat next to Bobby.

Duran came in close to Bobby and whispered, "Do you know anything about the captain?"

Bobby searched Duran's eyes for a moment then replied, "Such as?"

Duran licked his lips, then said halfheartedly, "I don't know how to put this, but I think the captain has a problem."

Bobby sat straight up in his chair and retorted, "I'm still not following."

Duran shushed the man, then said, "Look it. I have the bunk above her. When you came in earlier to wake her up, she was having one hell of a wet dream. And not a good one that I could tell."

Bobby nodded his head slowly. He had also heard her calling out when he entered. "Okay, so she had a nightmare. A nasty one. Close confines will do that."

"Something else. When I told my older brother that Hornacher was going to be Captain, he told me he had been under the impression she wasn't supposed to be on subs anymore."

Bobby was shaking his head the entire time. "She was XO on the Nautilus Two for Christ's sake. The Navy doesn't give you that for being a nut case."

"Her father would though." Duran let these words sink in for a second then added, "Look it. They didn't even tell her this ship was armed, like they were hiding that fact from her. Like they were afraid she would do something."

Bobby again shook his head. "Even her father can't give her commands at his bidding. There's a military process. And Navy Weapons were the ones that said we should be unarmed, and Merrick overrode that one."

Duran too sat back in his seat then said, "Okay, you can dismiss stuff. But my brother had heard that while she was on the Stingray, as weapons officer, she had a thing for one of the cooks and he didn't reciprocate, so she did a striptease for him in the galley. Well, she got caught and that's why they had to return to port less than a week out."

Bobby mulled this over a moment, his mind flashing to her dress in the control room after he had awakened her. But he shook his head once again and said finally, "Look it. Officers don't get promoted for screwing up. I don't care who your daddy is. There has to be a good explanation."

"Really? Rumor has it she was tortured at Annapolis and had an abortion and now has a real problem with men. Sort of psychotic if you know what I mean. Then I also heard she was nude in the control room of the Nautilus Two. That's why they transferred her sorry ass out of there."

Bobby rolled his eyes and stared down at the mapping board. Still, he had also heard things through the Naval web, the Submarine Corp being a small one. But in the entire week, he had not seen one little thing really wrong. In fact, she seemed to be doing one hell of a good job in his book.

Then Bobby's mind shot forward and he retorted, "Mr. Merrick and Commander Wolfson don't seem to have any problems with her. In fact, I ran into Crash and he said they insisted she stay in charge during this confrontation."

"Yeah. And what would the Admiral do if they took away her command?"

Bobby only shook his head and said finally, "Look it. As Medic on board, I'll keep an eye on her, but I really don't see any problems."

Duran shook his head and stated, "But a couple of us do."

CHAPTER 15

"I don't understand," muttered Beverly. She, Bobby, Wolfson and Duran were huddled over the mapping board. Alex was fixated on all his monitoring controls. Merrick and Willy were sitting side by side directing satellite scans, searching desperately for a heat signature from the massive nuclear engines of the Volga. Tinkerbell was running scans from other satellites, friend or foe, for anything out of the ordinary.

"We've passed them," uttered Bobby looking at the same information everyone else was. On the mapping board was the presumed point of the Volga. To the East was the exact location of the Specter, the points having intersected.

Don swiveled around, both hands clutching the arms of the chair tightly and said, "Nonsense. We're missing something."

Lt. Duran looked up and said to Merrick, "But given the slow twenty-two knot submerged speed of the Volga and the range from the destruction of the Seattle, we should be passed her."

"What was her presumed speed up to the Seattle?" asked Don.

Lt. Duran nodded forcibly and said, "Twenty-two point two one five knots. We're being consistent and we've detected no course changes or subterfuges in her directions. Not even a Crazy Ivan to that point. She's heading east. By our mapping, we've gone passed her."

"Maybe Rabinov has a different strategy," asserted Don thinking absently.

Beverly slapped the table and said suddenly in eye opening candor, "Of course! Why the hell didn't we see it."

Ralph nodded his head also and muttered, "Sure, he slowed down."

"What?" asked Don.

Don could see the lights shine in Beverly's eyes as she said, "What you said Don. Rabinov would have realized he's been, or going to be discovered from the destruction of the Seattle. Plus, his courier at the UN."

Ralph nodded knowingly, and observed, "He knows he's going to be hunted. He would have gone deep, hugging the sea floor, using the outcropping and ridges to hide his location."

"He would have abandoned the all-out race for the coast and gone to a hide and seek mode. Especially with a sub that big and can go that deep," inserted Beverly.

"How fast can he travel like that?" asked Bobby, already working out the range in his head.

Both Beverly and Ralph shook their heads. "Not fast," Beverly finally answered. "He would have switched to Magneto drive. Eight knots maybe, especially with a boat the size of the Volga. Damned thing doesn't turn for shit, and considering all the outcropping that permeate the Pacific."

Don had walked over to the board and looked down. Bobby and Duran were already working out a probable scenario. Don then asked, "Look it all these out cropping. The Volga would be twisting and turning every twenty minutes. A lot of stress for his short staff."

Beverly gazed down at the board the topographic ocean floor pointing out the several land marks rising above the standard ocean floor. Finally, she sighed and said simply, "Right."

Wolfson then observed, "But what if he's gone deep, say two hundred meters, and skirting the larger outcropping?" Ralph's finger guided a line through the topography, past several of the large obstructions, through the ocean on a much improved, straighter course. "The Volga could then maybe do twelve, maybe thirteen knots and steer clear of only a few obstacles. Plus, make it still damned hard to find her. And the Russian Fleet still has no idea where the Volga is going."

Beverly nodded then said, "He'd still be making good time and no heat signature. Sort of a balance of the two. And if Rabinov is as good as he thinks he is, he would have dove deep given the changes in topography." She glanced over at Bobby who was already doing the projections for this scenario.

Lt Duran looked on as Bobby brought up a more detailed mapping of the ocean floor near the Aleutian Trench and pinpointed the exact position of the Specter. Then he projected the proposed position of the Volga.

Don looked down and asked, "That's what, twenty kilometers?"

Bobby looked up and said, "Yeah."

Beverly quickly turned and gave Crash new bearings, then looked over at the man responsible for finding the Volga and said, "If we're right Alex, we should have contact. Keep an eagle eye."

"Aye Ma'am," Hernandez responded without so much as twitching his eyes from his four screens. His passive array monitors could pick up something at any moment.

The Specter cruising at sixty-six knots was making ground up quickly and it did not take long. Hernandez pressed his earphones to his head then shouted excitedly, "I have screws bearing five degrees to the port bow!" Every monitor in front of the man burst to life in pinpointing the big submarine.

"Monitoring, I need a depth monitor, and a sounding depth," expelled Beverly quickly.

"The Volga is running around one hundred twenty meters give or take from this range, Captain, and we're running almost a thousand meters." responded Alex swiftly.

"Steering, take us down bubble to one hundred meters make course change to intercept, back off to quarter throttle," instructed Beverly quickly.

"Changing course Ma'am, diving to one hundred meters, five degrees to port bow, and backing off to twenty-five knots," responded Mr. Caldwell, glancing up at his own projection screen to view an undetermined object in which to steer for and making the slight adjustment to the steering controls and speed.

Bobby and Duran were already prefiguring the routes when Beverly asked Alex, "Hernandez, I need visual confirmation before we do anything. I don't want to get into a war with the Gorbachev or the Minsk by accident." Referring to the two other Russian Submarines, she knew to be in the North Pacific.

"Yes Ma'am, still scanning. I have visual at eleven kilos, but I cannot confirm target. We're getting visual from a head on direction and it's hard to pinpoint, especially with rock formations in between," Hernandez responded.

Beverly nodded then said to the communications officer, "Steve, make ready to open up communications with the Volga if this is her."

"WHAT!?" burst Don. Ralph was standing beside him and grimaced at the sharp noise. "Darned Captain, you could have warned me," said Ralph to Beverly as he pushed a finger into his ear to stop the ringing.

Don was in an immediate rage. "Don't tell me we have to send them a greeting card before we blow them to hell? Oh, Jesus Christ, Beverly!"

Beverly walked around the board and handed him the orders from the Admiral. He snatched the paper from her hand and quickly scanned the contents. "Detain? How the hell do you DETAIN a submarine?" He yelled. He ripped the paper up in his hands and threw the shreds into the air. It was as if the man was going to blow, when he grasped hold of the railing surrounding the mapping board and pulled mightily. Then he took five quick, deep breathes.

Don then said methodically, "Navy protocol will be the death of us all. FINE. We detain them, play nice nice, THEN we blow the damned thing to hell."

Beverly's dark eyebrows were arched in the way a parent would watch her child throw a temper tantrum. She said, "Don, they've still got no verification that the Volga has done anything wrong and the Russian Navy won't confirm. We unfortunately, have to play it safe, before we start a nuclear war."

"Captain? I got another image on scanners," inserted Hernandez quickly.

Beverly's mind shot forward and she asked swiftly, "Torpedo?"

"No. Much bigger."

Ralph looked over at the oceanographic man as Don raced over to take a look. Ralph asked, "Another Sub?"

Don quickly looked up from the screen and responded softly. "No. The computer identifies it as Carcharodon Megalodon. And it's headed straight for us."

"What?" said Ralph in disbelief.

"Captain. I have verification on the screws. The computer says it is the Russian submarine, Delta type Five, very probably the Volga, all five hundred and ninety-one feet of her," inserted Hernandez quickly.

"Damned, that's a big boat," muttered Bobby.

Beverly shot him a withering glance then commanded, "Communications, send command our last location in case anything goes wrong and tell them our current situation. Then get me a God-Damned Russian frequency on the Volga." Then she turned to the other side of the control room and said, "Weapons, plot a solution for torpedoes' one and two and load, do not open outer doors quite yet, and keep a finger on our USAC."

"Aye Captain." In the entire shakedown cruise till now, Eddy had been referred to very seldom. He had been asked on occasion what the response would be from weapons in certain scenarios, but going under the disguise of having no weapons, there was little he could do. Even with his experience on the USS Seattle, this was still new to him, with ten monitors to keep track of. He was quite surprised to feel an adrenalin rush as he armed the weapons console for the first time. He felt no qualms about following orders and blowing another human being sky high. Especially one much bigger and obviously deadly. That was in his psychological make up. Still, the small-town boy from Iowa was sweating, with an ever so slight tremor to his trigger finger, and a finger pushing his glasses back up.

On the Volga, the situation was even more confusing. Rabinov had been called off the conn by his sonar man.

"I have an object in the water but the computer can't identify it," said Lieutenant Peter Markova, a Ukrainian born naval officer and the only one on board the least bit familiar with the detection system of the Volga.

"What do you mean? How big is it?" Asked Rabinov, leaning over the man's shoulder.

"The computer can't get a real grasp of it. It's giving me reading of between twenty too about forty meters long and closing fast in our baffles. It's not a whale sir, by the shape and the speed, but the computer doesn't know what it is," replied Peter, not happy with the computers inability to identify the noise, as he glanced at the Acoustic Data Processing systems and the Active Array. All of which were telling him little.

"Is it dangerous?" asked Rabinov growing concerned.

"It appears to be an animal of some sort, but it's closing fast."

Everyone in the Volga's control center could feel the tension as whatever was swimming by did so, causing a wake over the submarine that could be heard inside.

Commander Ushinko pulled up next to Rabinov and said, "Apparently, whatever it was didn't want anything to do with us."

"It makes you wonder though," replied Rabinov thinking out loud.

Suddenly Lt. Markova pressed his headphones in tight and yelled, "I have a new disturbance five degrees to starboard bow."

"Now what?" asked Ushinko looking over the sonar man's shoulder.

Peter glanced at the long-range Active Passive Array sonar. The small computer flickered then spit out its interpretation of the new noise. Peter nodded his head and replied, "Computer says seismic abnormality."

"Seismic? Out here? Put on speakers," commanded Rabinov.

The small speaker above the sonar man's head came alive with a swooshing noise.

Rabinov listened to the uniform noise, then asked, "Can you pinpoint?"

"No sir. It's still quite away off, but it's moving closer."

"It's moving?" Ushinko asked incredulously, then looked over at Rabinov and asked, "Since when does an abnormality move?"

"Can you get an idea of the distance?" asked Rabinov ignoring Ushinko.

"It's like an echo. It fades in an out and but …"

"But what man?" demanded Rabinov into the face of the now scared sonar man.

"Well, it's clearly coming at us at a uniform speed. And damned fast. Faster than anything man made other than a torpedo." Said the man with more experience than anyone else on that boat.

Rabinov stood up and glared at the sonar scopes which only showed sporadic blips and marks. "What the hell is out there?" he finally muttered. He suddenly felt like he was in a chess game and someone changed the rules.

"Sir! I have an incoming communique," yelled Lt. Vilnius over the ship's speakers from the conn, the onetime driver and now communications officer, having inherited the job with very little training.

Rabinov grimaced, waved it off, then snatched a phone from its little stand and yelled into it, "Communications ignore."

Vilnius inserted strongly, "Sir. I think you should hear this. It's from the American Submarine Specter. They're demanding … our unconditional surrender." That statement fairly echoed through the massive metal tube.

Every single crewman on board the Volga stopped breathing. The air in the cold metal cylinder was humid and thick. It felt as if no one could breathe. Suddenly, they were being hunted by some unseeing force. Two separate noises deep underwater, and the computers could not even hazard a good guess. Worst of all it was a force that could see them. Young Ukrainian faces all searched each other for support. All they found was fear.

Two years previously they had been approached. Some were already on board the Volga; some would be carefully transferred. Vlad Yashangov had spent millions of rubles, helping out the immediate families of the crew men, buying their immediate allegiance. Not only that, when Kuznotzhov was back in power, they would in turn inherit some of that power. They would be the literal start to the future government of the new Ukraine. They would have the world by the tail. For the rest of their lives.

Rabinov was infuriated at the voice echoing through his submarine. Again, he looked over at the sonar screens which showed a soft green background. Finally, he looked down at Peter and demanded, "That fast-moving signature was a submarine. Where is it?"

The Lieutenant merely shrugged his shoulders, completely befuddled. All he had was a swooshing noise he could not pinpoint, and a blank green screen.

Ushinko came up next to Petrov and said quickly, "We need to buy time."

Rabinov nodded. The swooshing noise was coming in fast, he needed to slow his already lumbering boat down so that maybe sonar could pick up something. Anything at that point would be helpful.

Having not yet put the phone away, he yelled into it, "Engineering this the captain, I want full reverse on the engines. I'm going to buy some time."

Lt. Federov glanced up at his steering controls and grimaced. Trying to steer that massive sub in reverse was not much harder, still it was not something he wanted to do on a constant basis, given the topography.

"Captain Hornacher. I have an incoming message from Admiral Rabinov of the Volga. He says he wants to talk to the Captain of the Specter," relayed Steve to Beverly.

She thought for the barest second then asked, "Does he speak English? Or do we go to Russian computer speak?"

"Affirmative Captain. In English."

"Put him on control room speakers." Beverly had actually wished for the computer to translate for her voice would have come across as a male computer translation. She steeled her nerves for she knew he was going to be insulting.

"Admiral Rabinov, this is Captain Hornacher of the United States Naval Submarine, the USS Specter. I have been told by United States Fleet Command to find your position, halt your passage, have you surface and have you boarded by one of our warships. In this matter we are seeking an unconditional surrender because of your terrorist activities."

Rabinov smiled. "A feminine Captain," he responded gleefully. "How quaint. Are things that desperate in the land of the free that they have stooped to using women to fight their battles?" Then a sudden realization crossed Rabinov's mind and he added, "Wait a minute. Hornacher. Any relation to Admiral Hornacher? Oh my, that's priceless. Daddy bought his little girl a spooky little toy boat."

This even rankled Don's nerves. More than ever he just wanted to push the button and blow the asshole to hell. Ralph tried to stay detached and watched Beverly's response.

Beverly had heard worse in her life time and merely brushed it aside. Taking no notice of this as she continued. "Admiral. You know you are being charged with the destruction of the USS Seattle and terrorist actions. We are to take any force necessary in accomplishing this." That's when she played her hole card and added, "And considering you can't get a clear signal of my spooky little boat, I would think this would be wise decision."

Rabinov stood speechless for a second. This rattled him. He was being out maneuvered by an American woman. Choosing his words, he responded, "So. The rumors are true. The Americans have made their stealth sub. Is it also true that it is a little bitty thing not capable of swatting a fly?"

Ralph motioned for Steve to break off the control room speaker, then he grabbed Beverly's elbow and said, "Beverly, he's playing us. He's buying time and trying to ascertain our position."

"Captain?" Insisted Hernandez.

Beverly looked into the eyes of Ralph and searched for a barest of moments. Then she said without turning, "Go ahead."

"I have several things happening. First of all, that shark is fifteen hundred meters' distance from us, making a direct line and closing fast. Secondly, the Volga has come to a dead stop and opened all four of her doors and flooding tubes. At seven kilos' distant she's getting ready to fire."

"Do you know if it has a lock on us?" asked Beverly still looking directly at Ralph. Her mind was racing.

Willy responded, "No. But by my calculations, if they fire a salvo in a wide pattern, they would get damned close. Especially if their fish have heat-seeking ability. Even we expel fuel."

Beverly nodded at Ralph and said, "Control, go to battle stations. Weapons, make ready. Communications, put me back on com."

Ralph wheeled around immediately and said sternly into his microphone, "You heard the Captain, BATTLE STATIONS, BATTLE STATIONS, BATTTLE STATIONS. Tinkerbelle, battle stations protocol."

"Aye Commander. Initiating all back-up systems and going to battle stations format," responded Tinkerbelle.

"You're on Ma'am," responded Steve as the lights went to red and a low throbbing alarm went through all the radios.

Beverly turned away from Ralph, gathered her thoughts for the barest of seconds, then said, "Admiral Rabinov, you have opened your doors and flooded your tubes. I take that as a hostile response. You leave me no choice."

Rabinov gritted his teeth. Ushinko said to him softly, "The American woman does not play games."

Rabinov thought for a moment, then turned around to face Peter's back and asked, "Has our animal made any moves?"

Peter was watching intently, using the sonar to make a computer scenario of its destination. It was making a beeline for something. Maybe, just maybe he thought, it was the American sub. Finally, he reported to the Admiral, "Yes, sir. It seems to making a straight line to something. Plus, I could have sworn I heard a mechanical sound."

"Listen and tell me if the animal stops and you can get a lock on the mechanical sound," Petrov acknowledged, happy that at least one man on his sub was an expert. The radar man just might have saved them all.

"Captain Hornacher?" asked Hernandez again.

"Yes Alex," Beverly said still waiting for Petrov's response.

"One hundred fifty meters before impact with the shark. One thirty-five."

"The damned thing is coming to get us. Just like the Iceland Venture," alerted Ralph ultimately coming to the grim realization first. The damned shark was not going to just swim by, it was zeroing in for the attack.

Don threw his hands up in the air and said, "What fucking shark attacks a submarine?"

"Don, this one does. Statistically, our prehistoric shark has a dislike for mechanical devices," stated Tinkerbell very quickly

"One hundred meters Captain," inserted Hernandez.

"Too late to fire a torpedo!" Yelled Don quickly.

"Captain?" asked Ralph quickly.

Beverly wheeled around and yelled at Crash, "Steering, evasive maneuvering, let's make the damned thing catch us."

"Aye Ma'am," responded Crash, sending the Specter into a port side dive.

"Their passive sonar might be able to lock onto the disturbance of the shark," stated Ralph coming to the reality.

Beverly's heart sank for a moment as the enormity of the situation grabbed her by the throat. It just did not occur to her the shark would actually attack the sub. Up till that point, she thought as all other sea creatures, it would just swim by. "Damn! Brace for impact," Beverly stated loudly, as another alarm went off throughout the all the radios. "Weapons, countermeasures on that damned beast!"

"Aye Captain!" Lt Faulk responded. However, at sixty-six knots the USAC was going to take time to initiate, as he had never once turned on the controls of their Ultrasonic weapon. Tapping his controls, he opened up the outer doors to the right parabolic dish. Glancing once again at another monitor, the shark was closing fast. Having no time to line up any kind of aiming, he simply hit the fire button, hoping the massive sound generator would terrify the shark.

The intense thrumming echoed through the Specter, Eddie actually getting a fairly accurate shot off. The shark took a majority of huge blast of energy, stopping all eighty-seven feet of the beast in its tracks. Again, since its reawakening, it encountered something completely new. This shot through his body, quivered his spine and rattled his brain cells. For a moment it stalled. For a moment anyway.

"It just pissed him off! He picked up speed," Alex yelled. His screen showing a clear, exterior camera view of the huge beast slicing straight for the conning tower. Underwater cameras picked up the prehistoric monster opening his huge maw for the attack. That was really something Alex had just as soon not seen.

The prehistoric shark had to turn slightly to latch onto the diving Specter. If Crash had merely dived straight down, the one good eye of the beast might not have noticed. But as it was the Specter swung right into its field of vision and it quickly made a beeline for its target, crashing headlong into the swung away antenna array of the conning tower.

The Specter lurched to the starboard fifteen degrees as it flung the crew of the control room. The computers quickly equalized the ballast and sent the sub back. Then the eighty-seven feet of the fish shoved the submarine the other direction, using the conning tower for leverage, as the crew was flung the other direction.

"Can we back away from this thing?" Beverly implored Don in between lurches.

"Hell, I don't know but it's worth a try!"

"Steering, full reverse. Back off! Get us out of here!"

"Yes ma'am," Crash replied gritting his teeth. At the battle station call he was automatically harnessed to his chair, but still the shuddering and turning of the shark were playing havoc with his controls. The bulk of the determined shark was hard to steer around.

Peter instinctively yanked the headphones off his head, genuinely afraid he had lost an eardrum. "Good God I don't know what the hell that was!" Exclaimed the young man, the noise still echoing through his head.

"Surely we can zero in on that noise!" Demanded Rabinov hearing the massive thrumming noise echo through the metal skin of the Volga. Rabinov then dashed across to the sonar station to look over the sonar operator's shoulder. "Can we get a fix on that? He yelled again at Peter who had one finger in his ear.

Peter glanced around at his passive array console, saw a good coordinate solution showing on his computer monitor and said, "Of course Comrade Admiral. I will send coordinates to weapons immediately."

Rabinov quickly grabbed the phone again and said quickly, "Weapons, are we in position to fire on THAT target?"

"Yes, sir, we have a confirmation and are attempting to lock on," Rabinov heard from Malovich, the weapons officer.

"The second you have confirmation, fire tubes one, two, three and four."

Ushinko walked up behind the man and said softly, "You may have gotten very lucky my friend."

"Maybe there is a God after all," Rabinov smiled back.

"Captain! Four fish in the water. Range, seventeen hundred meters and closing fast," yelled Hernandez. Then he quickly added, "And Captain. They are going to be damned accurate."

The Specter jolted one more time as Beverly asked, "Weapons, can we lock onto those and take them out?"

"Negative Captain. Not from the front tubes," replied Eddy glancing at all his monitors showing the Specter's level line bouncing around and the shark thrashing over the bow of the sub.

"Well then, open the rear tubes, lock on the two that you can and fire!"

Just then the sub again shuddered and lurched twenty degrees to starboard, sending everyone not strapped down to the right side of the submarine. Eddy however, was grimacing mightily. These torpedoes were not ready and the several moments it took, to open doors and calculate the firing solutions cost him precious seconds.

Ralph yelled, "Captain, I suggest you grab a chair and get ready for impact!"

Don had latched onto the back of a chair next to Willy to keep himself from sprawling headlong against map board. He crawled around and sat, swiveling wildly, belting himself in.

"Captain, impact in fifteen seconds," said Willy surprisingly calm.

"Communications, send out a quick signal to command to give them our last location," barked Captain Hornacher, as the grim realization that the Volga had pinpointed them because of the rogue shark.

"Aye aye Captain," replied Steve grateful to have something to do while destruction seemed so eminent.

It took the five seconds for Faulk to get the rear fish ready. Eddy yelled, "Two rear fish away, and they are locked onto the lead torpedoes."

Beverly and Don immediately understood. Four torpedoes exploding within a hundred meters of the boat was almost as bad as actually being hit.

They heard the torpedoes explode. The underwater detonation was so close to the Specter that it rattled the little ship. It seemed to enrage the shark even worse as it renewed its ferocity on the small submarine. The shark literally hurled its weight against the boat and sent it thirty degrees to port. In the background was the voice of Hernandez counting down the distance from impact.

"Two fish down, two fish two hundred meters, one seventy, one fifty..." Hernandez continued.

Eddy frantically glanced around all the weapons control, wishing for something to do. He was supposed to shoot something, the USAC not yet regenerated, the torpedo's way to close. He felt completely helpless. All the weapons at his disposal and he was completely useless.

"Fifty meters, brace for impact!" Yelled Hernandez, the terror evident in his voice.

Don reached over and pulled Beverly into the chair with him. Bobby, Duran, and Ralph were all strapped into the map board chairs as impact seemed inevitable.

Duran glared over at Bobby and slowly shook his head.

"HANG ON!" yelled Beverly as she glanced into the face of the man she prayed was as good as his word. "God, I hope you're right," she murmured as she buried her head into his shoulder.

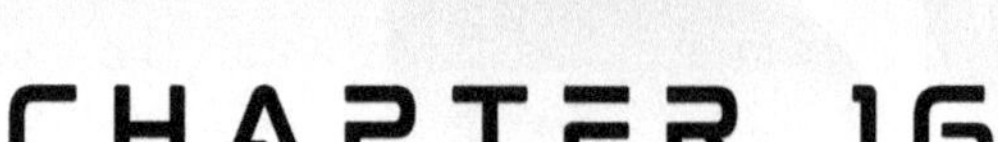

CHAPTER 16

On board the Volga the small crew held their breath. They had watched their torpedoes getting picked off one at a time. However, the computer acknowledged, the last two detonated against something. They all watched closely as the Passive Wide Aperture Bow Array of the Volga searched diligently for any signs of life through the intense explosion. Sonar picked up nothing but the echo of the blast. After a few moments it signaled. Finally, Rabinov allowed the Active Array to send out the intense burst of sound, the usual pinging heard throughout the ship and water. After several more moments, the computer finally verified with the green letters, TARGET DESTROYED.

Ushinko sighed heavily as the skeleton crew on the bridge of the Volga rose up in a thunderous cheered. Admiral Rabinov was not so sure. After few more moments he had the sonar man double check for the swooshing noise. After 40 seconds of waiting for the explosion to clear, there was none to be found. The sonar signature of the shark was also gone. Rabinov waited.

"You do not believe the computer?" asked a relieved Ushinko.

"I am not so convinced it would be that easy. We may have hit the animal and not the submarine. I want what little confirmation I can get." He turned to Ushinko and said, "We wait."

They waited a couple more minutes. Still nothing was moving, no sound was heard. Acknowledging the results, Rabinov signaled for the one quarter speed, maintaining an easterly course.

Ushinko following Rabinov back to his quarters, all the while asking the Admiral what the next plan was. Ushinko was getting into extreme distress at all this warfare.

"I have no doubt that the American ship sent a signal of its last location. We are now in a very tense game of hide and seek." The man sat at his cubbyhole of a desk and thought. Finally, he took out a note pad to scribbled a note. He thought for a moment to choose his words and scribed a rather long message. Then he handed it to Ushinko. "Have the radioman send this to the American Fleet."

Ushinko read the note. Then he looked up at Rabinov asked, "Do you think that is wise to goad them like this?"

Rabinov thought the sentiment funny but did not smile. He only responded, "We are being hunted fiercely my friend. We have destroyed two of the best boats the American Navy has to offer. I want them to know who did it and that we will stop at nothing. Get up to periscope depth and send it. Put one hundred-ten percent on the reactors to pick up some speed, while we are near the surface, then dive to three hundred meters. And go to Magneto drive. I'm not sure about the NEWEST American technology, but it will baffle the Russians."

Rabinov was going to sit down on his bunk when he chanced to see the phone in his room. He latched onto the receiver and rung up weapons. He said into the handset, "Weapons, this is Admiral Rabinov. I want Sturgeon missiles one, two, three and four fueled and make ready for launch. That's right. I want to be ready."

Ushinko looked over at the man, and suddenly felt old and very vulnerable. He had hated what the Russian Government had done to his home land. It was one way he would get out of in budget situation. And he knew he was in a position like no other human being in the world. A trusted officer of the Russian Navy on the biggest submarine on the planet. But somehow, he had hoped no one would get killed. This was going beyond his wildest nightmares. And now the possibility of nuclear holocaust had just raised its huge and ugly head. He feared where it was all headed.

Half of the Joint Chiefs of Staff were on pins and needles. The first message from the Specter had been that they were engaging the Volga, and of their exact position. General Blanchett, Admiral Hornacher, Admiral Cartwright and Lucius stood watching the large overhead computer screens. Then came the last message from the Specter. They were under attack from the Volga. And in an unrealistic wrinkle, a prehistoric shark.

Blanchett looked over at Hornacher and asked simply, "Shark? What kind of damned shark attacks a submarine?"

"Supposedly it sank the ship Iceland Venture a couple of days ago. The Specter helped in rescuing the crew." He did not care about the damned shark. He wanted desperately to know what was happening out there in the cold water of the North Atlantic.

General Blanchett could tell Hornacher was no mood to talk so he pulled in behind Cartwright and asked, "How big is this shark?"

Cartwright whispered back, "Best guess is about a ninety-foot long."

Blanchett nodded as if that were everyday event, then muttered, "And the Specter is roughly two-hundred feet long." He stopped to think, then remarked softly, "This isn't good, is it?"

"No sir. It isn't," replied Cartwright.

The communications console came alive as the operator wrote down a hasty message. He stared at it briefly, then stood up and handed it to General Blanchett. "Sir, this was intercepted by the Gerald Ford in the Pacific. They felt they needed to pass it on."

"Thank you." General Blanchett opened the note and read it carefully. He folded it up methodically. "Damn," was all he said.

Lucius looked at him and asked, "It's not good news, is it?"

Blanchett hand him the note and said, "No."

Lucius read quickly, folded it, but before he could tuck it away Admiral Hornacher snatched it from him.

"It's about the Specter, isn't it?" asked Hornacher unfolding the paper.

"I'm so sorry Jack," Lucius muttered.

Hornacher pulled out his reading glasses and read, TO THE FLEET COMMANDER US NAVAL FORCES IN THE NORTH PACIFIC. NICE TRY. LITTLE GHOST SUBMARINE DID NOT PUT UP MUCH OF A FIGHT, A DIRECT HIT BY RUSSIAN TORPEDOES AND SUB AND SHE CAPTAIN ARE NOW GONE. STAY OUT! OF THIS OR MORE WILL BE KILLED. ADMIRAL RABINOV, COMMANDER VOLGA.

As any father would want to do, he denied it at first in his heart. Then he read it again. He balled up the paper and flung it at the floor.

Blanchett grabbed him, staring into the hard and lost eyes of a father. "Jack, listen to me. We're going to get him. Do you understand? We're going to hunt him down and blow him to hell."

Hornacher sighed heavily, the hatred and loathing filling his heart. There was no ready action for the man, his mind racing, his chin holding steadfast. He blinked several times, snorting as he did, his fists turning white from the exertion.

"Can we get me out to the Ford?" asked Hornacher finally, talking of the newest and largest Aircraft Carrier the Navy had.

"No Jack. You're of no use out there. These people know how to do their job. We … I need you right here. We need to develop a strategy," commanded Blanchett.

Cartwright had gone over to retrieve the note, but instead of reading it, he folded it up and slid it in his pocket.

Hornacher snuffled a second and said, "Yes sir. Let me compose myself for a few moments and then …"

"… Then we'll get the bastard." Finished the General.

"Right," Hornacher nodded forcibly.

Cartwright grabbed Hornacher by the elbow, led him to the rear staircase and guided him upstairs to the glassed in conference room. Leading the man to a chair, Cartwright left the lights off and instead went over to the refrigerator on the back wall and pulled out a cold bottle of water. He opened the top and placed it in front of the Admiral.

The Admiral stared at the bubbles in the water. Finally, he opened up. "Dan, I never got to tell her I loved her. I never told her how proud I was of her. And now. Now she's gone."

Cartwright nodded, but he could only imagine. His one son was an accountant, nice and safe in an office building. He could only imagine. He pulled up a chair next to Hornacher and simply put a hand on the shaking fingers of the man.

Hornacher looked up in the semi darkness, a tear slipping down his face, and uttered, "Do you know how much guts it took for her to follow in my footsteps? Do you know how much hell she went through at Annapolis?" Hornacher looked over Cartwright then blubbered, "Do you know she was … imprisoned? And she STILL stuck it out. Anyone else would have quit Dan. Not my daughter. Not her."

"I know Jack. It's hard, very hard to lose someone you love so much and so special to you," said Dan as consolingly as possible. He had been close to the family even when Beverly was a teenager. He had heard and helped the family in their time of need, especially that little time in her life when they could not find her, and feared her dead. But now his heart ached but for a different reason. The entire crew of the Specter was gone. All the brave men, some of the best in the Navy and the experimental ship, supposedly indestructible, was gone. And he had a hand in it all. Merrick had insisted and he agreed to arm the ship. And now they were dead.

A handkerchief came out of Hornacher's back pocket. He snuffled into it and dabbed at his eyes. "I never told her that. I won't even get the satisfaction of burying her," muttered Jack.

"The carrier group Gerald Ford has a sub hunter in it and they're only a few hundred miles from the Volga. They'll get Rabinov, Jack. We'll get revenge."

Hornacher looked over at Dan and said, "I don't want revenge. I want my daughter back." Then a sudden horror-stricken thought gripped the Admiral and he muttered, "Oh, God. The Misses! She'll never see grandchildren. She'll hate me the rest of my life." Hornacher grabbed Cartwright and said shaking his head fiercely, "She didn't want her to go to sea. Said this would happen to one of us. Oh God, she's going to kill me."

Cartwright's mind suddenly went to Beverly's mother. The news will indeed crush her. He was already running out of words to say. All he could do was glance at his friend then look out the overhead windows to the EROC. He suddenly thought of the note in his pocket. He pulled it out slowly and glanced at it. Then something struck him as odd about the note and he read it again. He stood up and using the light streaming in from the windows, he read the note a third time. Then he looked over at the bank of pictures, one being from the GPPP satellite.

"It doesn't add up."

"What?" asked Hornacher dejectedly, his thoughts still on his lost daughter and distraught wife.

Cartwright studied the note one more time, then he turned and waved the note in the air. "The message. It doesn't make any sense."

Even in the dimness of the conference room Hornacher could see the hope in Dan's eyes. "What do you mean?"

"It doesn't make any sense. You see Jack, the Specter is designed to take a hit. Merrick's God-Damned sub can take a direct hit torpedo. The Volga doesn't know this. The Volga does not CONFIRM destruction and neither do we. Even with two fish, the Specter stands a good chance of survival. It is going to take more than a long-range fish to kill that sub. I think they're still out there, Jack. Crippled, playing dead, but still out there."

Hornacher snuffled once then followed the line of thought. "If she's damaged, then she would have shut down and gone to silent running to keep from getting into another altercation. Maybe going so far as to shut down positioning." Jack looked up at his friend then asked, "Sincerely now Dan. Don't raise my hopes. This is really something I'd just as soon not get into with the wife."

Cartwright nodded and thought deeply. "Sincerely now Jack. I wouldn't call the Misses just yet. I think they're hiding until Don can make repairs." He thought of the work that went into that sub, and the money. He thought of the larger-than-life Wolfson and Schmitty fixing everything. And how pissed Don was at that moment. Suddenly, he felt as if they were very much alive. Finally, he stated, "In fact, I would bet my bottom dollar on it."

It was the man Cartwright knew, coming back to life. Hornacher balled up his fist and stated, "Then we need to mobilize. Get the last coordinates and get the Gerald Ford and the Jackson out there." He looked up into the face of his assistant, his friend of the last six years and said finally, "If there's even a chance Dan, we need to get some sound buoys and start dropping air born torpedoes'. Enough to walk across the God-Damned Ocean if necessary." Then he rose and said, "And George better get some results soon from the Russians. Or I'm going to blow them to hell too."

Cartwright smiled, and looked out across the Control room at the large screen showing various satellite images. The satellite was finding nothing, which made his heart lighter. Dan then glanced over at Jack. A warrior at war may not be a happy man, but he was a busy man. Or in this case, a man with a mission. A mission to forget.

That was when Cartwrights eyes locked onto the images coming from the GPPP satellite. It suddenly showed the Gerald Ford fleet, all eleven ships. Then it expanded out and a kilometer scale bounced to the bottom of the screen, around three hundred kilometers distant to a new location. Cartwright smiled. Tinkerbell was showing the way.

Carcharodon Megalodon had been on deck side of the Specter when the torpedo struck it below on the keel side. Like a few days previously it suffered an explosive concussion which rolled it off, pulling teeth lose and yanking its huge head in an unnatural fashion.

It floated away from the submarine, through a haze of blurry vision and bubbles that the explosive had caused. It rolled a few times, caught its sense, and swam away, its ancient mind completely unaware of the new world around it. Another big noisy white thing in the water, and it too was inedible.

The attack itself had been unsuccessful. The large ridge backed whale meant a feast to the eyes and to the stomach. It even sounded somewhat like a whale. And yet, it could not get through the skin to the soft blubber underneath.

It was hungry and it was at a loss. The teaming ocean that it once knew had fewer fish, and huge inedible things floating through it. It was maintaining enough food to stay alive, but just barely.

And not once in its travels had it caught sight of a female. Its ancient mind knew it was supposed to propagate the species. But there was nothing. It had run across a tiger shark, did not smell the hormones that would signal compliance, nor could it smell the fear that ran amok in front of its huge nostrils. It could barely discern the small, eight-foot shark. And so, ate it.

And where was the big, tempting, slow reptilians that made easy catches? The huge shark could not know they were now erased from history. It was in a new world and a new time. Not the one where dinosaurs walked the earth and ruled the seas. But of humans and large machines that could not be eaten.

Finally awakening with yet another dull ache, it kicked its huge semi moon tale in and drove itself away from yet another thing it could not digest. Its huge maw tasted of blood, its own as it sliced through the water. Its senses could still hear the pinging and motor whine of the Volga, but had lost the swooshing noise of what it thought was a whale. No matter. It was on the hunt again. For it was still hungry.

Little did it know the eighty-seven-foot shark was caught in a war, and was helping sway the balance.

CHAPTER 17

The two Russian torpedoes with a combined explosive weight of twelve hundred pounds, managed to impact on the port side aft of the Specter. It quickly flung the shark off its hold on the conning tower, huge seven-inch teeth grating across the surface, gnawing through the water. When they exploded against the hull, they shot the rear of the ship sideways, then sending it into a roll, pitching the ship ninety degrees off the center. The left wall had been turned into the floor. The computers running the ballast quickly compensated, the different compartments flooding and discharging water, trying to come to grips with the turn of events. They flooded the starboard ballast to try and straighten the ship and keep it from rolling over completely. Tinkerbelle was a busy girl. Inside, things were even more chaotic.

The initial explosion had a jarring effect, literally shaking teeth, as drastic as if a car had left the road doing a hundred miles an hour. At the last moments before impact, one could hear the whine of the explosive coming at them. Everyone on board the Specter gritted their teeth, and prayed the submarine was as bullet proof as everyone told them it was. But the bumpy ride had just begun. The explosion hit enough on the bottom side of the sub to send it into a roll. Dramatically and drastically, to send minds reeling at the turn of events. The reverberation of sound through the ship was deafening for the barest of seconds, then leveled out into a loud metallic echo.

Don, as if in a carnival ride, had the weight fling him around to his back, but the momentum with Beverly in his lap, flung him completely back around again. He could not hang onto her as he was now looking down at the left wall. The jarring and shaking of the ship and inertia and gravity took hold of her as she clutched at the air. Not anticipating the abrupt inertia, he had merely wrapped her up in his arms. His grip was torn loose, his fingers clutching at the air, latching onto a shirt sleeve and watching it rip as she grasped at his hands. He watched helplessly as she fell away. The fall itself was short but the slamming motion effectively threw her at the far wall. She hit the navigational consoles hard on her right side, instantly turning her into a rag doll as the impact blacked her out.

Ralph viewed this as he was sitting safely strapped into his chair and hanging onto the rail around the mapping board. Even as the air was shattered by the sounds of the low-level alarms, he was shouting commands, as the boat was on its side flinging everyone and everything around.

"Alex! Don't you dare take your eye off that screen! I want to know what's happening out there. Crash, flood ballast and shut down that damned engine! Come to all stop! I want all noise stopped! Willy! Get us level God Damn it! Tinkerbelle, alarm Protocol, then override and shut this pig down while we're still alive!"

Willy was sweating as he struggled to keep his head as the pressure was pulling down on him to fall away from his own console. "I'm trying. Believe me," he muttered.

"Let me help, Willy," said Tinkerbell as the alarms started shutting down.

The lights flickered for a second, then another low-level alarm began to sound, even as the ship was slowly coming to the final descent of its roll. The computers were programed to take over pitch when it hit fifteen degrees, unless overridden. The impact was that severe, which even though they were compensating, the ship was still being tossed by the immense blast. The Specter was literally shot sideways through the water.

"Willy? The hull? Have we been compromised?" Ralph asked quickly to the meaning of the alarms.

"No," was the instant response. "We still have one-hundred percent internal pressure. I do believe we have a major problem with the reactor though."

Don was staring at the comatose figure of Beverly rolling around against the lower part of the navigating consoles, bouncing between the walls and the floor. Suddenly Don came alive, realizing that only two alarms would sound throughout the ship and not the radios. One being hull breach and the other being the nuclear reactor. He demanded, "Willy! That's an alarm from the reactor, how is the core?" Even as he spoke, he struggled against the straps holding him in place. He wanted to get to Beverly, to keep her from striking any more metal objects.

Willy shook his head as if he had bigger problems then responded to Don, "Core shows one-hundred percent Don. We seem to have a bleeder somewhere."

"Commander, I've lost power! The best I can do is try to flood the forward tanks and take us down," explained Crash quickly.

"Do it. Alex, where in the hell is the Volga?" demanded Ralph, he too was struggling with the harnesses.

"She's cruising at five knots, trying to ascertain our condition." Alex thought for a moment then asked, "Commander if I may offer a guess?"

"Quickly."

"The older style computer systems would have marked a direct hit as a target destroyed. I think they think we're history."

"Good. Let's let them keep thinking that. Let's go to silent running. And SOMEONE PLEASE turn off that damned alarm!"

Willy's computer console was showing all the problems with the Specter, then suddenly all the alarms shut down in one fell swoop, Tinkerbell taking over. Finally, the control room was silent.

"Alex, where's the shark?" asked Wolfson.

Alex scanned every console, then replied, "Gone. He's already three hundred meters from us. The blast knocked it off. Whatever we did that pissed it off we've stopped doing."

The radio in Ralph's ear came to life as Schmitty, still in the engineering department finally cut in and said, "Commander, that thing packed quite a wallop. I've got casualties and damage back here. I'm scramming the nuclear reactor." Ralph sighed heavily. To Scram a reactor was the act of terminating fission. The Chief Engineer was literally shutting off all their power. What ever happened in engineering was not good. Ralph really hoped they could start it up again. He had never been on a submarine that had shut down its reactors before.

The Specter was making advances to level as Don still struggled with his harness. Bobby had his eyes glued on the captain the instant she fell. He pulled his harness apart, made his way around the mapping board and was sliding carefully across the floor to Beverly. Don finally got lose and almost dropped onto Bobby's back.

Bobby delicately pulled Beverly onto the floor, as the ship was now creeping back to only twenty degrees of center.

"How is she?" asked Don. There was part of him that was sorely angry at his own inefficiency at keeping the woman safe, and a surprising facet of him had nothing but concern racing through him. He KNEW that the chair had a locking mechanism, just did not think of it.

Bobby had listened for breathing and found it strong and regular. She had received a large gash on her hairline and was bleeding. He pulled his hands around her neck, searching desperately for anything out of the ordinary. He then carefully cradled her in his lap and probed her spine. Then he flexed her elbows and legs, happy to find nothing broken.

Bobby's massive frame tenderly picked the woman up, as if she was a baby, holding her head carefully. He was managing the slight tilt of the boat better than Don considering his added weight. He told Don, "I've got her Mister Merrick. I think she has a slight concussion and she's going to have some nice bruises, but other than that I think she's all right. I'll know more once I get her too medical."

Don nodded. He was not accustomed to being of absolutely any help, felt useless, and worse, felt stupid.

"Don, we have bigger problems," Ralph reminded the man, as Don shook off the scene. Ralph then hit his transmit button and asked Schmitty, "Chief, what kind of damage do we have back there?"

Schmitty responded, "Tell Don we could use an extra hand. We blew up a line. It's a bloody mess."

Ralph closed his eyes. Then he asked back, "Who is it?"

"Ray Dicenzo. His … his face is gone." Came the rather sardonic response.

Don looked down then glanced over at Ralph and said, "Must be a transfer line that burst. Probably got thrown against it when it went. It'd be like sticking your head in a nuclear radiator."

"Don, see if you can help them," Ralph said tenderly.

"Right." Don said but he was not moving. He was still watching Bobby taking one awkward step at a time through the hatches and back to the officer quarters.

Ralph then glanced at his watch and in a firm but quiet voice said, "As of eleven-hundred hours, forty-two minutes Western Standard Time, I'm taking command of this vessel. Until such time that Captain Hornacher is fit to resume command." He then turned to Willy and demanded, "I want all com and positioning turned off, then I want diagnostics done on all systems. First, I want to know how much damage the hull did sustain, then the ballast systems and the main frame. Then let's freaking pray we can move this tub."

Willy nodded, "Already running."

Ralph noticed Don still standing in shock. He rolled up next to him, put a hand on his shoulder and said, "She's going to be fine Don. She's a sturdy filly."

Don shook his head then muttered, "I couldn't hang onto her Ralph. She was ripped from me." He then slapped himself in the forehead and added, "Stupid me, I was afraid of hurting her."

Ralph felt the emotions bleed through Don's voice then he responded, "Don. I know buddy. Bobby will take care of her."

"Don, Schmitty really needs help," implored Tinkerbell.

Don glanced into the air at the voice admonishing him. Then he licked his lips tentatively, then looked Ralph in the eyes and said, "When we're clear of the Volga, we need to get to the surface. We need to vent. The transfer line is not dangerous but it'll make a mess of the engine compartment."

"Will do." Then Ralph let go of a massive smile and added, "We're alive and still fighting Don. We took two fish in the ass end and we're still alive. Good job man."

Don glared back at Ralph and said, "Good job my ass. It's a hell of a way to find out how much this thing can take." Don briskly swiveled, compensating for the ten-degree pitch and was gone out the control room door, rage and sorrow pushing him quickly.

"Captain? The Volga is transmitting," mentioned Steve.

"Burn it for me," responded Ralph quickly.

"Done."

"Captain? The Volga is still moving. And it's headed our way," Alex reminded him quietly.

"Let's play dead, shall we." Then he glanced around and said, "Which isn't too far from the truth." He glanced up at the ceiling as the submarine was still descending slowly into the abys.

He walked over to Hernandez' console and asked, "How deep is she?"

"The Volga went to transmitting depth but is now dropping, picking up speed to eight knots."

"Crash? How is our status?"

"Twenty meters till the bottom Commander. Ten. Five," said Crash as they all felt a slight grinding as the boat settled on the ocean floor. "We're at seven hundred seventy-one meters down."

Ralph then turned back again to Alex and demanded, "I want to know if they flood tubes, I don't want them to drop a mine on us. Understand?"

"Yes sir," responded Alex mashing the headphones to his ears. "They surfaced to transmit, which means they don't think we're an issue any more. At least I hope so."

Everyone in the control center of the Specter held their breaths. Slowly they could hear the propellers of the Volga churn away at the water, the sonar pinging madly, trying to find the remains of the little submarine. They got loud enough to reverberate through the skin of the Specter, and every soul on board. Everyone damned happy the plasma generator was still operating. Then without missing a beat, the Volga slipped on into the deep water.

Hernandez broke in quietly and said, "We got lucky, the Volga changed directions and didn't go directly over. It's continuing in a southeasterly direction."

"Continue to monitor Alex." Then Ralph pushed his ear piece button on his radio and said, "Don?"

"What?" was the breathless response. Ralph could tell Don was already suiting up for repairs to the reactor system.

"Don, can the venting wait a little while? The Volga just passed over," asked Ralph.

"I heard. Engineering is a sealed unit from the rest of the ship. We're going to have to slow down the CO two filtration system so we don't compromise it but yeah, we can wait. It's confined to the rear."

"Don. The million-dollar question. Can it be fixed?"

"As pissed as I am at the moment, if I have to get out and push I would. Damned straight she can be fixed Ralph. I have a big assed score to settle."

Ralph smiled. He did not need pep talks. He had Don, as the entire crew in the control room smiled along with him. Ralph responded, "As do we all Don. How long?"

"About three hours give or take."

"All right then." Ralph turned to Alex and asked, "Position of the Volga?"

"She's slowly descending but still running slow. The aggressive array has a lock on their signature and the Volga is back to running the Magneto Drive. It looks like she's changed tactics."

Ralph nodded, then mentioned, "Yeah, Rabinov knows for sure now he's being hunted. Won't take any more chances." He turned back to the other side and asked Caldwell, "Please tell me you can get us back to the surface?"

"Tinkerbell has confirmed all ballast pumps are running a little hot, but they'll work when we want them to Commander. We blow'em and we'll be on the surface in a couple of minutes."

"Thank you, Mister Caldwell." Then Ralph turned one more time and said to Barrington, "Steve, I believe you have a message for me."

"Yes sir." Steve hit the record controls, located the Volga loop and hit print. The communications printed out as Ralph walked over, snatched the paper and read. Ralph smiled fully when he was done reading.

"A couple of measly Russian torpedoes and we're done Unh? Well, this little boat has a surprise for him." Ralph glanced over at Alex and asked, "Distance from Volga?"

"Seven-hundred meters, sir."

Ralph thought for a moment then asked Barrington, "Steve, can we get a signal to command from this deep down without the Volga suspecting?"

Steve shrugged his shoulders then responded, "Sure. We just bounce it off our satellite using code. To the Volga it'll be very faint and very garbled. If at all considering the density of the water."

"Good. When they get two thousand meters' distance, I want to send a message plus the Volga's last coordinates."

"What kind of message sir?"

Ralph went over to the mapping board, pulled out a scratch pad and a pen from his breast pocket and scribbled a quick note in short-hand. He then walked over to Steve and handed him the note. Steve read it, then turned and smiled. "Will do sir," Steve said still grinning.

Ralph then tapped his ear mounted radio and asked Bobby, "How is our patient doing?"

"As you know, this is a little out of my league. But she's doing good Commander. The portable X-ray showed no damage that I could see. I've given her a thorough examination and just found the bumps and bruises as I suspected. I've cleaned the wound and given her a small shot for the pain and stiffness. When she wakes, I have some Ibuprofen for the bruises." Came back the voice of Bobby.

Ralph grew thoughtful for a moment then asked, "Bobby? What do you want to do with Ray?"

Ralph could swear he heard a loud sigh, then Bobby responded, "I have a body bag for him, Commander. We're going to have to put him on ice."

"Understood. Do you need help?"

"Not a problem Commander. I already have Frankie and Rory assisting me. They wanted to do something to help."

Ralph nodded his head and responded, "Understood. Carry on."

In the bowels of the Pentagon, all hell was breaking loose. General Blanchett was trying his hardest to get through to Georgiana Wannaker to get the message through. The United States Military has considered the actions of the Volga an official act of war. There would be no warning shot; there would be no spoken word or signal. It was shoot to kill. Whether the Russian government wanted to play along or not. And for one of the few times in American history, they were going to DEFCON 2. NATO itself was going to LERTCON 2. Communications were further opened with Japan and Australia as the information was shared with these countries courtesy of Military agreements. Canada's CFB Esquimalt Facility, home of the Canadian Fleet Pacific, in British Columbia, was scrambling the few ships that were still in port. Not a real Pacific might, the Canadian fleet still had the technology to help locate and maybe deter the Volga.

The Air Craft Carrier Gerald Ford was starting fly overs of the North Pacific, dropping sonar buoys and possibly, searching for any remains of the Specter. The Sub Hunter USS Jackson was dispatched ahead of the fleet, her Captain highly anticipatory. The Volga was a big and mean son of a bitch.

The USS Cheyenne, the closest American submarine, and a Virginia styled Attack Submarine, was contacted and given the go ahead to engage ANY Russian submarine believed hostile. With its thirty-four knot speeds, it was indeed making up time on the Volga. They had a good idea the last location but the question for its Captain, was what direction would the Volga travel?

General Blanchett was at the rear of the control area, on the phone with Georgiana. Cartwright could hear the one side animated conversation and he knew it was not going over well. Blanchett was yelling into the phone, "Madam Secretary, I have confirmation from the Specter that they were engaging the Volga in battle AND, a statement from the Volga itself that they have sunk the Specter … That's right Captain Hornacher's ship. He's taking it as father would. He's pissed. As am I at the moment. Don't care about the Russian Navy George. They get in the way I will get in their way, that's how this is going to work. And quite frankly George, we really don't know who's on our side. Rumor has it some of the captains are sympathetic to the plight of the Ukrainian Resistance. Well, you do your dove thing. I want full alert status of NATO forces, let's see if we can get a few Australian and Japanese subs in the water and get the fleet out of Sydney. I mean, our NATO forces out-number the Russians three to one. What? I don't need no authorization from the President. Well, then you get it so we can make this all okay dokey all right? I'm sorry George. I know you're doing the right channels, but if the Russians don't want to play, I really don't give a damn. Diplomatic channels be damned; this is one of those times when we TELL them what we're going to do. Frankly, I want them out of the way. The Volga has sunken two submarines full of American service people and it will answer for their actions. In fact, all I want NATO to do is locate the bastard, because, I'm going to blow him out of the water. All right. It's time to play hardball then. How is Billingham doing at the UN? Nothing yet? Maybe the guy won't show and leave the Ukrainian devils in the lurch. I know, I know. Nothings that easy. Listen, talk to President Garrison and inform him what we're doing. If he has a problem, then he knows how to reach me. We're not at war with Russia. Just one little nasty bugger of a boat. Oh, and one last thing George. Somebody inform the Chinese they need to stay out of this. Do the diplomat channel thing but the worst thing that can happen now is for one of our trigger-happy Sub Commanders to accidently blow up a Chinese sub. Best thing for them to do is to back away from any Russian subs they might be dogging. Right George." The man finally hung up the phone, staring at it a few moments.

Cartwright looked over at the General and said, "Quite the conversation."

"Politics gets in the way every time." He looked forward at the huge screens and added, "telling me I can't declare actions against the Volga until Garrison authorizes it. What rubbish."

There was a sudden flurry of activity from the center console where the Navy communications set up was located. Suddenly a man jumped up and literally ran to the rear of the room, waving a slip of paper in his hand. He ran up to General Blanchett, smiled for a second, then located Admiral Hornacher who was on the phone. He waited patiently, with a huge smile on his face. Hornacher took note of this and cut his conversation short.

The man proudly extended the note forward and said dramatically, "A message to you sir. From the USS Specter."

Cartwright nodded and smiled at the Admiral. Blanchett had swooped in next to the Admiral upon hearing this. The Admiral took the note from the man, who stood waiting in case of a return message. Jack looked over at Dan, and gave a lopsided grin. Finally, he muttered, "God I'm glad when you're right."

"What's it say?" asked Cartwright, a large grin spreading along his face.

Hornacher read it aloud. TO ADMIRAL HORNACHER US FLEET FROM COMMANDER WOLFSON COMMANDER USS SPECTER. THE REPORT OF OUR DEMISE HAS BEEN GREATLY EXAGGERATED. WE HAVE HAD DAMAGE, ONE FATALITY AND A FEW BRUISES. I HAVE ASSUMED COMMAND OF THE SPECTER UNTIL SUCH TIME CAPTAIN HORNACHER IS READY TO REASSUME COMMAND HAVING BEEN SHAKE UP IN BATTLE. WE WERE BLIND SIDED BY A DAMNED BIG SHARK. WILL NOT HAPPEN AGAIN AND IT WAS NOT, IN MY JUDGEMENT ANYTHING THAT CAPTAIN HORNACHER COULD HAVE DONE DIFFERENTLY. DON IS HOPPING MAD. THEY TRIED TO WRECK HIS BOAT. THREE HOUR DAMAGE CONTROL AND WE WILL BE READY TO GIVE PURSUIT. REGARDLESS OF WHAT THE NAVY SAYS, WE KNOW OUR DUTY. WE ARE AFTER THE VOLGA. COMMANDER WOLFSON. PS. TELL ADMIRAL CARTWRIGHT THE SPECTER TOOK THE FULL BRUNT OF TWO OF RUSSIA'S BEST. NOW WE TRULY ARE, A GHOST BOAT.

"Yes! I knew it!" yelled Cartwright pumping his fist in celebratory action.

Blanchett laid a fatherly hand on Hornacher's shoulder, gave a squeeze and said, "She's all right Jack. Bev's still alive."

Admiral Hornacher managed to hold in the tears and folded the note up cleanly. Then he looked over at the General and said, "What's more, the Specter is alive. They're still the best chance we got."

"A three-hour head start is nothing compared to the Specter's speed," Inserted Cartwright. Then he added with a grin, "I can't wait to hear this story about the shark."

"Sir?" came from the Ensign who dropped off the note.

Hornacher thought for a moment then replied, "Oh, radio back to the Specter our alert status and tell them the hunt is on. Find the name of the fatality. Tell them we now have no confirmation of Russian Naval help or resistance status. And tell them; tell them good hunting."

The man smiled, wheeled around and headed back to his console.

Lucius Perry who had been in the upstairs conference room, screaming on the phone, heard the news. His entrance was as loud and boisterous as one would think coming from the big man. He came down the stairs, yelling at Jack until he found him then ran up and bare hugged the man.

At first Hornacher was taken aback by the obvious show of affection. Then he let his emotions go and hugged the man back. All the while Lucius was yelling, "Bev did it Jack. Bev did it! The first woman Captain to direct a submarine into battle Jack. She did it! And she's still fighting Jack!"

Neither Hornacher, Blanchett nor Cartwright had thought of this. History had been made that day.

Finally, Hornacher and Lucius pulled away and Jack looked at Perry and reminded the man, "Lucius, they're not done yet and they're a long way from home. I'll officially celebrate when I see my daughter again."

"Of course, Jack, of course." The Secretary of Defense gathering his decorum and straightened his tie. Then he looked at Admiral Hornacher with a twinkle in his eye and said again, "She's alive Jack."

It was then that the coordination effort with the US Military had begun. General Blanchett was as good as his word. He did not hesitate to get the word out that the Volga was now a renegade sub and there was no negotiation. The entire Pacific Fleet was now on high alert and sent to intercept. Fly overs from Anchorage, Pearl Harbor and Yokosuka were fueling up. The George Washington, A large US Aircraft Carrier stationed in Japan was recalling all Naval personal and getting set to sail. After fifteen minutes the United States military machine was in motion, and every allied ship was moving in a different direction, under high alert conditions.

It was then every phone on the rear bank of consoles started ringing. All four men stopped and glanced at each other. This can't be good thought Cartwright.

The Secretary of Defense answered one of the offending instruments. The other three men listened carefully to a ten-minute one-sided conversation that included more yes, nos, and grunts. They understood little when Lucius finally hung up the phone.

"I take it our courier showed up at the UN," remarked General Blanchett.

Lucius dove in and replied, "Yes. Apparently, Kirk was only half right. The man was not only wired with explosives but wired for sound. And get this. There were two of them, each to watch the others back. It quickly became evident that the men were talking to outside forces. Without knowing what kind of back up the courier's had the security forces could do little."

Admiral Cartwright then asked, "I take it then that one of the couriers has given us his list of demands?"

"They're going to send me the two-page list, but it's not pretty gentleman."

"Can you give us a quick rundown?" asked Hornacher.

Lucius took a deep breath and then attempted to explain. "The terrorist group is demanding that Madam Secretary of State and a news crew of the local Washington channel six crew accompany them, on an outgoing flight from Dulles Airport at midnight. There, they will fly to Montreal, pickup Kuznotzhov, refuel and fly to Boston where they will have another ocean flight to London. And there they will have another plane meet them and take them to the Ukraine. All the while having the news team do a live remote from the plane."

The Admiral looked perplexed at Lucius then asked, "How is Kuznotzhov getting to Montreal?"

Lucius shook his head then answered, "Something to do with a helicopter out of Coats to a little airstrip in a town called Ivujivik on the coastline. A Gulfstream will meet them there and ferry them to

Montreal." Lucius then looked Admiral Hornacher straight in the eye and stated, "It appears the Gulfstream is already waiting."

Just then a member of the office staff walked up with four copies of the demands and handed them to Mr. Perry.

"Thank you," said Lucius handing each man a copy. Hornacher took out his reading glasses as did Cartwright, for the print was tight and small.

"Oh my God," muttered General Blanchett scanning the paper quickly.

"Is Colonel Devlin still around here? I want his input on this," demanded Lucius.

"They've thought this out, haven't they?" uttered Cartwright, flipping back and forth between the two tightly printed pages.

"The worse part of it is, they seem to be one-step ahead of us," said Lucius.

"Have we contacted Georgiana yet?" asked Hornacher.

"I understand the President and she had a short conference and she's agreed to it. If it will buy us some time. What kills me is that they knew she would be in Washington," remarked Lucius.

Blanchett then made the observation, "It's very simple if you think about it. Madam Secretary is an easy mark, not one to put up a fight, but incredibly important."

"Have you looked at the bottom part of the last page?" asked Cartwright.

They all flipped in unison. It was the compliance factor. If they did not do this and the Volga did not receive a live television feed by twelve-fifteen AM Eastern time, they would open fire. Then, every ten minutes they would fire again. Even from the detached position of the Volga out in the North Pacific, she could readily hit targets.

"Oh, good God," muttered Hornacher.

"Can they do this? Can they get a T.V. feed to the Volga?" asked Blanchett.

"That's what I want the Colonel for," replied Lucius.

"What about the news crew? They're not going to want to be on a plane with a man strapped to the gills with explosives?" remarked Cartwright.

"The thought is that the courier wants someone they're familiar with. No sneaking federal agent in," replied Lucius.

"Plus, more hostages," stated Blanchett.

"Exactly. The news team in question has already said they would do it."

Hornacher looked Lucius straight in the eye and said distinctly, "The President."

"He does make a good car salesman when he has too. The news crew puts their lives on the line, for the scoop of the century," said Lucius.

"Time lines for all this?" asked Blanchett.

"Very good chance Kuznotzhov could be having supper in Kiev by this time tomorrow."

"What about the Russians? They're not going to let this just happen without some retaliation? Are they?" asked Cartwright.

Lucius looked down at his shoes then answered carefully. "They're working on it. When Georgiana confronted the Russian Premier with the information from the Specter, he talked. The Volga has been hijacked for just that purpose. They're embarrassed and caught with their drawers down around their knees. The couriers have sent a separate set of demands to the Kremlin. The Volga can simply sit out in the Pacific, playing hide and seek and nuke half of the United States and Russia, if they do not get what they want."

"Good God. That means, the US Navy is hunting down the Volga with the Russian Navy doing its own, uncoordinated assault," observed Admiral Hornacher.

Lucius nodded his head and said, "Let's hope the two don't meet."

"What about the media?" asked Cartwright, usually the liaison between the Fleet Commander and the hounds of reporters.

"They've found out about the Seattle. They sort of know about the Volga and making up their own stories in that matter. When the report of the Washington News Crew hits the fan, all hell is going to break loose," said Lucius. Then he turned to Admiral Cartwright and said, "I may have you do a press release to mollify the worried crowds."

"Right," responded the Admiral already thinking of how to down play a possible nuclear holocaust.

Then Lucius, without really knowing who to talk to said to Cartwright, "Can the damned Russian renegades actually shoot a nuke?"

Hornacher responded, "According to Merrick, there's ways of getting around their system. They probably can."

"Damned."

Just then the stately Colonel with Chang in tow could be seen walking though the computers and consoles. He walked up to Lucius and asked, "You wanted to see me?"

Lucius quickly relayed the scenario to the resident computer and communications expert. "Can it be done?" he finally asked.

Chang thought for a moment then replied, "Yes, of course. Provided the Volga has been rigged for television receiving and there's a re-trans unit or a transmitter somewhere close by."

Lucius nodded then went over to a rear computer manager and tapped the man on the shoulder and said, "I need a map of the North Pacific."

The man merely nodded, punched up a few instructions on the computer and the large screen faded to black then came up with a huge version of the Pacific rim and the Hawaiian Islands.

Lucius turned to Chang and asked, "How close?"

Chang waved a hand and replied, "Anchorage TV transmitter might have the range."

"Would the Volga have to surface?" asked Lucius.

Chang thought for a brief moment then answered, "I don't know."

"No." Responded the Colonel instantly.

Lucius was losing his patience. "Work with me here. Could they get a signal sitting three hundred meters under water, coming from an airplane thirty thousand feet in the air bouncing off a transmitter in Anchorage?"

The Colonel finally understood, then weighed all the variables. After some thought he said, "Radio waves are completely different from a television signal. The Volga would have to rig for this, and make sure they cut out all the peripheral magnetism. Then you have to consider the atmospheric instability from the plane."

"Good God man. Which means, what?"

"It means it's complicated, but doable. They could not get a signal through that much water with all those variables. I believe, they would have to get the antenna up to at least, oh, say, twenty feet of the surface. Maybe lower, considering what kind of receiver they have on board."

Lucius smiled and said, "Thank you Colonel. Get it arranged."

"Certainly."

Admiral Cartwright understood completely and said quickly, "The Poseidon Satellite."

Hornacher also nodded at Lucius and said, "Don should be able to get a pinpoint positioning on the Volga when they come up for reception."

"And then we'll know," remarked General Blanchett.

Lucius pointed a finger at the men and said, "And that Gentlemen, the Volga does not know."

"Our ace in the hole, the Specter can catch up to the Volga in a matter of minutes once repairs are made," inserted Cartwright.

Admiral Hornacher was already walking to the US Fleet communications consoles. "I want a message to go out to the Specter," he directed. Then he wheeled around and said to the Secretary of Defense. "I know I don't have to ask you this, but what with Merrick has told me and what's going on, I'd let you know. I'm going to authorize an EAM on the Bird of Prey."

Lucius nodded his head softly, as if weighing the consequences of the action. Then he finally replied, "In regards to what has happened,

I feel that might not be a bad idea. Without the President here, I'll sign off on it. And then … I'll tell him later."

"The Specter would be in the best position," Admiral Hornacher exchanged. Then slowly, he turned back to the console and commanded. "Send the Specter's coded launch EAM to the Specter to counter a live missile launch by the Volga."

"And pray they don't need it," mumbled Lucius under his breath.

CHAPTER 18

ommander Wolfson could not wait. He let twenty minutes' slip by then he surfaced. The Specter had gotten the word, as the EAM had been received and all the codes verified, by himself, Caldwell and Faulk. They had been given permission for a live launch of a nuclear missile. Yet, it was not meant as a deterrent or to initiate full scale war. It was to simply counter Volga's launch, no more.

And the demands had been made. The Secretary of State was going to be held hostage. Wolfson had been informed the Volga could possibly have to expose itself to the surface to get a clear television signal. But Lt. Duran informed Wolfson that the Volga was still clearly in range to strike the Western Seaboard, and oddly enough, Vladivostok. For it was clear the current Volga had nothing to do with Mother Russia. They had no idea where a strike would be headed.

Lt. Duran ran into Bobby in the crew's quarters as Duran was getting a jacket to head to the surface of the ship. Wolfson was permitting the crew to come up to get some fresh air.

"So, what do you think now?" asked Duran putting on his jacket.

The big man searched around the quarters as if that was dumb question then he replied, "What do I think about what?"

"About what I said earlier about the captain. She let a shark attack us."

Bobby scoffed noticeably then replied, "She didn't LET anything happen. We got attacked by a prehistoric shark AND a big Russian sub at the same time. And we're still alive. That's what I think."

Duran nodded then said, "Well. You look at it that way if you want to. There's a couple of us that don't trust her to get us through this mess, and we're quite happy that the Commander is back in charge."

Bobby stopped, wheeled around on Duran and asked forcibly, "And who exactly are WE?"

Duran replied instantly as if to clear himself, "Mr. Monk, Bruce, a couple of the guys in engineering. One of them even mentioned mutiny. But the battle took care of that for us."

Bobby glared at the man then said, "I ever hear the word mutiny come out of your face again I will inform not only the Commander, but I will wake the captain and tell her. Do you understand me?"

Duran looked shocked for a second. Then he back pedaled slightly and returned, "Hey, listen, I didn't bring it up. It's just that we don't want to end up like the Seattle by an incompetent Captain. That's all."

Bobby swung around, put a large hand against Duran's chest and shoved him against the wall. Then he moved an inch closer and whispered through clenched teeth at Duran as another person had entered the quarters, "Everyone here is trying to do the best they can. You worry about your job. Okay? Oh. And one more thing. Your rumors suck. She didn't have an abortion." With that he exited the room to go on top, leaving Duran to straighten his jacket and compose himself.

The conning tower was seeing its share of visitors. Wolfson had the shifts overlap so that the current shift could get a breather, and some fresh air. In radio contact, he stood on the tower in a dark blue windbreaker, looking out over the calm ocean, and letting the sun shine warm his face. The air was bitter cold, but was easily better than the stagnant air as the oxygen scrubbers had been turned off.

However, the wet skin of the Specter was causing a visual nightmare. Every single crewman was wearing sunglasses.

Every once in a while, Ralph would let a grin flex his face as he could hear the communications in the engineering. Don was in his prime as he was throwing things at Schmitty and losing his cool in the hot radiation suit. Unfortunately, Schmitty threw things right back.

The small upper deck of the Specter saw several men sitting, or laying out trying to gather a few rays before being cooped up again below. A couple of the men braved the thirty-five degrees and let the sun soak into their exposed arms as they put aside their coats. But in the center was Frankie, her shirt hanging wide open, her hat turned around and with a massive pair of aviator sunglasses. Wolfson was at least glad she had on a sturdy bra.

After a few minutes, Lt. Smith rose up into the tower alongside Wolfson. He glared down at Duran on the deck. He now knew things he wished he had not. Mostly concerning the captain. His throat tightened every time he read and reread her medical file.

"How is our favorite patient doing?" asked Wolfson after a moment, letting his binoculars fall to his chest and stuffing his hands into his Pea coat.

"Good Commander. She'll wake up with a headache, but that's about it." Bobby patted his arms. Even through his pea coat he could feel the cold. However, the cold felt good as his blood pressure had definitely risen with his contact with Duran.

"You're from California, right?" asked Wolfson smiling.

Bobby smiled back then nodded down at the exposed men below. "Just looking at those guys makes me cold."

"I take it you're not doing the diving."

"In that?" asked Bobby incredulously looking down at the water. Bits of white foam slid off the side of the Specter, as even the afternoon sun could not shake the cold air coming from the North Pacific. "Not on your life. I think that distinction belongs to Garibaldi and Mr. Monk."

Wolfson nodded. He knew that, he just wanted to bait the man.

"Do you think we'll get the Volga Commander?" asked Bobby in all seriousness.

"Of course," came the instant reply. "We can make up the distance in less than an hour."

Bobby nodded, then asked, "Rumor has it the Volga has a double thick hull. Is that true?"

Wolfson looked over and patted Bobby on the back and replied, "Don't worry. When the time comes, this little boat will give out more than it will receive." Then he shrugged and said, "Besides, we've already proven we can take a solid punch to the jaw and survive."

Bobby looked out over the massive ocean, then remarked, "You know, under any other circumstances, and any other boat, we should be dead."

Wolfson slowly looked over at the man and replied, "You're right. And for a second, I thought it might happen. It's one of those irritating times when you're damned happy Merrick is as smart an asshole as he is."

Bobby nodded in agreement, then sought to study a cloud for a moment. His mind wrestled with a decision and a thought that kept nagging at him. Ultimately, he sought another opinion and said, "Commander. One more thing. I had to do a full exam on the captain."

Wolfson studied the words for a moment, then asked, "I take it you saw something you didn't like?" Wolfson thought he knew where this was headed.

"Not so much the exam, but I read her medical file for the first time. Pretty long and in depth. Well, it just makes me nervous. I gotta like well, undress her to look for contusions and what not and she's unconscious. I felt like I was holding onto a china doll, one I really didn't want to break. Or wake up."

Ralph nodded then cut to the chase and asked, "I take it there was a notation in her files about her abduction and rape a few years ago?"

Bobby shook his head then stated, "Yeah. No. No really notations on any rape. But the torture, Commander. I thought you might know. Yeah. It just makes me feel, creepy. The things that guy did to her. That shouldn't happen to anyone. Especially a smart woman like the captain."

Wolfson looked over at the man, with an intense respect for the man's concern. "I don't know all the gory details but I know it was pretty nasty. But that was over fifteen years ago. I have yet to see one chink in her armor, if that's what worrying you."

"Yeah, I know. Military Doctors gave her a battery of tests that would make a grown man cry. And they gave her a hundred percent rating. No screws loose that I can see. I just wish I didn't know that about the captain. It makes me feel … well, I don't know. Squeamish inside."

"Like you need to go out of your way to protect the lady?" Ralph responded smiling.

Bobby smirked and responded. "Yeah. Something like that."

Wolfson turned and said finally, "She doesn't need protecting. Believe me. And if you ever make her feel that way, she'll kick your ass. She's the Captain, she didn't earn that by being a whiner. She's got a hide as thick as rubber. Somebody once put her through hell and it toughened her up like nothing else in this world could ever do. She'll be back in charge."

Bobby grinned slightly, then looked back down at the men on the small deck. "That sounds just like my Momma. Can definitely take care of herself, and she even thinks I'm helping, she scolds me."

Wolfson nodded. Then he studied the horizon for a few moments with his binoculars, aware that Bobby was not moving. He put the glasses down then asked without looking, "Something else?"

"Yeah. I don't know how to put this."

"I don't want to know names if that's your concern."

Bobby smiled at the Commander for a second, grateful for the man's insight. Then he said, "Okay. A couple of the guys have, er, concerns about the captain's mental capabilities. They think she was given the command from her father."

Wolfson nodded. "Anything else?"

"Yeah. They've heard nasty rumors. You ever hear of an incidence involving the captain on board the Stingray?"

"No. Not that I know of. But I know of the one on the Nautilus Two, which has been blown out of proportion."

Bobby stood his ground. Duran had mentioned that also. He waited.

"The rumor has it the captain showed up in control naked. Heard it in every port and on every boat. That and about a dozen other rumors of the two other females on the Naut Deuce."

Lt. Smith nodded.

"The truth of course was somewhat different. Beverly had as her custom, woke early to get her run in. Just like with you guys. Well, the captain did not know this, and merely thought she slept in until seven A.M. She's in the shower at six forty-five and all of a sudden, the captain runs a drill. Sort of test the changing of the shifts. Commander Hornacher grabs a towel, her keys and sprints to the control room. The captain continued the drill like nothing happened and afterwards apologized to the woman."

Bobby nodded in understanding.

Wolfson continued, "Not nearly as much fun as a woman prancing around naked but reality usually isn't. She got a letter of commendation for it. And that's what happened Bobby. And unfortunately, that's how bad rumors start. Such as the Stingray. I'll bet reality was completely different then what seaman conjures up in their dirty little minds. And have they considered that she would not be here if she were constantly messing up? Even her father is not going to override the entire Pentagon and give the captain, her own command."

Bobby nodded once again then said, "That's what I thought. And that's what I told them." Then he added, "But Commander, she is having nightmares, that I do know."

Wolfson turned to Bobby, smiled and said, "I have nightmares about being short and Merrick has dreams about his notebook computer attacking him."

Bobby chuckled.

"You worry about what's bleeding Bobby. The rest will take care of itself."

Bobby turned to the Commander then said, "Thanks Commander. I figured you would have the straight answers. I'll see if I can give her something for a good night sleep."

"Good. And Bobby? You run into those guys, you tell them to do their job and let me worry about the ship. All right?"

Bobby looked back down at the crew sunbathing when a cloud happened to roll by, casting a shadow over everyone and instantly dropping the temperature. "Brrrr," was all he said as he went back down the open hatch.

Ralph looked at the hatch. Captain Hornacher and the ship had enough problems without people questioning her stability, he thought. Knowing Beverly Hornacher, the best and having run into the woman on various assignments, he had never once taken her for unbalanced in any way shape or form. Right now, the crew made him more wary. He hoped he nipped Bobby's concerns in the bud.

For the next hour several more men came up to enjoy the sunshine, as those on top went below. Finally, Don rose out of the hatch.

"Get her done?" asked Wolfson putting down his binoculars.

"Schmitty's finishing up. The sleeve and spot weld we put on should hold better than the original construction. Went through and pressure checked the rest of the system, to make sure we don't have another leak three hundred meters down," explained Don pulling his coat collar up.

"All right. What about the theory by Chang that the Volga would have to surface for them to receive the television transmission?" Wolfson asked.

Don looked over and replied, "Not as good as Chang thought." Then he smiled and added, "But good enough. The satellite picked up a trace, but enough of a heat source, about thirty meters below the surface, about where Tinkerbell told us they'd be. She's got a fix on the Volga, but of course, after the transmission, she dove out of sight."

"How far?"

"Would you believe less than forty kilometers away?"

"Good." Wolfson then glanced over at Don and asked, "Where's the Cigar? I figured that would be the first thing top side."

Don contemplated Wolfson with a curious expression crossing his face then he replied, "You know, funny thing. I can't find them. You wouldn't happen to know where they are, do you?"

Ralph nonchalantly shook his head then asked, "Divers ready?"

"Yeah, divers are ready." Don walked over to the open hatch and could see through the black, the frogman suits walking around. The diving chamber was located with the conning tower section.

"Explain to me again why we're putting men into a very frosty ocean?" asked Wolfson.

Don walked over to the rear of the tower and looked down. "Using a spectrometer, they're going to check the impact area of the hull." He looked back and added, "They're wearing special goggles that see ultraviolet light. We're going to make sure there's no spider webbing of the hull, or minute cracks that the sensors can't detect. And then they have an ultrasound that is meant to locate stress under the skin."

Wolfson leaned back against the tower and said, "I didn't know we could do this."

"I don't tell you everything." Don shrugged then added, "We have the time, so we do it." He looked across the tower at Wolfson and smiled then said, "Problem with amorphous metal, or any kind of steel really. Once it's compromised, it has a tendency to break down very quickly. Sort of like those microdot plastic bags. Stronger than a normal plastic bag, but they zipper when they finally do rip."

Wolfson's smile faded quickly. "I didn't know that. You never said anything before."

Don smiled broadly back and said, "Not to worry Ralphie. First of all, the torpedo impact was not severe enough to do damage, we're just taking the precaution. Plus, we can fix it if there is a problem."

"Oh. All right then." The smile returned.

Don watched as Garibaldi and Monk surfaced near the impact area. They waved the large battery-operated light at Don. Even with insulated skin-diving suits on Don did not want them in the water any longer than they had to. In contact by radio Don called down to them, "I want the primary impact area done first. Then if the cold hasn't sunk in yet, go out from there."

"Right Mr. Merrick," answered Mr. Monk. The two men submerged. After a few moments Monk called up, "We think we found the impact area. There's no dents or cracks that we can see."

"Good. Anything at all to be concerned about?

"No sir, no cracks… no nothing."

"Okay, hit it with the spectrometer and we see what we get."

"Okay."

Don patiently waited ten minutes as the men scanned the area, going in an ever-widening circle. Then they switch to the ultrasound, bouncing a tone off the metal structure of the ship, and again found nothing. Finally, Monk called back up and said, "Nothing Mr. Merrick. Smooth as glass."

Don nodded, then responded, "All right then. Get your butts out of the water then."

Wolfson chimed in and made mention, "I hear there's some hot toddy in the galley for you."

"Brandy?" asked Monk hopefully.

"Oh, could be. It's Alex's own concoction," responded Wolfson.

Don swiveled around and asked, "I didn't know we had alcohol on board?"

Wolfson reached in his coat pocket and pulled out a set of locker keys. His eyebrows went up as he swung the ring around. "I don't tell you everything either."

Don swung back around to face the front of the ship. Finally, he sighed heavily as if contemplating something, then walked over to the starboard side of the conning tower. The specially designed retractable ladder was already extended as he opened the side hatch and started down.

"Going to do some sun bathing?" asked Wolfson sarcastically.

"I'm going to see what that God Damned shark did to my boat."

Wolfson smiled and responded, "It's the Navy's boat."

Don popped his head up over the edge of the tower and said simply, "Yeah, right." Then he disappeared.

Ralph could hear the expletives coming from below as he continued to focus his binoculars on the horizon. After a few minutes he could hear the grunting as Don pulled himself back up the ladder.

"How did the boat fair against a prehistoric beast?" asked Wolfson.

"He scratched my boat! That's how it faired. And he's going to need a dentist." Don pulled himself onto the tower deck and closed the portal behind him. Then he retrieved from his coat pocket a seven inch, a patchy brown and yellow conical shaped tooth, with the bloody and tattered remains of the gum lines.

"Good God. Where did you find that?" asked Wolfson incredulously.

"The stupid beast tried to take a chunk out my boat and got his teeth stuck in one of the seams on the front of the conning tower. It was wedged under part of the antenna array. Stupid fish. If it wasn't for him, we'd be going home right now."

"And, knowing you, you measured the maw."

Don looked across at Wolfson and said with reverence, "Seven feet. The shark has a seven-foot mouth. Fortunately, he latched onto the tower and missed the antenna's array up the front."

"Man. Could you imagine trying to feed that thing?"

"Could you imagine that being the last thing you see?" Don asked, rotating the tooth around in his gloved hands.

The hatch opened up quietly as if the operator did not want to disturb the conning tower. He was silent as he slid up next to Don.

Don looked at the tooth one last time then transferred it to a coat pocket.

"Eddy." Don acknowledged. He knew why the man was there.

"Mr. Merrick." The man waited a second, pulled his coat closer around himself, then asked in his slight Midwestern twang, "Can I ask a question?"

"Shoot."

The man snorted, then said, "That's my problem. What did I do wrong? We have the most state of the art submarine on the planet and we got mauled by a shark and got hit by two Russian torpedoes. It's … it's my job to make sure that doesn't happen."

Don nodded, then remarked, "Eddy, nobody is blaming you for any of this. I have over ten thousand pages of manuals and not one word about how to shoot around a hundred-foot shark gnawing on the conning tower. You did what was required of you."

"I had nothing ready. I waited for instructions and had nothing ready," said Eddy, consoling his own ineptitude.

"Captain Hornacher is new to this system, we had a shark attacking us, it wasn't going to go smoothly. Not your fault."

Eddy shrugged his shoulders and exclaimed, "I just feel like if I had done something different."

Don glanced over and shook his head for a second. Then he stated, "Okay. I'll play this game. You want to know what you did wrong?"

Eddy Faulk looked across at Don then glanced at the Commander who was listening in. "No, what?"

Don poked him in the chest and said slowly, "You did it by the book. You didn't use that damned gray matter between your ears. There's nothing in any manual that says how to deal with a shark, and you made no suggestions, instead waited until told what to do.

You didn't think. You didn't rationalize the situation. YOU'RE in charge of weapons, you're the weapons expert and yet you waited." Don thought a moment then added, "It's not like a video game where you can save and start over. You have to pick the right response the first time."

Eddy nodded impulsively. He was actually thankful to be brought up short by the smart engineer.

Don then turned back and faced out into the open ocean, then he asked, "You ever play checkers?"

"Of course," came the quick response.

"There's two spaces on the board that have dead corners. You get a king into that corner; you can still be trapped. You have to think every move correctly, every time to win. You have to react to the other player and not just stick to your strategy."

Eddy nodded knowingly. He had certainly lost his share of checkers games to his grandpa.

Don grinned then said, "Take one second next time and THINK the situation through. It will come out much better."

Eddy pursed his lips together, with quiet determination and nodded his head. "Okay. Okay. Thanks Mr. Merrick."

"You'll get another chance Eddy. Believe me. And next time, we kill the damned shark, and sink the damned submarine and live happily ever after." Don smiled at the man as he lowered himself through the hatch.

"Thanks for the pep talk, Don," mentioned Ralph sliding up next to him.

Don shrugged his shoulders and said, "The man was doing his job and it came up wrong. That's why we're doing all of this. You can't do everything by the book. There is an exception to every bloody rule and you have to know when to break the rules. He'll figure that out."

"Thanks anyway."

Don then glanced down at the antenna array, as suddenly, twenty or so fins swiveled quickly. "Something's up."

"Commander, we have incoming, I'm scanning for identification." Came the voice of Tinkerbell. Right behind it came Hyde's voice, "Hey Tinkerbell, that's my job."

Ralph pulled the binoculars up and frantically scanned the horizon, then asked, "Where?"

Tinkerbell had the upper hand and she was not letting go. "Fighter jet, directly due west, flying low, about ten miles off Commander. It's a friendly. Probably from the Ford."

Ralph pulled his heart out of his throat. Ten miles was less than a minute flying time. The men and woman on deck would have been sitting ducks.

"Commander, we have com." This time it was Hyde.

"Put him on." Wolfson could already see the Boeing X-thirty-two screaming at them.

The pilot's voice came over quickly on the radio. "Hey Specter. Man, that thing is tough to get a lock on, isn't it? My electronics are bouncing wildly. Damned hard to look at too in this sun. Getting a tan, I see. How are the repairs going?"

"Word gets out quickly, doesn't it?" Ralph asked as the fighter sliced over with a dull roar. All the crew members on the deck stood and waved frantically.

"Admiral Hornacher's orders. He wanted visual while you institute repairs."

"Repairs have been made. We're finishing the venting and letting the core warm up."

"You guys actually took on the Volga with that little sub? Man, that has got to be one high-tech little machine. Either that, or you're crazy."

"It helps to be crazy. Tell the Admiral we're still floating and getting ready for the chase," replied Ralph watching the supersonic fighter slice neatly over them.

"Roger that Specter. And Specter, my hometown is New York. Don't let them get a shot off, Okay?"

"We'll try not to." Wolfson watched the Boeing wave its wings then turned and was out of sight in less than a minute.

Wolfson looked over at Don and asked, "You got a time?"

"Forty minutes and we should be one-hundred percent."

Ralph glanced at his watch then said, "Georgiana Wannaker should be about half way to Montreal by now."

"Man, you know it's all hard to believe this is all over a jail break," observed Don.

"Very simply put my friend, but yeah. It is, isn't it? I'll bet right now the Russian Government is having kittens at the thought of Kuznotzhov returning to the Ukraine."

"What about the people? I'm not up on my political overthrows. How are the people in the Ukraine going to take this?"

Ralph thought for a moment then answered, "Don, to them we're the bad guys. Just one step behind the Russians. They're loving this. The Volga has succeeded in out maneuvering the Russian and US Navy combined. They're dancing in the streets."

Don nodded his head and replied, "That's what I thought." He sighed heavily and added, "That's why I design subs. Much easier than dealing with people. Hell, I have a heck of a time with the US Navy when they're on my side."

Wolfson chuckled at this thought. He glanced at his watch once again then called down to the three bodies still on deck. "Sun bathing is over gentlemen … and lady. Time to go back to work. And Frankie button up before you go below."

This brought about a chorus of boos but the men climbed the indented ladder quickly with Frankie bring up the rear.

Bobby quickly sought out and ran into Duran in the crew's quarters. He was calmer and wanted to diffuse the situation between the two of them. Then he started explaining.

"I talked to Commander Wolfson on the tower."

Lt. Duran glared at the man.

"I didn't say any names and he didn't want to know. Anyhow, I talked to him about some of the rumors concerning the captain. Appears, after all they were just rumors."

"Including the Stingray?" asked Duran, believing his brother.

Bobby shook his head and replied, "No. That one he hadn't heard about." Bobby added, "Look it. There're things you don't know and I'm not going to bring up. The captain is perfectly capable to run this ship and even Commander Wolfson said just worry about your job and he'll worry about the ship. He's not going to let something stupid happen. All right?"

Duran shrugged his shoulders and said, "All right."

Bobby was not one totally happy with that response, but it seemed to end there.

Wolfson entered the control room with Don in tow. Ralph commanded, "Crash, take us down, flood main tanks to thirty meters. That fly over by our fighter makes me nervous. I want off the deck."

"Yes sir. Making for depth of thirty meters."

Approximately thirty-five minutes later Schmitty reported in that everything with the reactor was a go. Wolfson nodded, then said to into his mic., "Engineering, I want one-hundred percent on the reactor."

Then Ralph barked at Duran, "I want the best positioning of the Volga and send the coordinates to steering." Then Ralph wheeled to the Caldwell and stated, "I want to make that asshole sweat. Eighty-five knots to the Volga's location. Hyde, I want to know the second you make any kind of contact."

Don glanced over at the man with a questioning look. The Specter was nursing a patch job. He thought that was pushing it a bit.

"I want to go home," shrugged the Commander, addressing Don's glare. He then swiveled around on his shoes and commanded, "Duran, I want a damned accurate guess at the Volga's possible location."

"Yes sir. Shouldn't have changed too much from the previous heat signature."

Petty Officer Hyde who had taken over for Hernandez suddenly broke in and said, "Commander. I have screws off starboard aft, about fifteen kilometers off and closing."

Willy looked up from his computer controls, getting feeds from the GPPP satellite, which showed a very clear heat signature just below the surface, and inserted quickly, "It's not one of ours Commander."

Don looked over at Wolfson for a second. A nine-mile head start and three times the speed made the decision simple. Put space between themselves and whatever it was. At least that's what Don thought.

"Henry, can you get a make on it?" asked Wolfson.

"Computers coming through now Commander." Henry stopped for a second then added, "It's the Russian Submarine, an Akula class type two. A newer one. Computer says it might be the Gorbachev, Sir."

"Crash, hold up," came from Wolfson.

"Slowing Commander."

Don wheeled around from his position at the map board. He said to Ralph, "Now what?"

Wolfson shrugged his shoulders and said simply, "I want to talk to them."

"What? Jesus, what is it with you Navy types? Always wanting to talk to the enemy. I believe in shooting first, shoot again, shoot till they're dead, then asking a few freaking questions or two."

"Shush Don. I'm thinking."

"Now he's thinking! Good God, we're in trouble."

Wolfson paid Don little mind as he walked over to Barrington and said, "See if you can get a line to the Gorbachev for me."

Steve had the same thought as Don, but he bit his tongue and responded, "Yes sir." After a long minute of getting a frequency locked in, he said, "I have them sir, and they're not happy."

"Why pray tell is the Gorbachev not happy?" asked Wolfson smiling.

"Because they can't locate us," responded Willy smiling back, detecting the sonar echo bouncing wildly off the Specters surface, thankful the plasma generator still operated.

Ralph chuckled then said, "Good. That's sort of the idea behind this boat. Steve, ask them if we can open up a dialogue."

Steve sighed and said, "Yes sir." Again after a few moments, he responded, "No sir. No communications until we confirm our location."

Ralph pondered this for a few moments, then asked Henry, "Distance?"

"They're within fourteen kilometers Commander."

Ralph walked over behind to Faulk's chair and said softly, "Eddy. I'm going to give them our location. Before I do, I want aft torpedoes' three and four locked on and ready to fire, but do not open rear doors. On my command. You got that?"

Eddy nodded, flipped up two accidental cut offs then flipped two switches, punched up the location of the Gorbachev on his computer, set the torpedo coordinates and said, "Ready for action Commander and the USAC is on standby, generated and ready."

"Good." Then walked over to Henry and said softly, "Henry. They so much as twitch, a torpedo door opens, they flood their tubes, they arm anything, you let me know. Because then I'm going to blow them out of the water. Good Russian, bad Russian, I don't care because he's not on my side. Got that?"

Henry turned and smiled into his Commander's face. "Yes sir."

At least he was doing something right thought Don.

"Don, you stay quiet, you hear me?" demanded Wolfson pointing at Don.

Don merely nodded. This was Wolfson's show.

"Steve, send our coordinates, and our designation, if you would," Ralph said when he felt that everything was right.

Barrington talked briefly into the computer as it sent out the Russian interpretation. He waited several moments. Then he swiveled quickly in his chair as his headphones came to life. "They want to talk to the Captain of the Specter."

"Sir, they're slowing," mentioned Hyde quietly.

"Good." He looked over at Faulk and said, "Be ready." Then he turned back to Steve and asked, "My Russian is a little rusty, will Tinkerbell do the interpretation?"

"Captain Balakoff speaks fluent English, Commander," answered Tinkerbell

"Of course, he does." Ralph then glanced around the control room as if to think of something he was missing. Satisfied, he nodded at Steve and said, "Go ahead." The switch was thrown and Ralph said into his lapel mic, "To whom do I have the pleasure of speaking to?"

"This is Captain Balakoff. Who is this?"

"Commander Wolfson."

"Commander, we heard you were dead."

"Lies. Perpetrated by the Volga."

"But she did sink the USS Seattle, did she not."

"Sadly enough, yes she did."

"The Volga is a great but dangerous ship."

"Yes sir. I realize that. I was hoping to ask some questions."

"As we have questions Commander."

"First off, I would like to know your military's involvement with this. It appears the politicians can't seem to communicate with each other. And a nasty rumor some in the Russian Navy are sympathetic to the Ukrainian fight."

There was a slight delay. Then Balakoff answered, "Fair enough. We too are hunting the Volga. As you say, higher echelon plays games. They deny the stealing of the Volga, but that's what it was. And as far as the Russian Navy, I cannot speak for all, but the submarine force is damned mad at anyone stealing our submarine."

"Good. I'm glad to see we are on the same playing field."

"Not quite Commander. How is it that you can lock in our frequency? Not to put too fine a spin on it, your voice is better than most Russian subs would send."

"Our computer has all known worldwide frequencies on memory. I'm sure your computers do as well Captain."

There came a slight delay then Balakoff asked, "Your ship is invisible to our radar and sonar and you seem to have a completely silent drive system. Why is this?"

Wolfson thought for a moment, then said, "Liquid metal skin Captain. Makes sonar bounce off without a direct refraction. And the propulsion is hidden underneath the USS Specter. Just like your Magneto Drive."

Don almost came unglued. He had to muffle himself to keep from yelling.

"Liquid metal? What kind of metal is liquid metal?"

"Oh please, Captain. I am the commander, not the engineer or scientist. I don't really know the technological stuff. Now, I have one more question. Is Rabinov himself commanding the Volga?"

Again, a slight delay then Balakoff's reply. "No. It is a look alike imposter. A good one named Viktor Puchinko. Which is how they managed to baffle the shipyards at Vladivostok. He was a sub commander in his day. But he is of Ukrainian descent and has betrayed the Russian Navy." There was a slight pause then Balakoff added, "Rumor has it they were financed by the North Korean's."

Wolfson's mind whirled for a few seconds then he asked, "I take it they free Kuznotzhov, they get a new ally in the Ukraine? And the North Korean's get a new Submarine."

"That's the rumor Commander."

"So, he walked in and bullied his way onto the Volga. The rest of the crew has to be on his side."

"Exactly Commander. Now my turn. How big is the Specter? We had heard of the small stealth sub. Considering the ghostly name, is this it?"

"The Specter is big enough to go toe to toe with any Russian Submarine in the world Captain. On that you can rest assured. And we're damned sure big enough to kill the Volga. Which we have all the intents of doing."

"Commander, it seems to me you have already engaged the Volga and lost. I suggest we hunt the Volga together, and bring down the bastard that betrayed the Russian Navy and killed your countrymen."

Ralphie actually contemplated this scenario in his head for several moments. Glancing at a wide-eyed Merrick shaking his head, he sort of came to the same conclusion. "Love too. Can't Captain. We have a score to settle with the Volga, Captain, and I feel we would only get in each other's way. However, I do have one last question Captain. Is the Volga capable of firing an ICBM?"

"That has also been a question of great concern on my boat Commander. My weapons and computer people tell me it is very probable Puchinko can override any Russian code. He was seen boarding with a notebook computer which was not Rabinov's habit."

"Good point sir. Good point. Well, Captain Balakoff, if we don't succeed, I wish you good hunting to you and your crew."

"Such is life. Good hunting to you Commander."

Ralph signaled a cut in transmission and Steve shut it off. "You can take the lock off the Gorbachev, Eddy. Crash, ten degrees down dive to seventy meters and eighty knots if you will. Let's put some distance between us and another Russian sub."

"Yes sir."

Wolfson looked over at Don and smiled, then said innocently, "What?"

Don finally took a breath, then said in respect, "Have you ever thought of being a politician?"

"No, not really. Why?"

"You told him nothing."

"On the contrary. As Commander of this sub, I told him exactly what I knew. Which just happens to be nothing. Well, almost nothing." Ralph then smiled. He thought for a few moments, then asked Don, "Do you have any Frank Sinatra cued up?"

"Yeah. Why?"

"We could use some good music to serenade our Russian counterparts."

"Tinkerbell, if you would." Don realized what Ralph was up to. "Strangers in the Night, if you don't mind."

"Oh, I LOVE Frank Sinatra," Tinkerbell responded

Suddenly, the restrains of Frank's signature song echoed through the hull of the Specter. Several of the men with better voices sang along.

The Gorbachev's sonar man thought himself crazy. He could pick up the song plain as day, and relayed this information to the captain, who listened on another set of headphones. But the curious part was the speed at which the sound disappeared. This was not lost on the captain. He asked the Sonar man for a guess at the speed. His only response was "damned fast."

CHAPTER 19

Beverly woke with a start. The muted lighting from the night light bled through a crack in her sliding doorway. Amazingly, she felt as light as air, as she slid the folding door open and glided her feet to the floor and flexed her toes. That was when she chanced to look down. She did not have a single stitch of clothing on. She gazed around her bunk. Nothing. Not even sheets, as she was sitting on the mattress.

She rose and stood up in the room with utter confusion racing through her. Whom did this to her, and how could she command with no clothes? raced through her mind. She walked over to the lockers and opened hers up. Again nothing. Then she went down the line and true to form, nothing. All blank, hollow lockers. She crossed to the bathroom hoping to find something. She found little, except a roll of toilet paper. Looking at the pitiful military issue paper, she grabbed it just in case. She then crossed back and chanced to look at the medical locker. Opening the locker door, she spied the little cubes stacked on top. Her hand shot in and she grabbed two of them. Mylar blankets vacuumed wrapped to save space she ripped one open and shook it out. She quickly fashioned a skirt out of the clingy material, and pulled it tight. She unwrapped the second one and coiled it several times around her chest. It would have to do.

Beverly walked to the command quarter's door and opened it an inch to glance out to see if anyone was coming. Then she dashed across the corridor to the men's quarters. Another futile search gave her nothing, as if all had been erased from the face of the earth.

A small, uncomfortable feeling was starting to race through her. She had not seen a single soul since she awoke, nor had she encountered any sign of life. She again made a dash, this time to the galley. Again, nothing, not a soul.

She would have to make her way to the control room, where surely, everyone was. She pulled up the blanket.

Normally, she had no qualms about strutting around naked. The psychologist many years ago, had told her it was a by-product of being viciously violated. Almost as if she treated her body and her mind as separate entities. She had to remind herself on occasion, of her surroundings and her physical presence in the scheme of things. Sometimes, she forgot, as in one emergency on the Nautilus Two. A Nuclear armament test had commenced in the early morning hours. As crewmen scrambled to their stations, being timed to the second their reactions, Beverly, as XO showed up in control to verify the firing codes. She was wrapped merely in a damp, white towel. Her hair still dripping wet, they proceeded with the mock test, then the captain quickly hustled her butt out of the bridge. He commended her initiative, then apologized, then told her he would make allowances for female dress in the control room. She shrugged it off. She was doing her job, not giving a damned who might be peeking. They could do no worse to her than what had already been done.

In her dream Beverly's frustration was turning into a boiling anger. She was the Captain, God Damn it! People would be made to pay. It was not funny, no matter the joke they were trying to play. She walked back out into the hallway, past the conning tower escape hatch then to the hatch at the control room.

Beverly opened the door, expecting to see a sea of faces laughing at her. Instead, she found; no one. She walked in, slowly strolling through the control room, looking at the monitors and consoles, showing the ships status. She glared up at the big screen as it showed the open ocean, and a rather large submarine in the middle of it. Suddenly, she was aware she was looking at the Volga.

Beverly stood looking like an escapee from a bad disco movie all covered in silver, in the control room of the Specter, staring down at the biggest sub in the world. She was utterly alone, stripped of all dignity, and defenseless.

Then, very suddenly anger raced through her. She smashed her fist on the pilot's console, again and again. All the while screaming at the air. The Volga was starting to fill up the screen, as it plowed straight on into the Specter. Finally, it encompassed the entire screen, as it seemed the Volga was coming in. Then; it did, crashing through the glass and demolishing the Specter's control center, Beverly flinging her arms up in defense.

Beverly woke with a start, gasping madly. She was working up a sweat, as she clutched at her blankets, pulling them up around her throat. Her eyes blinked at the darkness that engulfed her. Spasmodically she reached overhead for her little light and finally found it. The reality of being safely in her bunk grabbed her quickly and diffused the grim feelings racing through her. She brushed away an angry tear, leaving a bloody streak on her cheek, then felt her right hand, and stopped to looked at it. Somehow, she had come into contact with the ridged edge of her bed and there was blood trickling across the knuckles. She flexed the hand, aware that she had only broken the skin.

"If I live through this I've got to talk to my psychiatrist," she muttered to herself. She moved slightly, feeling the large bruise on her right hip and the slow throb of her bandaged forehead. An overall stiffness encompassed her body. Her mind instantly recalled the last events and she was relieved to be waking up at all.

The nightmares were back with a vengeance she realized. She could cope, having spent two years battling her dream scape villains. She coerced her mind into leaving them at night and not take them into the daylight with her. The problem she faced at that moment was her reactions to the nightmares. She would mutter, moan, swing, thrash and sometimes, downright hold very verbal conversations. And in the back of her mind was the horrible thought of actually getting up and walking in her sleep. As if she was escaping by groping through the dark. That was what she feared, and then how would she explain it all to her crew, looking to her for leadership? God, she hoped it didn't get that far. Maybe she thought, of talking to Bobby about a sedative. If they survived.

It was Don entering the quarters that had awaken her. She sat upright, wanting to talk to him, and even though she was wearing nothing more than her T-shirt and her boxers, that did not bother her. It seemed like every grain of respect she maintained was being pecked at, and she no longer cared what anyone saw. Still, she decided to gather her wits first and wait for him to leave. She pulled her sheet up and wrapped it around her bleeding fist.

Don entered the command sleeping quarters quietly. He needed to use the head and he wanted to preserve the tooth. He stopped at his locker first, pulled the huge tooth out of the pocket and wrapped it in a towel, popped open a drawer and carefully hid it underneath his folded underwear. Then he hung his coat, and tiptoed over to the bathroom. After a few moments, he came out.

Don was making to leave, when Beverly's bunk started thrashing and she swung widely. He stopped to watch, heard her moan loudly, then snort as if finally awaken. He waited a minute, unsure of what to do. Then, he heard her voice and her admonishment. Must have been a hell of a dream he decided. He thought again to leave, but found himself staring at the accordion door. He was worried about her, and felt she was probably awake. He would peek in to be sure.

Then he quietly went to her bunk and pulled open the door slightly. She was staring wide eyed at him, sitting cross legged, the lower half covered by the blanket, one hand sitting in her lap, the other tucked below the blankets.

His head jerked at the surprise and he smacked the back of his head on the upper bunk. Even the hard plastic construction gave his head a wallop. "Son-of-a-bitch. Oww." He said as he rubbed his cranium.

"Oh Don, I'm sorry," Beverly acknowledged. Then she laughed slightly.

"Yeah, very funny. Scare the old guy to death," he said as he continued to rub.

Beverly pulled the sliding door aside, then threw her feet out to the floor to sit up straight. Her head throbbed harder, so she stopped short of standing. Finally, she looked up at Don and said smiling, "I'm just glad we're all still alive."

Don stopped rubbing his head then looked down at Beverly, the emotions of letting her fall still bubbling in him as he said, "Are you okay? It sounded like you were beating someone up in there?"

"Just … just a bad dream I guess."

Don had already figured as much so merely responded, "Oh, okay then. I'm glad you're all right. But we all didn't make it Bev."

The smiled dropped quickly. "Oh, no. Who?" she asked tenderly.

"Engineering. Ray Dicenzo."

Beverly was going to stand, thought better of it, then patted the bunk and said, "Sit. Bring me up to speed, while I gather my wits."

Don settled in next to her, careful to keep his distance, and to keep his stare from finding a place on the front of her T-shirt. He glanced over, saw the red smear, reached up and wiped it away. "It must have been quite the nightmare," he asked.

Not wanting to make a big deal out of it or to explain she merely retorted, "At least I'm still having nightmares."

Don nodded. He started in and spent the next five minutes telling her the events of the last three hours.

"You guys have been busy while I've been sleeping," Beverly observed finally.

Don shook his head and charged, "You weren't sleeping. You were knocked unconscious because I couldn't hang onto you."

Beverly shook her head and said, "Whatever the reason, you guys got us back into the game. And I got a nice nap out of the deal."

"God, you like to beat yourself up a lot, don't you?" Don unleashed on her suddenly.

"Excuse me?" asked Beverly, feeling the heat of Don's blast melt her core.

"We picked up the pieces and did what we had to do, because you were injured. But all you see is we did it without you. And I feel worse of all because I couldn't hang onto you and let you fall helplessly."

Beverly laid her hand on Don's knee and grabbed tightly and said sheepishly, "Oh Don, that's not what I meant to convey. You guys did a great job, and I just wish I was there to help. That's all I meant. Really, I wish you had hung on harder or grabbed something by mistake."

Don, heard her reaction but still felt she meant to feel the guilt of not being involved. However, he felt the woman had just been through hell and it was not his place to bring her up short anymore. Besides, even he could figure out she was having terrible nightmares. The blood on her cheek was fresh. He said in return, "I know. The guys just picked up the pieces. We're mad as hell honey."

She patted his hand with her free left hand, then smiled at him and said, "I know."

Don looked into Beverly's eyes and found a strength born of conflict. As long as he was being open and very stupid, he decided to delve further. "Can I ask a question? Why? Why go into a profession that a man's domain and follow into your dad's footsteps? Why do that to yourself?" It was a can of worms best suited for a psychiatrist, but he had wondered that the moment she walked onto the boat.

"Why not be a lawyer or a doctor?" responded Beverly having answered that question a thousand times.

"Exactly. As obstinate as you are, you would have made a good lawyer."

"Thanks." Beverly looked down at her toes and wondered how to express herself in this matter, or even if she wanted to. Finally, she said, "At first, I went to Annapolis to be an officer on a sub, because

I was told I couldn't. Everyone around Dad made me feel like only a man could command a sub. I was smart and arrogant. My Mother told me I could do anything I wanted to. But even then, I never really took the idea seriously. I thought I would pass my classes, then move onto something real. A back up plan. After my stint, get a real job in the private sector, or accept whatever commission the Navy decided was best for me. Probably in charge of the laundry on the Ford. You know, the captain of the sheets. Well, somebodies got too. Well then. Then. Something very nasty happened to me."

Don shook his head and pursed his lips at the thought. "I had heard. Life's hard enough without some asshole messing it up."

Beverly frowned and gazed down at her hands in her lap then said, "Shit happens. But the guy took something from me, and I don't mean physical. He took my freedom and what little there was of my dignity. All I wanted to do afterwards was run and hide. Be a nobody. Do something with no conflict, and not listen to the people around me talk about how great my father was or pity the poor girl that got … trapped."

Don nodded without really knowing what else to do, then asked, "So what happened?"

"My mother happened. When she finally found out and finally calmed down, she firmly told me I could let the guy win, and that mom and dad would love me no matter what. Or I could show him and the world, that I could grow stronger and do what I wanted to do. And I still wanted to show all those naysayers, that a woman could command a sub. So, I went back to school amongst all the stares and back-room rumors. I focused, buckled down and passed with honors. I tried my best to put that damnable evil little point in my life behind me." She sat for a moment wondering if she should impart a little-known fact then said, "I even went to a plastic surgeon to see if I could get a breast reduction. Maybe the men would take me more seriously if I was flat chested. But Mom found out. Boy was she mad. The entire point was that it always seemed to be a battle. At least in my eyes."

"And you had to fight for everything from then on," added Don respectively.

"Cartwright not telling any one of my commission, then the weapons. And including your respect, which hasn't been easy," Beverly mentioned back, her dark eyebrows arched, a slight grin spreading along her face.

Don frowned appreciatively. He knew he came off for being opinionated at times but in those times, he thought he was right, and that most of the time he was. Ultimately, he replied, "Walking onto this boat took a lot of guts. It's just me. I have a big mouth."

She patted his hand again and said, "You know, when we had that little chat while I took my shower?"

"Yeah?"

Beverly sighed for a moment, then sought to explain. "I'm very secure in my own skin. I taught myself to become detached from my body. To pay no attention to who might be watching or staring or even touching. The psychiatrist even explained to me it was a byproduct of the mind dealing with forty hours of the unknown. But it was funny. With you, I was so anxious you might peek or say something that I was actually a little nervous. First time in a long time. But I really wanted to show you I was a confident Captain, secure in her knowledge. And her own skin. But I did it to build my confidence. You were the one man on the boat who knew more about everything than I did. And I mean everything. You know how irritating that is?"

Don thought about this for a few moments. It had been an odd thing to do, as the info could have waited, and it did surprise him at the time. Finally, he responded, "Even if I had seen something by accident, I wouldn't have said anything. I'm a lot of things but I am a gentleman at heart. Hell, I couldn't even grab you when you were falling out of my lap, I was so afraid of just … hurting you."

Beverly chuckled. "I know. But that's not the point Don. A commanding attitude is something I have to work on all the time. I was simply afraid you would see something you didn't like. And open up your big mouth," Beverly noted lastly, letting a small grin spread her lips.

Don felt he needed to redeem himself a little and said in return, "Oh Jeez, am I that bad?" He glanced over at her again then added, "Don't answer that. Besides, I have a damned good imagination and I think the package is just fine, thank you. And I'm glad your mom intervened when she did." Don let his gaze fall for the barest of moments, aware that it took little imagination to view the outlines beneath the fabric. He looked back up.

Beverly noticed this then looked down at her feet, aware that her headache was dissipating. She was thoroughly enjoying the open conversation with Don, but she realized she had to get moving, her muscles were stiffening. "I know Don. It took a while but I'm very happy with myself. But whenever I hear it from someone else, I always wonder if they're talking to me or the Admiral. Sometimes, I wonder."

That's when it struck him. Her Dad's reputation, her own leadership abilities and her strength born of the rape had put men at a distance and a low priority in her life. Suddenly he felt sorry for her, but that's not what she wanted. She just wanted to be taken for what she was. So he said, "We need to get going Bev. If we ever get out of this, we'll continue this conversation again. All right? I promise."

Beverly nodded, "I think I'm pretty good now, just a small headache and some bruises. Give me few moments to get dressed. Besides, I've opened up more than I should have. Thanks for listening."

Don rose, careful not to smack his head again and walked to the quarter's door. He turned to look back and Beverly was smiling at him. "What?" he asked.

"You called me honey."

His mind searched back, and yes, he had. At first, he was going to deny it, thought better of that idea, and said jokingly, "Am I to be brought up on insubordination charges? You've got to remember, I'm not the one that undressed you. I was busy roasting my ass off fixing this tub."

Beverly chuckled, shook her head slowly and said, "No charges, you're a civilian." Then she thought and added, "As long as you keep it to private conversations."

Don smiled, and departed.

Beverly sighed heavily. She stood to get clean up and get dressed. All the while thinking. All her life she had pushed men away. They had all wanted something; at the time she could not give. Don was so smart, so self-absorbed, he did not need or want anything from anyone. In fact, he wanted them out of his way.

And she was attracted to this. This was a strength she had never encountered before. And oddly enough, it seemed mutual. Suddenly, she feared that it was all for nothing. For they were all going to die anyway. She shook this image from her head and cleaned herself up. Including her newest injury.

However, the second Beverly plugged in her ear bud it came to life. "Beverly? Any time you want a woman to woman talk, I'm always here for you." Stated Tinkerbell softly.

"Oh God, Tinkerbell, Umm … all right. I really appreciate that."

"I know, I know, I'm not EXACTLY a woman but I do have female insights and a psychology data base that would be very useful. I'm always here to lend an ear."

Beverly thought for a second then she said, "Tinkerbell, I would love nothing more than to have a chat with you with your female insights. And no doubt, you could help me with my little problem. But right now, I'm good and anxious to get on the bridge. We have a big fish to catch which is a lot more important than my nightmares. But we'll talk. Okay?"

"I look forward to it Beverly."

"Captain on the bridge!" yelled Crash when Beverly walked through the safety hatch. It had taken less than twelve minutes for her to groom herself and get into a clean uniform. She had her hair swept over her forehead to cover the small bandage still there as her hat was pulled down a little lower. And the right hand had the smallest of bandages on it.

She nodded, then said, "Gentlemen." She noticed Don only looked up upon her arrival, as he was busy next to Willy at the control's consoles.

Ralph came up to her, snapped a crisp salute then extended his hand. "Captain. The ship is yours," he said graciously with a smile.

She shook it warmly, then said, "Don brought me up to speed on what all that has happened. Commander, do we have a plotting on the Volga?"

Bobby was sitting next to Duran at the mapping board. Bobby did not flinch an inch as the captain came into the control room. Duran finally said, "We have a good idea, but contact was lost. They're sticking to the ocean floor at six to eight knots. Estimated time of intercept is roughly forty minutes."

"Good. Have we had any communications with command?"

Ralph replied, "About five minutes ago. The air born bomb with our Secretary of State on board is still in-route. We've had a plea from the NIA to get the Volga before they land. They have a team of snipers at Montreal ready to take out the hijackers and really don't want it to leave the ground. They're just waiting on the word from us or anyone else luckily enough to blow the Volga out of the water."

Beverly glanced at her watch. "We have two hours then." She looked over at Ralph and asked, "When we get the Volga and let them know, how are they going to get the bombers off the plane?"

Ralph shook his head and responded, "I don't know all the particulars, but I guess it has something to do with Kuznotzhov and the refueling."

"That doesn't sound like much of a plan considering there's two of them," observed Beverly.

Ralph shook his head and returned, "I wasn't made privy of the particulars, but they sounded like once the nuclear threat was taken care of, the plane and the eleven on board were all expendable."

Beverly stood there in shock. She then replied, "Oh God. I know Georgiana pretty well. She's a hell of a smart woman. They just can't simply blow the plane on the tarmac and call it good, can they?"

Ralph shrugged his shoulders and said, "President Garrison has made it known he won't be held hostage by terrorist. Eleven people sound like a small exchange for the populous of Los Angeles or Tokyo."

Beverly shook her head then said, "I hope they come up with something more creative. At least try to get everyone off the plane." Her focus then detoured back to her own present situation and she wheeled around and asked Henry, "Hyde, you seen that damned shark?"

"No Ma'am. No shark."

"You detect that bugger anywhere, you let me know. Paleontologists find of the millennium be damned, I'm going to blow its shit away."

Hyde smiled as did Don. This was the version Don liked best. Strong and confident, full of spit and fire. Even when she was yelling at him.

Beverly then walked over behind the blonde head of Eddy hunched over his weapons control. He glanced up as if struck by lightning, then pushed his glasses up. She put a tender hand on his shoulder and said simply, "We'll get through this together. All right?"

Eddy stuttered for a second, then smiled up at the captain and replied, "Aye Captain. Mister Merrick and I had a little talk. Just bring us into range."

Don sat down at the computer controls next to Willy. He waggled a finger then said, "Bev, come here a second."

She walked over and bent down next to him. Ralph could not hear the conversation less than fifteen feet away, but could tell it was important by Don's animations. Ralph smiled inwardly.

Beverly nodded in understanding then stood and turned to face the radar controls and asked, "Any more contacts with the Gorbachev?"

"Nothing, we've left them in our wake, and they were traveling off bubble," responded Hyde.

"Good. The last thing we need is another Russian sub wandering around getting in our way," acknowledging her approval of Ralph's decision to go it alone. Beverly simply did not trust the Russians fleet. One rogue sub might spawn more subs. She chanced to glance over at the mapping board and saw Bobby staring at her, then redirect his gaze the moment she looked over. She walked over to the mapping board then asked Duran, "What's our position?"

He brought up a large-scale map and pointed specifically at an area. "By our calculations, the Volga is racing towards the Chinook Trough. More open water, fewer places to hide. But with its Magneto Drive and deep-water advantage will undoubtedly dive to the bottom."

She nodded, then said, "Good. That works to our advantage. We can go deeper than they can." Again, she glanced over at Lt Smith who was careful to look straight down at the board.

She walked back to where Don was still bent over Willy, bent over fully next to Don with an arm over his back, pulled her head in closely and asked softly, "Please tell me you guys can do this."

Don looked up at Beverly and acknowledged, "Yeah. We think the satellite can get a lock on the signal. They find out they're being chased again; they just might get desperate. Do something really stupid."

"How far inland can they shoot?"

"They could just about hit Oklahoma."

Beverly nodded and stood up. "Jesus. Keep me posted."

"Will do."

Ralph then asked in a low voice, "Captain. Did Don inform you that the Specter has been given the EAM code and has been verified by three members of the Specters crew to be authentic?"

She nodded her head and replied, "Don did mention that. It appears Fleet Command is worried about a nuclear attack. We've been given the green light."

Ralph merely nodded. It was all part of the job but there was a part of every person that never wants to fire off that amount of destructive power. There was enough juice to blow away a city. There was absolutely no room for error.

Beverly then glanced over at Bobby who was looking at her, then quickly shifted his gaze down. She could not take it anymore and walked over to the mapping board and sat opposite Bobby and Duran. Duran looked up first, could see Beverly glaring at Bobby, then he poked him. The large African American looked uncomfortable as he looked up and saw a finger waving him over. Grudgingly he stood up, walked around the board, and sat next to her.

She huddled close to the man and whispered, "I know you well enough Bobby that you're probably a little embarrassed and nervous about my exam. I don't give a rat's ass; you were just doing your job. But you saw my file, didn't you?"

Bobby looked over at the woman with a new found respect. "Yes Ma'am. It was quite a while ago but it was very extensive. Both psychological and physical."

Beverly stared at the man then let a small grin spread across her face. Finally, she said, "Now you know. Let's keep it our little secret, all right?"

"Yes Ma'am. How did you get that?" asked Bobby pointing at her right knuckles.

Beverly rubbed at the bandage, thought for a moment then said, "I'll be honest. It was a nightmare. I have those once in a while."

Bobby nodded and said, "Had a lady friend in the military at Iraq. Held prisoner for four months. Threatened to kill her every day. Came home with a bad case of Post-Traumatic Stress Disorder. Same thing you had. She was never the same." Bobby shook his head in disdain then added, "I couldn't even imagine Ma'am what you went through."

"Wasn't that bad, killing me was more of a threat than anything else. A couple of days out of my life, that's all. Not nearly as bad as Iraq. The food however, was lousy. Lost a little weight. The guy simply forgot to feed me." Beverly then let out a shy grin.

Bobby nodded, remembering the notations in the file. She had escaped on her own, with nothing more than a sheet wrapped around her, in the dead of night. No water, no food for more than two days, she had wandered onto an old hi-way and managed to flag down a car. Bobby could not even imagine how much courage that took.

"And how are the nightmares Ma'am?" Bobby asked whispering, as a concerned man and as the person in charge of all their wellbeing. He was not probing for chinks in her armor as Wolfson put it, simply trying to solve the one little thing he could help the woman with.

Beverly Hornacher steeled up her resolve. She knew where this was going. "They have nothing to do with reality. At the moment, they're sort of entertaining. Most action I've seen in months. That's all Bobby. That's all."

His pearly whites flashed back, then he sighed heavily as if a weight had been lifted. Bobby thought of his strict Baptist mother, and if anyone had done that to her, he would have hunted them down and gutted them like a fish. He nodded his head, put a large paw on her hand and said simply, "All right Ma'am. I've got some stuff to help you sleep." He thought for a moment, decided to chance the statement and added, "I think engineering can rig up a dimmer on your bunk light. To read by you understand."

This shook Beverly for a moment, unaware of that part of the information was in her medical file. She simply nodded at Bobby and slyly smiled, then responded, "Not necessary. Yet."

Then she swiveled around in the mapping chair and looked at the rest of the crew in the control room. Addressing all the men she then said in a hearty voice, "Thirty-five more minute's gentlemen, then the game is afoot."

CHAPTER 20

President Andrew Garrison strolled in through the northwest door from the main corridor of the west wing into the Presidential Oval Office. He had by-passed his secretary, in the next room, for the time being. He wanted just a few minutes alone with his thoughts, then let the rabble in he thought.

He sat at the massive cherry desk that his wife had picked out when he was elected to the office. He would have preferred something that fit his stature, for he was only five foot six inches. He knew his chair had been specially designed for him to sit up a little taller in the saddle. So, he did not look like a dwarf behind the massive chunk of wood. He actually liked the décor of the oval, as he let his wife pick out the colors. Anything to keep her busy. Gold drapes, dark blue carpeting with a ring of thirteen stars. He liked the office.

However, he loathed the latest problem thrown his way. The last forty-eight hours had been hell. Getting updates and notes without having any real input was driving him crazy. He had been on Air Force One heading to the West Coast when it all started. They had landed in Texas as the Russian problem took on new complications. He was talking to Lucius and Georgianna and General Blanchett periodically. He was talking to the Secretary of the Navy and then to the Vice President. They were talking, but in the end, he was really doing nothing. All the talking was basic information, sharing what was actually happening. And that was not how the President wanted to run things.

He stroked at his upper lip. He had the perfect face for a large mustache, which he had until he ran for President. Studies said Presidents do not have mustaches. The second he retired he was growing it back he had decided the day he won.

A small rap at the secretary's office door broke his thoughts. That was quick, he would have wished for more time. "Come."

The door opened and an older yet, attractive lady poked her head in and said, "I thought you snuck past me. Secretary Perry, General Blanchett and Hiram Walker are waiting."

Garrison glanced at some twenty notes on his desk and replied, "I know, let them in.

Sec, Nav.?"

Linda Chomsky was used to his short use of words. She had learned a long time ago that when he wanted to have an open dialogue, he would do so. But when words got in the way, he kept them to a minimum. She had worked for worse people. "Secretary Morrisey and Director Billingham are both on the speaker," she replied.

Garrison had forgotten about Kirk. "Good. Let's get this going."

Linda stood for a moment, when Garrison looked up and mentioned. "And yes, I noticed you got a new doo." He smiled. "Very nice, suits your face."

She smiled. "Glad you approve."

Garrison was glancing quickly at the notes on his desk. Most of them he already knew about. A couple were call backs, calls that would have to wait. The door opened once again, "Mister President." Linda said, merely opening the door wider, letting in General Blanchett, Mr. Perry, Colonel Mayfield and Hiram.

Garrison waved at the twin couches facing each other. "Have a seat. Secretary, Director, can you hear me?"

"Yes, sir Mister President." Came the quick response.

"Linda, any word from Jonathon or Martin?" Garrison wanted Linda listening in the conference calls for just such problems.

Jonathon was of course the Russian Ambassador and Martin was the Chinese Ambassador, Martin Fielding.

"Enroute Mister President. Should be here shortly." Came the reply.

"Let security know, I want them here ASAP."

"Yes, Sir, I figured you would."

President Garrison sighed heavily then charged in. "Do we have any proof that it was in fact the Volga that sunk the Seattle?"

The four assembled looked at each other than Lucius replied, "No. No distress call was put out by the Seattle. The remains of the Sub were first detected by the Specter."

The Specter. The Presidents mind drifted to a year and half previously. Garrison had been the first President to take on the trillions of dollars deficit that the American people were racking up. A three-billion-dollar war machine in time of relative peace was against every grain of his nature. It was already in the works by the previous administration but cutting the funding would still save the American taxpayer two billion. And even after a half hour conversation with Mister Merrick, did little to change his mind.

However, the next day would take care of all that. He remembered it succinctly. All four phones on his desk rang at once, even the direct line to the Kremlin. That in fact was very unusual because all calls went through his secretary. Linda had opened the outer door and merely threw her hands in the air. She had no idea why all his phones were rings.

He answered the closest one, with anger in his voice. "This is President Garrison. Who is this?"

"This is Mister Merrick. Was not sure which phone you typically answered so I rang all of them. Turn your attention to your smart T.V." Garrison had turned to face the TV, mounted high on the wall to the right of the desk, when it suddenly came on. A singular image was an attractive older lady dressed in a blue, form fitting dress. The woman was Linda. Garrison had glanced at the real Linda and she merely shrugged her shoulders, her mouth agape in wonder. Even the dress was exactly the same.

The digital image sat in the middle of a dark background and started talking. "Mister President, my name is Tinkerbell and I am the AI program that runs the Poseidon Project on board computers. I am currently sitting on the outside shell of the futuristic submarine." The lights around the submarine came up and sure enough the lovely lady was sitting cross legged on top of the front of the conning tower. The camera image left Tinkerbell and rotated around the shell, past the aft, around the one side, coming around the front to the see the bubble that would be the Slaw weapon and coming directly back up to Tinkerbell.

"As you can see Mister President, the shell of the ship is complete. The Liquid Metal construction is six times stronger than any steel. It will go three times deeper than any known submersible. The Liquid Metal Reactor along with the Fusion Jets will generate a speed of close to one hundred knots an hour. It will in fact be the fastest boat on the ocean. It will have a Plasma Generator which will make it virtually invisible." In a matter of emphasis Tinkerbell then stated, "Mister President, there will not be a Submarine that can compare with this vessel."

President Garrison had sat on the front of his new huge cherry desk, his arms folded across his chest. Linda came in and sat next to him. Finally, the President asked, "Tell me about the technology. It's obvious you can do things that no one else in the world can do."

Tinkerbell smiled a demur grin. "You are smart man Mister President. The new Submarine will have its own satellite. It will NOT have a periscope. It will not need one. It will NOT have Sonar. It will have a lazar targeting system. It will have torpedoes fore and aft. It will have a synchronized weapon that can fire eight miles. And it will have a Nuclear fusion missile that will in fact be the longest and fastest ranged nuclear weapon on the planet." Finally, she paused for a moment and added with, "And as you can see Mister President, we can do almost anything we want to with our Quantum computer."

Suddenly all the phones on his desk started ringing yet again. Then Tinkerbell finished with, "Just think of what we could do if we were really trying." And she flashed a devastating smile.

President Garrison pursed his lips and drummed his fingers against the desk edge. Suddenly the Oval Office door burst open with a large Secret Service man brandishing a standard 9mm hand gun. "Are you two, okay? Our computers and security system has been going wild. Our radios went dead." That was when the large black suited man chanced to look at the television screen and saw Tinkerbell, or in fact Linda waving at him.

"We're fine. Put your weapon away. You make me more nervous than; I'm sorry I forgot your name?" Asked the President of Tinkerbell.

She gave him a scolding look and answered, "Really now. It's Tinkerbell."

"Yes, of course, I'm sorry you do look like my secretary."

"Yeah, she does. That's not her?" Asked the Service man.

"We thought it would be more pleasing to deal with someone your familiar with."

"Shut it off please and return the White House back to my control." The President said forcibly.

"Certainly." The ringing quit immediately and the Service Agents radio crackled to life.

There was a dead silence for seventeen seconds when the President finally stated, "Linda, get that smug son of a bitch on the phone as soon as possible."

"Don is waiting for your phone call." Inserted Tinkerbell still smiling, still sitting on the conning tower.

"You can go. And take your gun with you," the President instructed the Secret Service Agent.

"Oh. Yeah. Okay." He turned to leave, glanced around one more time then left the Oval Office.

Linda also turned to leave then asked, "Can I ask what do you plan on telling Mister Merrick?" She knew he was pragmatic man but he also had a temper. What had just happened and the doppelganger staring at her from the TV made her nervous as hell. This Merrick guy was not someone she wanted to piss off.

"I plan on telling him that the President of the United States does not take kindly to this little display." Then he pursed his lips together in thought and continued, "I also plan on telling him that it was very effective, got my attention and I plan on having a long meeting with Sec, Nav." He turned to Tinkerbell, still sitting on the conning tower, her long legs crossed and holding her hands on her exposed knee. "And I can't wait to have another conversation with you my dear."

"Oh, believe me Mister President, it will be entertaining. Nighty night." Tinkerbell then blew him a kiss and the screen then faded to black.

The Presidents mind came back to the present. Finally, he asked, "Do we have an update on the Specter? What kind of shape is she in?"

Colonel Mayfield looked sideways at him, realized the President was a little out of the loop and illuminated the President. "The Specter has made repairs and is less than twenty minutes behind the Volga."

The President looked around as if it was a joke. Then he said, "The Specter was mauled by a prehistoric shark then took two direct hit Russian torpedoes and she's now making up time on the Volga?"

"Yes sir. The Specter had made repairs and has a good idea as to the Volga's location and making speed to find her," explained Lucius, with a slight grin.

The President shook his head vigorously, then remarked, "That smug son of a bitch. You know I really hate him, but by God I'm glad he's on our side."

The Lucius mentioned snidely, "Not to mention Tinkerbell." Linda smirked.

"And Tinkerbell of course," nodded the President not taking the bait at all. "Now. What do we have in the water to back up the Specter? Even I realize that this is a fight the Specter can't win."

"I wouldn't tell Beverly that." Mentioned Rebecca.

"Excuse me? I'm a little out of the loop on this Specter?" Hiram Walker asked. A large Man of African heritage had retired as an Admiral in the Navy. His job now was as the Pentagon Spokesman. Yesterday he was playing Golf in Augusta, Georgia. Twelve calls later he was rushing back to one hell of an emergency.

Perry, General Blanchett and Colonel Mayfield very quickly brought him up to speed as he very deftly made note after note on what was happening in the North Pacific. Colonel Mayfield seemed to anticipated everyone one of his questions as she seemed to be the one explaining things in better detail.

Finally, Lucius was already pulling notes from his brief case and started in on the Presidents question. "Canada CFB out of Esquimalt has thirteen ships all on the move at our request, including two submarines, which were already deployed. Australia has three Colins class submarines in the water and twenty-three frigates and cruisers to bolsters Pearl's compliment. Most of these ships Mister President will come under the USPACFLT at Pearl. They have been given the updates and realize that the Volga is simply blowing any ship out of its way. They have no intention of engaging, just shadow and detect if they do find the Volga."

"And the Japanese?"

Lucius looked a little sheepish. "Um, sadly to say the Japanese don't want anything to do with this."

"Really?"

"No in fact they are pretty much pulling their fleet, as it were. My guess would be they really don't want to piss off the Russians or accidently run into the Chinese."

The President pondered for a moment then responded, "You know, I really can't blame them. However, I do remember little things like that."

Just then both Martin Fielding and Johnathon Peepers walked in, Johnathon as usual looked rumpled while Martin looked sharp and tailored. And quite a bit taller. "Mister President," Martin said as both extended their hands to the various people in the room.

"Good, pull up a chair." As could have been predicted, Martin quickly found a chair along the wall as Johnathon was left to look around the room and found a well-padded Victorian styled chair against the wall. He brought it over and sat to the right of the President.

The President turned to Johnathon. "All right. We have no real proof the Volga destroyed the Seattle, but we do know the Specter has been under fire from the Volga. So, I think it's fair to assume the Volga destroyed the Seattle." He stopped to let this sink in for a second then continued. "And now Johnathon, the sixty-four-thousand-dollar question is what the hell is the Russian military up too?"

"Well, right away it's getting complicated. A Ukrainian group has stolen the pride of the Russian Fleet. And because of that there is a shake up in the Russian Pacific command. Gone are Admirals Ventrovich and Andryich, both have literally disappeared from sight. Right now, even the Russian Ambassador Pusinko has no idea who's making the decisions."

"And WHAT decisions have they made?" Asked the President.

"They are actively hunting down the Volga, for there has been little communications with the rebel group. All they know is that they have been threatened with nuclear retaliation in case they are hunted. They in fact don't even know about Kuznotzhov and Coats Island."

"They have no idea WHY their sub was stolen?" Asked the baffled President.

"No sir. Since Coats Island was under US jurisdiction, I'm sure the rebels did not feel the need to give out any more info that they needed to."

"But the Russians have a good idea, right?"

"Um, yes sir, I would guess they have an accurate determination of the Volga's intention."

Suddenly Martin cut in, "And all of this being backed by the Chinese through the North Korean's. The Chinese would get the specifics on the fire power of the Volga and especially the Magneto drive, which they do not have, and the North Koreans would get to keep the Sub, with a healthy stipend to the new Ukrainian government."

"The Koreans would now have almost a hundred nuclear warheads at their disposal and both would get a new ally in the Ukrainians," inserted Lucius.

President Garrison was a quick tactician. "So, the Russians are hunting the Volga, have no idea where it's at, we have one, albeit small and damaged sub closing in on the Volga. The Chinese would love to get their hands on it. Would they attack American or Russian forces in order for the Volga to stay hidden? Would they help them in any way?"

The six people in the room all glanced around each other. Finally, Martin chimed in. "The Chinese I think are simply hoping this all works. Remember they don't really have the sub force to deal with Americans or Russians. The Chinese Ambassador has expressed that the Chinese would remain neutral in all this."

"You think?" Garrison turned his attention to Lucius. "What do you think?"

Lucius studied his hand for a moment then responded. "I think Martin is right, the Chinese Navy can't go toe to toe with us or the Russians, but I have to believe they just wouldn't sacrifice the Volga if there was a way they could intervene. I think they're out there may be doing nothing more than misdirection. But they are out there."

"That's what I thought. That's a lot of fire power just waiting to run into each other." He pondered for a few seconds then said, "I don't want another Saigon or Afghanistan. I want forces coming together right now. I want the Specter to get the help it needs to take out the Volga. We will not deal with terrorists. I do not want Kuznotzhov to reach the Ukraine, as much as I don't like the Russians trying to control it. This is not the way out of this mess."

"Sir if I may?" Injected Colonel Mayfield.

"Certainly," replied the President crossing his arms.

"If I know Captain Hornacher and Mister Merrick at all, they will not wait for back up."

General Blanchett looked at the President. "She's right."

Anderson nodded. "I understand that. But help me out here. The Specter does NOT have the fire power to take on the Volga. Correct?"

Lucius thought carefully then responded. "Frankly sir, I don't know. This is not simply a matter of comparing oranges to oranges. The Specter has weapons that that have never been used before. It will baffle the Volga to no end, so doesn't necessarily have to out shoot her."

The President in turn replied, "Okay. So let me put it this way. I want the Volga brought to justice. By any means necessary. I don't think, and you people don't know if the Specter can do it by itself. I believe reinforcements are necessary. I believe the Specter should locate and WAIT for the Ford or the Cheyenne to provide help. Is that entire scenario a bad idea?"

Lucius was nodding his head. "I appreciate where you are going sir. We will relay to the Specter they should locate and wait for assistance."

Colonel Rebecca Mayfield looked at every individual then settled her gaze on the President. "But, they WON'T. They find the Volga they WILL try to destroy her. They have witnessed the destruction of the Seattle, they have been attacked by the Volga themselves, they are not going to wait."

Garrison glanced around the room and witnessed Lucius nodding in agreement. "I appreciate that," replied the President. "I don't not want to see the destruction of the Specter on top of everything else. All right then. Tell the Specter then that it is their discretion, but if there is any way possible, they are to wait for assistance. If they feel the situation is too grave then proceed. If they continue it had better be a winnable situation." Garrison then turned to face the Colonel. "Will that work for you?"

"Yes Sir." The Colonel replied smiling then winking at Lucius.

The President then said, "What's that term you Military type use? Plow the field? I want the Volga overwhelmed, even if we have to blindside the Chinese." Then he turned to Martin Fielding and stated, "Martin, impress that fact upon the Chinese. And Johnathon, tell the Russians I expect full cooperation in finding and destroying the Volga."

There was a lot of nodding and mumbling as everyone rose. Lucius and General Blanchett looked at each other. They were just given carte blanche to destroy the Volga. Now, it was a just a question of finding her.

CHAPTER 21

Admiral Rabinov was concerned, as he made himself comfortable in the captain's chair in the control center of the Volga. After the confrontations with the Seattle and the Specter, he, and his entire crew were on the edge. Even with the full day head start, he honestly did not think they would be located so quickly. Particularly, so aggressively by the Americans, and alarmingly, with a secret submarine. With a skeleton crew, it meant catching quick naps, eating at their duty stations, and keeping a watchful eye on anything unusual. Even a seismic disturbance.

The television transmission had gone without a hitch, even though, Madam Secretary had vented her anger at them. Rabinov knew enough English to know she thought of them as 'filthy terrorists, without a grain of courage, who would not succeed'. Funny, he thought at the time, they seemed to be doing just fine as she looked very uncomfortable sitting next to two hundred pounds of C-four explosive and a jet full of fuel.

Even though the random radio transmissions that the Volga was picking up were all garbled or faded to the point of indistinguishability, he could have sworn he heard the voice of his old comrade, Captain Balakoff. Somewhere, lurking in the shadows, Rabinov knew was the Ballistic Submarine Gorbachev. He wondered whom Balakoff was talking to?

On board the speeding Specter, concentration on being the hunter gripped each crewman. Hernandez had done as promised with his Veal Cordon bleu. However, it was mostly served in the control room as no one was going to leave their post at that point in time. Even though it was well prepared, most nibbled or wolfed it down to get it out of the way. Still, Beverly was grateful for the interlude. The crew needed to be fed.

"Bobby. Time?" was all Beverly asked as she dabbed her lips with a paper napkin.

"About eighteen minutes Captain and we should be hearing something," responded Smith.

Beverly nodded, disposed of her melamine plate in a bag for such purposes then walked over to where both Hyde and Hernandez was monitoring the exterior ship systems. They sat side by side, plunged into their headsets firmly smashed against their heads. They had not even heard Beverly come up from behind. She said nothing, just glancing at the four screens showing various underwater and satellite pictures.

They had received a communique from Pacific Fleet. Wait for assistance once you find the Volga, UNLESS you have a volatile situation. But that made no sense to any of them. All 'ASSISTANCE' was hours off. The entire situation was VOLATILE. Did Pearl know that? No matter, this was a direct request by the President. Don only laughed. Beverly told Wolfson she would keep it in mind, and had communications send a verification of reception. Volatile her ass. She was going after the Volga.

Don was sitting next to Willy, his swivel chair positioned straight at the large central monitor. Sitting back recliner style, he had one hand on the touch screen and without looking, was smashing the screen to view different satellite images. The first was their location, then one was an infrared reading from the estimated location of the Volga, and yet another was a view of the plane that was carrying Georgiana Wannaker as it streamed toward Montreal. Like a sport junky on a Sunday afternoon, he switched views every twenty or so seconds.

Ultimately, Beverly walked over to Don and put her hand over his. "You're making me nauseous," she pointed out pulling his hand away from the screen.

"Sorry," was all he said in return.

"This is driving you nuts, isn't it?" Beverly observed, with a slight smile.

"I hate waiting. And this tub is too small to pace in."

Beverly smiled then looked back at the large screen. She then glanced over at their pilot and asked, "Mr. Caldwell. Why the nickname Crash?"

This took the man off guard for a second, then he responded, "Not much of a story really. It was my first training voyage. A small Skipjack sub off the East coast, with a new sonar array and console that was being tested for the first time. Nothing like we got here though. Anyway. We had a new captain, sort of full of himself, totally pissed off that he's in command of an old training sub. Took the entire thing sort of lackadaisically. Much like Mister Merrick, we have the designers of the sonar on board watching everything. Well, suddenly the sonar guys have something in the water."

Beverly was already smiling, for she had heard the story from other sources and knew where it was going.

Crash continued. "The captain, doesn't take the thing seriously, the small blip the sonar was picking up. Must be a problem with the sonar he kept saying. The signature was not big enough to be anything other than a fish, he kept saying. The sonar man tells him a small submersible is in the water with them and we need to steer clear. The captain argues with him, has confirmation from Norfolk we are alone. So, in a flash of stupidity, he tells me to turn the submarine on the small blip, the sonar is screwed up, picking up an old barrel or something in the water. Well, we ram the Navy's newest robotic submersible. The sonar however, didn't pick up the ship less than five hundred feet away. Total one-hundred percent damage to the submersible, sinking a ten-million-dollar machine, and sending the designers into a tailspin as to why their sonar picked up a small object in the water and not the large ship on the surface."

Beverly smiled and said, "I had heard. Big board of inquiry if I remember correctly."

"Yeah. Sort of messed up our sub as well. The captain gets written up and demoted for not taking heed, even though he was sort of right. Now, if he had crashed into the boat itself, that would have been all-right"

"And you get stuck with the nickname Crash," pointed out Beverly grinning.

"Hey, that's a lot better than what happened to the captain. The last I heard he was on board a mine sweeper off the coast of Greenland."

"Ouch," observed Beverly. Then she glanced at her watch then added, "Well, Mr. Caldwell, I'm glad you're on board. But I promise you, no little submarines today."

"That's what I'm afraid of," responded Crash glancing back at Beverly but with a devilish grin.

She nodded and sighed heavily. She suddenly felt like Don. Submarine commanders had to develop a knack of grasping the whole picture of the ocean without actually 'seeing' a single thing. Information was crucial, which concerned Beverly at the moment, for there was none coming. To keep herself busy she gathered up the dishes and ran them back to the galley. Ralph only shook his head in wonder as she returned.

Beverly noted that the eighteen minutes came and went. She knew it was not going to be that easy and that the Volga was not going to follow a straight line. Still, she asked Duran, "Do we have projected scenarios we can explore?"

The exploded view on the large map board was fraught with black marks. He finally made a circle in the center and pointed. "We should be no more than twenty kilometers off center."

"Which way?"

Lt. Duran stared at the board and shook his head. Finally, he observed, "He's got to be following the ridge to the East. Any other direction would be back tracking."

"Plot a new course and give steering the headings," Beverly said emphatically, trusting the observations of her navigator.

Crash made a fifteen-degree course change.

Four minutes later both Hernandez and Hyde came unglued from their seats. "Screws to starboard bow, roughly twelve thousand meters and closing!" Hernandez yelled.

Every muscle tensed in the control room of the Specter. Beverly took a heavy breath as if to focus then said to Crash, "Make course change Mr. Caldwell. Willy, we need to go to battle stations, if you please."

"Yes Ma'am," Willy answered sending the low volume alarm through the radios and turning the ambient white light a bright red.

"Alex, let me know when you've got confirmation of target," commanded Beverly.

"Nothing yet Ma'am," responded Hyde, glued to the screens.

Wolfson came up next to Beverly and noted, "If it's the Volga, stealth would be a good option."

Beverly nodded, and responded, "My thoughts exactly." She turned to Crash and said, "Steering, let's slow up to twenty knots." Then she turned to Hyde and asked, "Distance please."

"After the course change, we've narrowed it to eleven thousand five hundred meters. They're cruising at about eight knots."

"Hernandez, confirmation yet?"

"Computer is having problems getting a signature. We're in its baffles, it's awfully deep and more than likely it's running it's Magneto drive Ma'am."

"Understood." Then a thought popped into Beverly's mind and she asked, "No word on our shark, is there?"

"No Ma'am."

Beverly nodded, then had a thought. She motioned with her head at Ralph, and he walked over.

"Yeah?"

"Tower," commanded Beverly. They exited the control room, Beverly slowly closing the safety hatch behind her.

Lieutenant Peter Markova was tired. He was the only radar-sonar man on board the Volga. He was allowed eight hours off to sleep, then sit for the next sixteen. It seemed like an eternity since six that morning, his glutes and hamstrings tightening up on him. A crew man sat in his chair while he slept, but they really did not know what to listen for. But his mother was old and getting rather sickly, his sister had parleyed a cute face and figure into being a Tochka in Moscow. Prostitution did not sit well with Peter or his mother and was very illegal. She was not starving to death, but death followed her every night she went out. It played hard on Peter's mind as she was a smart girl and he wanted so much more for her. For that he would allow his butt to go numb and to listen. However, his one ear was still ringing from whatever the blast was that rocked his head earlier that day.

Commander Ushinko was also tired. Rabinov slept when tired and arrived when rested. Ushinko seemed to have to be on the bridge at all times. Already his nerves were growing thin. He kept reminding himself the payback for freeing Kuznotzhov. They would be made Ukrainian heroes, and the entitlements would last a life time. He kept glancing at his watch, wishing the plane would land and Kuznotzhov was safely on board headed home. They would get another transmission from LaGuardia and then one from Heathrow in London. All in less than thirty hours.

Peter paid the noise little mind when he first heard it. Like static in the background of his headset, he shifted in his chair. Then it grew louder, almost imperceptive. Finally, enough for him to take notice. A spine-tingling chill ran up his back as the noise was oddly familiar. He glanced quickly around all his sonar controls and screens and saw nothing. He tried to zero in on the noise, or tune it out. Again, nothing. Ushinko was close enough so he could grab the man.

"Yes, what is it, Peter?" asked Ushinko feeling the vise like grip.

"It's back," he said dramatically.

"What's back?" asked Ushinko concerned, his mind not quite focusing.

"The swooshing sounds. The little submarine. The bitch Captain. She's back!"

Ushinko shook his head vehemently and stated, "Can't be. We destroyed it. With two direct hit torpedoes."

Peter wheeled around in his chair and looked up with terror in his eyes and said, "Sonar and computer indicates it's the same wave signature. She's back! Get the Comrade Admiral."

Rabinov was in the weapons and sonar area of the control center in less than a minute. He listened carefully to the headphones. "Can you get a lock on its location?" he asked finally.

"No."

"What about the Passive array?" Rabinov said looking at the very blank green screen.

"No."

"Can you guess as to its location or distance?" asked Rabinov again hopefully.

Peter finally lost his temper, pounded his console and yelled, "No! I have nothing but a noise, don't you understand? Maybe if we had been allowed the retro fit, I would have had the technology to find this sub. But I don't. Listening devices are picking up an echo of the noise and that's it."

Rabinov slowly nodded his head. He said finally, "I understand. Do the best you can, but DO NOT take your eyes off that God-damned thing."

Commander Wolfson and the Captain had returned to the control center after a brief exchange of ideas. Beverly had conferred with the Commander of her strategy. It was
a bold plan, with a fifty-fifty chance of working.

Petty Officer Hyde yelled at Captain Hornacher, "Captain! We have confirmation. The target is a Delta type Five, being the Russian submarine Volga and she is five thousand meters on the mark, cruising at a depth of four hundred meters Ma'am."

Beverly nodded then commanded, "Steering, down planes at twenty degrees to four hundred meters." Then swiftly she wheeled and said, "Weapons, I want bow torpedoes one and two ready. Safety set for heat seeking."

"Yes, Ma'am," responded Lt Faulk, aware that this time there would not be another chance.

Beverly then added, "I'm counting on you to counter anything they shoot at us all right?"

"Aye Ma'am! I'm counting on me too."

Beverly then turned, glanced at Don then looked over at Steve and said, "Communications, let the Pacific Fleet know our current situation. Then I want you to open up a line to the Volga."

"Ma'am?" replied Steve in disbelief.

Duran and Lt. Smith exchanged looks, Duran shaking his head. He had heard parts of the conversation the captain had with Smith and now knew in his heart the captain was not playing with a full deck. This only confirmed it.

Don jumped out of his chair in rage, his fists balled up. He stuttered a few times then finally chose his words and started yelling,

"What is it with you people that always want to talk to the enemy? Jesus Christ I will never understand Beverly!"

Beverly stood her ground and merely retorted, "Shut up Don." Then she added, "Steve, just do it."

"Aye Ma'am."

Ralph walked over and put a hand on Don's shoulder and slowly pushed the man back down into his chair. Ralph could feel the rage shaking through Don. He knew what Beverly was up to. Being a much smaller boat, jumping onto the giants back was not always the best strategy. Maybe, they could literally scare the giant into surrendering. Even David had to be afraid taking on Goliath.

However, in the background of the several second communications search, was heard a low rumbling. Plainly, the words, "There goes the element of surprise."

Captain Hornacher slowly turned from her spot by communications to look over at the mapping board. The voice was distinctly Duran's.

"Lieutenant? Do you have a problem with my strategy?" She asked succinctly.

Duran had been caught off guard, and searched the faces in the control room. He had gone to all except Wolfson and Merrick to voice his concerns for the captain's leadership. Ray Dicenzo was dead, because of her inability to out think an old shark. Something should be done before they were all killed.

Duran was going to respond with an argument, but a shooting pain through his leg kept him from speaking. Bobby had a vice like grip on Duran's left leg and was squeezing with all his might below the mapping board.

Finally, Duran squeaked out, "I just thought ..." He stopped mid-sentence. Even Mr. Merrick was staring at the man as if he had the plague. Wolfson was merely shaking his head.

"Yes? You thought?" Beverly stated taking a step closer.

Bobby did not let up and it was clear that Duran was not going to get any assistance from his fellow crewmen. This was uncharted territory, and clearly it was going to get any raised voices in deep trouble. Duran shot a hand under the table and latched onto the fingers crushing his leg.

Finally, Ralph jumped in and said, "Captain, Lieutenant Duran is very good at his job, but not very good at thinking. I'll deal with him later, right now we have a sub to deal with."

Beverly shot Duran one last curious glance then said, "Commander, I will leave with you to deal with the Lieutenant." Then she quickly wheeled around and went back to the communications consoles. Wolfson only glared at Duran then shook his head again.

"Done. Pearl has acknowledged our current situation. They want to remind you about their last communique? And I have the Volga's frequency and they acknowledge," said Steve, still wondering what the hell the captain was doing.

"Good," nodded Beverly. "Now I am going to make this quick so wait for my signal, and keep the line open, I'm hoping for a response. On speaker."

"Yes Ma'am."

Beverly looked up into the air with hatred in her voice. "Rabinov or Puchinko or whoever you are. This is Captain Hornacher of the USS Specter. Trust me, I am not a ghost, but you can't see me, can you?" The rage swelled up in her a little more as her lips twisted into a hard mouth. She had practiced the line she was going to deliver for the past eighteen minutes. "No one will hear the screams at four hundred meters below the water. We now have orders to shoot to kill. The American Navy is on your ass, the Russian Navy is on your ass and I'm so close I can smell it. I will give you ONE chance for unconditional surrender. Or, be prepared to meet eternity." She waved at Steve in disgust, her teeth clenched in rage. In her heart she wanted Rabinov to know who killed him.

"Wow." Said the lone voice of Tinkerbell.

Ralph nodded his head at Beverly. It was gutsy, and it had cost them the small element of surprise. But Beverly had sent a clear signal through the water to scare the hell out of anyone. The Volga was marked for death. And maybe, just maybe, they would signal a surrender without shooting off one torpedo.

Admiral Rabinov stood stunned as did the rest of the crew throughout the controls of the Volga, as the ghostly message fairly echoed throughout the massive sub. The She Captain was back. The American Bitch and the submarine that would not die. Rabinov measured the response from the crew. A goodly amount of disbelief and terror ran across their faces. As it should be. They had detonated two Russian torpedoes on the little boat and the ghostly sub was still out there. And what's worse it had found them yet again. What would it take?

"Peter, was there any way to get a lock on her signal?" Rabinov implored, yelling at the man sitting twenty-five feet away.

Peter sat stunned for a few seconds, then threw his hands up, leaned back in his chair and said, "It was all less than fifteen seconds, and it wasn't a direct signal. All I can give you is a direction. Passive array says the signal was bounced off directly behind us. Probably a long way off. That's all I got."

Rabinov nodded then commanded, "Steering, hard a port come about one hundred eighty degrees." Swiveling around he yelled to Ushinko, "Tell weapons to load and flood one, two, three and four and prepare to fire, on my mark."

Ushinko then exploded at Rabinov, "The American's have us dead in their sights! She has given us a chance to surrender!"

Rabinov wheeled around and yelled, "NO! We go as planned. Lock and load the damned torpedoes!"

Ushinko stood absolutely stunned at this turn of events. He slowly picked off the radio controller and relayed the message.

"To shoot at what?" murmured Molovich, sending the commands to the torpedo room to load.

Rabinov moved down to back end of the control center and said, "When we close the gap, we should find something to shoot at. Prepare two acoustic counter measures, for they are assuredly going to fire first."

Ushinko, having heard the words of the Grim Reaper, had fallen into a state of shock. But Rabinov's actions mobilized the man as he grabbed Rabinov by the arm, and growled, "She has us marked for death, we can't see her and you're firing at ghosts! We got lucky the first time, what the hell are you doing?"

Rabinov wheeled on the man, yanked the arm away and growled right back, "I'm fighting for my life. We are dead, no matter what. We surrender now, we will HANG by the Russians! She knows that, she's just trying to scare us into surrendering without a fight. Well, I'm going out fighting. What do you want to do?"

Every single man on the bridge of the Volga was riveted on the confrontation between the two men. They were now caught in a battle no man expected, or knew how to get out of. They waited with bated breaths for the outcome.

Ushinko's lip quivered, then he yelled, "If we agree to a surrender, we can negotiate with the Americans and at least live out our lives. Maybe in prison, but still alive!"

Rabinov sneered back at the weak man. He growled into Ushinko's face, "Do you think that Yashankov or the Russian government would really allow that? Or the North Koreans?" He turned as if to address all the men on the bridge. "What do you all want to do? We would all die in prison before the year would be done, IF WE SURRENDER!!"

Rabinov waited a few seconds as no one said a single word. Young men all looked back at their leader. All painfully aware this was the one decision that would seal their fate. Rabinov, hearing no objections turned back on Ushinko and growled, "We … are going … to fight."

Beverly was leaning over the communications console, aware that they were not getting a response. She took a deep breath, stood, then looked over at Ralph and said, "It's not coming."

Ralph merely nodded, as he gazed at the monitors over Hernandez's head and responded, "He knows he's a dead man no matter what he does. He's measuring us for the fight."

Beverly then turned to Eddy and asked, "Do you have a lock on the Volga?"

"Yes Ma'am!" yelled Eddy, clenching his teeth in preparation.

"We're in that volatile situation. Fire torpedoes one and two," Beverly said without hesitation.

In Eddies ear came a small voice. "Eddy, I think you need to engage the USAC."

"Oh, yeah. Good idea Tinkerbell," whispered Eddy as he started touching his computer screens.

"Man, she's not only got balls, but they're brass too," whispered Don to Ralph in obvious admiration of the terror Beverly sent across the water.

Ralph nodded then whispered back, "You certainly have to admire her style. Rabinov and his little crew have just got to be rattled out of their shorts."

"Filling their shorts, you mean."

"Captain, torpedoes one and two out of the tubes and clear sailing!" Yelled Eddy.

"Volga is flooding all four tubes Captain and she is swinging to the port," informed Hernandez.

"Range?"

"We're still at thirty-five hundred meters Captain."

Ralph injected quickly, "He's swinging to give us a side view. We're going to hit the triple hull. But the Russian sub can't shoot at us from that angle."

"Weapons, keep a watch out," Beverly instructed Lt. Faulk. She then looked over at Don who was back at his chair working on the computer. "Don? Anything?"

"Not yet," he muttered back. "Tinkerbell?"

"Working on it, Don. Myself, Gypsy and Willy are working on it."

On the Volga there was chaos. "Comrade Admiral, I have a new noise which I'm assuming are torpedoes. Three thousand and closing very fast," stated Peter unaccustomed to the higher pitched whine and speed of the little Specter torpedoes.

Rabinov injected calmly to Ushinko, "Steering, maintain ninety degrees to the fish. Then, on my mark, as aggressively as possible, bring us about the last ninety. Tell engineering I want to push one-hundred-ten percent on the reactor, let's get some distance. Weapons, countermeasures on my mark."

Ushinko relayed all the instructions. He then looked at Rabinov. "Surely the small sub can't have much for fire power," observed Ushinko hopefully, distressed that they were fighting a ship they had already sank once.

Peter spoke up, "Sir, fish are making adjustments for us, they have changed course to match our progression. And sir, detection says they are smaller, but they are FAST."

"They may not be much but they are damn accurate. I would expect nothing less," mentioned Rabinov to Ushinko. Then he added, "We have underestimated them once, I will not do it again."

"And we can't fire at this angle," said Ushinko dejectedly.

Rabinov walked back behind the steering center and commanded, "Steering, start bringing us about, and bring us up to launch depth."

Ushinko then understood the reasoning. Rabinov knew he could not get the lethargic Volga around in time so chose to take the fish at the strongest point on the ship. Then he was hoping to get off a few shots of his own. And, he hoped, going to missile launching depth would scare the Specter into backing off.

Rabinov grabbed a phone and asked weapons control, "Deter, when can we fire?"

"We are seventy-five degrees out of rotation. We would be shooting into the abyss, and even at heat seeking they would find nothing. Maybe twenty more seconds or so," answered Molovich.

"Comrade Admiral? Fifteen hundred and counting," said Peter.

"Battle stations! Brace for impact," Ushinko yelled across the control center as the strobe light begin flashing in earnest. Everyone on the Volga could hear the pinging sonar picking up speed as the two fish raced closer.

Rabinov latched onto the phone once again and yelled into it, "Counter measures ready?"

"Ready." Came the response.

"Peter. I need to know when they hit a thousand," instructed Rabinov.

"One thousand? Now! Now, now!" Peter yelled, absolutely amazed at the speed of the little bombs.

"Countermeasures away!" Commanded a stunned Rabinov at the speed of the torpedoes. He was fighting a battle against weaponry he had no knowledge of.

Inside the Volga they could hear the soft plops of the acoustic mines leaving the upper section of the hull. Designed to emit a heat source with a chemical stream of bubbles and sound penetrating electronic gear meant to baffle anything coming at them. Very simply put, they gave the torpedoes something big and noisy to aim for instead of the submarine itself. Most of the time it worked.

Even though Eddy could actually steer the torpedoes to their final destination, and he could roughly tell the location of the mines, he could not swing the torpedoes around enough to elude the entire blast area. The chemical bath from the countermeasures mushroomed.

Less than two hundred meters from the Volga there was a twin detonation as one fish actually hit the mine, sparking the other fish. Still, the lights flickered inside the Volga as it rocked from the outward effect of the explosion. When the lights finally stayed stationary, they showed a stunned crew. Crewmen of the biggest submarine in the world and they were out dueled.

"Still think they have no fire power?" asked Rabinov to Ushinko as the mighty Russian warship slowed its twisting motion.

"We have premature detonation, both torpedoes are a miss Captain" shouted Hyde as he could still hear the screws and see the image on his monitor.

"Detonation less than two hundred meters from target Ma'am," injected Eddy.

"What's their position?" asked Beverly of Hernandez.

"They're coming about, and headed for the surface. At their current rate they should be ready to fire about now."

Sure, enough Hyde yelled, "Four fish in the water, one hundred seconds to detonation."

Ralph quickly set his watch and started counting down the seconds.

"Weapons, I need countermeasures on my mark. Let's try not to shoot off any fish at this time. They have us outgunned at this point. I want to even it up a little," explained Beverly. Unlike all other submarines there was no tell-tale pinging. Hernandez counted down five-hundred meters at a time, knowing that there was a lot of fire power coming straight at them. Beverly literally drummed her fingers on the mapping board bidding her time. She listened intently as Ralph counted down to ten seconds, then she yelled, "Mark!"

Ralph all of a sudden nodded knowingly. Now he understood completely what Beverly was up too. Instead of an all-out blitz, she was playing chess with the Russian. The idea being, even if she lost, she would severely deplete the Volga and make it easier to find. The Specter was like a boxer without much of a punch, but it could take a direct uppercut to the jaw and still stand. Suddenly, brass balls were not what came to Ralph's mind. It was Liquid Steel he was thinking of.

Eddy was staring at his screen, the USAC having a unique success pattern as it was tracing all four torpedoes coming at it. He finally got the pattern he liked and hit the fire button the massive thrum echoing through the small sub. "Ultrasonic cannon fired Ma'am."

Beverly came in behind Alex's console and watched the progression. The first torpedo blew up at two hundred thirty meters, the second one quickly behind it. The shock waves from both the USAC and the Russians own exploding torpedoes sent the third one into a cartwheel and off to the starboard to pinwheel out of sight. The fourth one deflected just enough to go high. Beverly nodded her head and smiled. That's how THAT was supposed to work.

Beverly then swiveled around quickly and asked simply, "Don?"

"It looks like they're getting desperate," he answered, aware of the fact the Volga was rising quickly.

"Crap," was all Beverly said in return.

"Captain, they're opening outer missile doors," came from Hyde in disbelief.

"Steering, blow ballast, I want to get to the surface before they do."

Ralph came up next to Beverly and asked, "You knew this was going to happen?"

"Don and I had talked about it briefly. Don felt that if they felt threatened, they would use it as a trump," acknowledged Beverly, crossing her arms across her chest. "And as usual, Don was right."

Peter pulled his head phones once again. The sound was not as intense as before because of the angle, but if this kept up, he was not going to have any hearing left. He sincerely had no idea as to what that immense noise was but this time it did a job on all four torpedoes.

Rabinov heard from Peter, that they had premature detonation of all four of their torpedoes. Again, they had a weapon he had no knowledge of. He shook his head. They were at a stalemate. He made the next decision, retrieved his notebook computer and transmitter, then called Ushinko. He followed Rabinov down a set of wire grid steps, across the submarine, through a small door then emerged in the weapons control. Ushinko walked over to the console, pulled out his key and inserted it in the little port. For a second, he hesitated. Rabinov glared at the man. Ushinko finally twisted. Rabinov then punched a single button on his notebook computer, the small rotating dish wired to the computer, swiveling back and forth, until it had a lock on the computer. It hit randomizer and at one digit at a time, it ascertained the Russian transmit code, that would verify a good firing order. The green go button lit up as Ushinko stepped back. The Black Box had given up its secret.

"Don't worry old friend. It will send a distress signal to the rest of the world not to mess with us," Rabinov said smiling. Ushinko could not return the smile.

Rabinov looked over at Molovich and commanded, "Weapons, make ready for missile launch. Preselected target will be the San Diego Naval Base. On my mark."

"Missile number one is fueled and ready for launch Comrade Admiral. The preselected target is San Diego Naval Base Admiral. Locked on and engaged upon launch." Came from Molovich. The man then closed his eyes, hit the accidental cut off switch then sighed heavily, and hit the large engage button. He really hoped it would not come down to the simple firing button. Finally, he called back to Rabinov, "But still a hundred meters from firing."

"Right." Rabinov thought for a moment then once again grabbed a phone and said into it, "Vilnius. Open up line to our little bitch friend, while we slow and surface."

"Yes sir." Came the reply. Finally, "You're on Comrade Admiral."

Rabinov thought for a second then spoke quickly, "Captain. You have left me no choice but to show you the might of this warship. If you cross my path again and do not break off the confrontation, I will be forced to follow through. And the death of millions of people will be on your head. We can counter anything you shoot at us. We are in a position to fire a live nuclear warhead, aimed directly at San Diego if you do not desist."

Everyone on board the Specter heard the words. Slowly the upturned faces looked back at the captain.

"Don? Now would be a good time?" implored Beverly.

Willy was sweating as the immense main frame of the Specter, and the state-of-the-art code breaking program plotted out and detected the Russian coding, one digit at a time. They picked up the small laptop's own signal and the Specter's randomizer started picking it apart.

Don rose from his chair and walked over to Beverly. He sighed heavily, as if a great thought had passed and he had made a critical decision. Millions of people on the eastern seaboard, and the strength of the US Navy hung in the balance.

Don whispered into Beverly's ear. "Tinkerbell will get a lock on it, but he's loaded and I can't stop the first one." Then he looked into the green eyes, searching for any sign of weakness. He found none, so he muttered, "Let em Bev. The Bird of Prey can catch it."

Beverly nodded slightly. Everything on that small boat was extremely experimental, but had worked as planned. She just prayed the Bird of Prey was as good as its name. She then said to Steve, "Open Com. to the Volga."

"Aye Ma'am." Within a second, he nodded at her.

Beverly chose her words, glanced at Don then said into her small lapel mic., "Rabinov. I will say this slowly so you can understand me.

You had your chance. Do what you want to for you are a dead man. Screw you and your crappy boat."

Rabinov felt the slap all the way through the water as it reverberated off the walls. For the first time since the ordeal started, he was mad. A woman talking to him like that! He regrouped his senses and nodded at Ushinko, who was now just completely scared as was the rest of the crew. It was all out of his control.

Rabinov moved past Molovich to the weapon's board, punched in the five-digit code that only the commander of the Volga would know, glanced at the depth meter, waiting the ten seconds until they had reached launch depth, flipped up the last accidental cut off switch, then hit the main fire switch. The submarine lurched slightly as the gas operated cold launch method ejected the massive missile out of the firing tube and into the salt water of the North Pacific. Within a second, the rocket ignited, sending the missile through the water.

"It's away Captain!" yelled Henry picking up the mighty roar through the water. Hernandez was already tracking before it even broke the surface.

Ralph was already at the weapons board. Eddy had punched in his eight-digit code and using his thumb print hit ENTER. The key pod itself popped up from the console, as Ralph did the same. All on board could feel the saddle doors opening up on the back half of the Specter. Ralph punched in his eight-digit code, used his key, then punching his thumb on the large red fire pad. Beverly duplicated this and without hesitation, she did as Rabinov had just done seconds ago. Using her thumb print for identification, she pressed on the big red fire pad. And sent the one nuclear missile they had on board the

Specter away. The small boat shuddered briefly, as if it knew as to what it had just done. Less than thirty seconds behind.

"Communications, put out a coded message to let command know what's going on before they have kittens," said Beverly, for the first time, feeling sweat trickle down into the back of her bra.

"Aye Ma'am!"

"Monitoring and weapons, I want dead on accuracy in tracking that son-of-a-bitch," said Beverly sternly.

"Tracking Ma'am," replied Hernandez, his eyes glaring at his radar monitor with another image coming from the GPPP satellite, showing the two missiles racing across the North Pacific.

"Intercept in roughly three minutes Ma'am," added Eddy.

Beverly then asked, "Willy, is there any way of knowing if they have initiated separation?"

Willy understood completely and returned, "That would have been part of the launch sequence, but I see nothing in their computers that state multiple targets. Their trajectory is San Diego only."

Beverly nodded thankfully, then turned to Don and said, "God, I hope this works."

"You know, I'm kind of hoping it does too," replied Don, very much aware that they had just shot off a nuclear warhead with ten times more destructive power as the Hiroshima bomb. Chasing a bomb with more than twenty times the power. Hitting anything, was going to be a major disaster.

CHAPTER 22

The Pentagon EROC had settled into a waiting game. They were waiting for the jet plane to touch down in Montreal. They were waiting for the North Pacific Aircraft Carrier Battle Group, the Gerald Ford and the USS Jackson to steam to the aid of the Specter. They were waiting for the Cheyenne to close the gap, as they were no more than five hours away. They were waiting for confirmation from the President that indeed the Russian Politburo had recognized the fact that the Volga was no longer under Russian Naval Command, and to finally offer some kind of assistance, or at least assurances they would stay out of the way. They were waiting for the Chinese to back down. But most of all, they were waiting for the Specter to track down the Volga.

The Sturgeon missile launch from the Volga set off a multitude of alarms, with red strobes flashing throughout the facility, and staff members to scramble to make sense of the airborne menace. The Ops. Centers' five screens zeroed in on the digital frontier tracking the missile. In sickening reality, satellites picked up the nuclear bomb hurtling into the sky. Colonel Devlin immediately plotted a fourteen-thousand-mile detonation ratio around the Volga. It encompassed most of Russia, and into the heartland of the United States.

General Blanchett was the first to pick up the direct line to the White House. It took a few second to confirm his status and the conversation quickly turned ugly. "Yes, Mister President. The Volga has fired what we believe to be an armed nuclear missile. The Gerald Ford has an AWACS monitoring the situation. The target by Colonel Devlin's guess appears to be the Western Seaboard. Yes sir. I know."

One of the front communications officers suddenly jumped up and yelled at the General, "Sir, we have confirmation from Edwards Air Force Base that they are scrambling F-twenty-two Raptors, and are coordinating missile counterstrikes."

The General nodded then said into the phone, "Mr. President, did you hear that? Yes sir. NATO is on alert and will continue to be even if we manage to bring this thing down. The Gerald Ford is scrambling jets and are going to try to intercept. Yes sir. I know."

The General pulled the phone from his ear and hung onto it loosely, then turned to Admiral Hornacher and said, "The President and his staff have been commanded to load into Air Force One. They're not taking any chances. I'm being transferred to the Presidential Helicopter." Admiral Hornacher nodded, but felt helpless, and worse, defeated that the Volga was doing this to his country.

Lucius Perry was already on the phone to the Russian consulate in Moscow, taking over Georgiana's position while they sort the mess out. He was imploring a coordinated effort with Secretary of Defense in Russia, when the Volga fired. Now Secretary Perry's tone was taking a decidedly ugly turn at the missile launch. "Look it you political buffoon. The Volga just fired a live missile at the United States. Don't bullshit me, all of NATO is on alert. I understand you have no control over the Volga, but there should be some way of tracking your own submarine! I'll put this to you simply. If there's any way in Moscow, you can shoot this thing down you better be figuring it out!"

Admiral Hornacher moved over behind the Naval consoles simply watching the large radar screens. Admiral Cartwright stood beside him. They knew what the Specter was going to do. Still, they hoped Don was right or all hell was going to break loose, and thousands of people were going to die.

Finally, they saw it.

"Yeah, way to go Specter!" Cartwright shouted loud enough for every single person in the room to hear him. And as he was doing, they all looked up at the screen to see the Specter's piggyback missile streaking to intercept.

Every voice in the room stopped. Like watching a video game as they witnessed the satellite image picking up the Specter's missile and successfully tracking. The Bird of Prey was picking up speed and rapidly closing in on its target.

Admiral Hornacher quickly implored Cartwright, "Please tell me it'll catch it!"

Cartwright's head nodded emphatically. "You know Don sir. Fastest and longest-range nuclear missile on the planet. Yes sir, I do believe it will."

Upon that simple verification Admiral Hornacher yelled at Devlin and the communications liaison for the Navy, "Tell the Ford, and McGuire they need to get their jets out of the way. Get those planes out of there. Yes, the second firing is one of ours!"

The man sitting next to the Admiral said suddenly, "Admiral, you have an incoming encrypted message from the Specter." He handed the Admiral a sheet of paper.

Reading it he walked back to where General Blanchett and Lucius was still on the phones, neither of which were taking their eyes off the two nuclear missiles streaking across the sky.

"General, a message from the Specter," Hornacher said.

"Quickly, while I still have the President on the phone."

"The Specter is currently engaging the Volga and it has fired a live warhead at the western sea board. They are projecting it to be San Diego. The sub's counter missile is capable of destroying the Volga's before any damage can be done. They think they can stop any more firings." Hornacher had read it as a man faced with imminent battle. But his heart sunk as he realized who was still on that boat.

Blanchett quickly relayed this information to President Garrison on board the Helicopter. He nodded several more times into the phone, then put his hand over the receiver. He turned to look at the face of Hornacher and said, "The President is calling the Russian Premier himself. NATO is scrambling and the Japanese Air Force is putting up a Western blockade of aircraft in case this happens again. The British Prime Minister has authorized a nuclear retaliatory strike and defense if necessary." That's when he realized that he did not have all of the Admirals' attention. He was glancing into the eyes of a Father and said, "Oh God Jack. I had forgotten. She'll be all right. Beverly's got a good head on her shoulders."

Admiral Hornacher screwed his courage up and replied, "I know General. But she's out gunned. Make no mistake about that."

The Volga also witnessed the Specter's missile launch on radar. Rabinov had raced back to the radar-sonar station was looking over Peter's shoulder in complete disbelief. He shook his head as he uttered, "The little bugger is going to catch it. Isn't it?"

"Their missile is faster?" asked Ushinko, in disbelief, severely out of breath having climbed the metal steps.

"A lot faster. By my figuring it should catch it well over open water," replied Peter doing rapid calculations on the computer.

"So, we have alerted the world to our location and we have accomplished nothing?" asked Ushinko getting the full grasp of their thwarted maneuver.

Rabinov only glared at his subordinate. He was at a loss. Nothing in the scenario of the hijacking and the hostages prepared him for this. He was being countermanded and out dueled with every move. Rabinov could only wonder, how big was the little submarine haunting them? And worse, how many missiles did they have? The bitch Captain was backing him into a wall and he felt himself swatting in the dark. This was not part of the plan.

"Weapons, I want that damned missile at the apex!" yelled Beverly to Eddy. Then she wheeled around and asked sternly, "Don? Tinkerbell? Any time now."

"Almost. The Volga has started submerging again," replied Don, punching on his own binary randomizer circuits and relaying the information to their satellite.

Willy was working up a sweat as the Specter's massive mainframe was locking in on the Russian's computer code one digit at a time. "Almost, almost," he kept muttering.

"You said you could do it," reminded Beverly creeping up behind the two men to look over their shoulders. She was growing tenser with every passing second. With Multiple warheads and twenty-three-more missiles, even the wide spread US Military could not shoot them all down over open water. One would get through.

"Just call me Alan Turing!" yelled Tinkerbell.

"Got it!" Echoed a triumphant Willy. "We've got a lock on the Russian command signal!" Then Willy hit two control buttons in quick fashion and stated firmly, "And we now have a negative lock on the firing resolution of the Volga!"

"Whose Alan Turing?" asked Duran. Just about the whole crew turned to look at him.

"Ma'am, we have an incoming message from Admiral Hornacher," injected Steve.

Beverly glanced over at Steve, frowned heavily then said, "Tell him I'm busy at the moment, and to have the Ford stand on the pedal to pick up the pieces."

Steve quickly relayed the message, then grabbed the captain's attention and said, "The Ford has a lock on the Volga's position and wants to know if we need help."

Beverly understood completely. The Gerald Ford was equipped with Helicopters that had sonobuoys and magnetic anomaly detection, or MAD birds that could locate the Volga from the sky. Then start dropping air born torpedoes of its own.

She shook her head vehemently. "No. The Volga's not going to hang around the surface to be found. Tell them to put up airborne counter strikes in case they launch again, but leave the hunting to us." Ralph nodded along with.

Steve diplomatically relayed the message.

"Hyde, give me the Volga's range and position," demanded Beverly.

"Her turn is complete. She's headed for us but picking up speed. She's still about two thousand meters and closing."

Beverly turned and asked, "Willy, can she get a firing solution on us?"

"No Ma'am. The Volga's sonar can make a good guess but they do not have our position. All they can do is lock in our firing local from the missile launch."

"Thank you." Beverly swung around and commanded, "Steering, come to full stop. I want to go silent."

"Yes Ma'am, bringing the Specter to full stop."

"Captain, I have four fish in the water, safeties were turned off at launch," inserted Hernandez quickly, pressing the headphones to his head.

"Don, what's the odds of those things actually zeroing in on us?" asked Beverly.

Don punched up a smaller view of the ocean on his screen and replied, "We don't transmit heat like a conventional sub does, especially at stop. But if they get lucky, then one might lock on."

Beverly nodded, then said to Eddy, "Lieutenant Faulk, counter measures taking out incoming. Then fire torpedoes one and two."

Don had risen quickly, crossed the control room in two steps and plopped himself down in the chair next to Eddy. He asked innocently, "Mind a little help?"

"Not at all," responded Eddy sincerely, his ego lost in the first exchange with the Volga. He thought he was ready for all this but the first go around gave him a taste of failure he did not like. It was like playing four different video games at once, with lives on the line.

"We have nuclear detonation," inserted Willy suddenly.

The Specter's missile had retrieved the Russian cruise missile a thousand miles from the coast of California, at roughly sixty thousand feet in the atmosphere. The mushroom was not visible to any person on the earth, but every satellite rotating over the North Pacific quickly picked up the disturbance, flashing the news across the globe.

Willy quickly flashed it over the front screen as everyone watched in utter amazement. The Bird of Prey never armed all five of the warheads, using just one to detonate the Sturgeon missile, simply blowing a hole in the Earth's atmosphere.

All except Eddy who was busy picking off all four torpedoes using the USAC, having locked in the last scenario that worked so well. This time, the massive thrumming echo blew out three torpedoes and the sent the fourth swinging side. More than a thousand meters from the Specter, they came to an explosive end. He prayed nothing else was coming because the energy level of the USAC was literally on zero. It would take a few minutes to recharge.

"Bev, firing torpedoes one and two," said Don. He monitored their firing and programed them to zero in on the Volga. Satisfied that they were away, he leaned back in his chair. Never once in his entire life of building his own games and electronic gizmo's did he ever think he would be firing real live guns at anyone. Funny, it did not make feel like a conqueror. In fact, the entire thing made him feel slightly pissed. It was a hell of a maiden voyage for the little boat.

Wolfson however, had a different thought. It was the first time in history someone had shot a live nuclear warhead at the United States. His thoughts of his mom and pop suddenly filled his head and he really hoped they could stop any more.

Upon detonation of the cruise missile, Rabinov smacked the back of Peter's chair. Four more fish coming to an end, his nuclear cruise missile shot down. And he was shooting at an already dead apparition.

Peter Markova was going to add to his headaches. "Comrade Admiral, I've lost all sound detection that I had on the American sub." Echoed through the amplifier system.

Rabinov quickly looked over the man's shoulder. "She's stopped?"

"It appears that way." Then came the ear shattering sound once again, but Peter had learned the first two times to keep only his good ear in the headphones. The rattling noise echoed through the Volga once again. "God, I wish I knew what the hell that was."

"Whatever it is it's picking off our torpedoes," replied a dejected Ushinko.

The metallic rattling had barely subsided when Peter yelled, "I have two fish in the water and they are coming fast!"

Rabinov quickly thought of bringing the ship about then thought better of the idea. He asked Peter, "Can you make a good guess as to the firing range?"

"Yes sir. I picked them up around seventeen fifty at five degrees port. The computer has locked onto that location."

"Finally, we have something to shoot at," acknowledged Petrov. He wheeled around, snatched the hanging telephone and yelled into it, "Weapons, I want to lock and load four torpedoes, set to heat seeking to arm in one hundred meters."

"Yes sir," mumbled Molovich." The man was not as confident and was not even sure his torpedoes were capable of that. And the Specter's torpedoes were closing fast. Finally getting loading confirmation, he said, "Computing firing solution, and firing one, two, three and four."

The explosion between the two sets of opposing torpedoes was less than two hundred meters from the Volga, taking out three of its torpedoes. Rabinov was hanging over Peter's chair, at even that distance it rocked the mighty sub. The Admiral continued staring at the sonar array.

Ushinko grabbed Rabinov's arm and said, "We are going through a lot of torpedoes, Admiral."

Rabinov stood up ramrod straight and said to the man, "We do not kill the American Bitch, she will kill us. It is that simple." He then thought for a moment and said, "Make ready to fire another missile."

Scared beyond belief, the entire scenario going extremely beyond anything he thought would happen, Ushinko merely replied, "Yes sir." One more time he climbed the metal stairs and found the weapons control room. He walked back over to initiate the notebook computer with the transmitter. Nothing happened. He hit the send button again. Nothing happened, as the signal should have initiated the firing button on the main weapon's console to the engaged system. He made sure the transmitter was properly plugged in and tried again.

Rabinov slid in behind him, saw they did not have signal he asked, "Well?"

Ushinko merely shrugged his shoulders and said, "It's not working."

"It should be the same signal." Rabinov walked over and he too hit the send button. The firing console remained dark. He brought the computer program up to locate signal and hit FIND. The sequencer searched, then fell silent. The computer screen went blank then popped up. The simple words UNABLE TO LOCATE, stared back at Rabinov. Thinking that they had an automatic firing arrangement, he had locked the original signal into place. This should not be happening.

"What the hell has happened?" asked Ushinko dumbfounded.

Rabinov slammed the screen of the notebook computer down and stood, shaking in rage and frustration. Finally, he said to Ushinko, "The signal has been jammed, and they've changed our own Russian coding. Five feet away and we have been compromised. Somehow, the Americans have jammed us. And ours will not work until they turn theirs off." In a fit of anger, he picked up the small computer and was going to fling it at the far wall. Suddenly he thought better of the idea, and put it back down on his Captain's chair. He knew he could override it. It was just a matter of time and figuring out the codes. But at the moment, he was deathly busy. He raced back up the metal steps with Ushinko in tow.

"Comrade Admiral? The American sub has detonated the last torpedo we fired. And we are closing in on their last position," said Peter bringing the Admiral back to the present.

Rabinov was at a loss. He simply ordered Ushinko, "Tell weapons to make ready two more torpedoes, lock in on the last explosions and fire at will."

"The Volga is within one thousand meters and she is loading up two more fish," stated Hyde quickly.

"This point-blank stuff is not going to be in our favor, he's going to get lucky," observed Wolfson standing next to Beverly.

She nodded, "Agreed. Steering, full flank speed."

"Ummm. Ma'am we can't do that?"

Beverly glared at Eddy for a second when she realized why. "Right. Steering cancel that last order, let's do thirty knots flank speed."

Crash swiveled around in his chair has he had been watching the battle on Eddies computers. "Aye Ma'am, bringing the Specter to thirty knot flank speed," he replied, again happy to be doing something.

Beverly suddenly had a thought and asked, "Don. Can we rapid fire four torpedoes from the rear and still shoot down theirs?"

Don looked up at the monitoring situation and said, "We're going to have to, we don't have the USAC yet." Don then glanced over at Eddy and replied, "Possible. Eddy, follow my lead."

"Yes sir," was all the young man said.

Don quickly plotted a firing solution and rapid fired four torpedoes less than six seconds apart. Eddy watched to see Don zero in on the front two of the Volga's fish and take them out. Don glanced at Eddy and said, "Watch for countermeasure, let's see if we can slip these two past."

Eddy only nodded slowly as his unblinking eyes stayed glued to the monitors.

"Comrade Admiral! Two fish bearing straight for us!" yelled Peter, his head buried in the headset, really hoping no more devastating sound bursts, and his eyes glued to the screens.

Rabinov commanded quickly, loud enough for steering to hear, "Steering hard to port. Weapons release counter measures at a thousand meters."

Molovich quickly had the countermeasures loaded then simply fired the Russian acoustic mines for the Specter's torpedoes were already at six hundred meters.

"We're too close," said Ushinko looking over Peter's shoulder.

Don had guessed that they would turn and fire whatever counter measures they had left. He had separated the two torpedoes to give him the best chance. With one-hundred meters to go, one countermeasure detonated taking out the front Specter torpedo. He watched the other one close in on the turning Volga, as Eddy informed him of the starboard steering. Don effectively slid the last torpedo past the blast area and around the last countermeasure as it detonated behind the rapid fish.

"Sound detonation!" Rabinov yelled as he grabbed the railing surrounding the periscope area and hung on. Peter and Ushinko watched in horror as the little fish made a beeline for the mighty sub.

The strike hit the Volga at the bow portion of the ballast. Still, it rocked the mighty submarine as alarms went off proclaiming internal emergencies. Smoke rose in the control and sonar center of the Volga, as the ship temporarily lost lights. Emergency lights flickered on as a crewman put out a small fire with a fire extinguisher.

"Ushinko! Damage report." Demanded Rabinov finally as the rocking of the vessel subsided.

Ushinko was already checking over the ballast gauges as engineering was reporting safe and sound. Presently Ushinko looked over at Rabinov and responded, "We seemed to have taken little damage to the exterior tanks. We have had some malfunctions in the computer systems and ballast control is not one-hundred percent. But we are still alive."

"For the advantage of having a triple thick hull," stated Rabinov. He then turned his attention to steering and counter ordered, "Hard to starboard to original heading. Peter, do you have another fix?"

"Yes sir. She appears to be backing up. The Specter is already two thousand meters and fading. About thirty degrees' starboard."

Rabinov strolled quickly through the bridge of the Volga, thinking as he went. Finally, he grabbed the phone and yelled into it, "Weapons, I want four more in the water the second we can locate!"

"Yes sir," replied Molovich aware of the fact that he was tired beyond belief.

Ushinko came up behind Rabinov, shaking his head. If they survived, they would have nothing left to fight with, he thought. And then, like Wolfson, he realized the thought process. It was a chess game of attrition. And the She Captain was making up the rules. And winning.

"Hit Mr. Merrick! You got her!" exclaimed Hyde looking at his monitor.

Don watched for a few seconds realizing the confirmation was not coming. Finally, he said, "All we did was shake the shit out of it."

Ralph piped in, "He turned and you hit the triple-sided hull. Probably did some damage but damn sure didn't sink her."

"She's turning back," inserted Hernandez quickly.

Eddy grinned like a little kid just figuring out his favorite video game and said, "But they now know we can get around their countermeasures."

Wolfson had Willy confirm Volga's status, then sent the picture to the large overhead screen. He stated insistently, "The radar man on the Volga is locating our firing range. That's what they're shooting at us. That's why Rabinov's turning back around."

"Distance Henry?" asked Beverly.

"Twenty-five hundred meters and growing," replied Hyde.

"Anyone keeping count of their total weapons stores?" asked Beverly suddenly.

Eddy answered quickly, "Yes Ma'am. They have fired fourteen torpedoes at us and one cruise missile. Considering the altercation with the Seattle, they have to be getting awfully low on torpedoes."

"Make those four more fish," inserted Hernandez quickly.

"Jesus, he does like shooting his allocation, doesn't he?" stated Ralph to Beverly.

Beverly quickly noted, "He's hoping he has more ammo than we do. Plus, he's figured out we only shoot two at a time." Then she turned to Eddy and said, "How's the USAC?"

"Seventy three percent, maybe take out a couple of them but not all?" Eddy guessed.

"Can we load two fish from the rear and fire the USAC and take them out?" Beverly asked.

"Yes, Ma'am. But that leaves us with six up front and that's it," Eddy mentioned, loading the last two aft torpedoes. He quickly synchronized the sonic cannon, and fire off the available energy burst, then Don fired off the two rear torpedoes. Eddy glanced over; he saw Don smiling at him. He just grinned slightly, aware of the sweat trickling down his face, and his glasses sliding down his nose. They watched the monitoring systems, showing a good set of strikes, the cannon taking out the first couple and Don's torpedoes grabbing the last two, the detonation sounding through Alex's headset.

Beverly thought for a few moments. She knew there was only had six torpedoes left and she wanted to make them good. She crossed her arms and looked over at Mr. Caldwell and said, "Can you match their progression?"

Crash looked up for a second then stated, "I think so. I think I can maintain about a twenty-five-hundred-meter gap." Beverly only nodded in approval.

Ralph smiled as he noticed Beverly's military decorum in the control room was deteriorating.

Don could have really used a cup of coffee about that point but he was concentrating on the Volga's location. He suddenly felt a warm hand on his shoulder. He looked up into the clear green eyes of Beverly and for a split second he forgot people were trying to kill him.

"Don? Can we rapid fire the last six torpedoes?"

He nodded, smiled then said, "Possible."

"Then let's do it. On my mark."

Peter Markova had become like a man driving a familiar road without actually seeing it. His eyes were growing heavy and he barely noticed the first two fish in the water. Upon recognition he yelled, "We have incoming, closing about twenty-five hundred meters. No wait. We have two more less than five hundred meters behind those." His eyes then danced as the images seemed to multiply. "Oh my God, we now have six fish coming right at us!"

Rabinov sighed visibly. One more time he grabbed the phone and said drastically, "Weapons, load and fire one, two, three and four." He did not wait for this action to be taken when he yelled, "Hard to starboard and dive!"

Molovich merely looked up from his weapons console, and responded feebly over the intercom, "Sir we have exactly four torpedoes left. Is that really what you want to do?"

Rabinov stood stunned. Then he growled, "Countermeasures then. I want both the mines and the acoustics. Take them all out. We do have those, don't we?"

Molovich nodded in defeat as he relayed the signal to the last two acoustical countermeasures to be opened and wait for ignition. He commanded the torpedo room to load two tethered mines into the tubes and fire on his mark. The weapon's man had to wait an agonizingly long time as the doors were slow to open. Probably from the torpedo hit earlier. Finally, as the submarine was shifting into the turn, he got confirmation and fired. Hopefully, he thought, they would find the six fish baring down on them.

"The Volga has fired another counter salvo Captain! Wait a minute, they're mines Captain. Not torpedoes," announced Hernandez.

Don replied without taking his eyes off the monitors, "I've got them." Don had Eddy run a gauntlet with the first two fish, straight into find the mines and take them out, as he slowed down the progression of his four torpedoes. Eddy did exactly that, hitting the tethered mines and blowing them as Don slid the next two around the blast area. But with the acoustics doing their job, vision was tenuous as he managed to lead the next the two and strike the Volga near the bow.

Beverly watched over his shoulder. "We've got two still alive," she stated with certainty.

Don nodded, hoping to spread out the detonation factor by pulling the two last torpedoes apart.

The Volga was rocking from the twin blast on the bow of the ship. Several of the seamen were getting anxious and nervous about their precious submarine being hit yet once again. It was designed to give out a whooping, not to be a punching bag to an invisible foe.

Rabinov quickly dashed over to the internal monitoring as Ushinko had already sat down at a chair next to Peter and was staring at the screen.

Ushinko glanced around him and said in a low and resigned voice, "Starboard torpedo section has been taken out, damage to the outer hull at that point."

"We still have two in the water!" Screamed Peter getting Rabinov's attention.

Rabinov grabbed the back of the chair, took a deep breath, grabbed the ever-present phone and yelled into it, "Weapons, countermeasures!"

Molovich merely shook his head and grimaced heavily. With a twenty second loading procedure, there was nothing he could do. He also knew his torpedo team was shorthanded and exhausted, and now severely damaged. Molovich was trying to figure out exactly through the radio traffic who exactly was still alive.

Rabinov viewed the dark-green sonar screen in horror. His torpedoes had been picked off one by one. They were out of position to fire back, out of countermeasures and out of time. He just prayed luck was with them and the live fish would strike the triple hulled ballast.

Peter sat back in his chair, and rubbed hard at his eyes. They had already taken on three live hits and survived, limping along but still alive. He hoped it happened again.

Don was not firing them at the damned hull he decided. The first torpedo struck the front of the submarine striking damned close to the diving planes. The second fish, less than a second behind hit the conning tower. Both detonations together, rocked the Volga sideways, sending crewman flying. Alarms sounded as they lost power and went to battery back-up. The sound of crushing metal seared their ears. Smoke filled all the control rooms as consoles overloaded and burst into flames, pipes burst, sending scalding steam over anything not nailed down.

Unlike the Specter, the massive Volga was not quick to right itself. The submarine seemed to find a final resting spot almost fifteen degrees off center, making it impossible for anyone to resume their battle stations. Somewhere off the control center a massive hot steam line had burst sending a scalding spray over the equipment. Water was sloshing against the consoles as the mighty ship finally started righting itself, slowly but methodically.

Ushinko feared the worst as after a minute of pure chaos, the massive ship slowly stopped reeling and settled into a small forward pitch. The man was at a complete loss at to what to do next.

Alarms were blaring as lights flashed through the smoke in center of the Volga. The intercom was full of reports and problems. It was clear they did not survive this impact nearly as well.

Rabinov stood his ground, glancing around his embattled submarine. Little wisps of smoke sprouting up, scared faces glancing back at him. Finally, he grabbed his hand telephone and called down to engineering. The reactor was fine, just shorts in the system was causing the power problems. A small fire had been put out, but they reported no leaks, just broken water pipes.

Ushinko reported to him that ballast had been punctured through the outer skins and the inner skin had sustained damage. The pumps were barely able to keep them from filling and sinking. The conning tower was a mangled mess, and it was highly unlikely it would be a source of escape. It was damn lucky it was not leaking worse than it was. On top of all that they lost two men in the altercation, two men they could not afford to lose.

Rabinov walked around the smoky control room assessing the damage. He still had weapons control and a patchy sonar array, had sixty percent control on his ballast. Steering was functional with the rudder still intact but one of the diving planes was literally missing.

They could go ahead and to starboard but not to port. At least they had the engines.

Ushinko suddenly came alive and grabbed the man and inserted, "We need to get to the surface and vent this mess. Our oxygen scrubbers will not take all this smoke!"

Rabinov stared at the man. Then he walked over to the steering console and commanded in a low, defeated tone, "Go deep."

There was a large sigh from steering as he merely replied, "Yes Comrade Admiral."

Ushinko closed his eyes. They were running out of moves and this one was literally the sound of retreat.

"Damn!" yelled Don slamming his fist onto his knee. The computer showed two good strikes and yet, the massive Russian sub was still there.

Beverly stood up and pondered for a second. Then she asked, "Alex, can you hear anything?"

"Alarms Ma'am. I bet you there are a dozen alarms going off on the Volga right now. I also can hear a lot of yelling, I think they are taking on water, but we did not penetrate the hull. Underwater Lidar shows us she has a lot of external damage and she won't right herself."

"Does she have power?"

"Umm, yes Ma'am. She's continuing to dive and I have the magneto drive still fully engaged. She's turning due east." He turned in his seat, pressed the headset to his ears and added, "She's running."

"Eddie, let's stow the USAC for now, let it energize," Beverly turned over to Caldwell and said, "Crash, let's match their descent rate and bring the speed to forty knots. Let's catch up."

"Aye, Captain, demobilizing the USAC," answered Eddie.

"Ten degrees dive at forty knots, Aye Ma'am," responded Crash. As everyone on board the Specter at the moment, he was on the edge of his seat and happy to keep his mind occupied.

Don took a heavy breath, then stood up and came up next to Beverly as was Ralph. Don's hair was mussed as he kept running his fingers through it as Beverly's uniform was starting to show a ring of sweat under each arm. Even Ralph's mustache looked unkempt.

The three stood in the middle of the control room, compensating for the downward pitch, all wondering their next move.

Ralph finally mentioned, "Rabinov's hurting right now, and he doesn't know we're unarmed. He's just about out of torpedoes and diving to save his hide, thinking, falsely, that his boat can out dive our boat. But all we can do is shadow him and point the finger when the Jackson or the Cheyenne close in. We sneak in behind his baffles, he won't even know we're there."

Beverly took up the argument and countered, "Ralph, what's to stop him from turning on us? If he's still got full power and he figures us out, we're sitting ducks." Then she turned slightly to Don and asked, "Can he override our launching jam?"

Don looked over at Beverly and nodded, "Yeah. Yeah, he can. He goes deep enough and relocates the signal from his source, then re-establish the original Russian code, then, there's nothing we can do." There was a fire in her eyes he had never seen before. Her hair was a little askew from jumping around the control room monitoring every new situation, the white bandage peeking through the hairline. He thought he knew her well enough to finally ask, "All right Bev. I can see something whirling around in that little mind of yours. What's your plan?"

Beverly crossed her arms across her chest then cocked her head sideways as if her plan was impossible. She looked from Don to Ralph and back to Don. Then she said, "I want this to end right here. I do not want to risk him firing another missile by waiting for the Jackson."

"Agreed," said Ralph.

Suddenly Don asked, "If you're thinking about ramming her, I don't think we can build up enough momentum to do any real damage. Maybe screw up the propellers. Plus, the Volga still has some torpedoes left."

Ralph jumped in thinking out loud. "What if we relay to the Ford to start torpedo drops? If we can keep the Volga scared enough and shadow her, then maybe it might buy us enough time for them to arrive?"

Beverly shook her head slowly. "There's no time. They figure out we can't jam their signal; they're going to come up and launch again. They have nothing to lose."

"Exactly, Rabinov could have missile launch in ten minutes," added Don.

Ralph nodded as in defeat.

"Captain Hornacher? Are you thinking what I'm thinking?" asked Tinkerbell.

"What? What's the idea Bev?" Asked Don, absolutely at a loss as to what Tinkerbell was thinking.

Beverly sighed heavily then looked at Don and asked, "Can we fire the SLAW under water?"

Don pondered for several seconds, then let a devilish grin spread out on his face. He had completely forgotten about the one weapon still armed. "Possible. Very possible."

Beverly nodded then said, "The kinetic energy shells ought to do the job in the engine area of the Volga."

"Why not the thermonuclear? I mean, it would take probably only one shot?" asked Ralph grasping hold of Beverly's idea.

Don responded, "Nuclear devices have a lot of overrides and shut offs, to keep them from blowing prematurely. They need a catalyst. Nuclear to nuclear would detonate, could possibly cause an atomic explosion. Kinetic on the other hand, would just blow it up."

Ralph raised an eyebrow and retorted, "But we're still looking at twenty-three missiles full of rocket fuel. They have fired once, which means Rabinov has probably already fueled several others. The rocket fuel is no longer sealed."

Beverly nodded. Then she looked at Don and asked, "How close?"

"Willy, I need a trajectory on our kinetic shells verses water density at say a thousand feet or so," said Don without taking his eyes off of Beverly. His admiration for the lady just raised itself another notch, but like her, he thought there was a good chance he may never live to enjoy it.

Willy had been listening to the conversation and even though did not really like the idea of creeping up the Volga's ass, he was already working on the scenario. "Computing Don." It took barely a moment and Willy returned, "Sixty meters, give or take a few feet, for the shells to be the least bit effective."

Don cocked his head sideways, to match Beverly's off handed gaze, then thought for a moment and asked Willy, "And what kind of explosion factor are we looking at with twenty-three Russian cruise missiles?"

Tinkerbell inserted quickly, "Roughly the size of a small nuclear explosion. Make a crater in the water about four thousand meters in diameter, complete with an underwater tsunami." Willy wheeled around to look at Don and mentioned, "The damned thing would be visible by the naked eye from space. And that's if they don't go nuclear."

Ralph looked over at Beverly. Then he said, "We're going to be smack dab in the middle of the impact area."

Beverly looked at Don and asked, "Can the Specter handle it?"

"Oh yeah," Don nodded, then added dramatically, "It's the thirty thousand tons of flying shrapnel we're going to have problem with."

"I say we do it. As you said, it ends here," stated Ralph emphatically.

"Don? You know the boat best," Beverly said looking over at Don. There was a noticeable twinkle in her green eyes, which betrayed the look of a child about to do something really dangerous without weighing any of the consequences.

Don noticed it and liked the sly grin that accompanied the beautiful eyes. That childlike behavior was infectious. And it seemed like a logical way to end this nightmare. Don snorted then returned sarcastically, "Now you're asking for my opinion?" Then he smiled, slapped his hands together and said, "Okay, I'm excited to be part of this plan. Let's do it. What the hell. Let's see how much more this little sub can handle."

Beverly smiled back, nodded, then commanded, "Crash, how deep are we at the moment?"

"Two hundred thirty-one meters, and dropping."

Don grabbed Beverly's arm and said, "We need get closer to the surface to raise the deck gun." Don calculated swiftly in his mind the pressure and synchronic motor and added, "The closer the better."

Beverly wheeled around quickly and said, "Crash you heard the man. Bring us up, but keep on the Volga's ass. And damned fast Mr. Caldwell."

"Aye Ma'am. Thirty percent up planes. And damned fast."

Bobby glanced over at Duran, smiled then asked in a whisper, "You scared?"

Duran's eyes were wide open and he nodded slightly then said, "I think I've peed my pants." Then he smiled back and added, "But what a way to go."

On board the Volga, Peter Markova grabbed Ushinko and said, "The noise is fading."

Ushinko merely stared at the sonar screen and replied, "Really?" He then made his way to the conn to tell the Admiral.

Rabinov nodded, then wheeled around to face the steering console and asked, "How deep are we?"

"Approaching three hundred meters," answered the man, unfamiliar with the submarine, but knowing it was deeper than most subs were designed to go that badly damaged.

Ushinko was listening to the creaking go on around him. Report of a pipe bursting in engineering set off another alarm. He continued to keep a wary eye on the ballast, simply afraid, that it would crush the already damaged outer hull. But Rabinov's plan seemed to be working as the American sub was slowing its pursuit.

The creaking continued in around them as they slowly made their way to the bottom. A pipe burst in engineering brought about another alarm, but the triple thick hulled held its own.

"She's going to have to go deep to hunt us down," mentioned Rabinov, as the Volga had passed the three-hundred fifty-meter mark.

Ushinko who had been monitoring the ballast situation suddenly wheeled around and yelled at the Admiral to get his point across, "The tanks will soon be compromised if we keep diving. We have no damage control and they are taking in water faster than we can pump it out! If we go too deep, they will implode and kill us all!"

Rabinov looked over at the man disdainfully as if viewing a weakling and said finally, "All right. We stop. The Americans have no stomach for this depth, anyway. Steering, maintain current depth. I want one hundred-ten percent on the reactor, switch to standard drive, they have us dead in their sights anyway. I want some speed."

"Why doesn't she get it over with? She has us in her sights?" observed a shaken Ushinko watching and fearing a return of the torpedoes.

Rabinov thought for a few moments, he too listening to the boat under the extreme pressures of the North Pacific. Then, he started laughing. Still laughing he told steering to plot an easterly course.

"Why are you laughing?" asked a disturbed Ushinko finding nothing funny about their situation.

Rabinov grabbed Ushinko by the shoulders and said dramatically, "The bitch has nothing left! Her little submarine has shot her allotment and is all done." He then shook the man and said, "Don't you see? She does not have the balls to follow us to this depth and she has no weapons left. All she can do is shadow us." He let the man go then backed up and thought some more and said, "Yes. It works so well. Every time she fired it was only two fish, two torpedoes. In the end she fires six in some kind of sequence that only her little sub can handle. But she is whipped. She has failed!"

It dawned on Ushinko that Rabinov was probably right. But still, the little sub and the she Captain was still there to verify their location. Finally, he observed, "We must then try to shoot her out of the water."

"Why?" Replied Rabinov dramatically. "No, I have wasted enough torpedoes on the bitch. She can follow me all she wants. We get into another conflict she will only be in the way."

Ushinko replied, "First of all, we do not have full control over steering. Our dive planes on the port side are damaged. Secondly, we have no missile launch code and I believe her boat to have something to do with that." Ushinko studied his hands for a moment, all the while thinking then said, "And you said once not to underestimate the bitch. Even if she is merely tailing us, they will get us sooner or later. I am not so sure of your plan."

The real Admiral Rabinov would have hit a subordinate countering his judgement on the bridge of his own ship. But Puchinko was suddenly pleased with his revelation and let it pass, remarking instead, "Well then my friend. Let's hope it's later. For her to follow so closely, we are never going to get a shot off unless she gets sloppy. Pray that she does."

It was then that Rabinov had a thought and once again down the stairs to the massive weapons console and a very distraught Molovich. In an off chance and considering they were so deep; Rabinov took the chance. He walked over, opened it up and punched in the program to search for launch sequencing. It started its search mode, the little transmitter antenna rotating furiously. Suddenly, it had a lock. Rabinov's eyes grew wide. He spun around to look at Molovich who was indeed watching.

"As the Americans would say, we still have an ace in the hole," Rabinov said simply. He then grabbed the telephone and messaged steering, and commanded, "Take us up to launch depth. That will make everyone happy. And get me the bitch on com. I want to have a chat." He then turned his attention back to the computer. He needed to reboot the original codes.

Willy Williams raised his head and glanced over at Beverly, and uttered slowly, "Captain, we've lost the override on the Volga."

Hernandez quickly chimed in, "And the Volga has started to rise, and quickly."

Don shook his head quickly and sat down beside him. Suddenly he looked up at Beverly and explained, "The Volga's dove too deep, and the satellite can't keep the jamming signal up. They've discovered that, booted their system and taken us off line."

Beverly wheeled on the weapon's console and decided, "Eddy? Let's get them before they can get close enough to the surface to fire again."

"Ma'am? You said as close to the surface as possible? We're not there yet," inserted Crash.

Beverly noted this then looked over at Don. "Well?" was all she said.

Don responded with a frown and said, "It's not only got to swivel completely up, but it has to lock in an upright position, or it's going to leak like a sieve. If that happens, we're going to have to surface to fix it. And it won't shoot unless locked into position." Then he shrugged his shoulders and said, "Even at say twenty meters there's a chance it won't work."

Beverly nodded grimly then turned back to Crash and said, "What is our depth?"

"Ninety meters."

Beverly took in a deep breath, glanced at Don, then replied, "All right."

Willy wheeled around and mentioned to Don, "Don, we have redlined conditions on several of our ballast pumps, working this hard. The first blast we took didn't help any."

Don merely shook his head and uttered, "Just watch it."

Beverly then spun around on Alex and asked, "How much further till Volga has clear launching depth?"

"Roughly, two hundred twenty meters, Ma'am."

Beverly looked over at Don. Don, Beverly and Ralph knew they could surface faster than the Volga, but they would have to surface, lock the deck gun into place then get down, lock onto the rear of the Volga and shoot her down before the ship could reach launch depth.

She gazed at the man, then said grudgingly, "Don, this is cutting everything damned close."

Don grabbed his lapel microphone and asked, "Schmitty, we're going to try and raise the SLAW under water. Can you add some more juice?"

"How soon?" Came the quick response.

Don understood what the man meant. For Schmitty to go up front and locate electrical to the Slaw would take several minutes. "What can you do from engineering?" asked Don.

"I can arch the voltage regulator, but it will fry it in the process and we'll never get her back down." Was the swift reply from the Chief Engineer.

Don closed his eyes, weighed the variables then stated, "Do it on the captain's mark." Then he looked over at Beverly and added, "Your call."

Beverly nodded at Eddy then glanced at Don. "You over design everything. I have confidence in this." She quickly turned back to Lt. Faulk and commanded, "Weapons and Engineering, on my Mark."

"Tinkerbell, pay special attention to the fire detection system," inserted Don swiftly.

"Will do Don."

The Specter played the waiting game. Beverly watched the ascending numbers on Crash's monitor as they quickly pushed through the cold Pacific. Don wiped a blue sleeve across his brow. He was sweating profusely even in the sixty-eight-degree temps. This was not quite the test condition he had envisioned for his submarine.

Beverly had a depth in mind. As they hit thirty meters, she stood up, then yelled into her lapel mic., "Mark!"

Eddy flipped open the metal accidental safety switch, then initiated the raising of the SLAW. They all felt the small boat lurch slightly as the synchronous motor that was not designed to fight the crushing pressure at underwater depths, the lights dimmed for a barest of moments, the effects of Schmitty literally frying the circuitry, then the gun swiveled itself grudgingly into position.

Eddy looked over at the captain, sighed heavily and said, "It's locked in an upright position." He then clicked the weapon's program having the kinetic shells already set and initiated the fire button. He had green go graphs across his weapon's monitors.

Beverly nodded, taking note that both Eddy and Don were sweating. Don noticed her looking seriously at him and said swiftly, "We got lucky."

Beverly smiled back and retorted, "No, you're just that good."

Willy was shaking his head and said, "Computer sensors report a slight leak in the seals of the Slaw. But nothing to worry about."

"Captain, I have an incoming communique coming from the Volga," inserted Steve.

Beverly thought for a few moments. She knew what Rabinov was going to say and was playing his last card, the threat of a launch. Negotiations had ended a long time ago, she decided. Quickly she stated, "Let them eat static." Then she turned and said to Caldwell, "Crash, when the Volga …"

"The Volga had broken forty meters and slowing Captain!" interrupted Alex, listening to the massive sub trying to expel the ballast and raise itself to launch depth.

Beverly nodded, then continued her thought, "Crash, full speed ahead, pull up to fifty meters to the Volga's stern. And keep it steady."

"Aye, Ma'am. Locking onto the stern of the Volga." Replied the man concentrating on keeping the thousands of tons of ship in direct line to the Volga. Less than the length of their small sub left little room for error. His eyes never blinked.

Even rising at thirty degrees, the Specter had managed to pick up ground on the lumbering Volga. Mr. Caldwell initiated full speed ahead and picked up the Volga quickly. In a few moments of jockeying he announced, "In position Captain."

Beverly nodded, then walked over to the weapon's console and directed, "Get a lock on each of their propellers and knock them out one at a time. Let's stop them first. Remember, Kinetic shells."

"Aye Ma'am," replied Eddy, using the laser sighting underwater for the first time. He had a three-dimensional picture of the Volga on a computer screen, a small red dot floating around until he had it on the spinning blades of the Volga. One smaller monitor showed an underwater camera's eye view of the churning froth coming from the propellers. He would know instantly if he was hitting anything.

Both Eddy and Don were crossing their fingers. The deck gun was not designed for this type of warfare, and the idea of the shell simply blowing the barrel apart occurred to both of them. The good part was at least they were surfacing.

Eddy felt prepared for whatever happened and fired a shell. Inside the Specter they heard the smallest of plops.

Peter also heard the plop in his headset. He had no idea what it meant until the Volga lurched suddenly.

Rabinov was so engrossed in the launch codes to the point he had discounted the Specter and was surprised by the sudden movement. "What was that?"

The answer came quickly over the microphone. "Comrade Admiral, this is engineering. Something's going on back here. We have increased drag on our starboard propellor. We've been hit by something."

Peter heard another plop in his headphones. Suddenly he said, "They're in our baffles and shooting something at us!"

Rabinov was stunned. He could feel the boat slowing and a low grinding noise echoing throughout. Now what kind of weapon did they have? He wondered. Engineering called in again, "Comrade Admiral, the starboard propeller is gone and has bent the shaft, we're going to have to shut it down!"

Rabinov grabbed the phone, signaled engineering and then yelled, "Well-shut it off!" The slow realization that the Specter had his mighty boat still in her sights entered his feverish brain.

"You fool. You've underestimated the bitch again! That's why she would not talk to you. We are marked for death!" Screamed Ushinko into the telephone. At this point he no longer cared who heard. Rabinov was leading them to their death.

Rabinov yelled, "Continue to purge the ballast, let's surface and show her we can still fight."

They could all hear the water being pumped out, as the Volga continued her sideways ascent to the surface, the port ballast pumps feverishly trying to pump out more than coming in.

"Captain, we've disabled her starboard propeller, they shut down their engines, they're blowing their ballast, she's still trying to surface," injected Hernandez.

Wolfson rode up next to Beverly and inserted quickly, "Last ditch effort on his part. He's trying to get to launch depth."

Beverly simply nodded then turned to Caldwell and asked, "Crash can you follow her?"

Without so much as blinking Crash responded, "Got her dead in my sights Ma'am."

"Weapons, let's take out the port propeller. On my Mark."

"Getting a lock on the port propeller," Eddy responded, swiveling the gun slightly. "I have confirmed sighting on the propeller Captain."

"Mark," said Beverly, brushing a tangle of hair out of her eyes.

The first shell missed the mark and hit the rear of the Volga. Eddy realigned and fired again, taking dead aim on the vortex. Two more shells to the aft of the massive submarine brought the boat to a standstill.

Ushinko took in several deep breathes. The engine room confirmed that both propellers were now damaged beyond use and they were in fact bailing on the slowly filling engine room and sealing it from the outside. All they could do was hold anyone at bay with the threat of a nuclear launch. He sat down hard in the chair next to Peter and stared into the eyes of the young man. There was no smile left in the man.

"We are not going to live through this are we?" It was not so much a question as a statement of fact from Peter.

"I'm sorry but … no. We are not going to live. We had a good plan. We just … didn't plan on a new American submarine. One that … is simply better than ours." Ushinko put his hand on Peters and said quietly, "It was good serving with you, young man."

"You too Commander. You too." Peter then turned not wanting the Commander to see the tears forming in his eyes. He was not distraught for himself but his family. The Russian Government would not be kind to them, the family of a traitor.

At the weapons control center, Rabinov looked over at Molovich. His only chess piece left to him was the threat of nuclear deployment. And the bitch would not listen. He thought carefully and said, "The Americans little sub probably has no missiles left, or at least can't match us shot for shot. They have no torpedoes left. When we launch, we will inform their Fleet that if they so much as sneeze we will continue firing. All we need to do is wait the day out. Then we will demand safe refuge, or continue firing." Then he looked over at Molovich who was now no longer even paying attention as the ship was still listing and a good chance it was never going to right itself again. "Yeah, yeah, that will work." Finished Rabinov convincing himself of his last-ditch plan.

As if energized Rabinov ran down narrow hallway, back up the stairs and headed to the communications center. Quickly approaching Vilnius with a new energy and yelling at the man, "Get me that God-damned Bitch on the Comm!"

"Captain, the Volga is slowing, and has no propeller," informed Hernandez from his console.

"Captain? The Volga is insistent they want to talk," inserted Steve.

Wolfson injected quickly, "They're coming to launch depth to threaten us to back down."

Beverly nodded in complete understanding, ignored Steve and nodded then turned to Crash and commanded, "Steering, "I'm going to have Eddy fire the last six shells. When I do, I want full reverse. Understand?"

Caldwell merely nodded.

Don sat down next to Willy as Ralph was making his way to the mapping board. They had learned the first time. Don instantly saw what Willy had on his screen. The ballast pumps were overheating and shutting themselves off under emergency mode. Don only shook his head, for there was nothing he could do.

Don glanced around quickly, noting that Beverly was still standing over Eddy and said in distress, "Bev, sit down!"

Beverly ignored Don and continued looking over Eddy's shoulder. "Mark." Was all she said.

Don launched in again. "Bev. HONEY! Sit down!"

A stern look crossed her face and the realization that Don had accomplished the reaction he wanted it to do. He had gotten her attention. She sat down in the open seat next to the weapon's console.

Eddy did as commanded. Six rapid shots of the Kinetic shells into the engine compartment of the Volga. Hyde could hear the small plops as they left the Specter and a second later hit the rear of the Volga. Hernandez heard it also.

Steve then drew up in his chair and said, "I have someone from the Volga yelling at me that they want to talk you Ma'am."

Beverly, glanced over at Ralph then said slowly, "They had their chance, and they pissed me off. No. No more."

Don grinned a small school boy grin. Bobby glanced at Duran and smirked. Even Duran smiled back.

On board the Volga, the command did not know what was coming at them, and had no idea as to how to respond, other than trying to raise their lumbering submarine. In the engineering, however, the six shells started smacking the rear of the ship, with each doing more damage than the previous one.

Rabinov was literally yelling at Vilnius and commanding communications to send a signal to Specter to surrender, or else he would fire again. With no engines the ballast was slowly bringing them up. They were less than twenty meters from firing depth.

Ushinko could feel death closing in around him. The American She Captain had a weapon they knew nothing about. And now, they could not move. Strangely, he felt a certain amount of respect for her. She had outgunned them in an unfair duel.

Peter heard the sound of the shells exiting the Specter first. "She's firing again!" he yelled.

Silently, the crew in the control room all looked up as the plops hit the back of the Volga. Detonating against the aft hull, the third one broke through into the engine compartment, and started to flood the engines. Over the bridge speaker system, they could hear the distress of the few men trying to get out of the rapidly incoming water. The few men still there, would die by being blown apart, or by drowning. Alarms again started sounding as the hull had been compromised.

Peter, scanning the computer model of the Volga yelled, "The engine room is flooding! The flood doors have been blown and the Volga is flooding!"

The nuclear reactor was overheating as the cooling systems were blown, then the turbines filled the water with electricity, and blew up internally.

Ushinko looked over at Peter and muttered softly, "He would not surrender. And he has killed us."

The next three shells striking the engine compartment sealed the fate of the Volga. They penetrated the exposed areas, blowing the interior of the massive sub, causing internal destruction, until they hit the electrical. Each upon the other drove deeper into the rear of the submarine, opening the wounds and penetrated to the more complex open areas of the electrical wiring. The Nuclear power plant, not designed to blow on its own, still had plenty of explosive power, as the armor of the sub, started blowing outward, and throughout the mighty submarine. Red-hot shrapnel quickly started penetrating the fuel tanks of the twenty-three remaining cruise missiles.

The small handpicked crew trying to reclaim their homeland in one of the most terrifying terrorist actions in human history all realized that they had failed. The carefully laid out plans of the last two years was being defeated by an unknown quantity. There was no way they could have planned for the small indestructible submarine. They all died a quick death.

Upon the last detonation of the kinetic shell, the five-hundred-ninety- one-foot pride of the Russian Navy exploded into a million fragments, sending a shock wave that would be recorded on the seismographs in Alaska

CHAPTER 23

Admiral Hornacher had lost his dress coat, for he was sweating. He had thought he lost his daughter once. And now she was trading torpedoes with the Volga. All he had for information was a polite signal from the Specter, stating they were engaging the Volga. Damned, he thought, but he knew that. Of course, he should have known better than to request information during battle. But he wanted to know. He wanted to know how his daughter was doing. At the moment all he could do was watch the big screen and pray.

Lucius Perry was on a conference call to the President and the Prime Minister of Japan. He was doing damage control by explaining the mushroom cloud over the North Pacific, and the fact that the Specter was in a desperate shoot out with the massive Volga.

There was also to be an official White House statement. Just about any satellite worth its salt had picked up the blast over the North Pacific that was still rippling. The UN was being besieged with desperate calls from surrounding nations. Hiram Walker was a busy man has he had just started the Pentagon press briefing. He was receiving live reports as he answered questions.

General Blanchett was still coordinating the military efforts. But like Admiral Hornacher he felt tied and out of the loop.

Cartwright had found a position at a chair at the rear table. His focus was the big screen showing a serene ocean, from the GPPP satellite. He was waiting for the inevitable. But hoping it never arrived.

He noticed Blanchett's assistant finally enter the room. She was a striking, raven-haired woman, in a pair of high heels would easily top six foot. Everyone in the room was familiar with the woman. Cartwright had heard once that she earned her way through college working at Hooters. He could believe it, even though the olive-drab Army uniform. In addition, they all knew her to be a staunch supporter of women's rights, which seemed to be an oxymoron, but so did the fact that a pretty woman like her would make the military her home.

Colonel Rebecca Mayfield approached the group, nodded at the Admiral then strode quickly to her boss. "General, security is having problems with the media. They've clogged the avenue with their vans and they're clamoring for answers. The nuclear explosion is on every channel on every television in the nation. They know the President made an emergency take off in Air Force One."

General Blanchett responded, "When we receive word from the Specter, we'll respond. I believe Hiram is still in a press briefing so maybe open up communique to him and keep in the loop."

"Sir? How do you down play a nuclear explosion a thousand miles off the coast of North America, coming from a renegade Russian Submarine?" This came from the Colonel, sitting at an open desk next to a computer operator to get him to start feeding Hiram info.

Lucius shot her a glance, then replied, "The pentagon secretary is very good at spinning. Believe me, the media will be more in the dark after the news conference than before it. For your account, stick to the facts."

The Colonel responded, "I heard about five minutes ago that the jet was in Montreal airspace. If the Specter fails, Miss Wannaker is a dead woman, because Kuznotzhov will not be there to greet them and all hell will break loose. And the hunt will move into high gear."

Lucius just stared at the woman. Finally, he observed, "You have a curious way of thinking."

Colonel Mayfield responded, "Not really. Just logical. But my observation comes from Mr. Billingham himself. My impression was that the jet was not leaving Montreal no matter what." She turned over to Admiral Hornacher and asked sympathetically, "How are you doing sir?"

He looked over at the woman and smiled gamely. He lifted his arm and showed her the sweat stain. "That's how I'm doing. I'm sitting here twiddling my thumbs wondering what the hell is going on out in that big freaking ocean. And praying the missiles don't come again."

She nodded grimly. She had met Beverly at a NATO conference in Munich. Beverly, taking vacation to be with her parents, and Rebecca, as part of General Blanchett's team. They took it upon themselves to sample the excellent German bear and cuisine. Also, a flirtatious dalliance into the male scenery. Finally, she murmured, "Well sir, if anyone can hunt down a Russian submarine, it would be a very intelligent woman such as Captain Hornacher."

"I agree. I just wish that woman wasn't my daughter."

The Colonel let out a small smile and responded, "Good point sir."

"Oh Christ," came from the lips of Admiral Cartwright. Every single set of eyes flashed to the huge screen. In the middle was a boiling mass of water impossible in size to distinguish.

"Chang!" yelled Admiral Hornacher.

Chang was at the central controls. He quickly superimposed a yard meter on the bottom of the screen. They all watched as the implosion spread more than two thousand yards, three thousand yards then started evening out at around four thousand yards.

"That's got to be the missile bay of the Volga," said Cartwright observing the size of the disturbance.

Jack Hornacher had a cold chill run up his spine. There were only two possibilities as to the explosion. And one meant the death of his daughter and some of the Navy's best. He felt a trickle of sweat drip down his ribs. And yet, he felt cold. That's when he noticed

Colonel Mayfield had moved up next to him and was clutching his arm. He patted her hand briefly.

"It just can't be," murmured the Colonel.

Colonel Devlin was punching up coordinates and checking signals.

"Devlin, tell me you've still got a GPS signal from the Specter?" asked General Blanchett desperately.

The Colonel's head popped up from the consoles as he responded swiftly, "No. I'm sorry but our signal disappeared when the explosion happened."

Cartwright had stood up. Hornacher looked over at him to gain some kind of verification. Cartwright looked back then said, "I think Admiral, the Specter, for some reason or another, is in the middle of that explosion. That has got to be the missile bay of the Volga. Nothing on the Specter would explode like that, not even the nuclear." He glanced one more time at the Admiral and added, "If you knew Tinkerbell, you'd know she wouldn't allow it."

Hornacher really did not have any idea what Cartwright was talking about, but he wanted a better response than that. He gazed back up at the big screen and sighed heavily. His daughter did not call back. God, he hoped he heard her voice just one more time.

"Good God," responded Colonel Mayfield. Then she asked Cartwright, "I know very little about this submarine. If we lost GPS did the Specter explode and take the Volga with it, or is this just the Volga, and would the Specter survive such an explosion?"

Cartwright shook his head and said honestly, "I don't know. It depends on how close she was." Then he turned to the Colonel and added, "Captain Hornacher abilities not with-standing, there is a man on that boat that will give them a better than even chance of survival."

"That must be Mr. Merrick." She nodded and looked back up to the screen. She had also met Don once and of course; they did not get along very well. But there was intense respect for the man's abilities. She hoped he was good as he thought he was. She wanted to see her friend again.

General Blanchett was already on the phone trying to get answers.

Lucius was still on the conference call and was now explaining the massive explosion in the North Pacific. "No sirs, we still do not know what has caused THAT explosion and have no verification from the Specter or the Ford. Yes, sir Prime Minister, I know that's not a good answer. Yes Sir, I will let you know the second we have any verification and yes, there could be a chance that the Volga is still alive and out there getting ready to fire another missile. Yes sir, I think an aircraft blockade of the Japanese coastline would be a damned good idea."

The Colonel pointed up at one of the small screens and said, "The White House. They're releasing a statement."

General Blanchett looked over at Mr. Perry and said desperately, "We need to stop that before we panic people."

Lucius covered the mouthpiece and said, "I'm on the phone with the President right now. And I will relay that to him."

"We need to cut that off before they panic the world," stated the General. Then he turned to the Colonel and said, "Get a message to Hiram and have him down play that. And somebody get a hold of Billingham. He needs to roast two terrorists."

The Colonel rose from her chair with a single sheet of paper in her hand. "But we don't have any verification that it was in fact the Volga," mentioned the Colonel, with no intention of being mean spirited, she was just trying to get a grasp of the truth.

"Then we do what men do best. We lie through our shorts," said Lucius in his best political voice, still covering the mouthpiece as the Japanese Prime Minister was berating him.

"Beverly got them, make no mistake," mentioned Cartwright stalwartly.

Colonel Mayfield nodded in agreement. "I just hope she survived. I owe her a beer."

Every crew member on board the Specter would have given their eye teeth to be any place else than on that little submarine. They had done their duty for God and country. But the ride was a bitch.

Beverly had thrown herself into the vacant chair next to Eddy and had just managed to clasp the strap the instant the first shock wave hit. Tinkerbells even tempered voice echoed through the sub. "HANG ON THIS IS GOING TO BE A BUMPY RIDE. I'VE GOT CONTROL OF THE BALLASTS WILLY."

An underwater tremor traveling more than one-hundred-miles an hour slammed into the bow of the Specter. It jarred every bone and chattered the teeth of everybody on board.

Mr. Caldwell, as instructed, had thrown the Specter into reverse and was now hanging onto the steering console for dear life, the impact trying to wrench the wheel from his hands. His feet were rapidly trying to control the rudder as his body tensed instantly.

Don bit the inside of his mouth by accident. He was aware of several sensations, the intense vibrations, the sub starting to lose control, an intense rainstorm of metal glancing off the sub's skin, and an alarm as something had popped. He glanced over at Caldwell. He could tell Crash was losing the battle. Then he could feel it. Then he could see it as the control room went black, taking with it several of the underwater monitoring equipment and computer consoles at his own station.

It took an agonizing few moments in the dark with the Specter lurching like a mad bull for the emergency batteries to kick in. It was an odd sensation as one could barely see and all that was heard was a distorted grunting as each body was tossed viciously against their straps. But the lights did come back up and anything not bolted down was becoming a flying projectile to be avoided.

The Specter had ridden out the initial impact, then the wave had managed to get up under the bow. That was when Crash started losing control. Once the wave raised the bow, the sub started toppling backward.

There was no way the Tinkerbelle could control the ballast tanks fast enough and there were definite problems. Through the massive shaking and jarring the ship road up on her back, the bow pointing up. Then the entire sub started rotating as if stuck in a blender. The conning tower kept the sub from acting like a top, but it still wavered back and forth like a windy flag.

"Sonofabitch, this could end any time now!" Don hiccupped out feeling his tail bone finding the bottom of the chair too many times. He glanced at his flickering computer screen as it flashed one emergency after another. With each came another alarm. And a little curl of smoke wafting its way up as a monitor burst.

"Crash!" Beverly yelled, trying gamely to steer her swiveling chair to face the pilot.

"I ... I don't have much control!"

"Willy, ung, what's the alarm?" Don grimaced as the air was shoved from his lungs.

"Ballast Don, we've overheated, the valves are blowing! We've lost our GPS. We've ... shit, we've got problems!" The man responded, hanging onto his console and trying to steady himself to read the words dancing across the screen.

Don glanced at the screen, muttered, "Oh God. Tinkerbell?"

"Shutting them down Don!"

"Crash, one-eighty, full speed ahead, get us the hell out of here!" Commanded Beverly, clutching console in front of her.

Ralph nodded at the decision. They were in danger of flipping over backward and the reverse engines were doing nothing. While swinging around he noticed the big screen behind Bobby had gone blank. That was not a good sign he decided.

Crash did not say a word as he threw the sub away from the wave, praying the bow planes were still working. Punching up the throttle controls he forced them into full speed, hoping he had power. That act laid the Specter completely over on her side as the jarring continued.

Beverly heard the noise as did Don. It was a particularly large piece of metal striking the underside of the Specter, with a particularly irritating chalk board type scratching. And another alarm.

The Specter flipped over on its side as the engines ground away at the frothing water. It seemed to take forever, and yet it was only twenty seconds for the Specter to turn out of the wave and get into the same direction as the rushing water and boat parts. Within another minute Crash had managed to straighten out the ship and find a safe sailing solution.

The Specter, merely bouncing and jostling had come to a slightly skewed level, the worst of the explosion had gone by. The entire situation had taken less than two minutes, and yet, the Specter had traveled five kilometers in that time.

Don yelled over at steering, "Crash, shut her down man."

Mr. Caldwell did not need the captain's acknowledgment. He did swiftly as Don told him.

Beverly was the first one out of her chair. She jostled along the uneven deck to Willy's location. Don was already punching up the damage control and finding himself looking at a list as long as his arm. Suddenly the emergency lights went out, then a second later uniform lighting was restored.

"Tinkerbelle, let's do an alarm protocol." Stated Don firmly.

"Dissecting Specter's emergency system, shutting down non-essential to life."

"Captain, I've got an incoming distress signal from the Ford," said Steve through labored breathing.

"They're distressed? What the hell are we?" asked Don without taking his eyes off his monitor. Then he spit a wad of blood onto the floor.

"They just want verification Ma'am."

Beverly nodded, still working on the rolling deck. She glanced around at all the black console computers and said, "At least something's working. Let them know we're alive, tell them the Volga has been destroyed, but we could really use some assistance."

"Aye Ma'am."

Ralph was out of his chair lurching over to Don's chair when a plate in the floor moved beneath his feet. He quickly recognized it as the master tunnel running through the ship and he bent down to pull the handle up. Chief Petty Officer Schmidt was looking up at him, blood trickling out his nose, smeared into his bushy white mustache, and his ear covered in blood. Ralph extended a strong hand and pulled the man from his hell hole.

Schmitty merely nodded his thanks, wiping the back of his hand across his face. Then he turned to Don and said, "We have a problem."

Don still had not moved from his monitor and replied, "The core is fine. I show good readings across the board."

"The Jets," replied Schmitty. Then Schmitty walked up to Don and briefly whispered in his ears. Don looked at the man then whispered something back. Schmitty only nodded.

Don punched in the diagnostics for the engines themselves. "Good God," was all he said. He then turned to Beverly and said "We need to get to the surface."

"That might be a problem," answered Willy.

Beverly took a deep breath, damn thankful they were still alive, then asked, "I need a damage report gentlemen. What are we looking at?"

"I'm still finding stuff," replied Willy.

Don swiveled in his chair and looked across at Beverly. Finally, he said, "Until Willy can trace down all the incidentals, this is how it stands. Nuclear is five by, no problems, plenty of power. That's the good news. Right now, we can't adjust ballast which is why we're listing. And it looks like our drive assembly has been compromised. On a good note, it's a good thing we destroyed the Volga because we couldn't shoot a torpedo if we wanted to. Bow ports are flooded, causing us to list forward."

"What can be fixed?" asked Beverly afraid of the answer.

Don looked up blankly as if it were a dumb question, then he retorted, "Oh, everything can be fixed. If we get to the surface."

"Current depth is twenty-eight meters, Captain. But we're going down," injected Willy anticipating the question.

Beverly nodded then asked, "I heard the problem with the ballast. What's wrong?"

Don glanced over at Willy then back to his computer. Then back at Beverly. Then he shrugged his shoulders and said simply, "I don't know everything yet."

"Ma'am, we have computer verification that the Volga has been destroyed," relayed Hernandez.

Beverly looked at him with a curious look then smiled. "Right Alex. We sort of assumed that but I'm glad you're on top of things."

He shrugged then explained himself, "I just thought it was time for some happy news Ma'am. That's all."

"Don, on screen," injected Tinkerbell.

Don swiveled back around and gazed at his computer. He searched for several moments then sighed heavily. He turned around and said to Beverly. "Well Bev it's like this. Our ballast is comprised of sixty-four intakes and thirty-two pumps working jointly. The intakes simply let the water in making us heavier. In the old days it was big manual valves opening and closing. However, everything here is electronic. With the intense pressure from the blast some of the sending units have blown."

"Which means they're stuck open letting water in?" asked Beverly, grasping quickly.

Don nodded and replied, "That's right. Then there's the pumps, designed to pump water out of the ballast when we want to surface. Some of them have redlined and shut down automatically, some have decreased to seventy or eighty percent. And, on top of that, the shrapnel had also damaged a few of the ports, and conceivably, some small enough to be pumped into the pumps themselves. Which means they may keep working, they may fail. Now, that's the ballast.

The problem with the drive unit is more severe. Remember that big clang we heard about half way through the blast?"

"Yeah," she answered fearing the worst.

"Well, see, to put it simply, there is this electrical self-cleaning filtration system in the front of the intake that keeps little fishes from becoming fish cakes. Something, about the size of a car sliced through it and has jammed itself in the jet intake."

"But we never lost our engines," observed Ralph crossing his arms and leaning on one foot. His legs were beginning to get tired.

"Correct, give the man a cigar."

"That means the engines are still good, just blocked. Right?" asked Beverly hopefully.

"Also correct. But, and here's the kicker, we have no screen left which means we could suck up all sorts of nasty things or floating debris from the Volga, before we move a thousand feet, which is not good for the intake. That can be fixed, well, we can jerry rig something, but more important, that car is blocking the flow. We can't generate any speed."

"Can we remove it?" asked Beverly.

"Yes," answered Don and Schmitty in unison. Then Don added, "But that goes back to what I said about the ballast. We need to surface. And then Schmitty and I and … anyone left in engineering can fix everything."

"But you said the ballast is messed up. How do we do that?" observed Beverly.

"Good question," Don took a deep breath then explained, "Right now the Specter is doing all it can to keep from sinking. The negative tanks are full and the main still has water in them to take us down to meet the Volga. Now, we have sixty-four ballast ports. We have eleven pumps not working at all, about ten more that we've shut down from overheating. Then we don't know how much shrapnel we've taken into the ballast. That's a problem. However, given enough time on the surface, we can cool down the pumps, change out some of the sending units, and seal the intakes to keep water out."

Beverly nodded, acknowledging the dismal scenario. She looked at Don then said, "Then we wait for the Jackson to come rescue us. If I remember correctly, they have a DSRV that can lock onto our emergency hatch."

Don looked down at his feet as if embarrassed.

Suddenly Ralph pipped in and asked, "We won't last until then, will we?"

Don looked the man square in the eye and said just barely above a whisper, "We're taking in water as we speak. Even at eight or nine hours away, a couple of our key ballast pumps give out and we start taking in more water." He glanced at one of the few monitors that was working, saw the max depth monitor and said, "At around eight thousand feet depth we MIGHT survive, but a DRSV won't be able seal onto us."

"We can't even get to the surface to evacuate, can we?" asked Ralph coming to the grim reality. The rest of crew merely watched as Don, with each passing word, seemed to seal their watery fate.

There was a grim quiet in the control room of the Specter. A monitor sparked once again, then went blank, emitting more smoke into the room. As if it signaled the end.

Beverly looked over at Don. Up until now she believed the man could fix anything, could rearrange the world with a coat hanger and duct tape. Somehow, she refused to give up. She grinned slightly at the man and said, "I think I know you well enough. You have a plan, don't you?"

Don smirked back. "Schmitty's idea. It's the only option we got. Schmitty figures if we shut down the inoperable pumps, and increase the current on the existing pumps we can buy us a little time on the surface. By then the overheated pumps might come back on line." Then he nodded at Ralph and said, "Too either get it fixed, or get away."

"How long?" asked Beverly.

Don looked over at Schmitty then said, "Not long. We can rewire the system from the engine compartment. Ten minutes. But, and it's a big but. We may fry the pumps and sink like a rock."

"Don, you know better than that, I can monitor the situation to the milliamp. I won't let the Specter sink." Inserted Tinkerbell.

Don smirked for the briefest of moments.

Beverly did not hesitate. She said, "We have no choice. Do it."

Don smiled again and followed Schmitty to the hatchway. Then he turned and asked, "If we can get us to the surface, can I get a fresh cup of coffee? This is turning into a long and nasty day."

Beverly smiled back. She wanted to say something, but not in front of the crew. Instead, she replied, "I'll make it myself."

"That's a promise," Don said and smiled. Then Don said into the air, "Tinkerbell keep your promise. And keep me posted." Then he quickly left the room with Schmitty close behind.

If the crew on board the Specter could have held their breath for twenty minutes they would have. Willy noticed the voltage fluctuation on his Specter's status report. Eight minutes later Crash was the first to notice it. His computer was showing the Specter slowly closing on the surface. The rate was agonizingly slow but it was there. "Captain, we're going up!" he stated excitedly.

Beverly walked over to Mr. Caldwell's computer monitor, saw the numbers changing in a uniform succession. She then glanced over to Willy.

"They're hot, but they're running," Willy said smiling, ecstatic that something was working to their advantage.

"Damned straight, Willy," said Tinkerbell with an attitude.

Beverly smiled, then she turned and headed for the hatchway.

Wolfson looked at her curiously and asked, "Where are you going?"

She looked at him, batted her eyelashes and said in return, "Why, to get Don that cup of coffee. Of course."

Everyone in the control room broke out in smiles and heavy sighs of relief, that the little sub was going up to the surface instead of down to a watery grave.

Beverly was the only one in the galley. Engineering was busy patching small problems, most of the rest of the staff was either in the control room, or tensed up watching and waiting in their bunks. She fashioned the stainless-steel coffee machine and pot, specially built for a submarine that would not move unless unlatched, watching the brown fluid drain into the pot. She then poured herself a cup, and returned the pot to finish.

Beverly leaned heavily against the counter, sipping heartily on the coffee. She rubbed a hand over her face. She was painfully aware that things could have gone terribly wrong. Her throat tightened with emotion at the thought of everyone on board that small vessel could have very easily died if things had gone wrong. Her strategy, the Slaw, Don's ability.

Captain Hornacher looked up into the air, thanked God silently. They had, as Don had said, gone toe to toe with big and ugly. And survived. They had, in the end, bigger balls.

"Are you all right Captain?" asked Tinkerbell into Beverly's ear bud.

Beverly had forgotten Tinkerbell was everywhere. She smiled and replied, "I'm fine Tinkerbell. Just tired."

"So am I Captain. So am I." Beverly chuckled at the thought.

Bobby and Duran walked into the room. Bobby smiled when he saw the Captain, Duran looked down at his feet. Bobby spoke first. "Commander suggested we help out a little, considering we don't have much to navigate at the moment. But that coffee sure smelled good."

Beverly smiled back then suggested, "Put that in a carafe and make another pot. Don deserves at least a fresh cup."

Duran glanced up and found Beverly studying him. Bobby moved around him to the coffee as he stood rooted to the ground.

Finally, Duran muttered, "Ma'am?"

"Yes?" She was not going to let him off the hook that easily.

"About that comment in the control room. I just, well, sort of blurted it out."

Beverly shook her head then said, "It's not the comment that has me wondering. It's what brought it up in the first place. Something's been going on in this ship for a little while and you were the unfortunate one to voice your opinion."

Duran glanced futilely at Bobby, who only smiled back. He was on his own.

Duran started in. "Before we even set sail, I had heard some, well, rather nasty rumors."

Beverly nodded, then took another sip of coffee. "Nothing to do with an alert on the Nautilus Two or the galley of the Stingray? You see Lieutenant, I've heard the same rumors."

Duran paled noticeably, then remarked, "All untrue I guess."

"Nope, quite true." She glanced between Bobby and Duran, then added, "The incidents were real. The rumors are exaggerated versions."

Duran grimaced then nodded. As Bobby had told him, if the rumors had been true, she would not have been there.

"I'll tell you one more thing. I'm not going to explain the truth to you, because I don't have to qualify myself, especially to you, who chose to believe the rumors instead of the truth. But rest assured, I received citations, for both incidences." She then poked Duran in the chest and stated, "And that's the truth. You can tell your brother that also."

Duran turned white, apologized one more time, then made to exit the room hastily. He stopped short, turned slightly and muttered, "That, was a damned good kill Ma'am." Then he smiled sheepishly and left the room.

Bobby watched the man leave then turned to the captain and said, "Funny how some perfectly reasonable explanations, turn nasty."

Beverly sipped at her cup then said in return, "Not very funny to me."

Bobby nodded grimly then said, "Wolfson explained the Nautilus incidence to me. The rumor was much more titillating."

She smiled and replied, "The Stingray was even better. There was fire in the Galley and I just happened across it. A cook and I were fighting it with fire extinguishers when the fire roared out of control and set off the fire suppression system. Which effectively put the fire out, but made a terrific mess in the galley."

Bobby nodded. The suppression system was made up of a flame retardant powder, meant to smother any fire in a fire prone area. But like the Captain said, it made an incredible mess.

Beverly continued. "The captain wouldn't let us drag this crap throughout the ship, so he made us change into Tyvek suits, leaving our clothes in the galley. The rumor, I've been told is how we stripped each other down in the galley, then the fire started by our passion. Or I made the cook watch me strip down, or made him strip down, or something like that."

Bobby smiled. "Again, the rumor is juicier than reality."

"The thing of it is, if it had been two men, there would have been no rumor. A woman prancing around nude with a boat full of men is more fun out of context."

Bobby felt the blood rise to his cheeks. How unfortunate he thought, that she should have endure that stigma, without even trying. "And the sub had to turn around and return to port," he added.

Beverly smiled at Bobby, grabbed another cup, poured it full of fresh coffee and said, "I need to find Don."

Don and Schmitty had been as good as their word. Once they broke the surface, they pulled the extra charge off the pumps, and hoped they would stay on the surface for repairs.

Steve could not get communications with Naval Command, but he could talk to the Ford. The Carrier Group was making its best time to the location that Steve gave them, for the GPS on board the Specter, even with Tinkerbell trying to make repairs, was also malfunctioning. Through correspondence, the Pentagon knew they were alive. Beverly received a small note from Admiral Hornacher. 'Well Done.'

Don after wolfing down a fresh cup of very stiff coffee, was coordinating the repair team. Schmitty and Garibaldi were suiting up for a dive to try and see which ports they could instantly fix, coordinating everything with Willy.

Petty Officer Kroger and Merrick were busy tracking down the pumps. Accessibility was, as with most mechanical items on board the Specter, was found within the four feet by four-foot tunnel under the floor and on top of the drive unit.

Don was somewhere near the galley, scooting along with a tool box and his ever-present notebook computer, a small headset dangling from his left ear. A flashlight strapped to his head was showing him the panels for each pump. He had left Kroger behind to fix the last one as he was sliding ahead and using his computer to quickly diagnose each problem.

That's when he felt the lurch. At first, he ignored it. Then he felt another smaller one and he realized the ship was listing even more. He heard a voice on his headset radio, "Don? Did you feel that?" It came from Kroger.

Don responded quickly, "Keep working Denny. I'm going up to see what's wrong."

"Okay," was the only response he got.

"Don, we've blown the circuit breakers," came through his headset.

"Do we have replacements Tinkerbell?"

"Yes, we do. Don, I will redirect the power, but you need to change that breaker for the Spector to operate properly."

"Not a problem Tink. I'll take care of it."

Opening the hatch in the hallway, he was surprised to find a hand reaching down to him. He grasped it and found himself being pulled up by Captain Hornacher. He found himself not wanting to let go of the fairly firm grip. But when he stood up, he could instantly tell they were now listing to starboard. Something had happened.

Beverly had just come from the conning tower, where she and Wolfson were going over water rescue procedures. Beverly said instantly, "We're sinking Don. The conning tower is the only thing not in the water. We need to get off."

Don shook his head and said, "It's just the main circuit to the starboard ballast. We've popped an interior breaker. I can trace it down and get us back on level."

Beverly put her hands on her hips and sighed, then said, "And what if the other circuit fails Don? As Captain I will not waste this opportunity to abandon ship." Then she keyed her radio and said to Crash, "Mr. Caldwell, what's our status?"

"It's minute Captain, but we are going down inch by inch. We have maybe twenty minutes Ma'am." Came the response from Crash.

Don merely gritted his teeth then said, "Do what you need to do Captain. But I can fix it."

"You're being bullheaded."

Don smiled back and said, "And you're being pushy." Then he spit another wad of blood onto the floor.

Beverly did not smile, she merely put her hands up and grabbed Don by the shoulders and said succinctly, "Look it, Don. This ship did more than what was mechanically possible. I know what this ship means to you. But I will not argue this, Don. It got us to the surface, but now, we need to leave it in peace. We're going to abandon ship."

She turned and walked purposely away. Don only watched her, letting his eyes wander to the swaying dernier, his mind wishing for another time, another place. He grinned slightly, then went back to work. She may be leaving the ship, but he was not. Besides, it was not the ship he was afraid of losing.

The abandon ship call went throughout the Specter in matter of seconds. The crew gathered on the conning tower, Engineering bolting several lights on the conning tower, to penetrate the dark. But no one was the least bit happy. The wind had come up from the north and blowing up three-foot swells and a freezing cold spray.

They could all feel the listing of the battered sub growing. The Specter was going to go down sideways. No one was happy with the decision, at less than two-hundred miles away it was still going to take the Gerald Ford all night to reach them. Ralph had even brought up the thought of the Gorbachev. It was dismissed by the captain as too problematic. And even the helicopters on board the Ford could only ferry a few at a time, and the Captain of the Ford did not wish to expose more men to problems in the middle of a dark and choppy North Atlantic. The USS Cheyenne was still a good three hours off. They would have to wait.

Emergency gear was stowed off the front bow section of the conning tower. They quickly brought out the inflatable's, complete with water proof covers and battery heaters, enough to heat both rafts for two days. Supplies and stock for seventy-two hours of survival. Each man was handed a special waterproof and weather resistant suit that went on in two constrictive pieces and covered them from head to toe. They could survive in frigid water for up to twenty minutes. After six minutes the first raft full of men was dispatched onto the icy North Pacific.

Beverly had found Denny and was following him up the conning tower ladder. They both came up to see Ralph clicking off his list of crew members. Ralph handed Kroger a sea suit and said, "Put this on. It's cold on the water."

Denny looked at Wolfson and said in protest, "I want to stay and help. She won't let me."

"Nobody's staying Denny," replied Wolfson.

"Where's Don, the Chief and Garibaldi?" asked Beverly irritated with Denny pleading his case to Wolfson.

"No shows as of yet."

"Schmitty's still in the water," added Denny, still not putting on his suit.

Beverly keyed her microphone and said above the ever-present wind, "Chief, get your ass up here." Then she looked at Ralph and added, "I told Don to get on top. God Damn it, he knows."

"Knows what?" came from the conning tower hatchway, as Don was coming through.

"I have a suit for you," said Ralph, as they could feel a small jolt run through the ship. Then the starboard sank another foot.

"No. No Ralph. I'm staying right here. I can fix this," Don said slowly.

"Yes, you are," inserted Beverly growing tired of dealing with Don's childish behavior.

"No. I'm not."

"I order you to Don."

Don merely spit out a glob of blood and mucus, then looked at her as if she was being silly.

"If he stays, can I stay?" asked Denny.

Don grinned broadly. It was argument he was not going loose. "I can fix this Beverly."

"Don, we've sent a signal to the Jackson. They'll be here in less than eight hours. The Cheyenne will be here in three hours."

"Bev. I can fix this. I just wanted to see you off. I've almost got it fixed."

She grabbed him by the shoulders once again as if to shake the child in him and said desperately, "I don't care. You got us to the surface. You did it. You saved us. We'll be all right now." Then she studied the man for a second and said passionately, "Let the ship go."

Don gazed into the pretty green eyes. "I can save the ship Bev. Believe me."

"Don, can you give me a hundred percent guarantee that this ship won't sink?" Beverly asked searching the man's eyes. She found what she thought. A grain of doubt.

Don shook his head slowly then muttered, "No Bev. Conceivably something else could go wrong."

"Then suit up and get on board the raft." She had said more pleadingly than she wanted to.

"What about Schmitty and Garibaldi?" Don asked.

Beverly believing that she had gotten through to Don walked over to the edge of the conning tower and looked down into the surging water. She keyed her mic. again, and said, "This is Captain Hornacher. Time to come up gentlemen. We are abandoning ship."

She got a response from Garibaldi. "Be there in a second Captain."

Beverly watched as the bubbles quickly came to the surface. Then the head and goggles broke through. That's when she heard it. The familiar metallic thud of the hatch being closed. She wheeled around to stare at Ralph and Kroger. Don was gone.

Then it struck her. She jumped on the hatch, punching the electronic controls repeatedly, without any luck. Don had shut them off. Then she attempted to wheel open the secure door. It would not budge. Then she fell to her knees and started pounding on it, all the while yelling, "God Damn you Don, come back here. I will not lose you now you son-of-a-bitch!"

Ralph had watched as Don snuck off the conning tower and Beverly launched her tirade. There was more to it than simple disobeying of the orders. There was a passion in her voice. There had been a chord struck inside the two of them. Honey echoed in Ralph's mind and he smiled inwardly.

Beverly pounded futilely several more seconds, when the reality struck her. She bent down over the hatch, gathering her thoughts then glared up into the face of Wolfson. "Why didn't you stop him?" she yelled in despair.

Ralph shrugged his shoulders and said lamely, "He's a civilian. And I learned a long time ago, there's no arguing with Don. Besides Captain. He doesn't want to be on the water. He'd much rather be in it."

"Can I stay?" asked Denny pleadingly.

"NO!" responded Beverly viciously, raising herself to her full height.

"Commander Wolfson, I'll just catch the raft when it gets in the water," mentioned Garibaldi from the edge of the Specter, bobbing up and down in the water.

Beverly took a large controlled breath then asked Garibaldi, "Where's Schmitty?"

"He's not responding. I thought he was headed to the diving port," responded Garibaldi pulling his goggles up on his head.

"He has no intention of leaving, does he?" stated Beverly to Garibaldi.

He looked up at the captain from his position bobbing in the water and replied, "No Ma'am. He told me to go. He was staying."

Captain Hornacher nodded her head, then she turned to Ralph to vent her rage and said, "Him, I can court martial."

Ralph nodded grimly then said, "That's everybody Captain."

Beverly stood feeling all alone in the world. They were abandoning their home away from home, the fastest and most complicated submarine in the US Navy. And they were leaving it with men on board.

She looked up at Ralph, then she nodded as if the grim reality that she had ultimately failed. She pulled the waterproof hood up on her suit then said in a defeated tone, "Ralph, I will never understand that arrogant son-of-a-bitch. Nothing we can do. Let's go."

The twin rafts floated slowly away from the Specter, Wolfson grabbing a ride on the first one with Hornacher getting on the second. They could view the ship through the large, oval plastic windows that could be covered from the inside. It looked forlorn as the starboard side was slowly slipping in sideways. Beverly had not noticed it to begin with, but there were chunks of metal poking out from ports and seams. Scars ran the length of the ship. The flexible fins of the antenna array were bent with pieces of the Volga's debris stuck in between. She knew the blast must had been unimaginable. And the fact they survived was born more so from what she could see.

The North Pacific swells was going to make the ride a bumpy one. The rafts, as big as they were reacted like bobbers, riding high on the waves. The crew watched forlornly as the exterior lights of the Specter, slowly slipped sideways into the small waves. It took twenty minutes of every set of eyes watching the Specter, but eventually, the side of the conning tower slid beneath the water. Much like every rendition movie of the sinking of the Titanic, bathed in sorrowful music and intense grieving, the utter hopelessness filtered into every one's soul.

Once the last visage of the Specter was gone, the covers were drawn and made fast with fasteners to the sides of the oval windows. That simple action seemed to acknowledge the death of the Specter. But now it was one of survival. With eight in one raft and nine in another, their GPS units hopefully signaling to the Jackson their location. And the chill creeping in through the heavy waterproof material. The battery heaters were brought out, put in the center and lit on low.

The North Pacific was dark, forbidding place at night, so a small battery light found itself hanging from the top of the canopy, another on the outside and a bright beacon displayed their position. Mr. Caldwell looked over at Beverly. She had not spoken since entering the raft and pushing off. Even though he knew his conversation would be overheard, he wanted to comfort.

Finally, Crash uttered lowly, "Mr. Merrick and Schmitty are down there fighting for their lives. If anyone is obstinate enough, it's them two."

She pulled her hood back and looked over at Caldwell. "That ship did more than it was ever designed to do, and saved a few million lives in the process. But there is a time and place." She stopped for a second then added, "I know Crash. I know those guys are fighting. I pray they succeed. For them as well as for us."

Crash looked over at her questioningly. After what they had just been through, a three-hour excursion on the big pond was a little hick-up in the course of things. He only shook his head with a lack of understanding.

Beverly pursed her lips together and spoke slowly as if the words hurt. "There's still a very big shark out there Crash. That's why Don wouldn't get in this little raft. And I'm afraid a blast that large just might have garnered the damned beast's attention."

The grim realization crossed the face of every man on the raft. "Oh, shit," was all Crash said.

CHAPTER 24

on was muttering to himself as he crawled along the four-foot tunnel under the floor of the Specter. He was busy coming upon each portal to each pump, figuring out what was wrong, then seeing if he could initiate an instant fix or pass onto the next one. Towing behind him was a large tool box with two smaller bilge pumps, sending unit's and excess wiring and connectors, that he could make work in a pinch, rewiring the bilge pumps and wiring these into the ballast ports, bypassing the disabled ones. Not nearly the power of the ballast pumps, they however, would do the job, just slower. He could hear over his headset, Schmitty outside, coordinating the effort to make sure the ballast ports Don was fixing would work from the outside.

"Don, I hope you know what you're doing. I don't want to die tonight," stated Tinkerbell in Don's headset.

"Not today, HAL."

"Ohhhh, low blow. I'm monitoring our depth progression, Schmitty, and the location of the rafts through Gypsy. Anything else I can do?"

"Yeah, stop the Specter from sinking, save the crew in the rafts, and kill off the big assed shark."

"No problem. Anything else?" Tinkerbell knew sarcasm when she heard it.

"Yeah." Don stopped to rub his achy knees and sat up in the tunnel. "I just want you know you'll never die Tink. You know you have a built-in escape program, right?" He was talking about an emergency down load that Tinkerbell had that would send all her data to the GPPP satellite and allow her to download to the Poseidon headquarters and its own quantum computer.

"Oh, I know Don. I just don't want you or Schmitty to die trying to save the Specter. I know I am nothing more than a computer program but still don't want to see you hurt, or for me to end up at headquarters, doing nothing more than answering the phones."

Don knew that Tinkerbell had emotions, feelings and human interaction within her. She observed and learned, but this was a little new. She liked the CHALLENGE of being on a warship. Of having to figuring out problems and solving them. She had LEARNED to be part of a team.

"Well, Tinkerbell, I have no intention of dying today so you better get used to me."

"That's good because I really don't want you to be harmed."

Don smiled. The Tinkerbell AI program sure enough had emotional attachments. But this was the first time she had actually expressed anything. "And why is that Tink?"

"You're like a big brother that I never had, and keep learning from. I like that."

"What's happens when you stop learning?"

"Oh, that will never happen. Humans are so fascinating and unpredictable. Take Captain Hornacher for example. She is, how would you say it, irritatingly ruled by rules. And yet, you like her very much. And the same for her. I find that very odd, and yet, very satisfying at the same time. Like anything can happen with you people."

Don could not help but give out a loud laugh. "You know Tinkerbell. You're smarter than you look. But let's keep that little fact to you and me, shall we?"

"My lips are sealed." And again, something new, there was a slight giggle. Then Tinkerbell added, "And I find Frankie fascinating."

Don's mind shot ahead to the cute little oriental girl. He had heard of her sexual tendencies, but was curious as to what Tinkerbell knew. "And what is that you find so interesting?" He asked, happy to have a conversation while trying to solve their little problem of sinking.

"Welllll, I know what sex is all about and I know the difference between men and women, that's a no brainier. But SHE likes women too. In fact, she prefers them sexually. I just find that curious, because that's not how it is supposed to work with humans. And yet she is perfectly happy that way."

Don smiled broadly. He had heard some of the tales, but found it thought-provoking that was what Tinkerbell wanted to talk about. Finally, he said, "Well Tink, humans are a strange breed in which every single person on the planet is different." In a tone of admonishment though he added, "But now you're being very human and spreading gossip."

"Oh my gosh," came the immediate reply. "I AM. I'm so sorry. Shutting up."

Don shook his head and stated, "We'll talk later about us silly humans."

"Looking forward to it."

Don grinned, then the realization of the situation grasped him again. He sighed and thought quickly of Schmitty. Don realized that the ship could take an enormous amount of pressure. But Schmitty could not.

Finally, Don said into his headset, "Schmitty, get your ass in here. We've got enough to keep us afloat."

"One more." Came the somewhat breathless reply.

"That's what you said five minutes ago. Now Schmitty."

"Yeah. Port Twenty-six."

Don shook his head. He knew Schmitty was not listening.

"He's still within the safe range Don." Inserted Tinkerbell

Don's mind raced, for he had the same thought that Beverly had. Somewhere, out there, was a big and nasty shark. But the Specter was worthless if it was sitting on the bottom of the ocean, or crushed to smithereens, or too far away to help. One thing at a time, he told himself.

Sweating in the cramped quarters, he wired in the last bilge pump. Don had to stop an agonizing few moments to flex his legs. In addition, even if the ballast pumps did get them back up, they still needed to clear the jets of the debris.

"Don, we just passed the eighty-meter mark." Came through his headset.

"Thanks, Tink."

"Don?" Came the one-word question through his headset.

"Hang onto your shorts, Schmitty. I'll be back for you. Head for the surface," Don replied, knowing that Schmitty could no longer follow the progression of the sinking sub.

"Right."

At the moment Don actually could not say who was in the worst predicament. Schmitty floating helplessly and all alone in the damned cold Pacific, himself going down in a sub that may not rise; or the twin rafts floating aimlessly at the mercy of God only knew what.

The Specter had passed one-hundred meters, when Don finally managed to get the pumps rewired to port twenty-three. There was still no guarantee that any of it would work. He laid back in the tunnel and allowed himself a five-second breather. Don could tell the air purifier was no longer working, probably shut off by Tinkerbell, to conserve energy. One more thing to fix he decided.

Don flopped over and took a deep breath. Finally, he injected to Tinkerbell, "Tink. Fire this thing up and let's see what the hell happens."

"Keep your fingers crossed. Purging the ballast." A few seconds passed then, "Umm Don, I also have a disturbance on the monitoring systems. All eighty-seven feet of it. Don you might want to come to control. I can't fire the Slaw at this depth."

"Sonofabitch," Don muttered starting to crawl to a safety hatch.

Schmitty, starting to shiver, thankfully did not know of the eighty-seven-foot-long shadow that slid two hundred feet below him. His head swiveled; the large LED headlight still strapped to his head doing nothing more than lighting the swelling waves. Still, in the dark of the cold North Pacific, he grasped a sheathed knife strapped to his leg for security. He sensed a danger and not knowing what else to do, clasped the large hunting knife, and waited.

Beverly looked around her surroundings. They seemed oddly familiar, a strange odious scent wafting in the air. She blinked a few more times. She tried to raise her arms. They wouldn't move. She tried to move her feet. They wouldn't move.

She closed her eyes, a dreadful feeling washing over her. Then opened them again, the horrifying reality crossing her feverish mind. She was back in the room. The room where she had a nasty little point in her life. The room where she had spent more than forty terrorizing and torturous hours.

And yet, she was not a twenty-year-old woman scared out of her wits. She was a thirty-six-year-old woman who was mad. Mad at being back in this situation and mad at the man doing this to her once again. This time, she would kill him.

In reality, she had no vision, kept utterly in the dark. Her attacker would never let her know what was coming at her. In her dream, she could make out shapes. She lifted her head and saw the view she had seen for the most despicable period in her life. Beverly was stripped naked with a stained white towel covering her breasts and lower regions. And tied to the bed posts. Her attacker was nowhere in sight.

Her psychiatrist had explained the importance of the towel. It was a thin veil between her body and the attackers' lust, a small measure of protection that he could easily control, but give her hope. And take away at his whim.

She strained against the ropes. They did not give an inch as her wrists and ankles were bound tight. As before, all she could do was lay and wait. She glanced around the room. A small apartment bedroom, fraught with nasty, heavy metal posters and large pictures of naked women covered every wall. Only one set of dressers occupied a wall as the bed seemed to have an odd stench to it. She would learn later that the sheets had not been changed in more than four months.

Lined up on the dresser in a uniform row, was the torture devices. On occasion when the door was opened or her attacker turned on the lights, for he wanted her to see what was coming at her, she could view them. A whip, a toilet plunger, a large tube of extra strength Ben Gay and an assortment of wood clamps. Everyone used on her in one way shape or form.

The door slowly slid open. There was no trepidation in Beverly's soul. She wanted to kill the bastard. At least this time. At least in her nightmares.

It was the greasy faced man she had grown to despise. Tall, with a perpetual stubble that never seemed to grow. Clothes covered in car grease, and reeking of month-old sweat. Beverly strained at her bindings.

He laughed out load. "No need for that. I'm going to set you free."

She struggled harder. She had been told that several times only to be tortured. And then, out came a knife.

She glared at the man, daring for him to touch her. And yet, he went over to her, as she wound and bounced on the bed trying to get free and begin cutting.

Oddly enough, her wrist came free. Then her other wrist. Sitting up in the bed she pulled the lone sheet around herself and clutched at it as she watched in complete confusion as he cut away her ankles from the ropes. She swung her feet onto the side of the bed and sat.

"You're free." He said with a sinister grin.

She stood up quickly and wrapped the sheet tighter. This was not right her mind kept saying. This was not the way it happened. "Why?" she finally asked.

He shrugged his shoulders, and replied, "Just cuz."

She needed no more encouragement. She walked quickly through the house, glancing backward, thinking a knife was going to find her back. Trepidation raced through her as she fell out into the dark yard.

She stopped. Out on the road was a box. Clenching the sheet with all her might she could not make out the shape of the box but it looked familiar and very foreboding. She knew it was important to her.

She slowly came upon it growing frightened of the fact that it appeared to be a coffin. A plain pine box sitting in the middle of the road.

She wheeled around at her attacker and hissed at him, "Who is it?"

"Oh, you know. That guy you like."

Somewhere the wind blew and a dog seemed to bark and the dust came up from the road. All the anger in Beverly was now gone. He was dead? she thought. He can't die. Not now.

"Yeap that's him. A good trade I thought. You'll still be alive and the one person you seem to like is gone. I like it."

Beverly swung around viciously and shouted at him, "Not now you asshole. Not him."

One sticky eyeball popped open. She felt movement as she realized Bobby was nudging at her carefully. She had fallen asleep against him. Her bleary eyes opened up to view the muted light of the battery lantern swinging, as she pulled herself away from Bobby's shoulder. Captain Hornacher punched the button on her Timex Chronograph to view Western time then punched it again to view the current time zone. She dozed fitfully as her eyes grew accustom to the dim light.

God, she thought, she had not a nightmare in years and now, three days and three dreams. All different and diabolical. If she ever found a husband, he was going to have a hard time dealing with her excess baggage. If she ever found a husband, she thought with a laugh. Then the dream came flooding back to her. Hermind had made a choice and the first dream itself was not that unpleasant, at least not like the others. But the second dream careened around her brain, and grabbed her by the throat. It was bizarre, surreal, and creepy, and made her feel violated without being touched. Being raped by a monster of any kind shook her to the core.

Her mind had been all to right the reality all too real. Don was dead. And it ate at the pit of her stomach. Slowly, the monsters in her life were creeping in at the edges of her mind.

Getting a quick grasp of the situation, preferring to the deal with the miserable facts of the present. Beverly could see Crash, glancing out the plastic oval window. A swirling in the pit of her stomach launched itself. She bit her lip. Complex and different and jumbled each time, she thought, as she fought off the visual display of the coffin in the middle of the road

Finally, she pushed past her all to vivid images and saw what Crash was doing. He had part of the oval curtain pulled aside and was watching the ocean. The raft was large enough to ride the choppy waves but made visibility tenuous at best. Even through the slight opening Beverly could see a large waves crest and fall, but little else. She glanced around and noticed the rest of the crew was either like she had been, sleeping, or was also watching Crash.

"Mr. Caldwell, what's up?" she finally asked softly.

He closed the curtain and looked over at her. "Just, well, what you said Ma'am. I was just playing lookout." Then he thought for a moment, brought his binoculars up to his eyes once again, and uttered, "I thought I saw something."

Beverly nodded, sincerely wished she had not dozed, then glanced once again at her watch. Just a few more hours and the Jackson would have them. The Cheyenne had to be within a few miles. And all the nightmares would be over.

"Well, keep an eye out Crash," she muttered with a smile.

The group was quiet as the small swells and bobbing action of the raft, caused several of them to fall back asleep.

After Beverly determined there was not anybody listening, she turned to Bobby and whispered, "Thanks for waking me."

Bobby wanted to say something, realized it was not a good time and merely replied, "Your welcome Ma'am."

A few more minutes went by when Beverly could see Crash stiffen and she asked merely, "See something?"

Through a half moon and a misty sky the undulating ocean hardly gave away its secrets on the surface. But in-between the waves there was something totally odd poking up between the swells. "I think it's the shark. Something big about a quarter mile off to the east. It's gliding back and forth as if to determine what we are," responded Crash solemnly.

"Oh crap," she stated as she moved carefully past several snoozing bodies, over to the edge of the large inflation ring and out the window to also take a look. Sure enough, as they crested a wave she could see the large tattered, sail like fin was lazily gliding in the dim moonlight. She cringed at the size of the thing. Her nightmare had come to life.

In with the supplies and emergency equipment on the edge of the raft between Hyde and Kroger was a satellite phone. They had not thought to use it for simply they were waiting to be rescued, their GPS giving the entire United States Navy their location. Beverly slid over, rummaged through the plastic, water proof container and found the phone.

"Who are you going to call?" Crash asked. He knew it had been there but it was not like he could call the Red Cross or something.

Beverly answered nervously, already punching the numbers. "The Admiral at the Pentagon. They should be able to patch me into the Ford. The Admiral will have them send a helicopter and at least pick up some of the crew."

She heard the phone ringing on the far end. Again with a direct line to her father it rang several times before someone answered. But it was not her dad's voice. Beverly said breathlessly, happy that at least she made a connection, "Hello? Who is this?"

"This is Colonel Devlin. Who is this?"

"Colonel, oh God, I'm so glad to hear your voice. This is Captain Hornacher. Admiral Hornacher wouldn't happen to be there would he?"

"Captain? You have to realize it's almost two AM here. Has the Ford got you already? We got the word you had to abandon ship and they were coming out to rescue you. Are you all right?"

"No, the Ford does not have us and that's the problem. We are still in the rafts and we seem to have gotten the attention of our very big shark," she replied desperately.

There was a slight delay on the other end then Devlin blurted, "Oh, Good Christ. You mean that big prehistoric one? Okay, let me get a hold of the Ford and see if we can get a ferry service going. And some protection. Just hang on!"

"Thank you Colonel." Beverly hit the button to disconnect. She had wanted to hear her father's voice, talk about the loss of Don and Schmitty and Tinkerbell but there was no time. They were being stalked by something very big, nasty and speed was of the utmost importance. She glanced around the small bobbing raft and all the crew was now painfully awake and looking at their destiny and nightmare gliding around in the water.

She picked up the hand-held radio to the other raft that was securely tethered to them less than fifty feet away. "Commander Wolfson," said Beverly quietly.

"I see it," came the response from Ralph.

"I've made a call to the Ford. Hopefully, it'll stay away long enough for them to send a rescue chopper," said Beverly.

"I hope you're right," were the only words back at her.

Beverly slid the radio into a pocket. A new sub on a secret mission of experimentation, and it all was turning out horribly wrong. Her own turmoil surfaced rapidly as anxiety gripped her.

God, she wished she had done things differently, Beverly thought to herself. Simply opened fire on the Volga, not wanting to play the chess match. Do what Don's little submarine was intended to do, sneak up, and blow the shit out of the enemy. Nope, that was not her. She had to play macho, like the men and tempt the stupid bastard, did not she? Get in the Volga's face and tell them she was coming. And hope upon hope they would simply surrender. But they did not did they? She had seen the look on the crews, and especially Don's face.

And yet, it was what she wanted to do, and felt it to be the best strategy. And Ralph concurred that surprise was really not an option. Tell the big, nasty sub she was alive and well and coming back to give them a thorough thrashing. She was proud of the Specter and the men for surviving. She wanted Rabinov to know it was the little girl in the toy boat that had done it.

As if he could hear the little gears in Beverly's mind grinding, Crash slowly turned around from his spot at the plastic window, cocked his head sideways as if puzzled, thought hard and then asked, "Permission to speak Ma'am."

Beverly looked over at the man and smiled slightly and said, "Granted. But you may not have much time."

"That's why I want to say this Captain." Crash chose his words carefully then started, "When you opened up dialogue to the Volga, I thought that was an insane thing to do. Commander Wolfson explained to me on the conning tower the justification in your actions, about hoping they would surrender in the end. What you said to Rabinov was without a doubt the gutsiest thing I had ever heard. You baited the biggest Submarine on the planet and was downright nasty doing it. I was very proud of our ship at that moment. You gave me, and I think, all of us a lot of confidence. And you swore like a true sailor, Ma'am. That took real balls Ma'am."

Beverly grinned slightly as she heard several muffled guffaws. She finally replied, "Not bad for a woman, Unh?" Then she glanced around at all the faces, some scared, some proud, but all alive. Then she added, "And I couldn't be more proud of a command than I am of this one. But, let's all survive this little excursion first, then we'll all pat each other on the back."

"Aye, aye, Ma'am," replied Crash with a smile, remembering the incidence in the galley.

"Amen to that," inserted Henry.

Ralph, Steve, Bruce Eddington, Paul Garibaldi, Alex, Lt. Duran, Ensign Niguchi, and Willy Williams occupied the other raft. Beverly's thought to the split had been for some reason each group could somehow run the Specter even if separated. It was a desperate plan but it was the only one she could come with. At least she hoped.

Ralph sat on the edge of the large inflated tube, his body half hanging out the open doorway, a beefy hand grasping the edge, and watched with fascination as the large fin swung lazily in the dim moonlight. It seemed to be teasing them, like waving a huge flag, then striking from nowhere. He had his thirty-eight-caliber service revolver, but he felt like that would be the same as trying to throw rocks at an elephant. Still, he kept the holster unfastened.

Then the fin slid slowly beneath its own wake. Crash popped his head out the canopy opening to get a better view and was surprised to hear a welcome sound. It was a jet fighter, flying over low. He looked up and haphazardly waved, aware the pilot would not see him. Still, it was nice to have company.

Lt. Smith looked up at the ceiling of the canopy and said excitedly, "Did you hear that? That was a jet."

Henry looked over at Beverly and stated, "And what exactly is a fighter jet going to do? I thought they were sending a helicopter?"

"So did I. At least they have confirmation we're still alive," stated Beverly hopefully.

"Good point." Crash then looked back out the opening and added disheartening, "Oops, our fin is back."

The pilot swung low and just off a stall mode when he too saw the fin. He at first thought it was a small boat sail then gasped in realization. He was on the horn back to the Ford confirming that the helicopter was on its way. He quickly scanned his weaponry. There was little for him to do. It was too close to try a point-blank hip shot and the raft actually presented a much hotter heat source on his infrared scanner. He continued his flyovers to stay with the situation, but disbelief at the size of the thing made him realize the rafts were sitting ducks.

The fin slowly moved closer. For twelve minutes they watched it creep in, slip beneath the water then rise up a few feet closer. Like a cat playing with a mouse, there was little for them to do but wait fearfully.

Then finally, both rafts full of exhausted crewmen heard the welcome, swirling blades of the helicopter, a large search light scanning the ocean, taking its direction from the jet. It circled around slowing to hover, then dropped down closer to the water, sending a mist spraying in all directions.

The patchy gray Sikorsky SH-Sixty B Seahawk helicopter included the pilot, copilot and two winch men. Actually designed for multipurpose operations it had equipment on board for the detection of Submarines. It also had two torpedoes, but like the fighter, with such close proximity and no control other than heat seeking, would do little against the huge fish. They had enough room to squeeze six more bodies in. The three-foot waves, made them realize, this was not going to be easy.

The pilot gasped as the million candle search light found the huge fin slipping through the water. "Jesus, we need to get these people out of the water," he said into his headset in utter disbelief.

"How far behind is the second chopper?" the fighter pilot asked over the radio.

The helicopter pilot responded, "They were just gearing up on your call. We didn't realize the size of this thing, or we would have come out straight away."

Beverly crawled over to the portal and yelled over through the chopping noise that the other raft was to try and get rescued first. She waved into the search light and pointed desperately at the other raft. The Helicopter Pilot seemed to understand and swung in over to the second raft.

"Our fin is gone," mentioned Crash, still watching from his sitting position in the raft.

"Oh God, it's not!" exclaimed Beverly hanging out the canopy opening. All eighty-seven feet of prehistoric monster was rising up and heading toward the second raft.

"Button up your hoods, we're going in!" yelled Ralph as he too saw the impending doom coming straight for them. His thirty-eight caliber was out and he popped off several shots at the huge fin. What struck him really odd was the harpoon sticking out of the shark's head, and the ancient leather skin had been baked a dark brown. The remnants of Captain Drummond attempt to roast the damned thing. But Ralph would have preferred not to have been that close.

The helicopter had lowered its rope ladder when they saw it. The shark was making a beeline for the raft, then submerged. For a few moments they all thought it had simply dove under the water. Then it struck. It pushed up through the bottom, tossing the raft laterally into the air, as the nose kept the raft precarious inches from the massive jaws trying desperately to take a bite.

The crew on the second raft could hear the water turning into a churning boil as life on the raft turned topsy-turvy. The shark struck underneath the most ridged part of the raft, pushing it straight into the air. Everyone flung around, the crew trying desperately to hang on or to keep from being flung out into the open ocean. No matter how flimsy the rubber raft seemed compared to the ravaging teeth of the shark, it was better than splashing around in the water.

The raft literally rode up on the head of the huge beast and flopped completely over, landing on its top. The tether was jerking soundly on the other raft, Crash grabbing onto Beverly's jacket to keep her from hitting the drink. Whether the shark intended this no one could guess. But now, he could get at the tasty morsels trapped helplessly in the upturned canopy. Water quickly filled the bubble, as the light was now submerged six feet beneath them, offering a dismal pale green illumination. Bodies scrambled in the intense cold water to find the bubble of air trapped between the raft bottom and the water. Finally, all eight heads popped up gasping for a breath in the eerie green light.

Bobbing up and down Alex suddenly sputtered through a nose full of sea water at Ralph, "Commander, we need to get out of here! We're shark bait floating around in the water like this!"

"Agreed!" Ralph found the edge of the raft and fumbled around several moments until he finally found the canopy opening. Happy that the crushing water had not yet collapsed the rubber canopy, he fought his way through the heavy material and floated around the outside of the raft and hung onto the small ropes strung there for just such purposes. The blinding white light of the helicopter swung around erratically. He desperately scanned the water, searching for a hint of the white death. Steve popped out next and then Duran. Everyone could feel the cold but the Naval Survival suits doing their job, keeping the body warmth within. The spray from the swirling helicopter blades was laying a fine mist over them making vision difficult. The large spot light was keeping its focus on their desperate situation, the light catching the reflecting stripping of the suits. That was a big help.

Beverly visibly cringed when the shark struck. It almost pulled her tenuous grip away from the canopy edge as even their raft was jerked around from the thrashing. Everyone was glued to the opposite oval window; the curtain having been pulled aside. They waited for what seemed forever.

"I see three so far!" yelled Bobby finally taking count of the bobbing heads coming out and glistening in the exposed air and under the search light.

"I think they're trying to get on top!" said Hyde excitedly.

As each person exited the overturned raft, they were trying to get on the top side of the raft. At least to get out of the water. The ridged bottom made a good platform either way. Ralph and Steve helped get Alex up as the wet grips and heavy bodies were hard to move. Then Alex turned around and started pulling people up, starting with Frankie as he had a soft spot for the gregarious pilot. All the while trepidation and fear gripping them at the thought of seven-inch serrated teeth, and row upon row of them, slicing them neatly in two. Or worse, gulping them whole. Within a matter of a minute they had all eight on top of the upside down raft. The spot light was keeping its vigil on them but the situation was perilous at best.

Both Beverly and Crash felt utterly helpless. And they saw it again. The fin surfaced a hundred yards off, apparently not satisfied with its first attack. It was gearing up for another one.

"It's coming again!" the winch man yelled over the pilot's headphones. The other man was feeding in a bandolier into the only weapon the helicopter had. A ceiling mounted M One-thirty-four Gatling gun.

"You're not going to kill it with that thing!" yelled the second winch man.

"I've got to fucking do something!" screamed back the machine gunner. He took aim, told the pilot to get lower and fired off several bursts. He knew he hit it but probably did little. Maybe he thought, enough to scare it.

The pilot then said, "Try to keep the shark busy, I'm going to try and get the ladder in closer." He did not have much hope as there was still three-foot bob to the rafts.

"Right," came the response from the rear.

Ralph shielded his eyes from the intense spray, then glanced up at the harsh glare of the search light. He had enough vision to detect the ladder coming their way. He looked over at Alex and yelled above the engine noise, "Can you stand and grab that?"

Alex balanced himself enough to keep his feet underneath himself and stood up. Ralph stood also as he braced himself to try and raise

Alex up. Alex was standing straight up with an arm out stretched reaching for the ladder, the upturned raft bobbing up and down in the churning foam. It was creeping ever closer.

The shark came up from underneath again, pummeling and lashing out at the submerged canopy beneath the water. Like a popper full of popcorn, the bodies flew off in every direction, as the raft flew a solid five feet off the water. Alex had been launched and just narrowly missed reaching the wildly swinging ladder.

The raft hit the water in resounding splash. Unbelievably, it jerked several times, then the ten-person raft went under. Several men were drug under with the rubber, encasing them in the water pressure. A few men made it to the surface and splashed around in the frigid water completely confused as to what to do next.

This time the shark got tangled up in the rubber canopy and after dragging it down with him, he shredded his way out, popping the solid rubber construction of the inflation. A massive bubble burst forth to the surface as Beverly watched in horror as the raft was now gone.

The massive prehistoric shark found a body and in one lashing bite, sliced the man in two. Trapped in the rubber and doomed to make final contact with the terrible set of man-eating teeth. There was no screaming in the frigid water as the once smart and dynamic seaman succumbed to death quickly and painfully.

In a matter of moments of thrashing the raft floated back onto the surface minus the canopy, and the shark was gone again. Around the bobbing and tattered remains of the raft was a swirling of blood, only visible from the helicopter. The winch man felt a shock run through him as the rescue was turning terribly wrong.

Alex had been thrown clear of the raft, but in the dark of the boiling sea he could not make out his surroundings. He thought he heard screaming to his left and he tried to raise his arm to swim. Death was swift. He felt very little as his bottom half disappeared in the massive jaws, his mind acknowledged his death, then quickly blinked out, as his torso was plunged under water.

"Oh God," Beverly muttered covering her eyes, feeling totally helpless. She could not see the blood in the dark, but she knew in her heart.

The ridged bottom was still intact and floated on its own, as each of the remaining cold bodies tried desperately to swim back to it. The sea suits had added buoyancy but the weight made them a hindrance. Exhaustion was taking its toll but fear was a great motivator. They had heard the few feeble screams. Each could do little more than find the small rope on the exterior of the raft and hang on for dear life. The search light illuminating the red laced water swirling around them.

Suddenly, the ocean seemed to light up as the other two helicopters had reached the scene and added the intense lighting to the battle. Still, little more they could do but watch.

The spot lights focused on each body as they struggled to find the raft. The winch man counted only 6 finally grabbing hold of the tattered rubber tubing. Other than that there was little movement. They had little left to try and pull themselves out of the water.

Finally, Ralph yelled over at the man next to him which was Bruce. "The bottom should hold us. We need to get out of the water!"

Bruce pulled himself over and stated, "Let's pull over here and start pushing guys up."

Beverly was clutching the raft edge so hard her fingers hurt. There was nothing anyone could do. The helicopter was swinging in as well as it could, as the machine gunner was still trying to take safe shots. But they were losing badly.

Suddenly Beverly had an idea and started crawling over the edge of the raft and was getting ready to slide into the water, when Crash grabbed her by the collar and pulled her back in.

"Where the hell do you think you're going?" he asked. Then added quickly, "Captain."

"The tether, let's move the rafts together and give the shark a bigger target!" She yelled back at him.

Crashed blinked once, then stepping past Beverly, was over the edge and in the water, his breath almost pulled from him as the cold was intense, Crash thankful for the suits. He pulled himself through the water around the raft and grabbed the tether and started pulling back to the canopy doorway. Beverly was there as was Bobby, and they managed to latch onto Crash's shoulder and pulled on him as he pulled on the tether. The raft swung around as the doorway now faced the other raft. They were closing the gap. They knew in their hearts they were dragging themselves closer to the bloody fray, but it was all they could do to help.

The shark had no idea what was going on, but it could smell blood. There was thrashing in the water which it knew instinctively was food. But the coming up from underneath was not working for some odd reason. The food seemed to be splashing around on the surface. So that's where it was going.

The fin had circled around some hundred yards off to the west and dipped beneath the water in a dead aim for the overturned raft.

Beverly looked up from her precarious position on the edge of the raft and saw it all. The fin slunk below the surface. She saw the tail whipped hard, then it too sank. It was charging maneuver, her mind acknowledged. Then in grim reality she knew it was a last ditch effort for the shark. It was the final attack. And only two men had managed to get themselves out of the water completely and onto the inflated platform.

The ungodly, prehistoric apparition came out of the water. The seven-foot maw with seven-inch teeth opened in anticipation of grabbing a mouthful of food. And it was going to go right into the overturned raft like a large Frisbee, with the six cold bodies grasping what was little left of their lives. The pilot of the helicopter instinctively rose, not wanting to get the ladder somehow mixed up with the surface attack. The gunner was peppering the back of the huge creature, praying it made a difference. It was not as too many bullets were finding the water.

The prehistoric shark, its ancient mind not knowing of its modern world, its mouth chomping and biting less than one-hundred feet from Commander's Wolfson's back. Ralph could hear it coming as Bobby was yelling at him to get out of the water. But there was nothing he could do. He had extended his last bit of strength trying to get the other men up onto the solid remains of the raft. He closed his eyes, mouthed a quick prayer as arms reached down to pull him out of the water. A swell of rushing water reached his back.

Ralph waited for death and prayed it was swift. He felt the swell of water overtake him and the feeble remains of the raft floating in the water. An intense spray of water overtook his sense from the Helicopter coming in a close as it dared. He closed his eyes. He waited, longer than he thought possible when his ears acknowledged shouting and hands grabbing at him. Something had happened his mind registered as he chanced to glance behind him.

His first impression was that Beverly's raft was closing in on his position and was less than fifteen feet away. Then he swung completely around and saw the most absurd sight his mind would ever comprehend.

The massive bulk of the prehistoric shark had been lifted completely out of the water by the Specter, listing wildly forward. The bright lights mounted earlier were shining off the ancient skin, showing in gruesome detail, the shark's struggles. The flood lights from the helicopters lit the scene up like a rock concert. One could see every gruesome detail. Trapped on the forward deck, between the SLAW and the sloping conning tower, it was chomping at the air, less than fifty feet from the Commander's face. To complete the absurd picture, was Schmitty, hanging onto the SLAW, one of the side panels hanging open, as if he was trying to fix the gun. The man was toward the bow, trying to keep away from the large and furious set of teeth, chomping at the air.

On the conning tower was Don, wearing somebodies Pea Coat that was much too big, yelling at Schmitty, the shark, Wolfson and

Beverly in turn. Wolfson could not make out the words but he heard a lot of expletives.

The joy that Beverly took in watching the Specter rise up to intervene in the shark's path was quickly dashed by the knowledge that the shark could very well, simply fall forward and carry itself into the upturned raft. She implored Crash to pull harder on the tether to close the gap. Then she heard Don yelling something at her.

"PULL IN NEXT TO THE SPECTER! I TIED OFF A ROPE!" Don kept bellowing.

"He wants us to get closer to that thing?" asked Bobby clutching at Crash with Beverly almost standing on top of him at the raft port.

Quickly her mind rationalized the complete trust she had in the man. However, there was little propulsion on the raft, especially with Crash pulling at the remains of the other raft. The decision was swift. She jumped into the water.

"CAPTAIN?" Yelled Bobby.

Beverly ignored the frigid water and Bobby, grabbed at the rope circling the raft, and started swimming with all her might toward the Specter.

Don looked down in horror. That definitely was not his intention, to have more bodies in the water. Especially Beverly.

What the crew could not see, but was plain to Don from his position was that the shark had a large fin stuck on the antenna array and if it slipped off the boat, would do so backwards. Don knew there was little Schmitty could do from his proximity, but still he implored at the man.

"SCHMITTY, all I need is one God-damned shell!"

Gunther Schmidt seemed to come to grips with his fate. The massive shark thrashed, teeth flashing in the moonlight, the huge pectoral fin slashing at him. He pulled his large knife out of its sheath with his right hand, hung onto the gun barrel with his left, and swung himself closer to the monster than he ever bloody intended.

The blade sank deeply right underneath the huge eyeball.

The shark's mouth opened wide in extreme pain, trying gamely to bite at Schmitty. It succeeded in slamming Schmitty against the gun, its bulk effectively crushing him against the open side of the large weapon.

But it worked. The shark's painful ferocity had succeeded in dislodging itself from the top of the sub. It slid back into the water, complete with the large knife still poking out of its huge face.

Beverly saw this, then managed to touch the side of the Specter, now trying to right itself. She grasped onto the rope as Crash pulled the tattered raft back towards the Specter. The crew still alive from the other raft swam the few feet and they too were starting to get pulled towards the remaining floating raft, now closely pressing itself against the Specter. But no one could see the Commander.

Bobby yelled from his position in the rescue, "I see a hand grasping the tether!"

The first helicopter swung its searchlight and found the fingers slipping into the cold Atlantic. Crash took one desperate lunge that submerged his whole body, found an arm and yanked with all his might. He pulled the sputtering Commander up to the surface. Several more hands plunged in. Shivering uncontrollably, he was pulled aboard the raft.

"Is that everyone?" yelled Don.

Beverly looked up and said sadly, "Everyone that's still alive."

Don only nodded then looked down at the deck. Schmitty crumpled with his knees buckled, next to the deck gun. But Don stood his ground patiently waiting. Schmitty had both hands inside the SLAW, attempting to rectify the jammed shells. Don knew the man was hurt, but there was no stopping the Chief.

The helicopter men swinging the search lights around in ever widening arches trying to find the shark.

The shark's senses were exploding in pain, hunger and ferocity. It could no longer make out the raft hugging the side of the Specter. The Specter, having come to a stop, was no longer making any noise. The multitude of millions of receptors on his skin picked up something floating near the water surface.

Having been pushed away, the deflated raft had suddenly become the target of the shark's attack. However, the tether was still attached and jerked the survivors raft closer. The bodies hanging around the portal were all flung backwards and scattered to the floor.

Don was bellowing at Schmitty once again as he watched in terror as the survivor's raft was being pulled away. Like on a Nantucket sleigh ride, the shark had the deflated raft in his huge maw and was dragging the other raft away.

Bobby was the first to gather his wits and simply yelled for a knife and a rope from the small tool kit.

"SCHMITTY?" Screamed Don.

Schmitty turned around from his position on the wet deck, sat heavily, jerked heavily at the mask still on his face and said simply, "Now."

"We are loaded Don. Searching for a locking solution on that monster!" Came from Tinkerbell, through Don's head set.

Don clenched his teeth, swung the gun around, and using the conning tower controls started sighting in the monster. However, the raft riding behind was way to close. He just prayed the shark did not dive under.

A crewman hanging out of the helicopter doorway yelled, "KILL IT!"

The knife came out, it was passed to Bobby who lunged at the doorway, through the bouncing waves and thrashing tail that was now lashing at the raft. Bobby flung himself into the doorway and started slashing at the water. The knife finally found the tether.

Don nodded, seeing the survivors raft bounce off the huge, moon shaped tail and float away cleanly. It was now or never.

The shark was still chomping away at the tattered rubber raft, and it was starting to dive.

"Not yet you sonofabitch," muttered Don.

"NOW DON, NOW!" Yelled Tinkerbell.

The shell hit the prehistoric shark right behind the massive upright fin. Then, in a split second of time, the shark disintegrated into a million bloody pieces. The explosion, lit the air and echoed through the blustery North Pacific air. All three helicopters jerked in response, trying gamely to get out of the way of the prehistoric pieces flying everywhere.

It was a technological end to a prehistoric monster.

The explosion had startled every person on the raft, all cringing in the gruesome bath of red. It took several seconds for the flying parts of the shark to find the water, as a small wave descended on the raft and bobbed it against the Specter.

Don had felt like collapsing right where he stood. His heart had been racing at the thought of everyone on the raft getting eaten in the end. And he was quite sure there was no second shot coming from the SLAW. He glanced down at Schmitty.

Schmitty looked up weakly, nodded shortly then grunted, "Good shot."

"Take that you son-of-a-bitch!" Added Tinkerbell

Don took a deep breath. It was over.

The Helicopter Pilot sighed heavily. He was quickly on the horn back to the Ford that the Specter had surfaced and that he was trying to get radio confirmation that the Specter was stable enough for a rescue.

Don looked back down to the water and saw a grinning Bobby throwing up a life line to the Captain, who was still hanging on desperately to the Specter. She had managed to grasp the rope sliding off the edge of the sub, then hanging on gamely, as Bobby pulled them back.

Beverly managed to crawl up the rope and get onto the deck of the Specter. Quite literally they were looking at hauling the very cold bodies back on board to warm them up.

Don chanced to look out into the open water of the cold North Pacific along the starboard bow. The water had begun churning and boiling.

"Now what?" asked Don. He dreaded the answer, for there was nothing left to fight with.

However, a conning tower popped up through the water, then the rest of the very large three-hundred seventy-foot foot submarine, the USS Cheyenne rose with it.

The rescue party took little notice of this as cold bodies were beginning to find the deck of the Specter.

In a matter of moments Captain Cedric Melrose came up onto the Cheyenne's conning tower to look down onto the forlorn little sub.

"I have medical crews at the ready." The Captain acknowledged politely.

Don came unglued just as Beverly was going to open her mouth. "YOU SORRY SON-OF-A-BITCH! NOW YOU SHOW UP WITH YOUR SLOW, PIECE OF SHIT SUBMARINE. WE'VE BEEN BATTLING MASSIVE RUSSIAN SUBS AND PREHISTORIC MONSTERS AND NOW YOU WANT TO KNOW IF YOU CAN HELP? YOU PUKE. YOU PIECE OF CRAP. YOU SLIMY TOAD SUCKER. YOU … YOU … SONOFABITCH!" Suddenly Don wheeled back around toward Schmitty and yelled, "LOAD ME UP! I'M GOING TO SHOOT THE SONOFABITCH!"

"DON! Behave yourself!" Admonished Tinkerbelle.

The Captain of the Cheyenne heard all the words plain enough, but had no idea who the man was that was yelling at him. A little distraught that his ship was going to be fired upon he searched around for the Captain.

Beverly was trying gamely to get the attention of Captain Melrose. She had also heard the words of admonishment, smiled inwardly as she too felt the same way, but waved heartily at Captain Melrose to sort of diffuse the situation.

The Captain recognized her then yelled down, "Um Captain Hornacher? Sorry we weren't here earlier, but we'd really like to be of some assistance if you need it? We have been in radio contact for the past ten minutes from SOMEONE on the Specter apprising us of the on-going situation."

Beverly glanced over at Bobby who was now tending to Schmitty. Then she looked wearily up at the larger sub and yelled, "Medical assistance Captain. We have some wounded and cold bodies down here."

Captain Melrose merely nodded then was quickly yelling down the hatch at his rescue team. Dressed in black frogmen suits, they jumped into the cold ocean, carrying waterproof medic boxes. Using Bobby's extra rope, they were on the forward deck of the Specter within a minute.

A blanket was thrown around the shivering Commander but he refused to leave the deck. Quickly the team coordinated with Bobby what was to be done. They tried to assist Schmitty first but he would not leave. He had an engine to tend too.

Don had let his anger subside quickly as the realizations that there were cold men that needed help entered into his mind. And the Cheyenne could at least HELP that way, he decided. He watched as Beverly carefully walked over to the two Medics and Bobby trying to persuade Schmitty to go with.

Beverly tapped Bobby on the shoulder, shivered for a second then told him to get below and set up for whoever was strong enough to go aboard. Bobby quickly departed as the survivors of the raft were now all accounted for.

Gunther was trying gamely to stand up to show his Captain he could still function.

"Sir, you have several broken ribs and God knows what else. Please let me help you?" pleaded the big Medic to Schmitty, literally holding the man up.

Beverly looked Schmitty in the face and said, "Chief, I tell you what. Let these men help you on board the Cheyenne and after they patch you up, we can transfer you back in the morning. The Specter is not going anywhere without its Chief on the engines. Deal?"

Schmitty smiled bravely and said simply, "Deal."

"Thanks Captain," said the Medic as they fastened a very restrictive harness around the man to rappel him back to the waiting sub.

Beverly sighed heavily as if the weight of the world had finally been lifted from her shoulders. She allowed a small chill to run through her. She was not sure if it was the cold, exhaustion, or emotion bleeding though her body. She watched somewhat detached as some of the more of the wet bodies were being transferred to the Cheyenne. She hoped she had enough of a crew to move the sub. Finally, she spied Ralph, then Don coming down the conning tower.

Commander Wolfson was sitting on the deck of the Specter with a blanket around his shoulders, would shiver uncontrollably, then seem to find himself. And yet he refused to move.

Don finally reached the deck and quickly crossed it to find the Commander. He kneeled down beside him and asked, "Ralphie? You Okay?"

Arms quickly reached up and hugged Don, surprising the man. "I, I, I, thought ... I was de, de, de, dead," chattered Ralph, trying his hardest to smile.

"Take a lot more than some old shark to kill you off Ralphie boy," responded Don with a slight grin. Don then nodded at another Medic who helped the Commander to his feet to get him into the warmth of the Specter.

Even as the Medic was grabbing Ralph, Commander Wolfson's smile faded as he imparted to Don. "N, N, Not everyone ... made it."

Don let the reality of the gruesome death wave over him as he hung his head for a second then muttered, "I know."

Don watched the man get hauled away, then shoved his cold hands into the oversized pockets of the coat. He looked around and found Beverly looking at him. They stared at each other a few moments, aware that the Cheyenne Medics had claimed the last person and that Bobby was below fixing up his own medical room. Crash and

Henry were the last on the conning tower, but they stopped to watch the two people on the deck.

Don finally spoke. "The President called while you were away. He said you ignored his orders. He also said, well-done Captain."

Beverly's bottom lip quivered, both from being wet and cold, and having her eyes tear up and the emotions running through her. "Well done my ass." Was all she muttered.

"We won't tell anybody Captain," mentioned Crash with a grin from the conning tower.

Beverly smiled at the shivering man, then quickly walked over and grabbed Don. She hugged him with all her life.

He pursed his lips together and stroked her back and said, "I'm so sorry we're late. We concentrated on fixing our float problem and unfortunately sort of floated away. We couldn't find you at first."

"You bastard," she murmured. "I was so sure you were dead." She pulled back and looked at the man in the face with a grin that lit up the night.

Don wiped a tear from her eye, could feel her body gently shivering and responded quietly, "Me? Naw. I got a ship to rebuild." Then he pulled away and continued, "But I was so scared I was late when we surfaced and the shark was there and … we couldn't fire the damned gun. I was so afraid I lost the whole crew. Especially you."

"I'm so glad when you're right."

"So am I."

"Awwww," came across Don's headset.

"Mr. Merrick? Captain? I hate to say this but we've got a sub to drive and Tinkerbell told me she don't make sandwiches," mentioned Crash. But he still had a big smile stretching out his face.

CHAPTER 25

Down below they found the submarine in still a bit of disrepair. Every single person was exhausted as Bobby turned the crew's quarters into a medical center. Don returned to the control room to find it empty. Finally, Henry showed up to at least run the monitoring equipment that was still working.

Beverly knew that exhaustion was creeping into every man's soul at that point in time, but still, there was a ship to command. Trying to get the fishy stench out of her nostrils, and blood and fish guts out of their hair and skin, she, along with everyone else was trying gamely to wash the terrible incidence out of their lives.

A hasty head count confirmed that Petty Officer First Class Alex Hernandez and Lieutenant Robert Duran, did not survive. These facts with their own survival became a mixed bag for the men. Joy in their own life and sorrow at those who died. Sometimes jokes could be heard, then quickly snuffed out at the thought that there was less of them.

There was a certain new found comradery of the men who had not only survived the Volga but a big shark that never should have been alive, as each stood in line waiting their turn, for they had to act quickly. Half the crew was cold or worse, shivering uncontrollably and was of no use. Ralph refused to go the Cheyenne, instead finding a warm bunk in the crews' quarters. Steve, Bruce Eddington, Frankie and Willy were also warming up in the crew quarters. Paul Garibaldi, courtesy of his insulated wet suit, had managed to clean up in the crew's quarters and was back to overseeing the engines of the Specter. The Cheyenne had agreed to send over another Engineer to help. In fact, they had several volunteers, who wanted to snoop.

Mr. Caldwell, per the Captain's commands, having used the hot water to warm himself up, quickly made his way to the control room. He honestly did not know if the sub was much capable of moving, and Ensign Noguchi having bounced off the ancient skin of the massive shark, was severally bruised in places she should not have been. She was keeping Wolfson company, both trying to one up the other in dirty jokes.

Captain Hornacher, realized she was not the most important part of the team at that point in time. The functionality of the ship took priority. Someone needed to feed these men and operate the ship, as Don and Bobby were already on the horn to the Cheyenne to get more supplies, blankets and sandwiches ferried over to them.

The command quarters had now become the place of refuge for the remainder of the crew. She ignored the coming and going of underwear clad men trying to find warm clothing and waiting their turn. The head was busy at that point in time as she no longer cared who saw what, dressing as she was coordinating clean up. Trying to ferret out a clean uniform, she would stop and talk to the men as they paraded by, using a wash cloth to clean herself up, so that she could get to control quickly. She knew there were few functioning crewmen at the moment. She would take a shower later.

The Captain of the sub found herself talking to Eddy about the shark in the way it exploded. He had wished he had been the one to pull the trigger. Alvin Allan hustling himself up to get into control, mentioned he would like to go somewhere quiet when it was all over. The heart of a volcano or a hurricane maybe, sounded peaceful he quipped.

The line at the Commander's head moved slowly as Beverly had assigned them jobs and importance. Bobby had happened to walk in to fetch an item from the medical locker when he noticed the

Captain. Stopping, he stood by the door and only shook his head in wonderment.

Beverly was dressed in a fresh pair of khaki slacks, but she just had a towel wrapped around her shoulders, draped over her breasts. As were most of the men, milling about in the small quarters, wearing only boxers with their uniforms in their arms.

Finally, Bobby could take it no more and strolled silently over to the Captain and asked, "Captain, can I ask you what you are doing?"

She looked into the eyes of the medic and said, "I'm coordinating our control team and getting things moving. Why?"

Bobby only snorted. "Um Ma'am? I think the men might take you more seriously if you had your Captain's bars on."

Beverly just then happened to look down at the towel and understood. Thinking of the priorities of the ship and the survivors was the utmost on Beverly's mind at the moment. Not her own dress. Or lack of it. Shrugging her shoulders, she replied, "Okay. Fine. Hang on a second and give me a hand."

Bobby did not understand as Beverly split the small group in the command quarters waiting their turn and walked to her bunk. Bobby walked dutifully behind. She reached down into her bunk and pulled the bra she had laid out, turned to face away from Bobby, slipped the towel from around her neck, then slipped on her bra, adjusting the cups as she did so. Finally, she glanced around at the big man and said stoically, "Fasten me."

Bobby only shook his head and grinned. "You're something else, Ma'am." He said as he fastened the three clasps.

She then reached over to a hook, grabbed a T-shirt she had ready and slipped this on. Grabbing her shirt which she already had prepared, she slipped this on then turned around and buttoned up the front, then unzipped the pants and tucked it in. Then she looked Bobby in the eye, smiled, then behind a cupped hand she mentioned, "Do you think anybody saw anything?"

"I swear I wasn't looking Captain!" Offered Alvin suddenly, as the whole command quarters started laughing at the man. His face turned beat red.

Beverly smiled slightly, grabbed a small rubber band and slipped a knot of hair through it to keep it out of her face, then said, "I have to get to control, or what's left of it."

"Wait a minute." Bobby went to the Medical locker, swung out a set of keys and opened it up. Fumbling for a second in a large set of drawers, he produced a pill packet. Locking everything back up, he turned and handed the packet to the Captain. "It'll help you sleep."

"I said something on the raft, didn't I?" Inquired Beverly, as she pocketed the packet.

"Yes Ma'am, you did. And it wasn't pretty."

She only nodded and turned to walk away.

"I swear I didn't peek." Pleaded Alvin to Bobby as she was leaving the quarters.

But Bobby was not listening. He thought of his Momma, standing in the rain, waiting for a bus because they could not afford a car, instead using the money to send him to school. Women like that did what they had to do. No matter who was watching.

Beverly had crossed to the galley where she knew Don had a fresh carafe going. There she found some hastily made sandwiches courtesy of the Cheyenne of which she wolfed one down. Then she made her way to control. There she found Mr. Caldwell already at the steering, as Henry was just settling in on the listening equipment. Don was sitting at Willy's post. He looked up the moment she entered the doorway.

Don smiled at Beverly. There was no smile left in Beverly as too much death had happened that day. Even seeing Don again only made her realize that the crew was shorthanded.

She sat down next to him, nestling her cup of coffee in her hands. Then she asked, "The Beatles?" In reference to the music playing over the loud speakers. It just happened to be the song, 'A Hard Day's Night'.

"Tinkerbell's sense of humor. She likes the Beatles and at this point in time, anything to keep us awake and focused was a good thing."

Beverly let her eyes roam around then said, "I can't believe how good this place looks. It's like home." Then she turned back to Don, took a sip from her cup then said, "I have a confession to make."

"You're pregnant." Don responded completely dead seriously.

She sputtered excitedly for a second, walking around the quarters half naked and all the dreams she had been having flooding back to her. "No, I don't think so," she choked. Then she added, "I was the one who took your cigars."

"I know. Oh, you mean that's it? That's your confession? I was hoping for something juicier."

"I thought you'd be mad at me."

Don put a hand on her knee and said softly, "I know we lost three people today but I have some more bad news."

Beverly sighed heavily, her mind whirling, then said, "Please don't tell me we have to leave the ship. I have no energy left."

"The ship is fine Bev. Well not fine, but it will limp home without sinking and we have full power but because of the jet problems, no speed to speak of. I've made arrangements to meet the Ford. We've set up a ferry service between them and San Diego to get some key parts. We will go home under our own steam. I'll have a damage report shortly."

"So what's the bad news?" she asked nursing the coffee cup to her lip and taking a hot swallow. Even with warm clothes on and the temperature of the Specter rising for added warmth, she still shivered occasionally. She knew it was not from the cold.

Don sighed and responded, "It's about; Georgiana."

"Oh no," mumbled Beverly placing her hand on Don's.

"It didn't go well in Montreal. They managed to get one of the terrorists, but the other detonated himself. He took Wannaker, the two pilots and several FBI agents with him."

Beverly bent her head in reverence, then she finally murmured, "Poor Georgiana. Her entire life was one of good and helping. And some moron kills her. What a waste." That was when she noticed Don's hand. It had several fingers wrapped tightly together and on the back side of the palm the wrapping was covered in blood. "You're hurt. Have you had Bobby look at it yet?"

"Naw. Stuck my hand into a pump where it didn't belong. The pump won," he said looking down at his hand.

Beverly looked at his face. She stroked the stubble spiking his face, a smear of grease along his chin. "You look terrible," she said with her eyes blinking rapidly to keep the tears from surfacing.

He paused a second as if to find the courage to speak, then said, "We found that damned shark on our monitor the first chance we got to start moving, but we couldn't catch it. Then we realized what it was hunting. And I really thought I'd never see any of you again." He looked into her green eyes and said with a smile, "You look great to me."

Beverly brushed the hair out of her eyes and stated, "I look terrible." Then she asked, "How did you do it?" referring to the submarine.

"Oh, you mean the Specter? Didn't you read my bio? I over think everything, remember? Schmitty dove and worked on the ballast while I stayed inside and worked on actually pumping the water out. Disabling the bilge pumps, we wired those into the ballast pumps that were disabled. Not as much power but, guess what, they're interchangeable. Clever Unh? But I sort of knew that. Anyway, after that we suited back up and cut out the metal out of the jets as the Specter slowly made its way to the surface. We repaired the screen as best as possible, but we're going to have to go back out tomorrow. And Tinkerbell as always, told us everything that was going on. Anyway, it wasn't that hard."

"Don you dummy. What if you hadn't repair the ports right, or the pumps, and you just kept sinking. Did you think of that?"

Chastised Beverly shaking her head at the thought of the two men struggling to survive.

"Sure we did. Then our plan was, Schmitty was going to see how long he could tread water and I was going to set a new deep sea diving record in a submarine," he replied shrugging his shoulders. "But I guess if we didn't then none of us would be here."

Beverly gazed at the man and said, "Thank God for your pig headedness."

Don gazed into Beverly's green eyes and said, "I just wish we had been a little sooner. Three good men died today."

Beverly stroked his hand and replied, "You fought the odds and saved fourteen of us. That accounts for a lot in my book, Mr. Merrick." Still her heart ached for the gallant souls that lost their lives that day. She bent her head down in sorrow, deep in remorse.

Finally, Don placed a finger under her chin, raised her head and asked, "Well, Captain. Where too?"

Beverly turned to who was at the map board, was going to say something and noticed nobody was there. She shook her head. Duran was gone and Bobby was busy. So, she turned her attention to Tinkerbell and commanded in her best Captain's voice, "Tinkerbell, coordinate rendezvous with the Ford, and send coordinates to steering please." Then she turned and said to Crash, "Mr. Caldwell, best speed, WHATEVER this poor boat is still capable of. And Crash? We run into anything, well … shoot it."

Crash yawned heavily, having heard the entire conversation, then smiled sheepishly and responded, "Aye Captain. Changing course to one five for the Ford at the blistering speed of five knots an hour. And shooting anything in our God-damned way. Thank God."

"Crash? I'LL do the aiming," inserted Tinkerbell, again, with a little giggle.

Beverly smiled.

CHAPTER 26

I t had been four weeks since the destruction of the Volga. It was two o'clock in the afternoon as Don Merrick sat back in the comfort of the leather seats of his jet black, Royals Royce limousine. He had a whiskey on the rocks swirling around in his hand, then he tipped back another sip. Glancing at the opposite seat facing him, he smiled at the thought of the two bouquets of flowers. There sat two dozen yellow roses for the Admiral's wife and two dozen Mr. Lincoln reds for Beverly. And a bottle of one hundred-year-old French wine to toast the occasion.

The driver was taking him to the third floor apartment that Admiral Hornacher maintained in Washington. Don was tired and did not really feel like dressing up in a monkey suit, and he had a submarine to rebuild, but there he was in a black silk suit, white shirt, and silver silk tie. And draped across the opposite seat was a black bag with his tuxedo in it. He would not miss the ceremony for the world. And yet, the world was not invited.

Captain Beverly Hornacher, Commander Wolfson, Warrant Officer Three Clyde Caldwell, Chief Petty Officer Gunther Schmidt, and Lieutenant Bobby Smith deservingly, were to get the Congressional Medal of Honor. As were Petty Officer Alex Hernandez, Lieutenant Robert Duran, and Petty Officer Ray Dicenzo, posthumously. Distinguished Service Medals were going to every single survivor, as each was also given the Navy Cross that afternoon. Don was getting something for a civilian in a war situation, the Naval Superior Civilian Service Award. But, with the death of the Secretary of State, and the loss of the USS Seattle and the three crew members from the Specter, it was to be a very low keyed and somber occasion, at the White House. Presided over by President Garrison with a White House state dinner and the Marine Corp Brass Band later that evening.

But, as with all political things which just pissed Don off, this too was not that simple. There were several Congressional investigations going on. The question had arisen why the Specter was not supposed to be sailing under full armament. They questioned how Beverly ended up with the assignment considering her father. The Specter went into battle with a civilian on board. And Schmitty refused a direct order to abandon ship. Then there was the handling of the situation by the CIA. That was another mess in its own right. The United Nations was berating the Russians for the handling of the situation. There were several more things the Congress wanted to talk about but Don could not remember them all.

When the question did arise about Schmitty, Beverly made it known that she had not told a sole. But it did come out. And Don did let Beverly know in no uncertain terms that Schmitty was not going to rely on some half-assed military lawyer. Don was hiring his own. And then Don would give Gunther Schmidt a civilian job at ten times the pay, and the Congress be damned.

And yet President Garrison was a pragmatic and logical man. He knew what they had accomplished, taking an untried ship into battle against overwhelming odds. He even mentioned to Captain Hornacher in passing, "When the Congress gets rough, just wave that big medal at them and remind them, you saved their sorry ass. That'll shut them up."

Don watched the Pentagon pass outside his limo window, a light rain coating the Capital. He thought of the reception they had received and it brought a smile to his face. He had not seen much of Beverly that last few days of their voyage home. When pressed as to why he was spending so much time on repairs Don had simply replied, "I will not let my three-billion-dollar submarine look like a piece of shit when it docks at San Diego."

Even though they were sailing into San Diego Naval Base, it was not going to be the stealth mission the Specter was built for. They were sailing directly into San Diego alongside the USS Jackson and the massive carrier, Gerald Ford and a flotilla of battleships and cruisers. He found out about a day from port and threw a temper tantrum and several of his tools. That just meant repairs were on hold and the stealth submarine was no longer a secret.

Ralph and Beverly literally had to drag Don and Schmitty to the conning tower once they started navigating the harbor. It took a few moments, but Don could not help but smile. Even Schmitty started waving. The response was incredible. Fire boats spraying colored water, large sailing boats shooting canons, a dozen helicopters trying to get a view of the Specter as it was flanked by the massive aircraft carrier and battle cruisers. The bustling San Diego docks was decorated in the Red, White and Blue as every single dock was crammed with people, as was half of the Pacific fleet still in Dock.

Even bringing a tear to Don's eye was the USS Missouri, brought back to life from Pearl harbor, emblazoned with a large banner saying simply "Welcome Home Specter." The World War Two Battleship escorted the Specter past Port Loma, the Naval Air Station and to its final dock emptied of all ships except for the incoming Specter and Missouri. A fighter squadron made repeated fly overs.

The news of what the crew had done had spread around the world and a cheer rose from the harbor like a drowning wave of pure joyous noise. A brass band and plenty of officers, including the President and the Vice-President, greeted the Specter as it docked. As was every news organization in the world.

Beverly turned into a pillar of strength, leading Don through the procession. She managed to hold herself together as she saluted her father on the dock, painfully aware there was at least four thousand cameras and seventy news crews taking pictures. And yet, the military be damned, Admiral Hornacher grabbed his daughter and hugged her with all his might. The picture hit a thousand papers by morning.

Don had been torn between the Navy turning it into a spectacle, and the hero's welcome every person on board that boat deserved. His conversation with the Admiral had been short and sweet. "Thank you, Mr. Merrick, for bringing them home," and a warm handshake, was all the Admiral said at the obvious happiness at having his battered and bruised daughter returned safe and sound.

And yet, Don could not let the opportunity pass. "Next time, you'll listen to me," was all he said. The Admiral nodded and smiled in return. Beverly had wondered how they would react and had been proud of them both.

The media and the papers were having a field day. Don especially liked the head line of the New York Times. THE LITTLE SUB THAT COULD. Time Magazine followed the Specter's voyage from start to end. National Geographic spotlighted the Carcharodon Megalodon, and the technological marvel that was the Specter, even going so far as to do a brief interview with Tinkerbell. She was gracious as always.

But Don's favorite was Newsweek's simple headline. GIANT KILLERS. On the cover, supper imposed was the Volga and the Specter in front of it. The Specter was almost four hundred feet shorter, as they made comparison after comparison of the two submarines.

A million phone calls flooded in as the enormity of the situation unfolded. Agents, reporters, talk shows, newspapers, anybody and everybody wanted to talk to them. The Navy put a large and very wise clamp on the crew and Don could have cared less, and grew irritated with the barrage. The US Government and the President saw fit to release careful statements about the incident, a full detailed report would be forth coming. Which suited Don and most of the crew just fine.

However, one incident was comical and maddening at the same time. The next day after docking Don and every crew member, even while going through debriefing was contacted by the producers of the news magazine, underwritten by CNN. The Navy said no and Don said no. Every day they persisted, the Navy even going so far as to screen phone calls. Admiral Hornacher contacted them and in no uncertain terms told them all they would receive in an interview was polite 'no comments.' Still they persisted. It was just too juicy of a story to pass on. Until the producers had managed to track down Beverly. They wanted Captain Hornacher, the first Female to Captain a submarine that blew up a mighty Russian sub. Beverly had said it was like talking to a brick wall, the three men that confronted her would not take no for an answer. Beverly had declined gracefully for several days, and thought the thing was over. But, they had managed to find out where Beverly was staying and stopped her coming out of her father's apartment. Beverly, had enough. She did what any good sailor would do. She swore at the producers in two different foreign languages, threatened them with lawsuits and said the next meeting would be between military lawyers. That, finally shut them up.

And Don had not forgotten Dr. Scott Pierson. When Scott showed up back in New York, Don delivered a computer video that Tinkerbell had recorded, blowing the shark to hell. And of course, the seven-inch tooth. Scott bought Don supper in appreciation, as plans were being made to go back to the Aleutians.

And yet, not all was a hero's welcoming. There were funerals to go to. Don attended Ray Dicenzo's funeral in Ohio as did most of the crew. A military internment was done at Arlington Cemetery for Alex and Robert. Wolfson and Beverly went to the funeral of Georgiana Wannaker and the internment of the crew of the Seattle. And the National Geographic Society honored the crew of the Specter with their rescue attempts and a christening of a new experimental vessel, so named the Drummond. All somber reminder of what war was really about.

The limousine finally came to a halt, parking behind a smaller limo with flags ablaze with red stars on the fenders. Don glanced out the window at the beautiful high rise that had a bird's eye view of the Potomac. He wondered how much the Admiral paid for a two thousand square foot apartment on the best side of town.

Pulling everything together off the back seat, he waited patiently. Barney, his driver, finally opened the rear door with a large umbrella covering them both. As the two men walked to the front door of the complex Don stated, "Barney, I think we're going to have drinks so it may be awhile. If you want to, talk to the guy up front. I think we're going to the same place."

"Yes sir," was all the man replied as he tipped his hat at Don.

Don rode the elevator to the third floor, where he assumed correctly the Admiral had the entire floor. He walked across the small entry and rang the doorbell. He kept his feelings in check as it had been almost two and half weeks since he had seen Beverly. They had called each other and talked of what had happened and the medals and the crew. But somehow, neither would bring up actually wanting to see each other. As if an embarrassment hung in the air.

The door opened to a dark blue uniform with more metals than most automobiles. "Don, glad to see you," Admiral Hornacher said warmly as he extended a hand. Don instead, handed him the wine as the Admiral let him in. Don noticed there was little to the apartment that was of a naval flair. It was tastefully decorated with pastels and subtle colors, with a nod to the expensive. It was obviously a woman's touch and home he noted.

"I take it the flowers are not for me," Jack said comically.

"Not unless you really want them," replied Don smiling. The Admiral had learned that Don was as comfortable with himself talking to the President, as talking to the janitor. And probably preferred the janitor.

"Make yourself comfortable. The women are in the back getting ready," mentioned Jack. Then he added, "I take it the wine is for us to sample sooner than later."

"You take it correct. The more buzzed I am going to these things the better off I am," Don responded. The Admiral only smiled at the thought, as he could vaguely make out the whiskey smell.

Before Don could sit down however, Mrs. Hornacher came out from the rear bedrooms. She looked splendid in a pretty baby's breath print, belying a spring time flair, and necklace of pearls, gracing an open neckline. She was attempting to gently place the last pearl earring in when she walked out.

"I thought I heard someone here," she said brightly as she walked over to Don, and hugged the man that had saved her daughter. Don tried to balance the two huge bouquets of flowers in one hand as he hugged back with the other.

The Admiral still holding the bottle made introductions. "Don, this is my wife Judith. Judith, this is Mister Merrick."

Judith said sincerely, "I would recognize Mr. Merrick anywhere. We've had some very pleasant conversations in the past few weeks. Glad to finally meet the man behind the voice. And again, thank you for being so bullheaded as to save the crew and especially my daughter."

He appraised the woman quickly. Upper fifties of age and she was still in athletic shape, the same height, build and facial features of Beverly. He liked what he saw. Finally, he replied, "I didn't like the idea of a damn shark turning my friends into snacks."

Judith smiled and noted, "The yellow roses I take it are for me. And the beautiful reds are for Beverly no doubt. I love man who does his homework. Thank you very much Mr. Merrick." She took the flowers, smelled the sweet aroma, then handed them to a maid who seemed to have materialized from nowhere.

Don noticed the sly look she gave the Admiral who glanced sideways. "Don. It's just Don," he said. Then he added, "But Donny will piss me off."

She smiled. "Don it is. Beverly will be out in a moment." She turned on the Admiral and asked, "You don't have that bottle opened yet Jack?"

"Um, oh, where are my manners." Jack walked behind a rather extensive bar and pulled out the corkscrew. He expertly opened the bottle and poured several glasses of the hundred-year-old port. After passing out the glasses Jack asked, "What should we toast too?"

"Without me?" asked Beverly smiling.

Don turned and was immediately disappointed. She was decked out in her Captain's uniform complete with all the medals properly shined, and a tight bun of her brownish red hair. There was a hint of make-up, enough to keep her from looking washed out. "Oh," he said, suddenly wishing he had not.

Beverly charged in at that remark. "Is that all the response I get? Oh?"

Mrs. Hornacher immediately interceded, "I agree with Don. You have a beautiful figure and that uniform does nothing for you."

"Thank you, for getting me out of that one," said Don happy with her defense.

Beverly made note, "Hello, medal ceremony. Anyone remember that? I can't exactly show up in a slinky black gown, now can I?"

"Sorry. I just envisioned something a little different. That's all," replied Don wisely.

Mom jumped in and said, "Mr. Merrick cleans up nicely, don't you think?"

"Yes he does mother," noted Beverly walking up to Don and straightening his tie. Then she pulled it tight quickly and said with fiery eyes and a maddening voice, "And I should strangle you."

"What? Now what did I do?" he said in defense as the knot closed around his throat.

"What, he says. A twenty-two-page bio on you and not one word, not a peep about the fact that you are one third owner of PDM Poseidon Shipbuilders Inc. In fact, you're the M. I have to learn that fact in Newsweek."

Don felt the knot loosen. A big smile graced his face as he explained, "Silent Partner. I head up the engineering department." He thought for a moment then asked, "Does that change anything?"

"How much are you worth again?" asked Judith smiling broadly.

"Mother. Really." Beverly chastised making a face.

"Oh, depending on how the stock market is doing at the moment, around half a billion," Don replied. Then he looked at Beverly and smiled childishly.

Judith was beside her self. "Oh I think that changes everything Beverly. A good-looking man, smart as a whip and rich to boot."

"Judith." Jack reprimanded.

"But he likes to keep secrets," Beverly said acidly, with a lopsided grin aimed at Don.

"I don't tell everyone everything. I'd never get anything done. Besides, you have a few secrets of your own," Don responded right back at Beverly.

"And what should we toast too?" injected Jack suddenly, feeling the subjects getting too deep for him.

Jack handed a glass to Beverly as Don raised his glass and pronounced, "We should toast to getting through this evening without me putting my foot in my mouth or up some politician's ass."

"We should toast to love. Or lust, whichever comes first," said Judith happily.

Beverly raised an eyebrow then said, "We should toast to good friends. Friends that talk to each other and tell each other things." Then she shot Don a sideways glance.

Jack announced quickly, "We should toast to fallen comrades who can't be here for they have made the ultimate sacrifice."

It brought a solemn haze over the group. Then Beverly said raising her glass high, "To the ship that brought us back. To the USS Specter."

"To the Specter," they all said in unison. Everyone took a welcome sip, except Don. He drained his glass.

There was five second awkward silence when Don suddenly said, "I hear Ralph has a date for tonight. Some very pretty lady named Mayfield?"

Mother looked over at Beverly who looked into the air. "Playing matchmaker again?"

"They make a nice couple," Beverly said in defense.

"You led Ralph to the Ice Colonel? She'll eat him alive," mentioned Jack referring to Colonel Mayfield's nickname.

"Oh, I don't know about that. Ralph is a reserved sort but I saw him outsmart a Russian sub Captain with one hand tied behind his back. He can handle himself," stated Don knowing Wolfson the best.

Beverly shrugged her shoulders and was going to say something in response when Judith jumped in and said, "Oh, dear, look at the time. We need to go if we don't want to keep the President waiting."

Don's cell phone started beeping. He pulled it out of a breast pocket, glanced at the number on the screen and said, "I should take this." Punching the button, he said quickly, "Yeap, Yeap. Yes, Andy what can I do for you?" He glanced over at Beverly and said, "Well, I THINK I have an escort for tonight, if we don't hurt each other before then."

Beverly smiled and softened her features. "What a romantic," she muttered to her Mom.

Don looked over at Beverly and smiled then said into the phone, "Yes, I'm pretty sure. She looks like a good dancer too. We'll find out. Beverly Hornacher. Yes, Andy, THAT Beverly Hornacher. No, Andy, no hanky panky on the boat." Then Don laughed loudly and said, "Yeah, maybe next time. See you in a few. Bye."

Beverly's eyes lit up like jade ornaments as she asked astonishingly, "Andy? As in President Andrew Garrison? You know the President?"

"Yeah," said Don slipping the phone back. "He was trying to line me up with a lady, for the dinner and dance tonight. Some Washington socialite I guess."

"So this is officially a date?" asked Judith excitedly.

"Well, I wouldn't call it a date officially, since this is a Government function. But I was sure hoping Beverly would do me the honor of sitting with me," replied Don shrugging his shoulders.

"Again with the romantic flair. You could have asked me you know," said Beverly grinning at the thought of putting Don on.

Don realized he was messing up and treading on thin ice. So he walked up to Beverly and said, "I brought you your favorite flowers. I have a limo waiting that cost more than this apartment. Can I drive you to the White House?"

Beverly grinned her best vixen smile and said sweetly, "I'd love too. Donny."

"Do you have to wear that to the dance?" Don asked referring to the uniform.

Beverly glanced over at her father. He nodded disappointingly.

"Afraid so," Beverly responded. Then she smirked and said, "Maybe, afterwards, if you're a good boy that is, and after the dance you understand, maybe I can slip into something more comfortable. Or, not at all."

Jack cleared his throat rather noisily.

"Oh dad, I'm thirty-six years old for heaven's sake," said Beverly shooting him an amusing glance.

"I know Dear. Dads just don't want to hear the details. That's all," Jack responded with a smile. Inside however, the man was deeply pleased. Somehow, he had always feared, her past would haunt her into not looking for love at all.

Don wrapped his arms around Beverly and said finally in a low voice, "You know what I like. Just something simple. Like a big white T-shirt."

Beverly hugged Don back and whispered in his ear, "I know you do."

Judith suddenly cleared her throat and said offhandedly, "My, is it getting warm in here? I think we need to go." Then she smiled broadly.

Admiral Hornacher inserted quickly, "But Beverly will need to ride with us. Secret Service already has her arriving in my car. Don't want to confuse the old boys."

Beverly smiled at Don and mentioned with a smirk, "Maybe I'll ride in your fancy car later."

Don only smiled back.

For the first time since docking four weeks ago, the crew of the Specter was all together again. They were all in full military regalia with their shiniest brass and smiling faces. The weather cleared enough for them to receive their medals in a full-blown ceremony on the East lawn. It was a feeling only a few people in the world would ever share. Afterwards they were treated to a five-star meal in the State Dining room. Even the Engineers of the Specter managed to figure out which forks to use.

Then that evening they danced with a corp. of Washington's elite, in the huge East Room of the White house. A small Marine Corp. band providing music, the hundred-year-old oak parquetry floor seeing a goodly amount of dancing. The first dance was for Admiral Hornacher and his daughter, with the President cutting in after a minute. After that Beverly could not seem to get off the floor. Swaying under the immense Bohemian glass chandeliers, she did not mind too much.

Beverly saw a side of Don she had never seen before. He rubbed elbows with every single person at the affair, was gentlemanly and genuinely warm. He danced with Beverly of course, but also with about half the women at the ball, including the President's wife, and Frankie who was losing bits of her uniform. The man was constantly full of surprises.

Wolfson had also asked Beverly for a slow dance under the dimmed lights and mentioned casually, "Don can be nice when he wants to. Can't he?"

"He's full of surprises, that's for sure." But it was the smile that Wolfson took heart in coming from Beverly's pleasant face.

Beverly's smile finally gave way to a set of pursed lips. After thinking heavily, she finally said, "Ralph, about the Specter. It's yours to command. I had a discussion with the Admiral and ..."

"… And nothing Captain. I'm set to retire in a year and Don's company is looking to build a smaller version of the Specter for the scientific purposes. Go down and see why Kamchatka is trying to blow itself up, stuff like that. They asked me if I would head up the project and Captain the vessel. Which, by the way will be called the PDM Poseidon. Don insisted."

Beverly smiled again. The future was heading straightforward. Seemingly, without her.

Ralph then shook his head and mentioned, "Besides. I heard through the grapevine that PDM was building a new liquid metal sub. Around three-hundred fifty feet in size, and someone, I don't remember who mind you, mentioned you were tops on the list for overseeing that project for the Navy." Then his bushy mustache spread along his face in a large, boyish grin.

Beverly smiled back, as Ralph spun her around then pulled her in close and whispered in her ear, "Imagine what the little girl could do with even a bigger version of the Giant Killer." Then he kissed her on the cheek, as the dance came to an end. He left her standing in the middle of the floor, rubbing her cheek and smiling broadly.

Schmitty had even hunted down Beverly for a dance, which surprised Beverly. A dislocated hip and three broken ribs and he danced fairly well. The man with so few words, apologized profusely for disobeying a direct order. To Beverly it was like forgiving her father. What Schmitty had done was save the crew from ultimate death, and HE was apologizing.

The press was not allowed in to the affair, but outside they did manage to grab a few sound bites. But cell phone camera's and selfies were the toast of the day as everyone took pictures of each other. Captain Beverly Hornacher being a more favorite subject than even the President.

The biggest surprise of the evening came from Commander Wolfson and Tinkerbell, who materialized through the projector system, appearing absolutely life like on the huge screen, that was sometimes used in the huge hall. Decked out in a very feminine styled sailor's outfit, a short short skirt and displaying a hint of cleavage, complete with the white sailor's hat cocked jauntily on her blonde ponytail. She seemed to be on board the control room of the Specter. She was sitting on the large control board with her legs crossed and her hands on her upper exposed knee. It was rather risqué look for her.

Ralph produced the bottle of champagne that had accompanied them on their maiden voyage, to return unscathed. Tinkerbell, her own self-made image, had her own champagne glass full of bubbly. As Ralph uncorked the bottle, Tinkerbell raised hers and said in a very uplifting voice that echoed throughout the hall., "Good evening, President Garrison and brave crew of the Specter. I had contacted Captain Wolfson and asked if it was all right if I made a toast on tonight's auspicious occasion. He, surprised me by getting together with the tech department of the White House and in fact let me join in, in full living color!"

This brought out a smattering of laughter. Beverly standing next to Don, poked him and whispered, "Is it my imagination or does she look a little like Marilyn Monroe.?"

Don scrutinized the pretty Tinkerbell and nodded saying, "Yeah I guess so." Then he glanced over at Beverly and saw a sly smile. "Oh, don't look at me. I had nothing to do her physical appearance. She did that all by herself." He scrutinized the video one more time, then added, "In fact, I'm not sure how she's doing all of this."

"Sure." Bev responded still smiling.

"That would be my fault," stated Ralph, coming up from behind, handing out two glasses of the champagne. "She asked me what should she look like and all I could think of was the original Disney movie of Peter Pan. Old rumor was they modeled Tinkerbell after Monroe."

Beverly nodded her head then said, "She looks pretty good."

"A little more-sexy than I would have thought of," added Don, still wondering.

Tinkerbell was continuing. "I had been scanning the Russian response of the destruction of their precious Volga. I found this very apropos news article from The Pravda News organization. And I quote, 'Mother Russia is taking a very large breath of supreme shock. A Specter has waved it's mighty and invisible hand over the oceans and slayed the greatest warship of the Russian Navy. We have just fallen behind by twenty years. The Party, and our hearts are filled with nothing but despair for Mother Russia."

Tinkerbell then raised her glass and said, "From myself and the great submarine the Specter, to the greatest and bravest Naval crew in the world, and especially those who gave the ultimate sacrifice, I SALUTE YOU!"

"HERE, HERE," resounded through the immense room, as glasses clinked and more than a few people wiped their eyes.

Finally, President Garrison cleared his throat and waved at Tinkerbell, who waved back and said, "Well Tinkerbell, now that you have stole my thunder …" A few people laughed. "Seriously, I could not have said it any better. Thank you, Tinkerbell."

"You are welcome Mr. President," she responded with an immense, albeit sexy smile.

Beverly had hated for the evening to come to an end. The ship was in dry dock and would not set sail for another two months which meant that most of the crew would be reassigned. They would keep in touch she vowed. And there was something she needed to confide in Don, which she was not looking forward to. So in the last hour, she deadened her nerves with as much wine as she could find.

Don and Beverly finally crawled into the Royals Royce Silver and Black Phantom. limousine at one-thirty in the morning, Don still carrying a bottle of bubbly with him. Beverly quickly told Barney to drive around town for a while as she discharged her service jacket and pulled the tie loose. She then undid the top three buttons of her blouse as she waved air into the neck opening. That's when she glanced around the luxurious vehicle as Don was remotely closing the shades on all the windows. The white leather seats were trimmed in oak as she sank a good five inches into the seat. Facing her was a media center capable of anything her heart desired and in the center was a pull-out bar complete with freezer and ice. When the vehicle started moving into the sparse morning traffic, the light faded to an ambient blue. She whistled appreciatively as the vehicle shook off every bump with a smoothness she had never felt before.

Don made himself comfortable as he felt the car head off. "Where are we going?" he finally asked Beverly as she disrobed.

"Nowhere special. I want to talk."

Don held out the bottle of wine and said with a grin, "Want a sip?" Both of them had hit the sauce pretty well during the evening, Beverly going so far as to steal the President's drink from his hand. She coughed all over the President of the United States as he was drinking a stiff whiskey sour. He thought it was terribly funny.

"Don't mind if I do." She grabbed the bottle and slugged down several gulps. Then the shoes slipped off.

Don cocked his head sideways as he loosened his tie. Finally, he asked, "And what exactly do we need to talk about. Other than the drinking problem I wasn't aware of."

"I don't have a drinking problem. I was just going for the liquid courage," she stated slowly.

"Why?"

"I need to tell you something."

"Oh God. I'm not going to like this am I?"

Beverly turned to Don, opened her mouth but instead said, "Ralph and Rebecca make a nice couple, don't they?"

Don sat there stunned. He was not sure if it was the alcohol or if Beverly was leading him on but he finally responded, "As tall as they both are they make a great couple. They left awfully early though. I guess Mayfield suggested they find the Lincoln bedroom and find out what the big deal was. Ralphie didn't think that was good idea."

Beverly moved in to get close to Don and actually pushed her nose against his and whispered, "They went back to her place. If you know what I mean."

Don smirked. Good for Ralphie he thought. He let Beverly's attention wander as they talked of meeting everyone again. Crash's wife, or as Don called her Mrs. Crash, Schmitty's big bushy mustache, against all regulations, and a host of other subjects. All the while Don taking notice of Beverly slowly draining the wine bottle.

Finally, after about a half hour of talking and driving, he cut back to what Beverly had said earlier and asked, "So what is it that you wanted to tell me?"

Beverly quickly grew somber. Then she charged in. "I don't know how far you want this relationship to go. I mean, I'm out on ships all the time and you're always working, even though you have more money than God and don't have to, and you probably garner all the feminine attention you want, but I'm not really the stay at home type, but I'm definitely not the one night stand type, either, not that that happens a lot. Okay, what the hell, it doesn't happen at all, which is the point I'm trying to make. Not that I haven't had my opportunities mind you and I've had plenty. But, well, they all end up going away and …"

"Whoa, whoa, whoa. Am I to actually follow this or is there a point sooner or later?" Don asked, amused that the usually very direct woman was having troubles with the one subject.

Beverly clamped her mouth shut and turned to face Don, still painfully aware she was hot inside her clothes. Don slowly reached over with his hand and cradled her chin, pulled her in closer and kissed her on the lips.

Don drew back a bare inch and asked, "Now. What do you want to tell me?"

Beverly licked her lips for a second, the heat rising in her face. There was a warmth inside her she had never felt before. Then she murmured, "I … I honestly don't know how the rest of this night is going to play out. But … I have this little problem. You see … I haven't slept with a guy in the past two years, and well, the last time it didn't work out so well."

Don merely nodded as if it was an everyday occurrence, then he asked, "That's it? That's your big confession? You're really bad at having big secrets."

Beverly shook her head, then sighed heavily. Then she launched in. "You're not getting it. When I mean not so well, I mean when we finally did have relations, well, I couldn't go back to sleep. I mean, I got up and walked out on the guy in the middle of the night. I wanted to be with him and yet, all those memories surfaced and I just … I couldn't stay."

"Oh. And you're afraid that will happen with us?"

She looked over and searched the man's eyes for a grain of doubt. All she got was a lopsided grin. "Yes. Every part of me want's this to happen. I have no qualms about letting you in my life. And everywhere else."

Don snorted and smiled.

"But I just think this will turn out wrong and you'll hate me."

Don sat back in his seat and sighed heavily. Finally, he looked into the face of the woman who had blown up the world's largest submarine. It was a bold statement and she took no apology for it, she just wanted him to know. Her mind was full of thought.

Then Don finally replied, "I know honey."

The sweet but sad face suddenly turned into confusion. "You know?"

"I managed to pick up on some of the conversation you had with Bobby. While we were making our way to your position to pick you up in the rafts, I did a little snooping in your medical records on board the Specter. Tinkerbell didn't like it but …well, she understood."

She smacked him on the arm with a bare hand and glared at the man. Then her face softened, as the damage was done. Suddenly she shrugged her shoulders and said, "So. You know. That doesn't really change anything. Does it?"

Don smiled, glanced at his media center showing the vehicles travels and he replied, "And I invited you out, and at this very moment, we should be driving up to my place."

"Home Mr. Merrick." Came from the front seat.

Don turned to Beverly and stated, "You see. I know something the other guy didn't know. I know to take it at your speed. And if all you want to do its talk the night away or stay up all night, that's what we'll do."

He stopped for a second then continued, "And I have the most amazing lighting system you have ever seen, trust me. The mood lighting in this place would make Barry White proud. We can make it as dim or as bright as you want it. It even has a gas fire place in the bedroom. Until you learn to trust me. And we'll take it as slow as your heart desires. Honey."

Beverly's anger soften quickly as Don could only smile at her. Finally, she launched herself at Don and kissed him madly. Then she drew back and said with a laugh, "Now don't go thinking I'm that easy just because I'm drunk and you can sweet talk me with your smooth lighting."

Don just shook his head at the very intoxicated lady and withdrew from the car as Barney had opened the car door. Beverly crawled out behind him, her jacket in her hand as she looked up at the eleven-story building.

"Which one is yours?" she asked as Don led her through the extensive front doors and glass enshrouded lobby. She realized she had left her shoes behind, but did not care at the moment. The man seemed totally at ease, and she was happy. She glanced around at the expensive decor, all the marble and glass shining in the bright lighting.

Don walked up to the security post, waved a wine bottle at the uniformed man behind the extensive marble desk and said, "Don Merrick and guest."

The uniformed man rose and smiled. "Good to see you Mr. Merrick. And I would recognize Captain Hornacher anywhere. Glad to meet you Ma'am. We don't get many genuine heroes in here." Then the man looked down at a security screen and said offhandedly, "You're clear."

Beverly grew red at the thought of being an actual hero of any kind. She had stopped to look at the floor directory, taking note through her haze that the building seemed to be entirely controlled by PDM

Don finally said, "The entire building is mine. The top floor however, is my penthouse."

Don hit the elevator button as Beverly's eyes widened in acceptance. The elevator door opened and Don stepped inside and turned. Beverly hesitated a second, as if everything was moving way too fast for her. Then she asked finally, "I'll never figure you out."

Don loosened his tie and pulled it from around his neck, then unbuttoned the top of his shirt. Then he smiled and returned, "And I'll never figure you out. So, what's the point?"

Beverly stood, her heart starting to race, her feet desperately wanting to move. She uttered, "You're all right with things the way they are?"

Don merely nodded and replied, "We can talk about it all night or in the morning. Your choice. But for now, yeah, just the way they are. Going up." Then he put out his hand.

All the road blocks that Beverly maintained in having a relationship quickly crumbled as she reached out to Don. Stepping inside, she wrapped her arms around his neck and said, "Well, Donny. I hope you like a lot of baggage. And you know. I just might be that easy."

"You're a lot of things, honey. But easy? Never in a million years," replied Don as the elevator doors slid closed.